YA
F   Bond, Nancy. 021588
BON
            Another shore

$15.95

DATE			

TO RENEW THIS BOOK
CALL 275-5367

ANOTHER SHORE

By the Same Author

A STRING IN THE HARP
(*1977 NEWBERY HONOR BOOK*)
THE BEST OF ENEMIES
COUNTRY OF BROKEN STONE
THE VOYAGE BEGUN
A PLACE TO COME BACK TO
(Margaret K. McElderry Books)

ANOTHER SHORE

NANCY BOND

Margaret K. McElderry Books
NEW YORK

Copyright © 1988 by Nancy Bond

Margaret K. McElderry Books
Macmillan Publishing Company
866 Third Avenue
New York, NY 10022
Collier Macmillan Canada, Inc.

First Edition
Printed in the United States of America
10 9 8 7 6 5 4 3 2 1

Composition by American–Stratford Graphic Services, Inc.
Brattleboro, Vermont
Printed and bound by R. R. Donnelley & Sons
Harrisonburg, Virginia
Designed by Barbara A. Fitzsimmons

Library of Congress Cataloging-in-Publication Data
Bond, Nancy.
Another shore.
Summary: Seventeen-year-old Lyn, working in a
reconstructed colonial settlement in Nova Scotia,
suddenly finds herself transported back to 1744,
when the French inhabitants are at war with England.
1. Nova Scotia—History—1713–1763—Juvenile Fiction.
[1. Nova Scotia—History—1713–1763—Fiction. 2. Space
and time—Fiction] I. Title.
PZ7.B63684An 1988   [Fic]   87-3907
ISBN 0-689-50463-2

Kate, Tricia, Joan, and Kit—separately
and together, for all of you

→≫ ≪←

Lost time is never found again.
<small>BENJAMIN FRANKLIN</small>

⋙ Note ⋘

FOR YEARS I CARRIED THE IDEA BEHIND THIS STORY AROUND IN my head, looking for the right place to set it down. In 1980 I visited Louisbourg National Historic Park on Cape Breton, Nova Scotia, for the first time, and the idea found its home. Not a very convenient one, I must admit, but the place felt inescapably right. Over the next years, as I struggled with the emerging characters and story, and tried to learn everything I needed to know (impossible!) about living in Louisbourg in 1744, I sometimes despaired of making it all work, but I never doubted the geography. Many of the eighteenth-century people who appear in this story were real—their names are in the town records—others are entirely fictional, but in the end they are all the results of my imagination. The Bernards, Pugnants, Desforgeses left little behind them but their names. I hope I have done none of them an injustice. Through these people and descriptions of the town, I've tried to convey a little of Louisbourg's immense attraction and fascination. The effort involved in a visit to the fortress is repaid many times over!

I want to express my admiration for the planners and the builders of the reconstruction, and my gratitude to the people whose paths I crossed during my two visits: the animators, park staff, and guide (Kathy Fraser, who provided a vivid and enthusiastic tour); through them all, the past truly comes to life. Most especially, I must thank Mr. A. J. B. Johnston, writer, editor, researcher on the park staff, who patiently answered many questions, and directed me to much valuable information. Any gaps, lapses and errors in the result are my fault, not his.

Thanks to Patricia Runcie, who, although she "never really liked camping much," allowed herself to be steered off on a camping trip to Nova Scotia, and to Kate Paranya, who unhesitatingly agreed to go back again four years later. Thanks to Kit Pearson for her help when I was beginning my researches, and for sending me Christopher

Moore's book, *Louisbourg Portraits,* which captures so well the feel of the colonial town and its inhabitants. As a result of John Lynch's assistance, Dorrie Paget knows far more about photography and equipment than she is allowed to demonstrate (hers turns out to be another story, as is often the case). And finally, I have to express my enormous gratitude to those people who patiently bore with me during the long and sometimes painful process of writing this book, and who kept confidently expecting that I would finish it in spite of my doubts: my parents, Joan Tieman, Margaret McElderry.

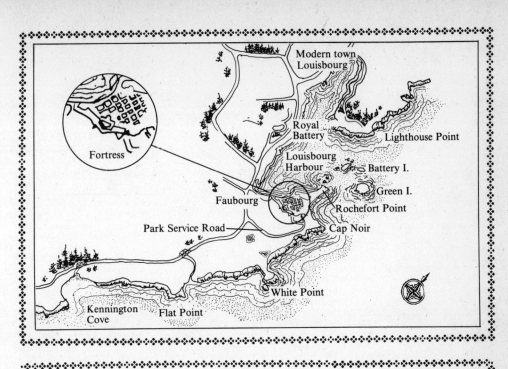

Modern town
Louisbourg

Fortress

Royal
Battery

Lighthouse Point

Louisbourg
Harbour

Battery I.

Green I.

Faubourg

Rochefort Point

Park Service Road

Cap Noir

White Point

Kennington
Cove

Flat Point

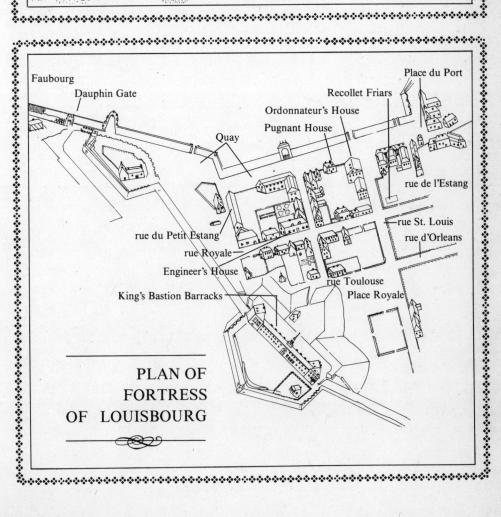

Faubourg

Dauphin Gate

Place du Port

Recollet Friars

Ordonnateur's House

Quay

Pugnant House

rue de l'Estang

rue St. Louis

rue d'Orleans

rue du Petit Estang

rue Royale

Engineer's House

rue Toulouse

King's Bastion Barracks

Place Royale

PLAN OF
FORTRESS
OF LOUISBOURG

ANOTHER SHORE

1

"DEAREST LYNNIE," MIKE HAD WRITTEN IN HIS CAREFUL script. "Not much has happened since I wrote you last—" Four days ago that was, Lyn reflected wryly, glancing at the five-page letter in her hand. How did he manage to write so much about nothing? A lot was happening to her but she could barely find the time to scrawl a postcard in reply. "—construction has actually started on the Aubuchon hardware store up Trapelo Road. My dad is very depressed about it. All he talks about anymore is money and how much everything costs when you run your own business. He's sickeningly nice to the customers and yells at us when he's home—not that he's home much. My mother keeps telling him it'll be ages before the Aubuchon opens, but then he yells about how they build things like that overnight these days. Maybe I won't have to go into the hardware business after all—though I wouldn't ever say that to him—he'd blow my head off. He's already accused all of us of not caring. Larry Calvert just landed a job at the Porsche-Audi dealership in Watertown—the one down by the mall. Do you know how much they pay their mechanics?" She hadn't a clue, but clearly it was a lot more than the minimum wage Mr. Hennessey paid his son for clerking in the hardware store. Mike was much too soft when it came to his father.

The sun was a smoldering bright spot high in the hazy sky. By afternoon Lyn reckoned the sea mist would have cleared off and it would be hot on the point. She sat on the wall at the end of the quay, beyond the last of the reconstructed buildings, beyond the rope that kept the tourists from wandering out of bounds. Already the fortress streets were full of them, in pairs and families and sightseeing flocks, come to experience—for a few hours or a day—life in an eighteenth-century French colonial port. She watched a group inspecting the stocks on the place du Port. With predictable jokes and laughter, they took turns photographing each other posing as miscreants, and several aimed their cameras further along, at Lyn as she sat in her costume: the shapeless unbleached chemise, with its wide sleeves, that served as blouse above her long, gathered skirt and petticoat beneath it, apron and crumpled white cap. Local color. She pretended not to notice so they wouldn't feel self-conscious. With an effort she pulled her attention back to Mike's letter and began to read it carefully. She felt guilty because it had been in her pocket since the day before—she had forgotten it yesterday and left it in her costume overnight, unopened.

Since the end of June, when she had telephoned him with her address: PO Box 189, Louisbourg, Nova Scotia BOA 1MO, his letters had come with gratifying regularity, twice a week. At least Lyn had been gratified at first: He was thinking of her and missing her. But her life was full of new people and experiences; she was busy all day until seven in the evening waiting on tables in the coffeehouse. After work, when they both happened to be in, she and her mother sat over a late supper and swapped news. Often Lyn walked down to the wharves to see what the fishing boats brought back, or she met some of the other park staff at the one bar in town for a beer and conversation. On her days off, someone was always going somewhere interesting: for a picnic by the lighthouse, or a swim at Kennington Cove, or shopping and a movie up in Sydney. But then there was Mike, reaching out with the long, inexorable arm of the postal service, to haul her back, mentally at least, to hot, dusty Belmont, Massachusetts, where nothing special was happening. It wasn't that she'd found anyone else to take Mike's place, nor even that she was looking, just that she was enjoying herself.

With a sigh, she read on. The Red Sox were fading halfway into the season, as usual. Mike was disgusted with them, but Frank, the retired MBTA bus driver who lived next door to Lyn and Dorrie on Waverley Street, still thought they could pull it out if they tried. The problem was pitching. Nothing new about that—every year the problem was pitching, as far back as Lyn could remember. They started out big, and then they fell apart, just when they had all their fans whipped up and full of optimism.

Lyn looked up to watch a battered trawler steam slowly past, between the rocky jaws that protected Louisbourg harbor, heading for the fish processing plant on the shore of the modern town: a blocky utilitarian construction, with a tall smokestack. When there was no wind to carry the smell away, the air was dense with an oily, pungent stench. After the first week or so, Lyn had stopped noticing it, but her mother had declared that after this summer she would probably never eat fish again. "It provides jobs for lots of people," Lyn had pointed out. "And probably drives at least as many away altogether," Dorrie replied. It was pointless to argue, so Lyn didn't bother. The fish plant was there, and so were they.

It was because of Dorrie that they had come in the first place. Back in March, she had announced out of the blue that she had been commissioned to do the photographs for a book about Louisbourg, a reconstructed French colonial fortress, somewhere in the wilds of Nova Scotia. "It's a museum," Dorrie said, "like Williamsburg. It's supposed to be fabulous." "I've never heard of it," said Lyn. "I expect there are lots of places you've never heard of," Dorrie replied airily. "To do the job properly, I'll have to spend the summer. If you come with me, we could take a little time at the end and have a vacation—before you go off to school."

Lyn already had a summer job lined up for herself at Fran's Pizza Palace, but she guessed shrewdly that this assignment was a big deal for her mother. The fact that Dorrie hadn't even mentioned applying for it was a giveaway—she wouldn't have to make excuses then if she hadn't gotten it. For the last three years she had been working part time in the Harvard news office while struggling to launch herself as a professional photographer. Her biggest break so far had been a project for the Kennedy Library in Boston. And Lyn wasn't deceived by Dorrie's casual invitation to her to come along; her mother thought she needed Lyn for backup. She didn't, of course, and once she got involved in the job, she'd forget Lyn's existence for long stretches of time.

Lyn could have fought it, stayed home by herself in their apartment, gone out with Mike, slung anchovies on pizzas, but the idea of going somewhere new appealed to her. In the fall she'd be a freshman at the University of Massachusetts, Amherst. The summer in Nova Scotia would mark the transition in a special way; and they'd never had money for official vacations anywhere. Lyn felt her horizons could stand broadening.

So instead of arguing, Lyn wrote to ask for a job at Louisbourg National Historic Park, figuring there must be something she could do to earn a little money and occupy her time while Dorrie was

3

working. Back came all kinds of forms to be filled out—getting work in Canada seemed unduly complicated, especially since it was only a job as a waitress in a coffeehouse. There was even an orientation program. "But you already know how to be a waitress," Mike protested. "You've spent the last two summers at the Pizza Palace." He wanted them to have this summer together in Belmont. Lyn shrugged. "Maybe they do it differently in Nova Scotia." The biggest thing in her favor turned out to be her four years of high school French; it was an advantage to be bilingual, the restaurant supervisor wrote, and Lyn was gratified by the idea of actually being able to put something she'd learned to use.

As it happened, the orientation wasn't for waitressing, it was for historical background. Everyone who worked in the fortress had to know something about its history and what life had been like in the colonial town in 1744, the year they had chosen to recreate. Even the waitresses wore costumes and were expected to answer questions—mainly about eighteenth-century food and eating habits, but anything else as well. It was like performing in an extemporaneous play: every morning, along with her chemise and long skirt, Lyn assumed the character of Elisabeth Bernard, a girl her own age, who had actually lived in the town. Even during her breaks she played the part, as now, sitting on the quayside in the sun, letting people take her picture and trying to be as unobtrusive as she could with Mike's letter. It was tiring—the days were long—but it gave waitressing a new dimension. Except on those rare days when the weather turned genuinely hot, Lyn much preferred her costume to the nasty little green-and-white nylon uniforms Fran had chosen for his employees. Those were easier to launder, but they smelled forever of onions and pizza sauce, and felt limp and clammy.

The biggest drawback, she quickly found, was that tourists didn't know whether they were expected to tip, so they often didn't. And they were so distracted by the eighteenth-century menus and ambiance, they tended to forget anyway. In the two restaurants they sat at common tables, elbow to elbow, and were served cold meatloaf, thick khaki-colored bean soup, dense slabs of brown bread and orange cheese, stews and rice, boiled vegetables, and tankards of beer or cider. The menus were simple to remember, but the work was not lucrative.

Still, Lyn was enjoying herself. That morning, before the coffeehouse got busy, she had had a long conversation with a couple from New Zealand who were making their way slowly around the world. New Zealand, they said, was so far from everywhere else they'd decided to see it all before they went back. They couldn't make up their minds whether to go west across Canada, or drop south and see some of the United States. Forgetting Elisabeth, Lyn told them about Boston and Concord and Lexington—all the things there were to see. They, in turn, told her about Rotorua where they lived—the geysers and the hot springs—and showed her a picture of their youngest grandson, knobby-kneed in shorts, standing in front of a tree fern. They gave her their address in case she ever got to New Zealand, and she vowed to herself that one day she would. When she was independent she wanted more than anything to travel—to pick a place and find out what it was like to live there, not just jog past the sights and buy a few postcards, but ride the buses and shop for groceries and use the laundromat—to have an address long enough to get mail.

She'd been delighted when the Parks Canada people had allocated Dorrie an apartment in the town instead of making them stay in the motel where they'd spent their first two nights. It was the top floor of a homely asphalt shingle house on Oak Street. Presumably there had once been oaks along the street—or someone intended one day to plant some. Dorrie had been critical—Dorrie was always critical until she began working. Lyn tried to be tolerant, but she wasn't entirely successful. Gracefully she had ceded the double bed to her mother, resigning herself to the foldaway cot. She didn't mind the mismatched furniture, the odd glasses and plates, the chipped porcelain bathtub with claw feet and no shower—only a rubber hose for hair-washing. Dorrie stopped complaining when she saw the darkroom at the park headquarters; the apartment was no longer important. Never before had she had free access to so much expensive professional equipment. She gloated. "It'll spoil you—you'll never be happy with your corner of the cellar again," Lyn predicted. "I'm sure you're right," Dorrie agreed happily.

The modern town of Louisbourg, where the house stood, was like a fish skeleton: a long main road that ran parallel to the waterfront, with little short streets coming off it on either side. It was not picturesque; it was the kind of place where real people lived and worked.

On the map, the road from Sydney was a black, nearly straight

5

line south to a tiny dot at the edge of the sea and an irregular strip of green labeled LOUISBOURG NATIONAL HISTORIC PARK. The tiny dot—the town—was where the black line stopped. In order to leave, you had to backtrack up it; there was no other way out. The farther along it they drove the Sunday they arrived, the more it felt as if they were driving to the end of the world. Houses were scarce outside of Sydney, and the flat, scrub-covered countryside surged in around them, enclosing the Toyota. It fell and rose gently, then slipped down into a ragged tide of graying fog. The windshield misted. Dorrie muttered something between her teeth and switched on the wipers and the parking lights, leaning forward, her shoulders hunched, her hands gripping the wheel.

It was difficult to make much of Louisbourg that first afternoon in the fog. They found later that there wasn't much without the fog: an untidy huddle of buildings on the edge of the harbor, stores, houses, a few churches, a post office. They came upon the town before they realized what it was, and were through it by the time Lyn managed to find the letter Dorrie had been sent just before they left—the letter that expressed enthusiasm at their projected arrival, hopes for a good trip, a desire to be of whatever assistance possible, and finally, buried at the end, the essential information about reservations and how to find the motel.

"It's the Mariner," said Lyn.

"So?" snapped Dorrie. "Did you see it?"

"I wasn't looking."

"I suppose we might not have come to it yet."

"But isn't that the park entrance? On my side—yes, there's the sign. He says the park's on the far side of town, so we've missed the whole thing."

"We can't have," said Dorrie firmly. "I don't believe it."

"Louisbourg's only a very small circle on the map," said Lyn, equally firm. "You'd better turn around; I don't think this road goes much farther." As she spoke, they reached the end of it. There was a large parking lot on the left, between them and the flat gray ocean. The single car parked in it made it look emptier than if there had been none.

"God," said Dorrie quietly. She pulled abruptly into the lot, turned the car, and they headed back the way they'd just come. "He does say the motel's *in* the town, doesn't he? This person?"

"Arthur MacGregor, assistant director, Fortress of Louisbourg," Lyn read. "Yes, he does. I think it's on the north side, where we came in. He says we can't miss it."

Dorrie snorted. She shifted down this time, and drove slowly through the town. They both peered from side to side. Lyn glimpsed wharves and boats down the streets to the right. The main road was hazardous with parked cars and pedestrians strewn all over it, doing unexpected and unannounced things. Several times Dorrie blew her horn irritably; Lyn gritted her teeth, determined not to start another fight. They found the Mariner where Arthur MacGregor said it would be: not elegant, but comfortable and doing a brisk business. "No vacancies," said Lyn. "That proves it must be good." "It proves nothing of the kind," retorted Dorrie. "It's the only motel in this place, as far as I can see."

She was right, it was. In order to come to Louisbourg you had to know ahead of time that you wanted to see it—you didn't happen on it by chance. There was nothing else out the road from Sydney except a scatter of houses and a few small fishing settlements on a back road along the coast. The amazing thing was how many people did manage to make their way to the park, in spite of the lack of convenience and amenities.

But even Dorrie, once she set eyes on the reconstructed fortress, had to admit it was worth going out of the way for. It was an impressive place, presenting her with endless possibilities and challenges. Once she settled down and started to work them out, her bitchiness wore off, as Lyn knew from experience it would. Dorrie always drove herself into a frenzy of nerves over photographic assignments because they meant so much to her and she felt compelled to prove her competence over and over, to everyone in sight. It did no good to point out the obvious: that if she weren't competent she would never have been chosen for the job in the first place. Lyn had learned to keep her mouth shut, but it put a strain on their relationship at times. This was one of the worst because it had taken them four days of steady travel to reach Louisbourg—four days during which they were constantly in one another's company, except when asleep or in the bathroom somewhere. The fact that Lyn had spent long periods in the car plugged into her Walkman had been a source of friction as well, but as she pointed out to her mother, it had helped to keep them from actually coming to blows.

7

On the south side of the harbor, across from the modern town, lay Rochefort Point, where, in the early eighteenth century, the French colonists had built the Fortress of Louisbourg. It had grown in a couple of decades into a thriving port, its economy based on cod fishing off the Atlantic coast of Canada. But the French and the English had continually fought with each other over the fishing grounds, and in 1744, France and England had officially gone to war. In the spring of 1745, a motley army of New Englanders, under the command of William Pepperell, had sailed up the coast to Isle Royale, as Cape Breton was then called, and landed south of Louisbourg. They then attacked the fortress on its most vulnerable side, coming across the marshes, instead of from the sea, taking the French completely by surprise. After a siege lasting seven weeks, the French surrendered and the English packed them all into ships and sent them ''home'' to France—never mind that many of them had never been there before, having been born in New France.

For a few years the English occupied the town, complaining bitterly the whole time about the vile climate and dying in great numbers from smallpox and scurvy. In the Treaty of Aix-la-Chapelle in 1748, they gave it back to the French and many of the former Louisbourgeois returned to take up life where it had been so rudely interrupted. But the English weren't through with them; in 1758, they reversed themselves, besieged the town again, recaptured it, and this time, after they sent the French army away, they leveled Louisbourg. By 1760 it was nothing but mounds of rubble and craters.

For two hundred years Rochefort Point lay bare except for some cows and sheep and a few fishing properties. Then the Canadian government took an interest in the site. Retraining unemployed Nova Scotia coal miners, it set them to work as masons, carpenters and blacksmiths, resurrecting the eighteenth-century town. One-fifth of the original Louisbourg, with its defensive ditches and walls, houses, inns, warehouses and soldiers' barracks, cobbled streets, quay, vegetable gardens and livestock, once again occupied the low spit of land at the edge of the North Atlantic. A seasonal staff of some three hundred people worked themselves to a frazzle making the town feel inhabited, giving visitors the impression that they were catching glimpses of life in 1744.

Lyn learned the broad outline of Louisbourg history quickly, like a homework assignment, because it was part of the job. On the whole, however, history interested her less than people: who they were, how they behaved, where they came from, what their expectations were. It didn't really matter whether they belonged in the eighteenth century or the twentieth—Louisbourg was full of all kinds. She enjoyed watching them, seeing how they reacted to the elaborate game of Let's Pretend in the fortress. There were always those among the tourists who couldn't believe that *some*where in the park they couldn't buy hamburgers, french fries, ice cream and Cokes; who complained at having to leave their cars at the visitors' center and take a bus to the town gate, even though that bus was free, and then walk around the reconstruction—women whose heels caught in the cobblestones and men who were bored by rooms of period furniture and were uncomfortable making conversation with the costumed "animators," as the staff members were called. There were also animators who were never completely at ease playing parts. But most people were willing to try. And really, the feeling you got every once in a while, just for a minute or two, of having slipped time somehow was uncanny. It didn't happen very often, never predictably, Lyn found, and as soon as you stopped to think about it it was gone. It was something you saw only out of the corner of your eye.

She kicked her heels gently against the planking and watched the gulls swarm and swoop around the trawler. From time to time someone threw a bucketful over the side—garbage, fish guts, it didn't matter—and there'd be a screeching flurry of wings and beaks as they plummeted onto the water in pursuit. They always seemed to know well in advance where to gather. Often the first sign of a returning fishing boat was a cloud of gulls on the horizon.

"Hey! I think they're looking for you."

Lyn jumped and found Rob Gowan grinning at her. He wore the ill-fitting blue uniform of a private soldier in the Compagnies franches de la Marine, his tricorn set rakishly back on his coppery hair.

"I lost track. Is Phyllis furious? I haven't finished reading my letter." Lyn shuffled the pages and glanced quickly at the end: ". . . went to see Mr. Lawton yesterday—he's a bit strange, but Gilbert looks fine, so I guess you don't have to worry. They seem to be getting along all right, though you forgot to tell Mr. Lawton about the salad bowl on top of the fridge. He was revolted by it

9

when he took it down to use—all black inside and full of cat hair. He scrubbed it out—'' *''Poor* Gilbert!'' exclaimed Lyn in horror.

''Gilbert?''

''My cat. The salad bowl was his special place. You'd think Philip would have noticed! Why else would we have another one in the cupboard, for heaven's sake!''

''Why indeed,'' said Rob gravely.

Lyn looked up at him and laughed. ''At least he seems not to be sulking.''

''Philip? Or Gilbert?''

''Gilbert, of course. I don't worry about Philip. After all, we did him a huge favor by letting him have our apartment while they're tearing his up and turning it into a condo. Our rent's much less than his.'' At the bottom of the page she saw, ''All my love, Mike,'' and hastily folded the letter over and stuffed it into her skirt pocket. They wouldn't have had skirt pockets in the eighteenth century; it was a concession made by the costume department under pressure. The staff was full of agreeable fanatics, obsessed with getting all the details right. Those animators who wore prescription glasses had to get their lenses fitted into special wire frames if they wanted to wear them in the park, and even that was a concession because very few eighteenth-century people had spectacles at all, no matter how bad their vision. Dorrie was inclined to take a dim view of the whole business; she thought they carried authenticity too far, and she absolutely refused to get her lunch in either of the so-called restaurants after trying it once. Instead, she brought her own peanut butter and onion sandwiches and potato chips, and ate them in one of the hidden offices, closed to the public. Lyn sometimes joined her, when business at the coffeehouse permitted. She didn't see Dorrie often otherwise—in the evenings at the apartment now and then, and from time to time as Dorrie wandered about the town with her Nikon and camera bag. But when she had the camera, she was oblivious to everything outside its scope. Lyn could hail her until she was blue in the face and Dorrie wouldn't hear a sound.

She stood up and brushed her skirt. ''Back to the fray.''

Rob slouched along beside her. ''There's a bunch of us going up north camping next break. You want to come?''

''Of course. But I've never gone camping before in my life—the only thing I've got is a day pack.''

"That's all right. You can borrow a sleeping bag from someone on the other shift—George has one, and a foam pad. We've got three tents among us—one's too small to sit up in, and the big one leaks, but you're supposed to be uncomfortable. That's the romance of it."

"I'm glad you told me ahead of time," said Lyn with a grin. "Who's going?"

"Sandy, Jean, Simon, maybe Roger, and Richard."

She made a face. "He doesn't like me."

"Richard? Of course not, you're an American. It isn't *you* he doesn't like—it's your heritage and national character. You're an oppressor and a bully, and you give him a painful inferiority complex. Nothing personal, you understand."

"But that's ridiculous!" Lyn protested, half laughing. *"You* don't feel that way, do you? Or Sandy?"

"Certainly. We're too polite to show it, that's all."

She gave him a good-natured thump.

"Actually, it's true—you Americans are rather overwhelming when viewed from this side of the border," said Rob. "There are so many of you and you have so much of everything."

"Not us," said Lyn firmly. "Dorrie and I, we hardly have anything at all. Just each other and some shabby furniture."

"And a cat with his own salad bowl."

"True," she conceded. "But I earn my wages, you know. I bet I work harder than Richard." She ran up the four steps to the Pugnant house. Rob raised his hat in farewell. "I'm off to demonstrate a flintlock. Save me a custard tart, will you? I'll be by this afternoon."

In eighteenth-century Louisbourg, Nicolas Pugnant had been a baker; he ran his business out of the stone house on the quay where he lived with his family. After his death in 1740, his widow had continued it with the help of a son-in-law. Only the two front rooms, with their whitewashed plaster walls and big bake ovens, were open to tourists in 1983. Here people could come and sit when their feet gave out, or it rained, or they couldn't decide what to see next. They could order coffee or cider and various kinds of tarts. The hardest part for waitresses was keeping track of the customers; it was very informal, the rooms were cramped, and people had to share tables. The back of the house was a big, businesslike kitchen, with stainless

11

steel sinks, an enormous dishwasher, refrigerators and counters. Realism in all things except sanitation and food preparation, as Kathy Gagnon, another of the waitresses, said. Her husband, Steve, was in charge of the animators. You could not risk giving the public an eighteenth-century case of food poisoning.

Up the central staircase were an office, a bathroom and a staff lounge. Even there—behind the scenes—the fanatics had left their mark: the lounge was full of books and reports on different aspects of daily life in the colonial town, invitingly strewn around for the staff to peruse while they lounged, and the walls of the bathroom were covered with maps and plans of the fortress and its environs so you could put every bit of time to constructive use.

From midmorning until late afternoon, the coffeehouse was usually busy, with a slack hour or so around noon, when the tourists crowded into the restaurants for lunch. All the food was brought in precooked every morning before the park opened, and the leftovers taken away after closing. The three eating establishments were close to each other in the center of town, with an enclosed common courtyard to camouflage the modern mechanics of the operation.

"I hear you're coming with us," said Sandy Ferguson, settling herself on the bench beside Lyn a couple of days later. It was noon and there was enough sun to cast watery little shadows, so Lyn and Kathy had taken their lunches out behind the coffeehouse, where no one could see them roll up their sleeves, discard their bonnets and hitch their skirts over their knees. Sandy worked next door, at the Grandchamp Inn.

"I haven't told Dorrie yet," said Lyn. "I've barely seen her since Rob mentioned the camping trip."

"She wouldn't say no, would she?"

Taking a mouthful of ham sandwich, Lyn shook her head. Dorrie might not be wildly enthusiastic about having her daughter go off on a four-day trip with a mixed group of people she hadn't properly met, but she wouldn't prevent her, either.

"Where are you going?" asked Kathy.

"Cape Breton Highlands," Sandy said. "Ingonish. We might even stop and see the Giant MacAskill this time."

"Oh, no!" cried Kathy, rolling her eyes. "*Not* the Giant Mac-Askill! Hullo, Madeleine, have a seat."

12

Madeleine Charbonneau joined them, spreading a napkin carefully over her lap before she unpacked her lunch. Like Lyn, she was new to the fortress; unlike Lyn she had a husband, a little boy, and a relatively nervous disposition. "Is this a real giant?" she asked warily.

Sandy's mouth twitched. "Angus MacAskill, the Cape Breton giant. He's in the Celtic College at St. Ann's. For years I've wanted to stop and see him, but every summer it's the same—I get voted down. But"—she looked encouragingly at Lynn—"if *you* say you want to stop, too—"

"Is it a sideshow? I hate that kind of thing," said Lyn.

"No," Kathy said. "He died in the eighteen sixties. They have a full-size plaster model of him in a little room. I went there once, years ago, and believe me, Sandy, it's not worth breaking your heart over. Seeing him actually ruins the mystique. It's the kind of goal you should never attain."

"It sounds awful to me," said Madeleine. "Why do you want to go?"

Sandy sighed. "There's a terrific postcard of him, but it's cheating to send it until I've seen him. I've got a friend in Vancouver who's crying out for a card of the Giant MacAskill."

"Tacky, tacky," said Kathy. "You'll never get Richard to agree to stop."

"He can wait in the car while the rest of us go in."

"I'm game," said Lyn.

"Actually, the Giant MacAskill aside, I wish I were going, too," said Kathy. "I haven't been camping in ages."

"Come along then—we'll fit you in," offered Sandy.

"I can't just go off and leave Steve. And I'm on the wrong shift anyway."

Sandy shook her head disparagingly. "What it is to be married."

"Suppose it rains?" said Madeleine.

"We get wet." Sandy was cheerful. "It's only three nights. You can put up with anything for three nights."

Madeleine said nothing, but the look on her face made it plain that she did not agree. Sandy and Lyn exchanged glances.

Just then Rob and another soldier clattered around the corner. "Aha!" cried Rob. "What are you loitering back here for? Haven't you got work to do, the lot of you?"

"Oh, please, sir," said Sandy, "we're not up to nothing bad, sir."

"What'll you give me not to report you?"

"How about a kiss?" She fluttered her eyelashes at him.

"Nah," said the other soldier. "How about some coffee and a couple of custard tarts?" Rob nodded enthusiastically.

"I think we can manage light refreshments for the troops," said Kathy, and disappeared into the coffeehouse while the soldiers spread themselves comfortably across a bench. Madeleine watched them over her sandwich with cautious interest. Lyn had noticed that she never took part in their nonsense; it was as if she didn't quite understand it and didn't really want to.

"I don't know where they're getting recruits from these days," Sandy complained. "Soldiers around here sure aren't what they used to be. At least the sailors are still game for a good time."

"You want to watch your step," warned Rob. "Girls like you can get into a lot of trouble making advances to a man."

"I was *supposed* to be a lady of quality when I first came, last summer," she said. "They were going to make me Madame de Gannes—the dress fit with hardly any alteration."

"Why didn't they?" asked Madeleine, curious.

"Because when I put it on everyone kept telling me that I walked like a peasant, and I never could get the hang of it. So they took the dress away and gave me a skirt and chemise and stuck me in the des Roches house instead—the fisherman's cottage. I was Ann Fourtier and had to learn nine hundred and ninety-nine ways to prepare salt cod and how to cane chair seats with rushes."

"More respectable than being a servant in the Grandchamp Inn," said Rob.

"But I like this much better. It gets pretty hairy at des Roches's when the buses stop. It's the first place everybody comes to and they don't spread out, they just cram through the door on top of each other. Sometimes it's so packed you can hardly breathe."

"Just because you didn't walk properly?" Madeleine sounded disbelieving.

"She didn't mince," said Kathy, reappearing with a grin and a tray laden with mugs and tarts. "Sorry, no custard—we have to save them for the afternoon crowd. They're the ones that run out first."

14

"I'd much rather be Madame de Gannes," Madeleine said, collecting her lunch bag and thermos.

"You'd probably be perfect," Sandy said blandly as Madeleine got up.

"*I'm* glad waitresses aren't required to *be* anyone," Kathy declared. "I've never felt comfortable with the whole idea."

It was Sandy who had encouraged Lyn to look up the Pugnant family in the park archives, to see if there wasn't someone she could pretend to be. "It makes it all seem much closer," she said, "like getting the focus right when you look through binoculars. Instead of all-purpose servant, I'm Marie-Thérèse Lajoie. She used to work at the inn; she was a couple of years younger, but near enough."

So, on one of her afternoons off, Lyn had gone to the park's library to see what she could find. The librarian, Joan Pearson, was a spare, weathered-looking woman in her fifties whose mind moved with lightning speed from one subject to another. She never finished a sentence because, before she could get to the end, her thoughts had leaped ahead to something else. She ran the library with good-humored efficiency, keeping track of what everyone wanted or needed or had taken off and squirreled away in one of the maze of offices in the various buildings in the compound.

There was a file of material about the baker and his family, and in it Lyn had discovered Elisabeth Bernard, the eldest granddaughter. In the summer of 1744 Elisabeth had been seventeen years old, just as Lyn was in 1983. Coincidentally, they had both been born in February, although Elisabeth's exact birthdate was not recorded. It amazed Lyn that the archives were so complete. "Actually it's because of the English," Joan explained. "When they sent the French back to France, they sent all the town records along with them, so they were preserved. Some are still in Europe, but we've gotten a lot back. There's so much stuff—" She waved her hand at the shelves and file cabinets.

In small doses, Lyn had to admit it was fascinating. But she felt no compulsion, as many of the animators did, to spend all her free time digging among the documents. Still, Sandy was right about having an identity: Elisabeth was a specific link to the past.

"But why?" the soldier with Rob was asking Kathy. "Why should it make you uncomfortable to impersonate someone? It might be different if that person was still alive somewhere, but after two hundred years—''

Kathy shook her head, her face clouded. ''It's too frivolous somehow. I don't know—''

''Steve doesn't think there's anything wrong with it, does he?'' asked Lyn.

''No. He thinks it's fine, but I can't help feeling—''

''You don't think we're being disrespectful, do you?'' said Rob.

''Don't be silly,'' Sandy said. ''I wouldn't mind if someone two hundred years from now wants to pretend to be me. At that point I'm sure I won't care in the least.''

''It's not the eighteenth-century people that bother me, it's the animators, if you want to know. I can go along with authenticity up to a point, but sometimes it gets too intense. It's hard to tell where one stops and the other begins, the way some of them go into it. And I'm not the only one who doesn't like it. Remember Simon?''

Sandy rolled her eyes. ''Do I ever!''

''Who was Simon?'' Lyn looked from one to the other.

''He was a soldier last year—Rob, you knew him.''

''Not as well as you did,'' said Rob with a grin.

''Dear heaven, yes. He had only been here two weeks when he decided he hated this place and almost everyone in it. Couldn't wait to go home. He used to come and talk to me about it by the hour— he was a pain really because soldiers haven't got much business around the fishing property. But he was just homesick, Kathy. And he didn't know how to make friends. He was pretty pathetic.''

Kathy frowned. ''There was more to it than that. He told Steve he didn't want to take the name of a real person. He refused. That's when we began discussing the whole thing, and Steve happened to mention—'' She stopped abruptly.

''Mention what?'' prompted Rob.

''Nothing.'' She looked as if she wished she hadn't gotten onto the subject.

''Come on, tell us,'' he urged. ''I do like a bit of gossip.''

Sandy gave him a repressive look. ''What happened?''

Kathy hesitated. ''It isn't something that gets talked about. It was two years ago, before any of you came and before Steve got promoted. There was a woman working at des Roches's who sort of went off the deep end. She got so involved with her character she

16

couldn't separate out of it. Her husband was terribly upset—he took her away in the middle of the season.''

"So? Where is she now?" asked Rob.

"I don't know. They just left."

"No one at des Roches's said anything about her when I was there," said Sandy. "Who was she?"

"Steve never said and I didn't ask. She was an older woman—her character was Agathe something. That's all I can tell you, and I shouldn't have said that much."

"She was probably having personal problems—trouble with her husband, or menopause, or a kid on drugs," said Sandy. "You never know about people underneath."

"I'll say," agreed Rob. "Look at you lot!"

Kathy shook herself. "Come on, Lyn, we've got to get back before Phyllis gets annoyed. We're already late."

→» 2 «←

"JULY TWENTY-FOURTH, SEVENTEEN FORTY-FOUR." JOAN Pearson stood on a bench at the front of the room, holding an open steno pad, frowning at them over her half-glasses. "For those of you who are purists, it happens to have been a Friday." Her voiced carried above the shufflings and mutterings of the animators as they buttoned cuffs and laced waistcoats, pulled up stockings, combed hair and gulped hot coffee from Styrofoam cups, preparing to shed the twentieth century for another day in the fortress.

"You are there," intoned a voice from somewhere near the windows.

"Okay. You've now got three Compagnie des Indes trading ships in the harbor: the *Philibert,* the *Argonaute* and the *Pientieue.* They cause quite a stir—you hadn't known they were coming, and there are three more on the way. They're huge, and they've come all the way from the Far East with cargoes of tea, porcelain, coffee, spices and cloth. Each one carries more than a hundred sailors, and they make a real impression on the town. A lot of the men are in rough shape—it's been a long trip around the Cape of Good Hope—but they've got terrific stories to tell, even if you don't believe half of what they say. The really sick ones are carted off to the hospital— the Brothers of Charity are going to be run off their sandals before

17

this is over. The ambulatory sailors are all over the town—mostly in the cabarets and taverns.''

"Singing lewd songs, pinching girls and getting plastered," observed Sandy. She held a pocket mirror for Lyn, who was twisting her straight brown hair into a knot and skewering it with bobby pins. It would begin to slither down before lunchtime. Lyn envied Sandy her thick, wiry curls; they sprang from under her bonnet in a becoming and suitably blowsy way. "Oh, *merde.*" Sandy rolled her eyes. "Madeleine's brought the brat with her today."

"Her husband's at a dental conference in Halifax and she can't ever get a sitter on Sundays," said Lyn around a mouthful of pins.

"A whole conference for teeth? Crikey!"

"It isn't Alexandre's fault that he's obnoxious. He'd be a decent enough kid if she'd just leave him alone."

Sandy made a rude noise. "Then he's doomed to brathood."

"I suppose. If only Madeleine would loosen up and let him enjoy himself when he comes—the other kids have a ball here, dressed up in costumes, charging around, having their pictures taken. Alexandre's eight years old, but she won't let him out of her sight." Lyn was sorry for Alexandre and irritated by his mother.

"The other event is the arrival of the warship *Caribou* from Canada," Joan continued. "Governor Duquesnel's plan is to send the *Caribou* and a second warship, the *Ardent,* after the Duvivier expedition, to support the French attack on the English at Annapolis Royal. Duvivier will set out on the twenty-ninth—officially the townspeople don't know this, but it's a safe bet you're all talking about it. When it comes to information, Louisbourg leaks like a sieve—somebody *always* knows what's going on. And it's important because it's your last big attempt to drive the English out of Isle Royale altogether."

"Does it work?" asked a soldier, and was greeted with good-natured jeers and cries of "Go look it up!"

"First year," said Sandy sagely. "He ought to know the answer."

Joan shook her head. "Another thing you don't know is that John Bradstreet has finally reached Boston with Duquesnel's request that the English and French exchange prisoners. You're all sick of having the town warehouses and outbuildings full of English soldiers under guard—you want to get rid of them well before winter

18

sets in and supplies get tight. Before the ships from France can no longer make it through the pack ice with provisions. Okay? Questions?''

"Any babies born in town?'' asked de Gannes's cook.

"Not today.''

"How are the privateers doing?'' asked Ordonnateur Bigot's secretary, buckling his knee breeches.

"Really I should make you wait and see. All I can say is that you French are doing much worse out there than you think you are. You had a banner month in June, capturing English ships left and right, but now they're getting more of yours. You just don't realize it yet. And you don't know that there are Massachusetts reinforcements at Annapolis Royal.''

"You mean it's all downhill from here,'' said Rob cheerfully.

" 'Fraid so,'' Joan agreed. "Bad fishing year, too. But not to worry—the worst of it happens after the tourist season, when you've all gone home to the twentieth century. Right now, most of you are merry as grigs.''

"What's a grig?'' asked Lyn. Sandy shook her head.

Every morning, Joan came to brief the animators on the events of the day in 1744, to help them into the right frame of mind and give them appropriate things to talk about among themselves and to tourists. It was a painless way to absorb Louisbourg history, and like many other things at the park, it was designed to make the past seem less past. At eight-thirty, they all trooped out and climbed onto the buses to be shuttled the mile or so from the compound to the turf-roofed cottage outside the fortress's main gate. Once across the drawbridge, they scattered to their various locations in the town and got ready for the invasion of visitors.

Lyn still felt a faint shiver of anticipation each time the fortress came into view across the low, marshy land at the southern end of the harbor. It grew out of the point: a jigsaw of roofs and chimneys, crowned at the top of the slight rise by the long line of the citadel with its slender clock tower. Approaching from this direction, people saw it very much as it must have been two hundred years earlier, with the open sea beyond. None of the distractions of the modern world were visible, except the narrow tarmac road the bus traveled. The present-day town, with its traffic, telephone poles and fish plant, lay in the other direction, out of sight. The effect was quite extraordinary.

All visitors left their cars, vans and RVs in big, well-screened parking lots near the park entrance, and were transported, like the animators, on buses to the des Roches's fishing property to begin their exploration. Once they had safely negotiated the soldier on guard duty at the drawbridge—who could at whim give people a very hard time; Dorrie with all her camera equipment had gotten the third degree on her first unaccompanied visit and had not been amused—people had several choices. They could proceed at their own pace, following the guidebook in a systematic fashion or wandering at will in any direction or taking one of the fairly strenuous tours led by French- and English-speaking guides in khaki uniforms. Wherever they went, they kept stumbling over eighteenth-century inhabitants gossiping, making nails in the forge, whitewashing walls or shingling roofs, concocting meals in the demonstration kitchens, making lace, hanging out laundry, gathering herbs, cleaning flintlocks, feeding chickens. Visitors were welcome to stop and watch, or to interrupt with questions, and the animators would reply in character as much as possible, though allowances were made for questions like where's the nearest bathroom and for tourists not fluent in either English or French. What, for instance, the flocks of Japanese thought of it all, Lyn was intrigued to imagine.

During her morning and afternoon breaks, if she had nothing special to do and it wasn't raining, Lyn usually roamed the streets to see what everyone else was up to. There was almost always some sort of pudding or cake to be sampled in the de Gannes's kitchen, or soldiers to exchange friendly insults with at the guardhouse near the barracks. One of the resident cats had four kittens in the ordonnateur's stables, and Lyn often smuggled them bits of cheese or meatloaf. Sometimes she ran into Dorrie, prowling the town behind her Nikon, assessing textures and shadows and interesting angles. At such times Lyn was struck in how unfamiliar her mother looked. Absorbed in her photography, Dorrie became a different person, someone unattached to seventeen years of motherhood. Lyn had never observed her at work before, but she supposed this was more and more what Dorrie would become once Lyn was launched as a college freshman. It occurred to her that they were *both* embarking on different lives. She wasn't sure how she felt about that.

Out on her afternoon stroll that Sunday, Lyn stopped to talk to a couple of the litter squad by the ornate wooden gate at the entrance to the town's main wharf. They were boys about her own age, dressed in baggy laborers' clothes, whose job it was to scour the streets for discarded film cartons, Kleenex and cigarette butts— twentieth-century debris of all kinds, which they collected in burlap sacks. Overhead the sun blazed in a clear sky and a light breeze wrinkled the harbor. Gulls sliced the warm air on knife-blade wings, alert for the return of the fishing boats. They were out after swordfish at this time of year. Lyn's only previous experience with swordfish had been in the Belmont supermarket, where it turned up from time to time as innocuous, expensive, grayish steaks, shrink-wrapped on plastic meat trays. She had never pictured them as pieces of the huge sword-bearing monsters that were hauled out on the Louisbourg wharves of an evening.

"What do they do with the sword part?" she asked John Duncan curiously. His uncle was a fisherman and lived in a bright blue house in the area of town called Havenside, on the road to the lighthouse.

John shrugged. "Toss it. It isn't good for anything. You want one, I'll get it for you."

"Really?"

"Sure. Why not?"

"You'd know why not if you'd ever smelled one after a few days on land," warned Roger Fiske with a grin. "Phew stinko!"

John said, "It wears off."

"How long does it take?"

"Six weeks maybe."

"That's about right," said Lyn considering. "Dorrie won't let it in the car if it smells, but if you get me one now—" She smiled, pleased by the idea. "It would be much more interesting on a dorm room wall than a hockey stick."

John was eager to oblige. "Tell you what, if it still smells when you leave, I'll send it to you. You can give me your address."

Roger snorted. "You wouldn't get it through customs."

"Why not? I'll send it in a map tube."

Out of the corner of her eye, Lyn saw Madeleine Charbonneau emerge from the coffeehouse. She stood on the top step and scanned the length of the quay, first one direction, then the other.

"Alexandre must have given her the slip," said Lyn.

"Alexandre?" Roger glanced around.

"Madeleine's son. She barely lets him go to the bathroom by himself, but every now and then he manages to escape while she's busy. She's terrified that something dreadful will happen to him."

"Like what?" said John. "The place is lousy with kids—nobody worries."

"I suppose one might fall into the harbor." Roger sounded dubious.

"Or that evil-minded goat up at the citadel might gore someone—he's figured out how to climb the fence now, and it's only a matter of time before he attacks a tourist. I wonder if our insurance covers that." John grinned.

"She's waving at you," Roger told Lyn.

She borrowed Sandy's favorite expletive. *"Merde."*

Madeleine would have been pretty if she hadn't looked so tightly sewn-up all the time, but Lyn had never seen her relax. Kathy said she was homesick for Montreal; she hadn't adjusted to life in the country. This past spring, her husband had decided to move back to Glace Bay, where he'd grown up, and open his own practice as an endodontist. Rob said he must have come looking for his roots. But instead of accepting what she found on Cape Breton, Madeleine talked endlessly about everything she'd left behind in Montreal. It seemed to Lyn that she was missing the point.

"Carolyn, you haven't seen Alexandre, have you? I don't know where he's gone." Madeleine hurried across the quay.

"He can't have gone far," said John helpfully.

Madeleine ignored him. "I've *told* him not to wander off, I can't understand—"

With an effort at patience, Lyn said, "It's only three, and John's right—he's got to be nearby."

"He's probably pinching nails off Sam at the forge," said Roger.

"Or hanging around the engineer's kitchen—Janet and Ann are making gingerbread this afternoon," Lyn said. "Kids always turn up where there's food. Does Phyllis know you're out here?"

"But he didn't ask," said Madeleine ignoring the question.

Because he knew you'd say no, thought Lyn. Alexandre's not stupid. Aloud, she said, "There's Phyllis—looking for you. She wants you back inside."

"I must find Alexandre first. Carolyn, would you mind—"

22

"Go back to the coffeehouse and *I'll* find him," Lyn told her firmly.

Madeleine looked doubtful; Phyllis looked impatient. Before Madeleine could argue further, Lyn set off in the direction of the artillery forge. John and Roger went with her. "Sucker," said John.

"It's *my* break and I'm not giving it up for no good reason. Alex is off enjoying himself. If Madeleine found him, she'd land on him like a ton of bricks, but if I bring him back, she'll have to keep her temper in front of the customers." She made a wry face. "Keep an eye out for him, will you? He's wearing blue breeches, a white shirt and clogs—about so high, with blond hair."

"That narrows it down to seventy-five percent of the little boys in the fortress," said Roger.

"Try calling him Alexandre—if he runs the other way, you'll know you've found the right one."

They separated in front of the king's storehouse, John and Roger continuing toward the main gate, while Lyn turned left to check the forge. Sam often conscripted boys to work the bellows for him— they seemed to think it was a great privilege. The courtyard in front of the forge was full of a walking tour, clumped around Sam and his anvil. Alexandre was nowhere in sight. Lyn spotted the tour leader, Kate Runcie, lurking on the edge while Sam did his stuff, and asked her if she'd seen Alexandre anywhere along her route. Kate shook her head. "Madeleine doing her hysterical mother act again? If he were mine, I'd push him out the door and good riddance. But I'll watch out for him," she promised. "Okay," addressing her group, she briskly pulled it back to her with the skill of long practice, "now we're going to the storehouse. Any building with a slate roof and a fleur-de-lis on top belongs to the king—that's how you can tell. The storehouse is where they keep all the supplies for the soldiers: uniforms, blankets, tools, lumber, dried peas and beans—if you know the right people, you can get just about anything you want for a price. . . ." A flock after their bellwether, the tourists followed Kate out of the yard. Lyn asked Sam, with no better luck. "Haven't seen him today. Try the guardhouse, why don't you?" But Lyn headed first for the engineer's residence. Gingerbread was a strong lure—she wouldn't mind a slab herself. But she'd have to be careful of the time. Phyllis got quite starchy when people forgot.

Of all the houses in the reconstruction, Lyn liked the engineer's best. It stood on the corner of the rue Toulouse and the rue Royale, an imposing L-shaped stone building. Monsieur Verrier, the fortress's engineer, had seen to it that he lived in considerable comfort at the king's expense while planning additions to the town and its fortifications. Besides living quarters, he had stables, an office and an elegant little garden planted in geometrical vegetable and herb beds, with a sundial in the middle. Despite his perquisites, his wife had declined to bring their daughters and come out from France to join him. Sometimes he spent the winter with her, but for twenty years they had basically lived apart. Without telephones and airplanes, their lives must have been quite separate. Nor was Verrier the only man in Louisbourg to have left a family in France: Governor Duquesnel, gouty, one-legged, veteran of many campaigns, also had a wife "at home." Lyn often wondered what kind of people they were, what kind of marriages they had, why they bothered—

Ahead of her, in the rue Royale, she could hear Kate's voice again, lecturing about colonial government. "—but it's Ordonnateur Bigot who doles out all the money, not Governor Duquesnel. He's—" As she turned the corner, Lyn had the oddest sensation. It flashed through her and was gone almost before she could grasp it— it was as if she had performed that precise action before. But of course she had, many times—that wasn't it. More as if she was *watching* herself do it—inexplicably detached. She shivered and suddenly the street gave a violent lurch. She collided hard with something she couldn't see—it knocked the breath out of her, and someone—it might have been Lyn herself—gave a muffled exclamation. The ground dropped under her feet, she stepped wrong, her right ankle twisted, she fell.

At the same instant, the air thickened and became a heavy impenetrable gray. It closed down on her like a fist, her vision blurred. People my age don't *have* strokes, she thought wildly. Panic burned the back of her throat. Blindly she thrust out her hands and hit the wall close beside her. Rough, wet stones scraped her fingers painfully. Her skirts tangled in her legs as she thrashed and she felt something rip. She forced herself to be still. Her chest was heaving and her pulse thundered in her ears; her mouth was full of the taste of cucumbers. Lunch. That calmed her.

The ground was slimy with mud, her hand stung and her ankle

throbbed, but otherwise she seemed all right. Except for her eyes. She blinked. The dimming of her sight was external, she suddenly realized. It was fog. Damp, chilly fog, filling the street, mopping up the light like a sponge. An overpowering rank sewage smell clogged her nostrils. She must have run into someone from the group, lost her balance. But the *fog* . . . And where was Kate? She couldn't hear her. . . .

People approached behind her. Practically on top of her, a man's voice said something unintelligible, the syllables oddly accented and slurred. Before Lyn could sort it out, hands grasped her by the shoulders and pulled her roughly to her feet. There was more ripping, and laughter—loud masculine laughter. She tried to wrench free to see whose fingers were digging into her flesh, but the hands shifted upward to cover her eyes, and the voice spoke again, alarmingly close to her ear. The man's fingers were strong and callused and stank with an oily fishy smell; his breath blasted her. He'd been drinking. He wasn't speaking English. It sounded a bit like French, but she couldn't untangle the words. Whoever he was, she was in no mood for teasing. The chaos inside her head organized itself into anger. "Let go of me!" she demanded. "You're destroying my costume, and if you don't get your filthy hands out of my face I'm going to throw up all over you."

To her indignation, he only laughed again, trapping her hard against him with offensive familiarity. She struggled with his hands, not caring if she scratched, and another voice said, *"Are you sure you want her, my friend? She is a cat, that one!"*

Some distance away, a third man called out of the fog. The one holding Lyn gave a grunt of annoyance. The second voice, the clearer of the two, said, *"Leave her—come on, André! You do not know who she is!"*

André spat something through his teeth. Without warning, he released Lyn and gave her a sharp little shove between the shoulder blades that sent her staggering forward. Recovering herself, she turned to confront him. He was dressed in costume, but he was no one she remembered seeing before. He wore a sacking cloak over his shoulders, and a knitted cap from which his hair hung lank and wet. When he grinned at her she could see uneven gaps between his teeth. *"You want to come with us, hein?"* he said, with a gesture so plain she could not help but understand. Her stomach clutched

25

unpleasantly. She didn't even glance at the second man; there was something dangerous about the first. She felt shaken and confused, disoriented. Too much had happened too fast. Before he could stop her, she backed out of reach, then walked quickly away. "Kate?" she called. "Kate?" But there was no answer.

At the corner of the engineer's house, she stopped to steady herself, taking deep, even breaths. To her relief, neither man had followed. She brushed the damp hair back from her face, and too late remembered the state of her hands. There was greenish brown mud all over her apron, and her skirt had ripped at the waistband. She must be a frightful sight. She'd have to mop herself up in the engineer's kitchen before going back through the streets—Janet would have a couple of safety pins, but the costume department was not going to be pleased when they saw what she'd done to her clothes.

A man and a boy with a handcart rattled past, vague in the gloom. The lop-eared brown dog with them paused to sniff the hem of her skirt, but when she spoke to it, it shied and growled. The boy whistled and it slunk away, tail down. The sight of it disturbed her. Before she could think why, three soldiers waded out of the fog, wearing their heavy gray greatcoats, tricorn hats pulled low over their ears. Twenty minutes ago, the soldiers had been sweltering in their blue uniforms. One of the three called something to Lyn. She looked at them, then quickly away, seized with an irrational fear that she would not recognize any of them. After a month in the park, she knew *all* the animators, at least by sight.

Leaning against the cold stone wall, she shut her eyes for a moment. Forget the fog and the strangers, and the jerk who'd given her such a dandy set of bruises. Concentrate on what she'd come for—to find Alexandre Charbonneau. Madeleine would be catatonic by this time if Alexandre hadn't reappeared, and Phyllis would be in a temper because Lyn was missing. "Shoot!" said Lyn aloud. The sound of her own voice was encouraging. As long as she was there, she might just as well check the engineer's house.

Not surprisingly, the garden was deserted and the door to the kitchen closed against the thick, wet afternoon. It was unlocked, of course. Visitors were told to try all closed doors; they were welcome behind any that weren't locked. Inside, the room was dim and smoky. There were no tourists hanging over the rope barrier, watch-

26

ing Janet and Ann prepare food. There was no rope barrier. For an instant Lyn thought she had mistaken the house, but she couldn't have. The garden lay behind her, where it belonged, its sundial ghostly and useless in the center. The room was the right size and shape, with the big stone hearth on the left, but the furniture was different. The table had been shifted closer to the fire, and there was a bench—and the people—

The man sitting with his elbows on the table and a mug in front of him wasn't Mark Baldwin, the gardener—he was older, the wrong build. And the woman at the hearth wasn't Janet. She raised her face, red from the heat, her mouth opening in a question, and Lyn stared at her blankly.

The man spoke. He said, *"What is it?"* The language *was* French, but not as Lyn was used to hearing it. What is it? her brain translated with difficulty. But she couldn't begin to find the words to answer. There was a peculiar buzzing in her ears, like a fly against a window-pane. Raising her voice above it, she demanded, "Who are you?"

The surprise on their faces was turning to something more complicated as they looked at her, absorbing the details of her appearance. The man scraped his stool back and got up, and Lyn's presence of mind deserted her altogether. She slammed the door shut on them and fled out of the garden, back into the street. The buzzing went with her. Suddenly, unavoidably, she was sick to her stomach.

Up came the cucumbers and all the rest of her lunch. She gasped and spat, trying to rid her mouth of the sour taste. The tuna salad must have been off. She shuddered, hoping that was the end of it, and glad there was no one to see her. The water in the air was just short of rain and her chemise was wet through; her hair clung vinelike to her neck, and her woolen stockings were in lumps around her ankles. She could hardly have felt more miserable. Perhaps she was coming down with something—flu, or a summer cold. She'd have to cancel out of the camping trip. Blast Madeleine Charbonneau anyway!

It was pointless to stay out any longer—she'd go back to the coffeehouse and throw herself on their mercy. When they saw she was sick, they'd put her to bed on the cot in the staff room for the rest of the afternoon. The idea of being taken care of suddenly appealed to Lyn tremendously. Wrapped in misery, she made her way doggedly back to the rue Toulouse, ignoring the figures she passed in the murk. At the bottom of the street, the bright, glittering harbor had disappeared. She could see the dark shape of the Frederick Gate, and beyond it a gray blank. She hunched her shoulders and hurried toward it, trying to close the rest of the world out. It was cold and it dripped, and it was full of sounds and movements on all sides that she couldn't think about. People shouted, carts clattered on the uneven cobbles, the air was sticky with salt and tar and the smell of fish so strong it was almost tangible—like trying to breathe soup. Lyn's skin was clammy and sensitive, as if she were feverish.

Out in the invisible harbor there were things happening: squeaking and scraping, disembodied voices calling and answering and cursing, the splash of oars and creaking of oarlocks, waves slapping against wooden planking, gulls muttering, and ropes groaning as they stretched taut. Without meaning to, Lyn began to run. She bumped into someone who grunted and swore, but righted herself and kept going. She caught her foot in a tangle of wet rope on the corner of the quay, but managed to shake it off. There was a nasty fluttering under her breastbone. She passed Madame Grandchamp's little inn, where Sandy would be entertaining tourists with her mildly bawdy stories about the local fishermen, and there—right where it should be—was the coffeehouse, solid against the fog, standing apart from its neighbors. Lyn bunched up her bedraggled skirts and climbed the steps. The door was closed. For just a second she hesitated, her hand on the metal latch. Suppose, when she opened it, the coffeehouse had changed, too—

A billow of warm, yeast-smelling air enveloped her as she pushed the door inward, smothering as an eiderdown. The little central hall was dim with shadow. There was no cheerful bubble of conversation, rattle and clink of dishes. Lyn's people weren't there—Kathy, Madeleine, Phyllis—smiling, apologizing because the custard tarts had run out, complaining because the tankards came out of the dishwasher too hot to handle, clinking coins in a hidden pocket to remind customers about tipping. Lyn froze in the doorway, transfixed. Faces swam toward her out of the darkness. None she recognized. They were ghosts, pale and shimmering. Lyn's teeth began to chatter with a chill that struck right through her. One of the apparitions came weaving at her, white hands outstretched, reaching. The figure made noises, but the buzzing in her ears was too loud—she couldn't understand. The walls surged up at her, the floor pitched, hands caught hold of her as the fog swept in.

28

⇶ 3 ⇷

SHE HAD FAINTED. SHE KNEW IT ALMOST AS SOON AS IT HAP-pened, but she couldn't do anything about it. She was outraged by her helplessness. Only once before had she ever come close to fainting. The first time she gave blood, no one had remembered to warn her about sitting up quickly and the church hall had spun. They'd made her breathe into a paper bag and lie with her knees drawn up for half an hour on a swaybacked Red Cross cot, even though she felt perfectly all right in five minutes and embarrassed by the fuss. It gave the nurses a chance to be professional, but it ran counter to Lyn's self-image of competency.

This time she was sick. She had a fever and a pounding headache and she felt dizzy and nauseated. She was being carried like a sack of laundry between two people. Fingers dug painfully into her armpits, and her legs were bundled together awkwardly with her skirts. There was a confusion of voices—male and female—urgent, excited, foreign voices, exploding with exclamations and question marks.

Without ceremony, she was dumped onto something hard—a bench it felt like—and propped upright. The voices went on and on, shredding the air, beating at her skull. She struggled to free herself from the darkness, but before she could get her eyes open, the sharp metal rim of a cup was thrust between her lips and a bitter liquid tipped into her mouth. It stung her nose. She choked and spluttered and jerked her head away, her eyes wide and watering fiercely.

She tried to ask, "What is that stuff?" but all she could manage was a thin wheeze. There seemed to be a great many people pressing in on her, breathing her air, staring at her. She had no idea who they were. The ghosts—there were two of them—turned out to be men wearing floppy white caps and things like bedsheets tied around their middles. Their bare forearms were smudged with white pow-der. Kneeling on the floor in front of Lyn was a young woman, her soft anxious face framed in white ruffles. Her eyes were a beautiful, intense blue. She held a tankard in one hand and there was a wet brownish stain on the front of her chemise. Behind her stood a barrel-shaped woman with a sharp, unforgiving face, and a little girl who peered solemnly at Lyn over the head of the large baby she was clutching. In the background, Lyn glimpsed a crooked, wispy old man, who quite obviously had no teeth in his mouth.

For a long, silent moment they stared at Lyn as she stared back at them. They seemed to be waiting for something. She straightened her back and her ears sang; her stomach felt like the inside of a washing machine. She swallowed hard, willing everything to stay put. The young woman blinked, set down the tankard and caught Lyn's hand between her two before Lyn could resist. *"Elisabeth,"* she said, and then a lot more Lyn couldn't begin to follow. "No!" cried Lyn in alarm. The woman's voice trailed away and she looked frightened. Cautiously Lyn gave her head a shake. "I don't understand." Her tongue tasted furry. "What did you give me? Who are you?"

The young woman uttered an exclamation of distress. One of the ghosts pulled off his cap and said something to her in a low, urgent tone. He had a mournful face and his hair was thinning on top, Lyn noticed irrelevantly. Why did none of them speak English? Everyone in the fortress spoke English. But these people paid no attention to her questions—it was as if they didn't understand her. The older woman interrupted, her voice irritable, and the young one turned back to Lyn. *"Elisabeth, you must tell me what has happened,"* she said earnestly. *"Did you not find Pierre? Do you know where he is? Was there an accident? Are you injured?"*

The vowel sounds and inflections were French, she was sure—if only she didn't feel so awful. . . . Somewhere nearby a baby began to wail: a needle of sound that drove excruciatingly into Lyn's head. On and on it went. When did it breathe? The two women were discussing her. If only the baby would shut up, Lyn thought desperately, she might be able to understand what they were saying. Although they kept calling her Elisabeth they seemed to know her, but she was sure she'd never seen any of them before. Her stomach lurched and she shut her eyes tight, willing it not to heave.

When she judged it safe to relax a little, she took a long breath and looked up to find the younger ghost regarding her with undisguised curiosity. He was, she guessed, a year or two older than she, dark-skinned beneath the powder, narrow-faced, good-looking. The little girl was watching her, too, but when Lyn caught her eyes, she flicked them away and retreated to the hearth. The toothless man seemed to have disappeared.

The room was a kitchen, typical of the eighteenth-century Louisbourg kitchens, lit by the fire sinking to coals in the wide, soot-blackened fireplace and by the thin, gray, rain light that leaked in through two windows in the wall behind Lyn. The hearth was cluttered with cooking pots, trivets, roasting forks. There was a long plain wooden table in the middle of the floor, surrounded by benches, and two straight-backed chairs. On the wall opposite Lyn was a tall, dark dresser lined with crockery and pewter, and next to the hearth, to her left, a large rectangular thing which she recognized as a *cabane,* a cupboard bed. It had sliding doors that shut to keep out drafts. She searched her mind, but although she knew there were a couple of them in the reconstructed houses, she couldn't remember such a bed in any of the kitchens. It wasn't de Gannes's and it wasn't the engineer's, but where else—

The voices stopped. Something had been decided. His face very long, the middle-aged ghost left the room through the door beside the dresser. With a mighty effort, Lyn collected her wits and cleared her throat. So far she had had gratifying success with her French and had managed to converse with tourists at a level considerably more sophisticated than *"Good-day-welcome-to-the-Pugnant-house-what-do-you-wish-to-drink-thank-you-very-much."* The new teacher at Belmont high was a genuine Frenchman and had given the fourth-year students a solid grounding in idiomatic French, encouraging them to read newspapers, magazines and paperback mysteries, as well as Gide and Sartre and *Les Carnets du Major Thompson.* Rummaging for the right words, Lyn said distinctly, *"I believe there is a mistake. I do not know where I am. Can you tell me?"* As an afterthought, she added, *"Please?"*

The young woman gasped, then uttered a flood of agitated words. They cascaded over Lyn, knocking her breathless. She caught the name Elisabeth several times, and Pierre, but that was all. She put up her hands to protect herself. *"Too fast!"* she protested. *"My head—I can't—where is Kathy Gagnon? Or Phyllis? Where's Phyllis?"*

31

The flood stopped abruptly, and she was met with a blank stare. The older woman tapped her own head significantly, her mouth zipped tight.

"Dorrie," said Lyn. *"Dorothea Paget. My mother. Where is my mother?"*

"Oh, Elisabeth!" cried the young woman, the brightness in her eyes spilling over and running down her cheeks. *"Françoise,"* she said faintly.

"Françoise?"

"Elisabeth, my poor one. I know that you miss her. I too cannot believe that she is gone—she was such a comfort to me. But she does not suffer—she is in heaven now and we must not grieve. Remember what Père Athanase said to us."

"Who?" Lyn was totally lost. *"But I'm not—this isn't—"*

The door opened and a small, straight figure in a long skirt and starched white cap marched into the room. Behind her came the first ghost. Hastily, the young woman stood up, brushing the tears from her face with her fingers. *"Maman—"*

"Marguerite, what is this?" Despite her size, the woman dominated everyone the moment she entered. She walked carefully, with a tiny hesitation on every other step. The ghost started to speak, but she cut him short with an impatient gesture. He gave the young woman an apologetic look, then frowned at the other ghost and the two of them disappeared through another door on Lyn's right. *"Louise, can you not stop that noise?"* The little girl began at once to rock a cradle on the hearth, whispering into it, and the wail gradually faltered into hiccups. *"Good. Now, Marguerite. Explain to me what is going on."*

In a low, hesitant voice, the young woman began. Lyn tried to follow her but soon gave up the struggle. Mother and daughter, she guessed, watching them. She noticed the way the skin of the old one's face was pulled tight and smooth over her prominent cheekbones and drawn up in tiny puckers around her eyes and the thin, straight seam of her mouth. It was not a sympathetic face. She kept firing terse questions at the young woman, Marguerite, that caused her to stumble. It was quite clear that the old woman was not pleased with the answers. At one point, she turned her head and glared at Lyn for several minutes, and Lyn was first to look away. But *I've done nothing wrong,* she thought indig-

32

nantly, why should *I* feel guilty? If only they'd all stop talking and let me *think*—

"Mon dieu, *you silly girl!*" exclaimed the old woman sharply. *"Florent? Where is Florent? We must find Pierre, then I will deal with you, Elisabeth!"*

There was a movement in the shadowy corner opposite the *cabane,* and the little bent man shuffled across the floor, grinning toothlessly. His clothes hung on him, limp and frayed, as if he were a badly made coat hanger. He stood, ducking his head, grinning and grinning, as the old woman gave him a string of orders, then he shuffled out of the room. Lyn watched him go. If only *she* could do that—just leave—shut the door on all these incomprehensible people. The edges of her vision wavered peculiarly as if hazed by heat; her hands were cold and her skin clammy with sweat. She felt lousy. She wanted to go and lie down, sleep the whole thing off. Well, why not? Sucking in a deep breath, she stood up and a swarm of tiny bright flashes filled the room. Her skirt was sodden and stank, her hands were sore, her ankle ached; she was perversely heartened: the discomfort was very real. No one expected her to make an awkward dash for the door. No one moved to stop her. On the threshold she paused momentarily and announced in clear English, "I don't know what's happened, or who any of you are, but I'm Carolyn Paget, and I'm getting out of here." She limped hastily down the dark hallway to the door at the far end. Behind her someone called out and she heard footsteps. She fumbled with the latch and pushed. Nothing happened. She threw her weight at the door and heard something thumping against the other side. The latch shook vigorously under her fingers. She swore softly. All the doors in Louisbourg opened inward—it made the hall in the coffeehouse extremely awkward to negotiate when there were crowds. As she stepped back, the door swung toward her. She dodged it and ran out, straight into the arms of the man who was on his way in. He grabbed her to keep from being swept off his feet, and for a moment they grappled precariously, glued together by their opposing force. Rain fell cold and steady on Lyn's face. Over the man's shoulder lay the edge of the quay, the Frederick Gate, the harbor, just where she expected them to be. The fog had lifted a little with the coming of rain, and through it Lyn could see tall dark shapes on the water—lots of them. Big, unfamiliar things. Ships. Their masts were blurred pencil strokes against the shifting gray. On the street below a wagon trundled past, drawn by a pair of oxen, its wheels sizzling in the mud. Cloaked, anonymous figures hurried around it. Somewhere a dog barked and barked, then gave a yelp as someone silenced it. There were no dogs in the park.

The man—another stranger—had Lyn firmly by the arms now, his heavy wet cape enveloping her, his breath moist and sweet with the smell of wine. Under the dripping brim of his tricorn he scowled at her. "Sacredie! *Elisabeth! What does this mean! You have almost knocked me down—what goes on? Where are you going?"*

She stared at him stupidly. If he had let her go at that moment she would have fallen in a heap on the steps; her legs were boneless. He gave her a shake that made her head wobble and throb, and thrust her roughly back into the house. When he removed his hands, she stumbled backward and sat down hard on the bottom of a staircase. The women from the kitchen crowded the hall, and the two ghosts had reappeared in the doorway where Lyn had first seen them. It's starting all over again, she thought, faintly hysterical. How many times would she have to go through it? She'd never hallucinated before, not even when she'd been so sick with measles that she'd lost two whole days. She wondered if she had actually fainted, or only imagined that she'd fainted. How could she tell? What was going on? Why couldn't anyone see she was ill and do something for her? She felt rotten. Maybe it was food poisoning? She could still taste that cucumber. . . .

All the while the voices raged around her, angry, accusing, apologetic, argumentative—the new one loudest of all. She clutched her head, not trying to sort them out. The man who had just come in took off his cape and hat, spraying her with drops of water, and smoothed his hair with stubby fingers. It was tied back in a queue. Glancing down at Lyn with obvious distaste, he brushed the front of his coat, twitched it straight, and shouldered his way peremptorily down the hall. The old woman stood still for a moment, then snapped angrily, *"You smell like a sewer, Elisabeth! Go and change your clothing. I will speak to you later."*

When Lyn didn't move, she demanded, *"Dear God, what is the matter with you? Have you lost your wits? Are you dumb? Can you not hear me? Christophe! Take her upstairs and be quick!"*

Before she could prevent him, the mournful ghost gathered her up

34

clumsily, not quite sure where to put his hands, and half carrying, half pushing, he took her up the stairs. The air at the top was dank and heavy; she shivered, chilled to the bone. She kept seeing the harbor full of ships and the rain beating down on the muddy street, and her knees wobbled. What could it mean? She leaned against the wall and he opened a door in front of her, then retreated without a word.

The little room was vaguely lit by a single window. She felt inside for a light switch, hoping to find one and sure she wouldn't. Nothing. She took a couple of steps forward and barked her shin on something hard and sharp. She said "Shit!" with great feeling. Soon there wouldn't be a square inch on her body that wasn't bruised or scraped or covered with lumps—she was tender and sore all over.

It was a bedroom. There were beds in it anyway—and not much else. She made out a fourposter with a canopy, a cot in the far corner, and the thing she'd fallen over—a trundle, one of those boxlike beds that could be pushed out of the way during the day. There was a blanket chest under the window, and a clothes cupboard beside it, about four feet high. Lyn sneezed and rubbed her arms, wincing at the bruises. Dry clothes. That was the first thing. No matter where she was, if she didn't get out of that wet stuff quickly she'd have pneumonia on top of her other troubles.

The cupboard had paneled doors—it should have looked antique but it didn't. On the shelves inside were piles of clothing. She rummaged through them, searching for something to change into, pulling various garments out, then wadding them up and stuffing them back again. If only she could find a pair of jeans and a T-shirt, a moth-eaten pullover, a turtleneck. But everything she touched was more of what she had on: bits of costume. Shapeless muslin chemises, heavy skirts, thick hairy stockings, aprons of coarse striped material, white cotton bonnets. There was a pair of knickers, but when she held it up it was much too small. Baby clothes, squares of cloth, handkerchiefs, a worn brocade waistcoat . . .

In the end there was no choice. She stripped to her underpants— she drew the line at underwear, and anyway she hadn't found any— then stopped, suddenly immobile. The things she'd chosen were roughly the right size: Clothes of this sort always were only roughly the right size. They got handed around from person to person, taken

35

in or up, let out, patched and darned, until they were past salvage. But Lyn hadn't a clue to whom these belonged. She felt as if, by putting them on, she was signing her name to a document she couldn't read. Still, she couldn't just stand there, rooted to the spot, naked and freezing to death. Especially with her head pounding like a jackhammer.

The fastenings were troublesome—they weren't quite like the ones she was used to. There were no little hooks artfully hidden inside where they wouldn't show, only buttons and ties. Her shoes were wet, but all she could find to substitute was a pair of wooden-soled clogs that were about size three. In spite of her reluctance, she felt better once she was dry. She left her discarded things in a miserable lump on the floor, then remembered her pockets. She dug out her few possessions: a wad of fuzzy solidified Kleenex, a large safety pin, the stub of a well-bitten pencil, a handful of coins—three quarters, four dimes and six nickels, all Canadian. Her last customers, a nice elderly couple from Mystic, Connecticut, had tipped her sixty cents in spite of being worried about the cairn terrier they'd left shut in their camper. She closed her eyes and wondered where they were at that moment. Miles away. The only other things were her order pad with LYN #7 on the cover in Phyllis's square capitals, and her key to the apartment on Oak Street. Nothing of value—the key could easily be duplicated, and there wasn't enough money for a hamburger, but it was all she had to prove who she was. There were no pockets in her borrowed skirt, so she tied the little collection carefully in her damp neckerchief and thrust it far back in the cupboard on the top shelf, where it was hidden. All except the key and the safety pin. Using the pin, she fastened the key inside the waistband of her skirt where she could feel it dig into her.

Outside the window the dismal afternoon was ebbing fast. Grays and blacks ran together in the dissolving light. Directly below was a yard surrounded by a high stockade fence with a huddle of sheds at the far end. Beyond them rose the dark angles of rooftops, shouldering each other back to meet the low slate-colored sky. The only moving things she could see were the ubiquitous wind-blown gulls and dirty rags of cloud. It was a bleak, unpromising view. Lyn was overcome with a paralytic heaviness. She ached all over. There was no way she could force herself back down the stairs to face that roomful of strangers. She simply couldn't cope. Her grasp of time had slipped completely—she had no idea how long she had been in that chilly little room, but they seemed to have forgotten her. Maybe they weren't there anymore—or maybe *she* wasn't, wherever there was. But she wasn't where she belonged, either, and she had to be somewhere. Her head was clogged with a slippery, mushlike applesauce.

She didn't bother to undress. She pushed her shoes carefully under the canopy bed so she could find them again. It was a good-sized bed, big enough for two people, with curtains tied back on each side. She got into it, curled herself up tight under the coarse blankets. The pillow rustled and scratched and smelled musty, but she ignored it and closed her eyes, sinking into a bottomless oblivion. Twice she felt the surface ruffled: once someone came to the door with a light and called *"Elisabeth"* softly several times. The second time there were people actually in the room, moving around, making little noises, scrabbling, creaking, coughing, causing the floorboards to groan. There were whispers, a muffled exclamation, more whispers. It seemed as if someone got into bed with her, nudged her, but it might have been part of the peculiar dream she was having. She plunged deeper, out of reach.

The sound of footsteps overhead dragged Lyn out of sleep into the darkness. People were clattering around on the bare floor above, making no attempt to be quiet. She felt thick-headed and her mouth tasted awful; for some reason the bed smelled stale and there were lumps where she didn't expect them. She rolled onto her back and was instantly wide awake. There was someone in it with her, someone who wriggled and moaned softly and burrowed against her. She only just managed to stifle a yell.

For the count of a hundred, she held herself perfectly still, breathing deeply through her nose, while her pulse gradually slowed. When she opened her eyes again, she noticed that the room was tinged with the faintest gray, and the window was a pale rectangle on the dark wall. Early morning. She remembered crawling into the bed, but she had no idea how long ago that had been—except the day before. Clammy fingers of disappointment closed on her throat. She had been hoping to wake up in the foldaway cot on Oak Street, in the room papered with cake-frosting roses, with Dorrie snoring

37

gently in the double bed beside her. She had been hoping that everything that had happened to her since she fell on the rue Royale and the fog had clamped down had been a product of delirium. But if that were true, then she was still delirious. She didn't believe it— she felt too genuinely awful.

Gradually she became aware of noises in the house around her; people were stirring. The room was growing distinct dimensions, and outside, very close, a rooster gave a half-hearted crow, as if he wasn't sure why he was doing it. A clock that sounded very much like the citadel clock chimed a quarter hour. On the other side of the thin wall just behind her head, Lyn heard a baby begin to cry. It was the penetrating, fretful wail of the day before, taking up where it had left off. The body next to her didn't move.

But somewhere, in the same room, Lyn heard a tiny gulping sound—a cough or a hiccup. It came again, muffled, but distinctly unhappy. Someone—a child—was crying. Carefully Lyn pushed back the blanket and sat up. She waited, gripping the edge of the mattress, until the room stopped heaving. Various parts of her body registered outrage, her ankle most of all, as she set her feet on the floor, and her stomach rumbled mournfully.

The sobbing came from the cot in the corner. As she limped gingerly around the trundle, Lyn saw that it was occupied by a very small child—boy or girl, she couldn't tell—sound asleep, with its hand curled next to its cheek like one of the little crabs she'd found washed up on Rochefort Point. No misery there.

But the boy, clenched in a tight ball under his bedclothes, was throbbing with unhappiness. "Here," said Lyn softly, sitting on the cot beside him. "What's the matter with you then? What's wrong?" She brushed the spiky brown hair off his wet face. His eyelashes were webbed with tears. He looked about six—the same age as Mike's youngest sister, Julie. "Shhh, don't cry so hard—you'll make yourself sick. It can't be that bad, whatever it is."

When she touched him, she could feel the tension holding him together, then suddenly he relaxed and hitched himself into her lap. She put her arms around him and rocked gently while he clung. Little by little, his tears subsided and he began to sniff in a recovering sort of way. "Better?" she asked. "Can you tell me?" But he only wiped his nose on the back of his hand and peered up at her. His eyes were watery and pink-rimmed and his ears stuck out like

38

mug handles. His face wore an anxious expression. "What's your name?" she asked.

A sudden loud volley of thumps under her feet made Lyn jump. The little boy's fingers tightened on the sleeve of her chemise; his eyes were round.

From the big bed came gruntings and heavings and a girl about fifteen sat up. She blinked and rubbed her face and exclaimed irritably, then she turned and shook the hump in the middle. *"Louise? Louise—up! Up!"* Flinging back the covers, she jumped out and ran to the cupboard, all the while talking as if someone had switched her onto play. She glared at Lyn but didn't seem in the least surprised to see her.

A second girl, much younger, emerged from the bed, her face full of sleep. She was the body Lyn had felt next to her; could there possibly be more under there? Rabbits out of a hat— But that was all. The older girl had long, thick, gold-brown hair and a delicate-featured, pretty face. The smaller one looked rather unfortunately like the little boy, quite plain. She pushed her straight brown hair back and looked at Lyn, still sitting on the cot. *"Ah, Blaize, what are you doing?"* she said. *"Have you been weeping again? You are such a baby, is it not. You will make Grandmother cross."*

"It is true, Elisabeth, you should not encourage him—it will only make him worse," the older girl said as she pulled her chemise over her head.

Lyn's heart sank. Neither of them spoke English. She glanced down at the boy, but he wriggled free and got up without looking at her. The older girl was staring at her, however, her eyes narrowed, her mouth quirked in annoyance. *"Zut, Elisabeth! That is mine, that apron! Why are you wearing it? Look at it! I cannot wear it myself now it is so crumpled. You are a disgrace—have you slept in your clothing?"* As she scolded she was busy with her hair: combing it, pinning it back.

The baby in the trundle bed was awake by this time, making happy little crowing noises and waving its arms about. It rolled free of its blanket and tumbled onto the floor. It pulled itself upright, grabbing the nearest thing it could find: unfortunately the older girl's skirt. She let out a cry and smacked the baby quite hard. The baby sat down with a thud and howled with indignation.

Lyn's head was pounding again. The room was like a kettle

coming to a boil, seething and bubbling. Even if she had felt well, she would have found all of this difficult to cope with. She was used to mornings that began in tranquility: the waking-up click of her clock radio, the kneading of Gilbert's gray mittens on her chest. As soon as he heard the radio, he would come to crouch over her breastbone, a warm, gently vibrating weight, his gold-green eyes less than a foot from her own. All she and Dorrie talked about in the mornings was weather, shopping, errands, who would start supper. They saved the rest for the other end of the day. Their bathroom schedule was carefully worked out to avoid friction.

Lyn wished she hadn't thought about the bathroom. She was absolutely sure that the kind of bathroom she had in mind didn't exist in this house, and wondered uneasily what there was instead.

In a flurry of words, the older girl departed, flouncing out of the room with a disapproving glare at Lyn. With considerable skill, the other girl was dressing herself and the baby simultaneously, while the boy struggled into his clothes by himself. He came and stood in front of Lyn, clutching a pair of breeches in handfuls around his middle. They had been intended for someone larger and hung loose past his knees. His stockings were wrinkled around his skinny legs like the threads on a screw. Giving herself a shake, Lyn pulled them up for him and tied his makeshift belt snugly. "All right?" she said, then, *"C'est bien?"* He gave a shy nod, then a sudden blinding smile. He was a homely child, all nose and ears, his hair sticking up in a cowlick, but the smile transformed him briefly and Lyn couldn't help returning it.

"Blaize, where are your shoes?" demanded the little girl.

Sabots—shoes, Lyn translated, and remembered to retrieve her own from under the bed where she'd pushed them. She also found a lot of dust and a thick white china pot with a handle. Her stomach contracted and she hastily backed away, afraid of what might be in it. There had to be some alternative and she'd have to find it soon. She would also have to find food; her insides were cold and hollow, and it occurred to her that she hadn't eaten since lunch the day before and she'd lost that on the rue Royale. Whoever these people were, they had to eat breakfast, and she was sure she'd be able to think better after toast and cereal.

"Here." The little girl thrust the comb she'd been using into Lyn's hand. The boy found his shoes and left. There didn't seem to

be a mirror in the room—perhaps that was just as well. Lyn had gone to bed with her hair damp and it had tied itself into knots during the night. When she was eleven she had refused to have it cut anymore, pointing out to Dorrie how much money they would save as a result. Dorrie believed in short hair—so much less fuss. But Dorrie's hair was springy and full of flattering little waves, while Lyn's was fine and limp and plastered itself to her skull like a bathing cap. Cut short, there was nothing she could do with it. Once it grew out she could braid it or pin it up or let it hang loose. . . .

"You will be all morning! What have you done to your hair? Elisabeth, let me. It is not good to begin the day with Suzanne in a temper." The girl snatched the comb away and began to work the snarls out. She was not particularly gentle, and Lyn closed her eyes, enduring the sharp little tugs. *"You frightened Aunt Marguerite so badly yesterday, coming back as you did. And without Pierre. She did not want Uncle Joseph to know that Pierre was missing. She was so upset. And now he is angry."*

"Pierre?" said Lyn cautiously, sifting a name out of the words.

"Yes. You were sent out to find him, is it not? So there would be no trouble. And instead, you return looking as if—"

"I was looking for Alexandre," said Lyn. *"Who is Pierre?"*

There was a silence. The combing stopped. Lyn opened her eyes to find Louise staring at her with a very peculiar expression. *"You do not know your own brother?"*

Brother? Lyn stared back, feeling utterly blank. Louise retreated behind her and began to yank again, hard and fast. *"It is very late,"* she muttered. *"We must go—it is nearly done."*

Choosing her words carefully, Lyn asked in French, *"Louise, what day is it today?"*

Louise did not reply. She put down the comb, took the baby by the hand and crossed to the door. She paused and looked at Lyn, the fear plain in her face. *"It is Saturday, July the twenty-fifth. Yesterday was Friday, July the twenty-fourth."* she answered finally, then hurried the baby downstairs.

⋙ 4 ⋘

T HE DATE WAS RIGHT, BUT ALL THE PEOPLE WERE WRONG. HARD
as she tried, Lyn could not recognize any of them. It was like
something out of a bad dream, a nightmare party where she knew
none of the other guests, but they all seemed to expect her to be
there. The kitchen was full of strangers. Some of them she'd seen
the day before: the florrid, red-haired man at the table shaving
himself with a wicked-looking razor—he was the one she'd wres-
tled with on the steps. And the blue-eyed woman setting crockery
around him—Marguerite. The other woman, the hatchet-faced one,
was stirring a cauldron over the fire. With the steam rising around
her and wisps of gray hair escaping from her cap, she made Lyn
think of the Weird Sisters in *Macbeth*. The little crooked man sat
hunched on a stool in the corner spooning something gloppy into his
mouth, and two more babies staggered and crept around the floor,
getting underfoot. The young woman looked up and smiled as Lyn
hesitated on the threshold, ransacking her mind for the right word—
bathroom, john, toilet—none seemed likely somehow, but her need
was acute by that time. Just then a door across the room opened—
one she hadn't noticed before—and the older girl came in, straight-
ening her skirts. Beyond lay the yard, dripping and woolly with fog.
Lyn took a chance. *"Pardon,"* she muttered, escaping out into the
early morning air. The salt-smelling silence was an immense relief
after the closeness of the kitchen, but she hadn't time to savor it.
There was a path between raised vegetable beds, leading to the back
of the yard, to the cluster of sheds she had seen from the upstairs
window. She picked her way among the puddles, figuring that if all
else failed she could crouch in a sheltered corner, unobserved. The
first shed was a chicken coop; inside she could hear the hens moving
around, making rustling, prooking noises in the darkness. Behind
the next door, Lyn found the astonishing angular brown-and-white
rump of a cow. She gazed at it, momentarily stunned. She'd never

42

been so close to a cow before. From the rear it made her think of the old sprung green sofa they used to have, its hipbones thrusting out above bulging sides. Its tail hung down like a piece of frayed rope, and its udder was swollen. It turned its head and peered at Lyn out of white-rimmed eyes, and moaned softly. "Not me," declared Lyn, backing away.

She recognized the rich, dark, sewage smell for what it was before she opened the third door. Inside was a plank with a hole cut in it—primitive but adequate. She sat gratefully and listened to the almost-rain drip off the roof of the little building, and wondered how in the name of heaven she had come to be there: in the outhouse behind the bakery in Louisbourg. In the right place at the wrong time. It seemed pointless to waste energy pondering the *possibility* of what had happened to her. Much more urgent was deciding how to deal with it.

The language, the clothing, the house, the people—everything was familiar and unfamiliar at the same time. She knew where she was, she was *sure* she knew where she was, but it was different from the way she knew it. And all those people treating her as if she belonged there. They kept calling her Elisabeth. That was really disturbing. The only Elisabeth she could think of was Elisabeth Bernard, the baker's granddaughter, born in February 1727. Serendipity, Joan Pearson had called it when they found her in the family records. A seventeen-year-old girl, living in the Pugnant house. Lyn wanted a character, and *voilà!* there she was, tailor-made. With a sister named Louise, and a brother named Pierre . . .

Sitting in the dark little outhouse, feeling a cold draft on her backside, Lyn shivered. She remembered Kathy Gagnon's story—about the woman who'd lost herself in her eighteenth-century counterpart, got so involved she couldn't disengage anymore. She'd slipped a cog. . . . Lyn gripped the plank with both hands. That couldn't have happened to *her*—she'd never taken it seriously, never spent hours and hours immersing herself in Elisabeth's life. She'd chosen a name for the fun of it—because Rob and Sandy had them. . . .

If only she didn't feel so lousy—her head wasn't working right. But the pain behind her eyes refused to let up; she rocked back and forth, hanging on. Footsteps scrunched on the wet gravel outside,

43

stopped, the latch clicked up. *"No!"* she called in alarm. *"Um*—je suis ici."

"Pardon, *Mademoiselle,"* said a deep male voice just the other side of the door.

She couldn't put it off; she pulled herself together and got up. His was another face she recognized from the day before: he was wearing a loose white shirt and an apron, but no cap. The fringe of hair around the crown of his head was coarse and graying. She guessed he was one of the bakers; the powder on his arms was flour—there was a smudge on his left cheek. He carefully avoided looking at her as she came out, studying his feet instead, and didn't go in himself until she was halfway along the path. She wondered what his name was and if he belonged to Elisabeth's family. There seemed to be an awful lot of people in the house.

Outside the kitchen door was a round, brick-walled hole in the ground, with a winch-and-pulley arrangement mounted above, and a bucket of water beside it. Lyn's hands were still blotched with grime. She washed them as best she could without warm water and soap, then took a deep breath and splashed her face. The cold made her ears ring. She dried herself on her apron, hauled up her sagging courage, and went inside, hoping for breakfast. Food might ease her headache.

While she'd been out, the household had expanded still further. Including Lyn and the three babies, there were fifteen people in the kitchen—sixteen, when the man from the yard returned. And instead of sitting down to eat, they all gathered in a semicircle and knelt on the bare wood floor. Hiding her dismay, Lyn took the place left for her between the young woman and the older of the two girls. The man who'd been shaving read something utterly incomprehensible from a scuffed brown leather-bound book—Lyn guessed it was prayers in Latin. Of course they'd be Catholics. If Dorrie hadn't been so adamantly lapsed Lyn might have known what he was saying—but the church didn't use Latin anymore, and with a French accent . . .

Lyn gave up on it, and instead covertly began to study the faces in the circle. She tried to remember all the names on the piece of paper Joan had photocopied for her in the library. It was called a reconstitution sheet—Sandy joked about frozen orange juice. On it were the names and dates of all the family members who'd lived in the Pugnant house in 1744, so far as they were known. The more she dredged out of her memory, the more peculiar she felt. There were more people than names, but each name fit someone. The old woman was there, pencil-straight, her clasped hands knobbed and misshapen. She'd had trouble kneeling, but had refused help. She could be Marie Pugnant, the baker's widow; and the man reading could be her son-in-law, Joseph Desforges. He was married to her daughter, Marguerite—the blue-eyed woman. Louise, the little girl upstairs, had mentioned Uncle Joseph and Aunt Marguerite . . . Lyn tried to swallow, but her mouth was dry. There was a horrid fascination to this.

Elisabeth's mother had died after childbirth, in June, leaving six children. She was Marguerite's sister, and her name was Françoise. Lyn could see it on the sheet. The children had left their father, who was an artisan, a roofer, and gone to live with their grandmother at the bakery. Lyn had asked Joan why. And Joan had said they would probably never know for sure . . . perhaps he couldn't look after them, or didn't want to. Maybe they were needed to work in the bakery. He would have had the money to take care of them, but their prospects might have been better with Madame Pugnant.

The girl next to Lyn must be Jeanne, the second eldest, and the boy next to Madame Pugnant would be Pierre. He looked like Jeanne—the same gold-blond hair and delicate good looks. Pierre should be eight, the same age as Alexandre Charbonneau, thought Lyn, staring at him. Was it really possible that she *had* lost her grip—gotten everything muddled up together? How could she be imagining people who were two hundred and fifty years old? How could she conjure up real bodies from nothing but a handwritten list of names? Mike had always accused her of lacking imagination—he claimed that was why she didn't like science fiction. A bubble of laughter rose in her chest, threatening to choke her. Across the circle, she was suddenly aware of Louise. She blinked and for an instant their eyes met, then Louise bent her head, deliberately withdrawing. She's afraid, Lyn thought; she looks at me and she isn't sure who I am. It steadied her.

At last they sat down at the table to eat, at least the adults did. Hot, gritty cereal with salt on it, and a little milk—straight from that cow out back, no doubt, and tasting faintly of garlic. Lyn was too hungry to worry about what you got from unpasteurized milk. But once the hollowness in her stomach eased, she could no longer ignore another apparently unanswerable question: where was Elisabeth Bernard? Lyn *knew* she wasn't Elisabeth—that was comforting; no one else seemed to realize it—that was disturbing. What had become of the real Elisabeth? If only she had been there, it would have been obvious to everyone that Lyn didn't belong. Even without her, if these people were truly Elisabeth's family—her brothers and sisters, her aunt and uncle and grandmother—how could they possibly make such a mistake? There was only that flicker of doubt in Louise's eyes, nothing more. The headache began to thunder inside Lyn's skull.

For the rest of the day she drifted, letting herself be carried along without a struggle. She waited for people to tell her what to do, and if she didn't understand—which she usually didn't—she waited for them to repeat themselves—which they usually did: angrily sometimes, impatiently always. Except for the woman she had decided was Marguerite. She was unfailingly kind.

Straight after breakfast, the men cleared out: the two ghosts and Joseph, taking Pierre with them. They disappeared into the big room off the kitchen, where, Lyn knew from the coffeehouse, the bake ovens were. Every time the door opened, a great billow of warm bread-scented air wafted through it. Jeanne wrapped herself in a hooded cloak and went out, and was gone until evening. The old woman, Madame Pugnant, left as well, although she and the men came back at midday for dinner. And they were joined by a potato-faced young woman Lyn hadn't seen before, who ate with them, but only opened her mouth to stuff food into it. She seemed intent on working her way through as much as possible in the time allowed. She did not reappear at supper.

Elisabeth's place was in the kitchen, where she was assigned a string of unskilled chores—nothing Lyn couldn't handle with her eyes shut once she understood what was expected. But everything was done in peculiar and unaccustomed ways, and she didn't know where anything was kept or what the odd-looking utensils were used for. The kitchen was ruled by the tough, bad-tempered, witchy woman, whose name was Suzanne. Lyn's first task was to wash the stacks of breakfast dishes. She was given a handful of sand, a bunch of twigs and a copper tub of water that started out too hot and quickly turned greasy and cold. The sand and the twigs were for scouring. Suzanne kept an unforgiving eye on her progress and scrutinized the results, rejecting anything she thought wasn't clean enough. *"You may have been able to clean halfway in your household, my girl, but not here,"* she declared, running her finger around a pewter porringer. *"Pah! You are lazy, that is your trouble!"* She thrust it back at Lyn, who took it in frustrated silence. She was finding it easier to understand what was said, but she couldn't translate fast enough to reply. Which was, she reflected, scrubbing away grimly, just as well.

"I am sure she is doing her best, Suzanne," murmured Marguerite placatingly. *"It is hard to learn the ways of a new household."*

"But of course, madame, if it is good enough for you . . ." replied Suzanne.

The young woman turned pink and glanced apologetically at Lyn. She spent much of the day on the settle under the window where the light was best, embroidering tiny silk flowers on a pale yellow garment. She had no pattern to follow, but her needle never hesitated; the beautiful flowers blossomed under her fingers like magic, even though she had to hold the fabric only inches from her nose to see it.

It was Louise's job to watch the babies and fetch and carry for Suzanne. The fretful child—the one who wailed all the time—was teething; otherwise they were very hard to tell apart, swaddled in layers of clothing and all about the same size. Anne and Marie were Marguerite's daughters, and Renée was Elisabeth's youngest sister. The little boy from upstairs was Blaize. For the most part everyone ignored him—everyone except the raggedy boy of about twelve who chopped and piled firewood, brought in buckets of water, cleaned the shoes, and was in and out the back door all day. Blaize followed him around like a puppy, practically treading on his heels, and every now and then the boy would give him a grin and a word or two of encouragement. At such moments if Blaize had had a tail, he would have wagged it in delight.

The other person in the kitchen was the little old man. Lyn found it easy to forget about him altogether; he sat on his stool in the corner, sucking his gums, smiling to himself, tying bundles of twigs around broom handles or whittling pegs out of pieces of wood. Occasionally he'd go into the yard, throwing a piece of sacking

47

around his shoulders. Once he came back with a basket of muddy carrots and onions which Lyn was told to wash and chop. Suzanne criticized her roundly for not chopping them right, though what difference it made when they all went into the stew pot on the hearth, Lyn really couldn't see.

Only the young woman was patient with her ignorance. When Suzanne told her to go and make the beds and Lyn stood looking blank, Marguerite put down her embroidery and smiled. *"Come, Elisabeth. We will do them together. Then the task will go quickly, is it not. My eyes need to rest."*

Suzanne glowered. *"That one,"* she said, shaking a ladle at Lyn, *"that one is useless. She cannot do even the simplest thing right. Six more people in the house—as if I had not more than enough work before! Pah!"*

With the door safely closed against the tirade, the young woman said to Lyn, *"You must forgive Suzanne, Elisabeth. She is getting old. She has a short temper, but she does not mean what she says."*

Lyn doubted that very much. She had Suzanne pegged as a sour old bitch who liked to bully people; she knew the type. There was one in the Belmont drugstore where Lyn had worked for a couple of months after school before getting fed up. Marguerite gave her a warm smile and put a hand on her arm. *"We will all learn to live with each other, you will see. You have not been here long yet— only a few weeks. In God's time it will work. I am so glad you have come, Elisabeth. It is much better than if you had stayed with your papa. Here you are not alone to carry the burden of being mother to the young ones; Maman and I can help. You are my sister now, like Françoise—only this time I am the older one. I can help you as Françoise helped me, is it not."*

Experimentally, Lyn said, *"Françoise—your, your sister—my mother—"*

"Oh, Elisabeth, I do miss her. I know that she is with God and that it is selfish to mourn. . . ."

Lyn frowned. Whether she liked it or not, each piece fit the pattern. At least she knew where she was, though how she'd gotten here, or why, she hadn't a clue. If only she'd had some aspirin in her pocket with the Kleenex and loose change. . . .

Downstairs, the house was divided in two by the hall which ran from the front door, past the curved staircase, to the kitchen at the

48

rear. To the left of the door was one long room, front to back, filled with two masonry ovens, kneading troughs, trestle tables, barrels and bins. Inside it, Lyn glimpsed the men at work: Joseph with his back to her, working over something on a table, the two ghosts pummeling great masses of pale, sticky dough, and the boy, Pierre, measuring flour. Across the hall in the small front room, Madame Pugnant stood behind a high counter, talking to a woman in a bonnet and shawl. The back wall was lined with shelves that were piled with cloth-covered mounds and stacked with loaves like cobblestones and bricks. Lyn had no doubt: this was indeed the baker's house.

Upstairs, where there should have been offices, a lounge and a modern bathroom, there were bedrooms: the one Lyn knew already, over the kitchen at the back; another very much like it in front; and a third over the bakery that was larger and more elegant, with its own fireplace, a small settee, and a desk with a straight-backed chair by the window overlooking the quay. While Marguerite tied back the heavy green brocade bed curtains, Lyn dared to open one of the books on the desk. The stiff pages were covered with columns closely written in a thready hand: words, dates, figures. She couldn't begin to decipher them. But each page was headed by the year: 1744. Although she had already worked it out, Lyn felt her heart give a sudden kick. Beyond the window the day was a gray, unpromising one. The fog had cleared completely in the night, and she saw that the harbor was full of ships: dark, high-ended hulls, masts like trees in a forest. There were several enormous ones swarming with little figures like termites, and dozens and dozens of smaller vessels. Rowboats and barges wove in and out among them and gulls slid over and through their rigging. Far away, on the other side of the water, a funnel of dirty smoke rose, thinning and widening as it lifted from an invisible fire. And near the tip of the opposite point she could just see the thin white finger of a lighthouse. But however hard she looked she could make out no sign of the modern town and the fish-packing plant anywhere along the shore. There was nothing out there that belonged to her world.

"Elisabeth, you must not touch those," said Marguerite, coming to her. *"Only Maman—and Joseph, of course. But she will be cross if they are not as she left them."*

Lyn shook herself, letting the cover fall shut. *"What are they?"*

"The accounts," said Marguerite reverently. *"They are very complicated—I could never understand them. Françoise was good at figures—do you take after her perhaps? She kept the books for your papa. I am not so clever."*

Lyn helped her straighten the bedcovers and they left the room, carefully shutting the door. When Lyn paused outside the next room, her hand on the latch, Marguerite said, *"No, Elisabeth. There is no need. There is nothing in there but trunks and crates, do you forget?"* She cocked her head. *"Ah, I hear Anne. Poor little one, her teeth hurt her so! I must go down to her. Do you mind finishing alone?"*

"Finishing?" Lyn glanced around the landing. In a dark corner she noticed a ladder that disappeared through a square hole in the ceiling. *"The attic?"*

It was a narrow space under the rafters, like a long tent. Lyn could stand upright only under the ridgepole, and even there her head grazed the roof. Two tiny dormers on each side let in a meager light, and at either end was the solid stone wall of a chimney. She laid her hand against one and it was warm. The space was empty of the usual dusty clutter she associated with attics. Instead it contained three narrow cots and two straw-filled mattresses spread directly on the floorboards. There weren't many clues to who slept there—a few pieces of clothing, a pair of clogs even smaller than the ones she'd found downstairs, a worn leather satchel, a couple of battered trunks and a heavy chest. Men's things, she decided, probably belonging to the bakers, and they were the ones whose feet had woken her.

At suppertime, Jeanne returned, her cheeks becomingly pink, her eyes bright and lively. She chattered incessantly to Marguerite and Louise and Lyn, although Lyn didn't even try to follow the tumble of words. She was by that time much too tired and muzzy-headed. The meal was simple: cold meat, cheese and bread and mugs of beer. The youngest children—the babies, Louise, Blaize and Pierre—ate earlier, and Suzanne and the old man did not come to the table. The boy, to whom Blaize was so attached, had disappeared altogether. Conversation was just a blur of sound to Lyn; she couldn't sort anything out anymore. She remembered Mr. St. Cloud, the French teacher, earnestly advising his classes that the way to

50

learn a language was total immersion. "Go and live among the French!" he would cry. Lyn had visions, when she was a college junior, of a year in Paris or one of the provinces in the south of France. . . .

She woke to find someone shaking her. To her utter amazement she realized she must have fallen asleep as soon as her head touched the pillow, and she had no memory of anything afterward: no sobbing in the dark, no footsteps overhead, no cockcrow. She opened her eyes and felt the sting of disappointment. She was still there, in that strange room. Over her head was a reservoir of darkness: leftover night trapped under the bed canopy. And there was Louise's face close to hers, wary and unsmiling. *"Elisabeth, you must get up. It is soon time for Mass."*

Lyn sighed and swung her legs cautiously over the edge of the bed. The headache exploded, sending bright little sparks up behind her eyes. She waited for them to fade, then got up and began to search for her clothes; she could think of nothing else to do. The night before she had undressed with the others and gone to bed in a voluminous unbleached nightgown.

"No!" cried Jeanne as Lyn began to pull on the crumpled striped skirt. *"You cannot wear that to Mass. Whatever are you thinking of, Elisabeth?"*

"Mass?" Lyn echoed feeling stupid. *"But—"*

"Where is your green skirt? Do you not care at all how you look? If you do not care for yourself, then think of us who must be seen with you."

"I do not—" began Lyn.

"Here." Louise thrust another skirt at her; it was heavy, dull green material, and there was a plain mud-colored jacket to go with it. The skirt wasn't too bad—something it might be fun to wear if Lyn had found it at a secondhand clothing shop—but the jacket was narrow across the shoulders and tight under the arms, and not a color she would ever have chosen for herself. She struggled into it and felt as if she had been trussed.

Jeanne examined her critically and shook her head with a disapproving *"Tchk."* She was wearing a pale rose skirt and jacket that set off her complexion and gray eyes most becomingly. *"You must ask Grandmother for some new clothes, Elisabeth, really you must.*

51

Those are a disgrace. You could never go to work for Madame Duvernay looking like that—except perhaps in the kitchen.''

In the modern park Sundays were treated like any other day of the week. The visitors expected to find everything going on as usual, regardless of the Sabbath, so, to the distress of the purists on the staff, authenticity was sacrificed to tourism. The French inhabitants would have spent Sundays in prayer and pious contemplation, attending at least one of the Masses in the barracks chapel, or drinking and gambling in the cabarets, depending on the strength of their religious convictions.

Now as the bell in the clock tower rang, knots and clusters of people came out of houses and began to sift upward through the streets toward the chapel. Almost everyone was dressed in best clothes; to many that meant neat and decent, but to the well-off it meant silks and velvets in pale impractical colors and elaborate uncomfortable-looking styles: elegant bonnets and lots of lace and ruffles, polished brass buttons and buckles, powdered wigs, intricately embroidered waistcoats and stomachers. The social structure of Louisbourg was very plain to see. Lyn decided the Pugnant family fit somewhere in the middle: better dressed than many, they were nowhere near as smart as some.

They went up the rue Toulouse in procession: Madame Pugnant leading the way at her slow, deliberate pace, her stick clenched tight in one gloved claw, the other clamped on Joseph's rust-colored sleeve. Since she had cannoned into him on his front step two afternoons before, Joseph seemed to have forgotten Lyn's existence. He was, she guessed, too important to pay any attention to a niece by marriage. He walked with his chest thrust out and his chin tucked in, like a large rufous pigeon, nodding and speaking to people along the way. Always, they were the better dressed people, and they didn't always respond.

Next in order came Marguerite and Lyn, then Jeanne and the two little boys, Pierre and Blaize. Bringing up the rear were Joseph's assistants from the bakery. One was Thomas and one was Christophe—Lyn wasn't sure which was which. Louise and the babies stayed home with Suzanne and the old man.

Although the sun wasn't shining, it was visible behind thin clouds, like a silver dollar in the pale sky, and the unpaved streets

52

were dry. The air smelled of fish, and underneath the fish, of salt, tar and woodsmoke. It was full of the whining of gulls and chittering of swallows. All around Lyn spread the town in its entirety. She recognized the rue Toulouse by the houses on it. But the *feeling* of it was alien and overwhelming.

Solid as the modern reconstruction of Louisbourg had felt to Lyn—stone and timber, plaster, slate, and shingle, chimneys that smoked, doors that latched, windows with glass and shutters, yards planted with vegetables, livestock—all that had been only a shadow of the real thing. Behind it lay the modern world, ingeniously camouflaged but right there, working away to support an illusion: underground electric cables, caterers, dishwashers, supply vans that came and went under cover of darkness, flush toilets, audio-visual programs—all of it so familiar to Lyn she barely noticed it. But now that none of it was there, suddenly she missed it keenly.

At the rue Royale Lyn looked left. As far as she could see along it there were buildings, and above their roofs she glimpsed a second spire, twin to the one on the citadel. Joseph gave an exclamation of annoyance as she trod on his heel. Flustered, she muttered, *"Pardon."*

The spire could only belong to the hospital—the hospital that had not been rebuilt. She remembered a discussion she and Rob and Kathy had had about it one morning not long ago. Steve, Kathy's husband, yearned to rebuild the hospital. As far as he knew no one anywhere had reconstructed one—it would be unique, a wonderful opportunity to study eighteenth-century medicine. "It would be fairly gruesome though, wouldn't it?" said Lyn. "I mean, things were pretty primitive then—no anesthesia or antibiotics—even sterilization." "Hacksaws, purges, bleeding, leeches," said Rob with grisly relish. "Only tourists with nerves of iron and stomachs to match admitted." Kathy said, "Yes, I know, but Steve's right—it was a part of life." "And death," added Rob. "Who ran it?" Lyn asked. "The Brothers of Charity," said Kathy, "and only for men. It was mostly soldiers who got sent there. I guess if you could make a choice you stayed home and had a doctor. Anyway, there's not much chance. The reconstruction's finished except for the fiddly bits around the place du Port. Steve has to be content with what we've got, unless he can convince someone to give us an enormous grant for the project." It was too bad, Lyn reflected wryly, that Steve wasn't the one who was here to see it.

Along with everyone else, she found herself being funneled through the narrow passage in the earthworks that surrounded the citadel. Shoes and boots and clogs echoed hollowly on the planking of the footbridge that crossed the dry moat.

There were no pews in the little gold and white chapel. The congregation sorted itself out according to sex and status; women and children on the left, men on the right; the expensively clad in front, the poor at the back. The Pugnant family stood in the middle. On the other side, in the first row at the altar rail, Lyn noticed a short, stout figure in crimson and gold. He wore a white wig and leaned on a cane until someone in his party brought him a chair; he was the only person to sit. Lyn was watching him with mild curiosity when it suddenly struck her that she was looking at Jean-Baptiste-Louis le Prévost Duquesnel, the governor of Isle Royale. He had a wooden leg—and gout and bad teeth and abscesses and hardening of the arteries. His wife, like the engineer's, had declined to follow him to Louisbourg. Before the end of October 1744, he would be dead—buried under the floor, right where he sat. They had found his skeleton when they excavated the site. The hair on the back of her neck stirred and she shivered involuntarily.

"Elisabeth." Dimly she heard Marguerite's urgent whisper. A moment after those around her, she knelt and bowed her head.

The Mass was in Latin. Its rhythm was vaguely familiar to her, thanks to Mike, not Dorrie. That was one reason, Lyn suspected, that Dorrie was less than wholeheartedly enthusiastic about Mike: he and his family were all good Catholics. Lyn sometimes went to Mass with the Hennesseys. Dorrie herself had grown up in a strict Catholic family, choked by rules. She was always being forbidden to do things without being told why. It had taken her years to break free of it, if in fact she actually had, which Lyn sometimes doubted. That was one of the reasons why Mrs. Hennessey, Mike's mother, was less than enthusiastic about Lyn.

What she didn't know, which would have made her genuinely opposed to both Lyn and Dorrie, was that Dorrie was not only a single parent, she was an unmarried single parent. When, at twenty-two and just out of college, she had found herself pregnant and involved with a law school student too absorbed in his studies

54

and his career to want a wife and baby, she had broken with him, struck out on her own, and kept the baby.

Her family was horrified. They didn't want Dorrie without a husband and Lyn without a father, so Dorrie had broken with them, too, and raised Lyn by herself, without benefit of a religious education of any kind. "When you're old enough, you can decide," she told Lyn firmly. She almost never talked about her family, or about Lyn's father, Nick.

Several times in their relationship, Lyn and Dorrie had approached perilously close to, and always shied away from, what exactly had happened when Dorrie discovered she was pregnant— what scenes had taken place, what choices had been made. Lyn knew that was why Nick disappeared—or Dorrie had left him— because he hadn't been ready for a baby. It took no great powers of deduction to see that. He hadn't known who Lyn was, but he hadn't wanted her, and Dorrie had. If Dorrie ever felt any regrets—about Nick, about her estranged family, about her lost freedom—she never let them show. Lyn kept thinking that should be enough. And it almost was.

⇝ 5 ⇜

THEY EMERGED FROM THE CHAPEL BLINKING IN THE SUNSHINE OF midday. The scrim of cloud had vanished, leaving the sky an endless blue; the slate roofs of the town shone dully and the harbor, spread out like a great saucer, was speckled with brilliance. Lyn's spirits rose like the gulls that rode the warm air currents high overhead.

Outside the walls of the citadel, in the large open space called the Place Royale, an open air market had appeared. Around the edges, men, women and children were selling all kinds of things: vegetables, round wheels of cheese, sausage, fresh and salt fish, rabbits and pheasants, cherries and strawberries, live hens in coops, limp ones trussed, plucked and ready for the pot. People bargained and argued, laughed and gossiped; it was a scene bright with movement and color, and Lyn would happily have lost herself in it. It reminded her of the Haymarket in Boston, early on Sunday mornings. But the family paid no attention to the vendors. The place was also full of chapelgoers visiting with each other, eyeing their neighbors and

55

showing themselves off in their Sunday splendor—an open air parish hall, Lyn thought, mildly dazed. Joseph deserted them with alacrity, joining the fringes of a group of men—prosperous civilians, most of them, but several wore officers' uniforms. As he approached, they broke apart in a roar of laughter, then pulled inward again. Lyn watched him shift from spot to spot around the circle, seeking a way into it, and was reminded of the kids at the high school—the ones who didn't belong to a clique but desperately wanted to, hangers-on, unnoticed unless someone needed a scapegoat. They never seemed to realize the hopelessness of their yearning, nor how obvious they were.

Marguerite and Madame Pugnant struck up conversation with a middle-aged couple. Although she had attempted to hide it with a thick layer of powder and rouge, the woman's face was deeply pitted. She felt Lyn's eyes on her, and Lyn looked quickly away. Pierre stood at his grandmother's elbow, stubbing his foot in the worn grass, watching with undisguised envy a gang of boys about his age, who were playing some game in and out of the crowds. She'd seen that same expression not long ago on Alexandre's face when Madeleine had her eye on him. She felt a sudden sharp pang; she was much more lost than he'd ever been. A small, confiding hand worked its way into hers. She glanced down and found Blaize close beside her, not looking, as if unaware of what his fingers had done. "Blaize?" she said softly. He started and glanced up guiltily, ready to withdraw if she scolded, but she smiled and curled her fingers around his.

Jeanne tugged Marguerite's arm and whispered something urgently to her. Marguerite tried to follow her gaze, wrinkling her nose with effort. The couple moved on, and Madame Pugnant said in a severe undertone, "Have you no manners at all, Jeanne Bernard? You were unpardonably rude to Madame Corbin."

"I am sorry, Grandmother, but—"

"I should have made you apologize, but I was hoping that perhaps she might not notice as I did, so I did not draw attention to you."

"But, Grandmother, Lieutenant Duvernay is over there. Should we not pay our respects?"

Madame Pugnant frowned at her. "I suppose we should. But you remember what I have told you. Do not get above yourself."

"No, Grandmother," said Jeanne, not quite managing to sound chastened.

Lieutenant Duvernay wore the blue coat with red facings and brass buttons that marked him as an officer in the Compagnies franches. He had a dark, smoothly handsome, slightly bored face. His wife wore a full-skirted blue dress and an elaborately mounded hairstyle, and she hung on his arm possessively. Lyn was introduced by Madame Pugnant as Elisabeth Bernard. When Jeanne glared at her expectantly, she managed an awkward little bob. The conversation sounded extremely polite and stiff; as far as Lyn could tell it was about the weather—how good to have the sun shining. Lieutenant Duvernay left the talk to his wife, rocking gently back and forth on the balls of his feet, not bothering to hide his lack of interest. He gave Lyn a quick but practiced examination of the kind she found particularly offensive, then dismissed her. He spent rather more time on Marguerite, who blushed and looked down in confusion, causing him to smile a little.

"Who is he?" she demanded in an irritable whisper when he turned to Madame Pugnant for a moment.

"Who?" Marguerite sounded surprised. "But he is Lieutenant Duvernay."

"I know that," said Lyn. "I mean—"

There was a sudden disturbance on the edge of the place as a man pushed his way into the middle. He was not dressed for Mass; he wore a rumpled, none-too-clean shirt, breeches and a shabby leather vest. His thick, unkempt hair was dark gray. He had broad shoulders and large, powerful hands, and he came straight toward them, his narrowed eyes fixed on Madame Pugnant. Lieutenant Duvernay's expression became interested; his wife looked fearful. Madame Pugnant's thin, straight mouth grew so thin it almost disappeared, and Marguerite gave a tiny gasp. The color left her face and her eyes were wide and frightened. Blaize's hand stirred in Lyn's like a mouse. Jeanne had gone pale too, but her face was sharp with anger.

"I wish to speak to you," declared the man.

"I am engaged," said Madame Pugnant crisply. "We can speak another time, Jean Bernard."

He shook his head emphatically. "Now. We must speak now."

"He has been drinking," remarked Lieutenant Duvernay as if they were still discussing the weather.

57

The man gave him a contemptuous glance. "I have come to talk about my children, Madame. It is important."

"I should not think you would want your children to see you as you are now," replied Madame Pugnant.

"It does not matter to me what you think."

Jean Bernard. Another piece of the puzzle. This was Elisabeth's father. Lyn's own interest quickened. Madame Duvernay was pulling discreetly but insistently at her husband's arm, eager to leave the confrontation. With some reluctance he went, nodding to Madame Pugnant.

"Anything you have to discuss with me," she said to Jean Bernard, "would be better discussed in private, and when you are sober."

"I *am* sober!" he exclaimed angrily. "Mathieu, tell her I have not had a drink all morning. I have not touched a drop. Tell her."

Lyn hadn't noticed the lanky man who stood behind Jean Bernard. He was younger, dark-haired, with a chiseled, angular face and a beaky nose. "I am not sure this is so wise, my friend," he said mildly.

"I did not ask you if it was wise! *Sacredie!*"

Mathieu sighed. "It is true, he has not been drinking, Madame."

She glared at them both. Everyone within earshot of the group was listening with undisguised curiosity, and people too far away to hear turned their heads to see what was going on. "Now then, Jean Bernard," Madame Pugnant said, making up her mind. "What is this about?"

"You should know. It is that man. I watched you talking to him. It is true that you have arranged for my daughter to work in his house?"

"You know that it is."

"I will not have it."

"Jean Bernard." Her voice was calm, but there was an edge to it that could have cut glass. "You evidently forget that your children are under my roof now, and it is for me to make the decisions about their futures—what is best for them. We agreed this, you and I, when Françoise died."

"*You* agreed!" He gave his head a furious shake. "But I will not argue that with you now."

"For Jeanne it is a good position. She is learning much in Madame Duvernay's household—"

"Yes, I can believe that! Are you sure, Madame, you know what is taught? Jeanne?"

"Yes, Papa," said Jeanne in an icy voice. "What Grandmother tells you is true. I like to work for Madame Duvernay. You should not disapprove—they are good to me. I am learning to make lace and to dance—"

"Dance, is it? Why do you need to know such a thing? What use is this?"

"I am learning to be a lady," said Jeanne stiffly.

"But you are *not* a lady! You are the daughter of a roofer—do not forget that. It is respectable. But that one? No. I do not trust him. He is—"

"This has gone far enough," interrupted Madame Pugnant. "If you wish to discuss family business, Jean, you must come and see me."

"I will take them back, Madame. I warn you—"

"Back to where?" she snapped. "You have left your house. Do you want to have them live with you above Lopintot's tavern? In a single room? With your disreputable friends?" She flicked Mathieu with her angry glance.

"I can provide for my own children," Jean Bernard growled.

"Money, perhaps. But that is only one thing. Look at you! You do not care for yourself—how can you care for your children? Pull yourself together and be sensible! Sometimes I cannot understand what my daughter was thinking of when she married you."

Mathieu laid a restraining hand on Jean Bernard's arm. He shook it off. "Elisabeth? There you are. And Blaize, too. You will come with me now. Jeanne."

No one moved.

"Will you not do as your father tells you?" he roared. "Elisabeth!"

"No, Elisabeth, you must not," Marguerite whispered fearfully.

Jean Bernard's chin was covered with stubble, his fingers bunched themselves dangerously at his sides. He glared straight at Lyn and showed not a glimmer of doubt. She stared back, then slowly shook her head. "I—no. I cannot. I am sorry." But she wasn't, not really. She certainly had no intention of going off, heaven knew where, was this rough-looking, belligerent person. He might be Elisabeth's father, but he was no relative of hers. She shifted her eyes and found

59

Mathieu watching her; his were the color of river water, a chilly brown.

"What is this? What is this?" Joseph came rumbling up; he checked when he saw Jean Bernard, and his face lost much of its assurance. He harrumphed audibly.

"It is all right, Joseph," said Madame Pugnant. "We have been conversing with Jean Bernard, as you see. It is time for us to go home now."

Joseph scowled, aware that he had missed more than a conversation, but unwilling to admit it. "If he has been causing trouble, Maman—"

"No more than usual," she said, permitting herself a tiny, grim smile. "Marguerite, Elisabeth, come. Where is Pierre? Jeanne, go and find him. Quickly, girl! In future, Jean, we will discuss such matters not on the Place Royale, is it not." She gave him a curt nod and walked stiffly past, her steps uneven but firm. The rest of them followed. Only Blaize hung back, pulling at Lyn's hand, his small face anxious, but he kept his fingers locked around hers and let her tow him along.

"Very well, Madame! Very well! But this is not the end, I promise you! I will indeed come to see you," Jean Bernard called after them. Madame Pugnant did not turn her head; she marched across the place, her arm through Joseph's, her spine straight. But Lyn looked back at the two men. She couldn't help wondering who Mathieu was.

All the way down the rue Toulouse, Madame Pugnant's cane punctuated their progress with exclamation points. Joseph huffed beside her. Behind them Jeanne positively blazed with indignation. "What will they *think*, Marguerite!" she cried. "Whatever will they think? How could he *do* that? It was horrible. I am mortified! How *could* he?"

"Why was Papa so angry?" asked Pierre. Jeanne had extracted him ruthlessly from the game he had slipped away to join. "I do not understand."

"If you do not keep still there will be even worse trouble, Pierre," she warned him. "Do not mention Papa, or Grandmother will be so angry with you!"

"But why?" he asked plaintively.

"*Because,* you stupid boy!"

60

By the time they reached the house, Marguerite was beginning to show a little color again, although she still looked frightened. Puzzling over what had happened, Lyn wondered what she would have done if she had found herself fainting across Jean Bernard's doorstep instead of Madame Pugnant's. She shivered. Having no known father would certainly seem to be preferable to having a father like *that*, but she did agree with him on one thing: Lieutenant Duvernay was not a man to inspire trust. She liked him even less than Jean Bernard.

Joseph closed the front door with a decisive thud, latching it firmly, then turned on his mother-in-law. "You ought to have had him arrested on the spot," he declared. "Why did you let him get away with such outrageous behavior?"

"It was not necessary to involve other people, Joseph." In the dimness of the hall, Madame Pugnant's voice sounded thin and tired. She leaned with both hands upon her cane and her shoulders drooped.

From the kitchen came a muffled crash followed by the angry sound of Suzanne's voice and a panicky wail from one of the little ones.

"Maman?" said Marguerite.

"Go. All of you, go. I will speak to Joseph upstairs. There are matters to discuss. Elisabeth—" She held out a hand to Lyn. "You will help me." She leaned heavily on Lyn for support, negotiating the steps slowly, pausing on each one. She had exhausted herself.

At the top, Joseph turned and said, "We will be the subject of the worst sort of gossip in town because of this. Do you not care what people say about us? I will not have it. I will not have my name blackened by such a scoundrel. I have a reputation to protect. Business interests. Investments."

Pausing to catch her breath, Madame Pugnant said, "And a wife and children."

"Yes, of course. A wife and children. That goes without saying."

"Of course," she echoed dryly.

"You should never have taken the brats from him in the first place. If he wants them back, let him have them, I say. Let him worry about them, not us." He held the door open, and Lyn helped Madame Pugnant to the chair by the fireplace. She sat down slowly, as if her joints did not want to bend, and sucked in her breath as she

61

did so. The skin around her mouth was drawn in tiny puckers, and across her cheekbones it was translucent and faintly blue, but her eyes were sharp. "We have discussed this, Joseph," she said when she had collected herself. "They are family—as are you. Jean Bernard pays their expenses, but he is not fit to look after them alone. We have done the Christian thing and taken in my daughter's children."

"Christian!" snorted Joseph, pacing up and down. "You need not pretend with me, I know why you want those children. It is for the boy. And you cannot have him without the others—Bernard will not let you. Well, I can tell you that he is little better than useless in the bakery, Pierre. He does not want to learn. Where was he Friday afternoon, eh? Along the quay, watching the sailors come ashore. I ask you! What good to me is such an apprentice? Give them all back to their father, I say." He turned and glowered at her. "What was he shouting about this time?"

"I am really not certain, Joseph," said the old woman blandly. "It is often difficult to tell with Jean Bernard. But you need not be concerned for your reputation. The only harm he did today was to himself by making such a spectacle."

"I hope you are right." With a flourish he left the room.

Madame Pugnant closed her eyes; a muscle twitched in her jaw. She muttered inaudibly under her breath. Suddenly she said, "Elisabeth—you are still there?"

"Yes," said Lyn, then added, "Grandmother," with an effort.

"I will have my dinner up here. You will tell Marguerite. And you will send Pierre to me now."

"—and I shall be at Grignon's tavern for dinner. There are people I must see—I have business to discuss," Joseph was announcing in the kitchen.

"But, Joseph," began Marguerite anxiously, "suppose Jean Bernard—"

"Jean Bernard! Do not mention his name to me. I have heard enough of that scoundrel to last me a lifetime. If it were not for *you*"—he shook his finger at her—"if it were not for you, I should have nothing to do with him at all. There would be no need. If you would do your duty—"

The room was very quiet when he'd gone. Marguerite stood still, holding one of the little girls in her arms, her face hidden against the baby's head. Suzanne, who had been watching avidly, turned back to the roast she was basting. Pierre turned the spit and Jeanne set dishes on the table. The other children were in a subdued huddle near the hearth.

"Marguerite?" said Lyn tentatively.

Marguerite gave a tiny sniff. She raised her face and Lyn saw tears on her cheeks. Joseph was certainly no prize either, she thought crossly. "What is it?" It was such a disadvantage, being dropped in the middle of other people's lives this way. Especially since all the other players assumed she knew the rules. "I do not see—how can this be your fault?"

"Oh—it is very complicated," said Marguerite sadly. "He is so disappointed that he has no—children."

Thoroughly confused, Lyn said, "But are not—" She groped for the right words. "Do you not *have* children?"

"Anne and Marie. Yes, of course, but you must remember they are not Joseph's children. They are daughters of my first husband, Elisabeth. And Joseph—he wants sons of his own." She bit her lip and glanced apprehensively in Suzanne's direction. Although she had her back to them, Lyn could feel her listening. To distract everyone, she said, "Madame—Grandmother will have dinner in her room. And she wants to see Pierre."

Pierre made a face. "Why? Why does she want to see me, Elisabeth? Because I was playing?"

Lyn shook her head, and Marguerite said, "Go to her, Pierre. Your grandmother needs you. You are a great comfort to her, you know."

Looking doubtful, he went. Marguerite's tears had dried and she seemed to have recovered her composure. She set the baby down— Anne or Marie, Lyn hadn't a clue which—and said, almost cheerfully, "All will be well, I know. God will make it so. We must have faith in Him."

Good luck to God, Lyn thought irreverently but with genuine feeling as they sat down to dinner. Nothing to do with people ever turned out to be simple once you looked beneath the surface. She wondered if He'd known they would turn out this way when He'd created them.

It was an awkward meal. She and Marguerite and Jeanne shared the table with the two men from the bakery. Long-faced Christophe looked middle-aged to Lyn, while Thomas, the olive-skinned, handsome one, she judged to be about twenty, though it was hard to guess ages—people tended to be younger than they looked. Marguerite, her cheeks pink with self-consciousness, asked a brief, unintelligible blessing. Jeanne was still seething over her father's behavior. "He could not have chosen a worse moment," she complained to no one in particular. "I do not ever want to see him again. He has ruined everything for me. What am I to say to Madame Duvernay tomorrow? How am I to face her?"

"You did nothing to be ashamed of, Jeanne," said Marguerite soothingly. "It is over, and by tomorrow it will all be forgotten. You need say nothing." But Jeanne refused to be soothed. She pushed her food around on her plate with angry little jabs of her fork and ate almost none of it. Marguerite glanced appealingly at Christophe. Thomas kept his head down.

Christophe cleared his throat and made a valiant attempt at conversation, speaking about the *Argonaute* and the *Pientieue,* names that caught Lyn's memory. Ages ago—two days, in another world—Joan Pearson had told them about the *Argonaute* . . . "Is that—it is a ship, is it not?" she asked boldly.

"Yes, that is so, Mademoiselle. She was lucky to arrive Friday morning before the fog. One of the Compagnie des Indes, and they say that more are on the way," said Christophe.

"I should like to see them sail in," said Thomas suddenly. "I do not see why we must stay inside and miss such a sight."

"Because there is work to be done, that is why. And you are paid to do it."

"From India?" said Lyn.

Politely Christophe answered, "Yes. That is why they are called Compagnie des Indes, Mademoiselle."

Lyn sighed. From the way people treated her, it was clear that they did not expect a great deal from Elisabeth. Her hesitations and idiot questions, her not knowing where things were kept or how they were done, or even what clothes to put on, were accepted with hardly a shrug. Instead of finding these lapses peculiar, people found them irritating if they took any notice. Lyn was forced to conclude that Elisabeth was not all that bright.

It still baffled her that no one was able to look at her and see that she was not Elisabeth Bernard; that she was a stranger they had never laid eyes on before. First thing that morning, sitting on the privy, she had decided to confront them. She would go back in and explain to them who she was and where she belonged and get it all straightened out. But in the kitchen again she lost her confidence. With her tentative, awkward French she wasn't sure she would be able to make herself understood. And wouldn't it be better anyway to try it on one person privately than on everyone at once? The whole thing was very complicated and required a willingness to believe she wasn't convinced any of them possessed. If they hadn't noticed on their own, how could she expect them to grasp it? And the ultimate question: Even if they understood, what could they do about it? Until she had some answers, she concluded reluctantly that she was better off keeping still. It wasn't as if she was in danger, or even very uncomfortable. The summer of 1744 had been a good one in Louisbourg—that's why the park had chosen it: the war was still distant and the siege undreamed of, the harbor was full, the town was busy. The French privateers were out capturing English ships and sending home all kinds of prizes. . . .

"—so many sailors in the town," Marguerite was saying. "They are very noisy, are they not? I hear them on the quay at night under our window. I wish they were not so close to us."

"They have been at sea a long time," said Thomas. "They have seen amazing things. I have heard such stories—" His face was suddenly animated. "A man was telling me about this animal—big—so huge it was. It had a tail at each end—you could not tell which was its front—with feet like tree stumps. So!" He gestured with his arms. "Can you imagine that?"

"No," said Christophe bluntly. "Sailors are very good at telling stories, Thomas. When they are at sea for months and months they have little else to do."

Lyn almost said "Elephant," then thought better of it. They would think she had lost her senses.

"It is a fine adventurous life for a man," declared Thomas.

"It is a hard and a dangerous one. Did you not hear how many of the sailors have been taken to the hospital? The brothers work night and day caring for them, they are so ill," said Christophe.

Marguerite looked alarmed.

He added quickly, "It is quite safe, of course. No one in town

65

need worry. It is nothing like the smallpox. They would not be allowed ashore if it were, Madame.''

Lyn choked on a mealy-tasting bean. Smallpox was a danger that had not occurred to her. She had remembered what they told visitors about the water and had avoided drinking any, but people used to die of smallpox before there was a vaccine.

Conversation faded after that. Thomas went back to his meal with a brooding expression. But several times Lyn noticed Christophe watching Marguerite with a serious, steady gaze, and once Marguerite looked up and met his eyes for a moment and blushed. The color beneath her fair skin was most becoming.

In the afternoon, once dinner had been cleared away, they went for a walk along the quay. Marguerite had gone upstairs to fetch Madame Pugnant's dinner, which came back almost untouched, making Suzanne mutter disapprovingly. "She does not eat enough to stay alive, your maman. Why does she think I bother to cook, eh?'' "I am sorry, Suzanne. She has no appetite today,'' Marguerite apologized. "It is not your cooking.'' Suzanne sniffed. "Maman wants us to go walking,'' Marguerite said after a moment. "The weather is too fine to waste, she says.'' She did not sound eager, but Jeanne at once began to get ready. They gathered up Louise, the babies and Blaize. Christophe and Thomas had disappeared, and Suzanne was settling herself for a nap as they left.

Lyn, who'd been afraid they were going to spend the rest of the day cooped up in the kitchen again, was delighted. It seemed as if the whole town was promenading past the bakery, on the broad harborside street. On the front steps, Lyn paused to watch the spectacle. No matter how hard they tried, the hundred or so costumed animators in the park could never hope to achieve the real thing: the bright colors and constant movement. Like the pieces in a kaleidoscope, people moved together and apart, forming and reforming patterns, shifting constantly. Lyn wished Steve Gagnon could have seen it.

It was certainly a far cry from the Sunday crowds she was used to—along the banks of the Charles River in Boston, where people dressed up or down as they chose and did what they liked, disregarding everyone else. Couples tangled in undisguised passion, families having picnics, graduate students flying kites, kids on skateboards, joggers, cyclists, people walking dogs and sometimes cats, and once a parrot, Frisbee games and softball on the grass, nearly naked bodies soaking up the sun. What would Marguerite make of that, she wondered. It would probably scare her witless. She wouldn't have any idea what was going on—there was no room in her world for it because it had never happened. At least Lyn, belonging to the future, could understand what she was looking at here. She felt momentarily dizzy; flecks of light dazzled her eyes.

"What is it, Elisabeth? Do you see him?" Marguerite asked fearfully.

"Who?" Lyn blinked.

"Your papa. I am a terrible coward, I know, but I do not want to meet him again."

"We will not, Aunt Marguerite. He is not here." Jeanne, impatient, was below them on the quay. "He would not dare to approach us after this morning. He would not *dare*." Her chin was set in defiance.

"But you will look out for him just the same, will you not?" begged Marguerite. "My eyes are not so sharp as yours. I do not recognize people at a distance."

"Yes, of course. But let us not stand here. It is so *obvious*, is it not?"

Blaize attached himself once more to Lyn, this time giving her his special smile. "Oh, Blaize, you are such a baby," said Louise with scorn. "He is only a little boy," said Lyn mildly.

"He will *always* be a little boy. Even when he is grown," said Jeanne. She walked with her head high, pulling her baby sister, Renée, along. "He is an idiot."

"Jeanne, you must not say that," Marguerite protested.

"Do you mean—?" began Lyn, looking doubtfully down at Blaize. He was staring at the ships in the harbor, seemingly oblivious to his sisters.

"He does not speak," said Jeanne. "I do not think he understands anything. He does nothing but follow Michel around. He is old enough to be useful—but no, he can do nothing." She gave her head a shake, dismissing the subject. She had something else on her mind; she seemed to be looking for someone. From her expression, Lyn suspected it was not Jean Bernard, but someone she wanted to find.

Marguerite said, "Perhaps he will grow out of it. Françoise used

67

to worry so about him. Since the fever he has been silent—I do not know. God's will is often mysterious to us, but we must have faith. We are being tested, is it not.''

''Hmm.'' Lyn did not want to get into a theological debate with her. She had done so many times with Mike to little avail: He did not like to argue about his beliefs; they were simply part of him like his arms and legs. In a half-resentful way, she envied him. But if she had trouble with Mike in English, she knew she hadn't a hope with Marguerite in French. She wasn't, however, convinced about Blaize; there was something too alert and quick in his eyes. Just because he did not speak didn't mean he couldn't understand.

Various people greeted them as they made their deliberate progress along the quay toward the Dauphin Gate, and although she smiled and nodded and replied, Marguerite never stopped to visit with anyone. Lyn, to whom they were all strangers anyway, turned her attention to the harbor. All the way around it, the shore was littered with little fishing properties: cottages, landing stages, fish drying racks and boats. Several miles from the town, she noticed a massive, gray structure, squatting just above the water, and realized it was the Royal Battery—nothing but a foundation and some lumps of masonry in 1983. There it was, entire, its cannons facing the harbor mouth, ready to splinter any English warships foolish enough to try to attack Louisbourg. Time wavered over the landscape before Lyn like a heat mirage.

''You are so quiet, Elisabeth,'' said Marguerite. ''I wonder what you are thinking. You seem very far away.''

With an effort, Lyn dragged herself out of the future. ''I only look at the ships.''

Marguerite smiled. ''It is a fine sight. Louisbourg is an important city, is it not. The center of commerce from all parts of the world.''

Curious, Lyn asked, ''Have you ever been anywhere else?''

''Me?'' Marguerite was surprised. ''But, Elisabeth, where would I go?''

''To France—or to Quebec. To Boston, perhaps. Do you not want to travel?''

''No. I am content to stay at home where I belong.''

''No one goes to Boston,'' said Jeanne flatly. ''We are at war with England. It is against the law even to trade with New England.''

"But people do it," Louise said. "Many people in town. Papa's friend Mathieu Martel is one, I know. Michel says so."

"Michel!" said Jeanne scornfully. "That man Martel is a scoundrel anyway. I cannot understand why Papa took him in. Why could he not have found someone respectable to work for him? I do not know why Martel is not arrested and thrown into jail, or at least deported."

"It is because Antoine Bigué went off to Port Toulouse," said Louise. "And Papa had no assistant."

"That was his own fault for getting so angry with Antoine. Who can blame him for leaving?" said Jeanne. "I would leave, too."

Marguerite sighed. "It is so peaceful, all of this. I do not like to think about the war. Perhaps it will never come at all."

"It is already here, Aunt Marguerite, and we are winning it. The town is full of English prisoners, and almost every day a captured English ship sails into the harbor. Soon we will chase the English out of New France altogether." Jeanne was positive.

"People have said that for a long time," Louise pointed out. "It does not happen."

"But *this* time"—Jeanne glanced at them, her eyes bright—"soon there is to be an expedition against Annapolis Royal. There will be warships and the Acadians and the Indians will join with us and drive the English away forever."

Lyn had an uncomfortable feeling that it hadn't worked quite that way, but she wasn't sure. Joan had mentioned that expedition, but Lyn couldn't remember what she'd said about it; it had nothing to do with her.

"How do you know this?" Louise sounded skeptical.

"I know," said Jeanne mysteriously. "I hear many things these days. But I should not have told you—it is secret. You must promise to say nothing of it to anyone. With all the English in town—the wrong people must not learn of it."

"Then I wish *you* had said nothing," declared Marguerite. "Why can we not just live our lives quietly? Why must there be a war at all? If they wish to fight on the other side of the ocean, let them."

"It is the *English* who wish to fight. It is they who threaten us. We must defend ourselves, is it not? We have many brave soldiers who will defend us. The English will learn that we are too strong for them."

Lyn felt the start of a headache: pressure behind her eyes, hammering against the inside of her skull. She didn't want to think anymore about any of this. She didn't want to wonder what happened—to the town, to these people—when war actually did come to Louisbourg. "I am tired," she said. "Can we go back?"

"Elisabeth, are you ill? Why did you not say?" Marguerite was instantly full of concern. "We will go at once."

In front of the King's storehouse a group of officers stood talking and laughing, enjoying the sunshine and each other's company. As she approached them, Jeanne began suddenly to chatter about the fine afternoon and the people they had seen, going to great lengths not to notice the young men. Eager to forget the war, Marguerite joined her. Lyn's headache eased slightly as she reflected that some things, at least, hadn't changed much in two hundred years. She wondered which of the officers Jeanne had her eye on. Whoever, it was clear that they had all noticed that Jeanne wasn't noticing them. It was the sort of mutual nonrecognition that had great significance. Once they were out of earshot, Jeanne said breathlessly, "Did you see him?"

"Who?" Marguerite was poised for flight.

"Which one is he?" asked Lyn, playing the game like an old hand.

"His name is André Philippe de Caubet. He is *enseigne en second* to Captain Duvivier. He is going on the expedition next month and I will not see him for a very long time," she said tragically.

"Jeanne, who is this man?" asked Marguerite. "How do you know him?"

"He comes often to see Lieutenant Duvernay, Aunt Marguerite. I have not mentioned him to *any*one—not even to Madame, although I think she has guessed there is something."

She would have to be stone blind not to, Lyn thought wryly. Jeanne shone with excitement.

"But you have not spoken to him, Jeanne?"

She sighed. "Of course I have not, Aunt Marguerite. But I have seen him look at me, and Madame has told me about him. She tells me about all of the officers who come to the house. His family is very good—and he is not yet promised. Grandmother can have no objection, I am sure. I would be the wife of an officer—"

"Wife? How old are you?" asked Lyn, amazed.

"I have fifteen years, Elisabeth. Maman was only sixteen when she married, and Aunt Marguerite." Jeanne looked down her nose at Lyn. "You are jealous, Elisabeth, that is all. You are seventeen years and you are not yet engaged."

Lyn closed her mouth with a snap.

↠ 6 ↞

B Y CONCENTRATING HARD, LYN WAS DISCOVERING THAT SHE understood more of what people said than she had thought she could. Her ear adjusted quickly to the cadence and sentence structure, and she became quite adept at figuring out unfamiliar words from their context. She was hampered by the headaches which burst on her without warning, like sudden thunderstorms, drowning out everything else until they passed. Although still severe, she was relieved to find that they came less frequently.

But understanding the language was only part of the problem. She didn't *think* in their French, so it was necessary to translate mentally whatever she wanted to say, and the more complicated it was, the longer it took. Most people hadn't the patience to wait. Although she often felt like stamping her foot and shouting at them, instead she gritted her teeth and pushed herself as hard as she could, and it got easier.

The work wasn't hard, it was boring. Elisabeth's days were filled with repetitive household chores—nothing requiring the least imagination. At night, the family went to bed soon after dark, and Lyn fell asleep almost as soon as she was horizontal, worn out mentally and physically by her efforts to stay afloat. A couple of times she roused to hear Blaize crying and stumbled out of bed to sit with him; his need of her was comforting.

And every morning, before it was light, the footsteps echoed overhead. They belonged to Christophe, Thomas and Pierre, who slept in the attic with Florent and rose before dawn to fire the bake ovens and knead flour into the yeast sponges for the day's bread. By breakfast time they had done several hours' work.

At the end of a week, Lyn decided that what she missed more than anything was twentieth-century plumbing. People didn't seem to notice each other's smells, even though they lived on top of one another. But then, why should they? They knew nothing of talcum powder, washcloths and antiperspirants, Lyn reflected as she thought with longing of a hot shower and lots of soap and shampoo. She did what she could in the way of washing with cold water from the well, and whenever she washed dishes or clothes—which was often—she managed to do a bit of herself at the same time. She even gave herself a kind of shampoo with a piece of the coarse yellow soap they used for everything. Suzanne, noticing her wet hair, shook her head and muttered disapprovingly. Normal people obviously did not do that kind of thing; not only was it unnecessary, it was unhealthy. But in the warm weather, under all those layers of clothing, Lyn found she itched oppressively.

The privy she could cope with. It could have used a daily shot of Lysol, and she was glad it wasn't the dead of winter, but it was definitely better than a chamber pot. And inside the earth-closet with the door shut, she could count on being alone for a few minutes during the day. Normally she liked noise and company and people around her, but she was also used to having space and quiet when she wanted. In the Pugnant house there were people everywhere; all rooms were common rooms, and there was no such thing as free time, when you could go off by yourself, even just to sit in the bedroom upstairs with the door closed. The nearest she got to solitude was the day she spent mostly in the privy with stomach cramps and diarrhea after rashly eating some odd-tasting dried meat, and it wasn't worth it. After that she was cautious about food, deciding it was better to be a little hungry than deathly ill.

The best thing, she decided, was to treat the eighteenth century like a foreign country: one she was visiting for an unspecified but relatively brief period of time. It couldn't really be much different from a stint in the Peace Corps—living in some underdeveloped country with primitive sanitation, no electricity, no cars, no supermarkets, no telephones. You learned to live with what there was. You tested yourself in an unfamiliar culture and you grew. Lyn resolved firmly to grow.

One of the first things she did, however, was to steal a length of cord from Marguerite's workbasket so she could unpin her apartment key and hang it around her neck, under her chemise. Everyone else might persist in thinking she was Elisabeth, but she *knew* she was Lyn Paget. The key lay against her skin as a comforting reminder of her real self.

On Monday morning, another of the enormous Compagnie des Indes trading ships entered Louisbourg harbor, joining the three already lying at anchor. They dwarfed everything else on the water. Lyn was peeling onions in the kitchen, tears slowly dripping down her cheeks, when the *Mars* came in. At home in Belmont, Dorrie was in charge of onions because they never bothered her; Lyn mashed the potatoes because she hated lumps and Dorrie never let them boil long enough. In Louisbourg they had not yet discovered potatoes, but there were lots of onions.

The boy, Michel, who turned up again that morning at prayers, told them about the *Mars* while they prepared dinner. He had, by apparent luck, happened to be on the quay when the ship sailed in. "Hmmp!" sniffed Suzanne. "Wasting time as usual!"

"Madame sent me on an errand. What should I do—close my eyes?"

"You should come straight back and get on with your work, that is what."

"You cannot blame him for watching, Suzanne," said Marguerite, who was embroidering by the window. "It must have been a fine sight. I would like to have seen it myself."

They all had the chance that same afternoon, when the *Baleine* arrived, her banks of pale canvas visible above the low line of Rochefort Point, blowing silently through the long warm light like a huge moth. Thomas came with the news soon after she was sighted, and everyone went out to watch from the front steps, even Joseph and Madame Pugnant. By the time the ship came about to enter the harbor, the quay was crowded with people, materializing as if by magic from all parts of the town. The Island Battery fired a salute as the *Baleine* slipped past, and the ship answered. Pillows of white smoke bellied into the air, followed by a succession of flat thuds, and the crowd cheered.

"A waste of good powder," said Madame Pugnant, her arms folded tight across her narrow chest. "We are likely to regret that later when we need it for serious matters."

"Nonsense, Maman," said Joseph. "Why are you always so full of gloom? There will be enough powder and to spare. The summer

73

is far from over. Think of all that our privateers have captured for us." He seemed to be in unusually good spirits, his anger of the day before forgotten. Lyn had heard him singing in the bakery in a light and not unpleasant tenor; he had even absent-mindedly smiled at her once or twice, and he had not shouted at Marguerite when Anne began to wail during dinner.

"That was last month. Before the English knew to be on their guard. Now it is *we* who are losing ships, so I hear. People talk of a blockade. If the English close our harbor we will have a thin winter, Joseph. You mark my words."

"Blockade!" Joseph was scornful. "Why must you always be borrowing trouble, Maman? Is that not a warship in the harbor? Why do you suppose she is there? To look at? The Comte de Maurepas will not abandon us to the English, we are too important. There will be no blockade. And when the *Cantabre* returns home with her prizes, you will see how right I am about these things."

Lyn saw Madame Pugnant give him a penetrating look which he ignored. "I hope you are right, Joseph."

"Why do you think I am not?" He sounded annoyed. "We cannot lose, I tell you. Go to Monsieur Bigot and ask if *he* has doubts. Or to the Governor himself. They are the ones with experience and knowledge of such matters, not you. I am only sorry I did not have more to invest in the *Cantabre*."

Madame Pugnant pursed her lips and stared out at the calm sunny circle of water. The sky was flecked with little foamy clouds. On the deck of the *Baleine* little figures danced from side to side and over the rigging, securing lines and stowing canvas. Small boats schooled around her like herring around a whale. At last, with reluctance, the people on the quayside began to scatter and drift away, back to the work they'd interrupted. Madame Pugnant turned suddenly. "What is this?" she demanded. "Have you nothing to do, any of you? Why are you all standing here with your mouths hanging open? Go—all of you! Get back to work at once!"

The streets were clogged with hundreds of sailors off the ships. They spent whatever money they had in their pockets in the shops and taverns and cabarets; they drank and gambled and argued with each other or anyone else they met, sang rowdy songs in a bewildering variety of accents and languages, and told fantastic stories about exotic places and wild adventures. They described islands fringed with palm trees and giant ferns, where the sun lay warm and gold on dazzling beaches, and the water shone like topaz, and the friendly brown-skinned natives wore hardly any clothes. These visions were all but incomprehensible to people who lived their lives huddled on the thin edge of the cold, choppy North Atlantic, where fogs unrolled off the sea in thick wet blankets, and storms swept the rocky land bare of all but the hardiest growth.

Word of these wonders filtered tantalizingly into the kitchen, brought by members of the household who had access to the town. Thomas frequented the quayside taverns in the evenings, and when he talked about the sailors and their voyages his eyes would lose their focus and a kind of hunger would creep into his face. When Christophe was around, he would interrupt Thomas with a frown and send him back to work again.

Marguerite did not like the sailors, they made her nervous. They were rude and foreign and noisy. She did fine sewing for the wives of merchants and officers, and when she ventured out to deliver her waistcoats, caps and christening gowns, she begged Lyn to accompany her. Lyn needed no urging; the town was an endless source of fascination, and Marguerite's customers were scattered all over it. There was no particular order to the streets: respectable town houses, builders' yards, shops, taverns, shabby dank little cottages, warehouses, were strung together anyhow. Marguerite hurried past them all with her eyes down, clutching her shawl and her basket, while Lyn lagged behind, wanting to see everything. She was particularly curious about the taverns. From the outside, they looked like ordinary houses, but in fine weather their doors stood wide open, affording intriguing glimpses of murky smoke-filled rooms. Snatches of conversation and masculine laughter floated out on currents of warm, sour-sweet air.

Marguerite would implore her not to stop. "Elisabeth, you will be noticed!"

"Is it wrong? Are women not allowed? But I am certain I have seen—"

"*Please* come away!"

Resignedly Lyn allowed herself to be pulled along. "Joseph goes, does he not? Do you never go with him?"

"No, I do not. And anyway, it is for business that he goes—to make contacts."

I bet, thought Lyn, remembering the heavy smell of wine on his breath.

One morning they were on the way home from Monsieur Biron's apothecary shop. The rue de l'Estang was hazy with a mist that smelled of iodine. Unexpectedly, from somewhere over their heads, a voice called out, "Good morning, Madame Desforges."

Marguerite froze like a rabbit, and Lyn peered up through the grayness to see who it was. Above her on the roof sat Jean Bernard, a hammer in his hand. "Let us pretend we have not seen him," whispered Marguerite, but it was too late for that.

With exaggerated politeness, he conversed with her about the weather and the state of everyone's health, inquiring particularly about his children and Madame Pugnant, and Marguerite tried very hard to be polite back. Lyn supposed that almost anything she might say would sound odd—after all, the man thought he was her father— so she kept her mouth shut. He seemed pleasant enough, certainly not drunk, but she could feel Marguerite's discomfort and she was sure he felt it, too. At last he said, "But I must not keep you, Madame. Please take a message to your mother for me. Tell her that I will call round to see her as soon as I have the time. I have not forgotten our last conversation, but I have been very busy these weeks."

Behind him, a head appeared above the rooftree and shouted something that Lyn did not catch. He gave an abrupt nod and got to his feet. "I am coming, Mathieu. Wait until I can show you how it is done." He looked again at Marguerite. "I hear that the *César* has taken three ships, Madame, from under the noses of the English. That is very good news, is it not? Next will come word of Captain Doloboratz and your husband will be a rich man, I think. He can buy himself a place on the Superior Council and be a gentleman. He will not need to work like me." He turned and climbed easily up the steep slope of the roof and disappeared.

Marguerite breathed a sigh of relief. "Françoise would scold me for being afraid of him, but he is so harsh and he has such a temper. She knew how to manage him—when he shouted, she would shout back and make him laugh, but now she is gone and he does not laugh." She gave a little shiver. "And you, Elisabeth—are you not afraid of him either?"

Lyn didn't know how to answer. She could hardly say that she

76

didn't know him well enough. "What about Joseph? He shouts," she said instead. "Does he frighten you?"

Marguerite blushed. "But with him it is bluster. I know this even if sometimes I forget. Joseph is different, Elisabeth."

Bluster it was, but Lyn wasn't convinced that made Joseph preferable.

Late that afternoon, when the fog had frayed and broken over the ocean, a small ship made her way into the harbor, driving three others. She was the *César,* a French privateer, bringing home her prizes: merchant traders intended for Boston, that would instead fill Louisbourg warehouses. The *César* wasn't much to look at: her hull was scarred, her sails patched, and one of her masts was oddly crooked, but news of her arrival spread like fire along the waterfront, causing great excitement and jubilation.

At supper that evening Joseph looked smug. "What did I say? Next will come the *Cantabre* and our fortune is made! I told you this from the beginning."

"Money is all very well, Joseph," replied his mother-in-law in her dry, deflating voice, "but we must have the supplies to purchase with our money, or it will do us no good, is it not. We cannot make bread from gold—we must have flour."

"Are you never satisfied? Perhaps we will no longer need to make bread from anything!" cried Joseph in exasperation. "Or had you not thought of that, woman?" He banged down his tankard. "I will not sit here and listen to you talking this way. I will go and have a drink with my friends and hear the news from Beaubassin himself. I will celebrate. You can worry yourself to the grave for all I care!"

Breaking the silence that followed his departure, Marguerite said, "Perhaps he is right, Maman? Perhaps our fortune is made?"

"Perhaps," was all Madame Pugnant would say.

They sat silently in the kitchen until it was time for bed. Lyn was struggling with the stiff, raspy, gray stocking Elisabeth had been knitting. Marguerite helped her, expressing mild surprise that Lyn had trouble with double-pointed needles and decreasing, and Louise gave Lyn a very peculiar look when she asked about a pattern to follow. There was none; she was just supposed to know. As she folded it that evening to put away, she discovered that she had dropped a stitch two inches back and would have to rip it out again.

77

It was all she could do to keep from hurling the wretched thing into the fire. It would have smelled terrible.

She woke the next morning to the sound of voices on the other side of the wall: Joseph's loud and angry, Marguerite's barely audible. Then Anne started to howl and Joseph bellowed something, and a few minutes later slammed the door so hard Lyn felt the vibrations. Turning her head, she met Louise's intense, apprehensive stare. "He is very angry. It is not good."

"Do you know why?" asked Lyn.

Louise didn't answer. Instead she pushed Lyn out of bed and began to dress quickly.

Joseph's face was heavy with bad temper, and Marguerite's eyelids were swollen. Lyn guessed that he'd been bullying her. Dorrie would have had no patience at all with Marguerite; she would say Marguerite got what she asked for if she couldn't stand up for herself. Part of Lyn agreed, but not everyone was as strong-minded as her mother.

Joseph mumbled through prayers. At the table, he ate his breakfast with great deliberation, lost in his own thoughts, seemingly unaware of the rest of them, until without warning, he suddenly jerked his head up and shouted at Blaize, "What do you think you're staring at, boy?"

Blaize, who had been sitting cross-legged on the floor, cleaning a boot, was obviously not aware that he had been staring at anything. He looked at his uncle in alarm and his eyes filled with tears.

"He is doing nothing wrong," said Lyn. "Do not shout at him!"

Furious, Joseph turned on her. "You! Hold your tongue! Who are you to answer me back?"

She wished she had adequate French to tell him what she thought of him right there on the spot, but her vocabulary failed her. She could only glare at him.

"That is enough, Elisabeth," said Madame Pugnant, her eyes on Joseph. He refused to meet them. "It is time we all got to work, is it not?"

Thomas vanished at once, taking Pierre with him; Christophe followed more slowly. At the door, he paused. Lyn saw Marguerite look at him, for just an instant. He frowned; she straightened her shoulders and attempted a smile. He disappeared into the bakery. Florent had melted into his corner, where he sat sucking his gums nervously, and Suzanne, with her back to the room, wasn't even pretending to be busy. The air was electric.

Michel came clattering in from the yard with an armload of kindling. Like a fox, he lifted his head and sniffed the signs, immediately alert. Dropping the wood by the hearth, he picked up the milk bucket. "Will you help me with the cow then?" he asked Blaize, and Blaize vanished like smoke out the back door. Lyn wished she could follow. She had forgotten about Michel, but if anyone knew what was going on this morning, he would. He was about twelve—thin and wiry, nondescript, with a ragged fringe of brown hair that shadowed needle-sharp eyes. When Lyn questioned Marguerite about him, Marguerite replied rather vaguely that Michel lived somewhere outside the town walls in the faubourg, with his widowed aunt and her children. His aunt took in laundry to earn a living, and that was all she knew, nothing about his parents. Evidently it hadn't occurred to her to wonder. He did odd jobs around the house and bakery, tended the cow and hens, ran errands and delivered special orders. Lyn envied him his freedom; it seemed he could go anywhere in the town—he had contacts all over, and knew about things almost before they happened.

Joseph drew himself up. "I suppose," he said reluctantly, "that I must spend some time with the books this morning. You have the accounts up to date, have you?"

Madame Pugnant gave a nod. "It would be as well. If you can spare the time, Joseph." Her face was expressionless.

Once they'd gone, Marguerite's brave smile dissolved. She twisted her apron in her fingers, her face full of tragedy.

"What is it?" asked Lyn. "Tell me what has happened."

"He had such plans, Elisabeth. It is a terrible blow."

But she was interrupted by the young woman who worked in the shop. Marie-Marthe's head appeared around the hall door. "Madame says that you are to come and help me, Madame Desforges. She is busy and I cannot work alone. It is too much for one person."

"Oh, but I cannot—" protested Marguerite. "The babies—"

"Go on," said Lyn briskly. "Louise and I will watch the babies. I know nothing about the shop—*I* cannot go."

Marguerite drew a long, shaky breath. "Do not let Marie near the fire, and if Anne begins to cry—"

79

"Yes, we will manage. Go." When she was safely out of the room, Lyn turned to Suzanne, who was being very quiet. "What do *you* know about this?"

"Me?" Suzanne gave an angry grunt. "Who would tell me?"

Lyn regarded her speculatively. No one needed to tell Suzanne something in order for her to know it. She, too, had her contacts. The Widow Grandchamp next door for one. Suzanne scavenged all kinds of gossip by the fire at the inn; the widow dealt in it like any other commodity, and Suzanne then used it to buy herself importance. Michel was fond of needling her: hinting at things he knew that she didn't, or questioning the accuracy of her information. "I have heard," he would say, "that Marie-Thérèse Lajoie had a visitor last night. But you must already know, is it not." And he'd go out to feed the cow, leaving Suzanne, red in the face, to brood over who the dressmaker's visitor might have been. It seemed to Lyn a rather dangerous game—Suzanne could be shrewish and vindictive when roused—but Michel was unbothered.

"Why do you just stand there like a lump, eh?" she demanded, scowling at Lyn. "You are good for nothing! It is late—clear the table!" She really didn't know what had happened, and she was crosser than ever as a result.

And because, of course, Michel did. "What? You have not heard the news? It is all over town this morning," he said, pretending surprise. He set the milk down. "It is no wonder that Monsieur is in a black humor."

Suzanne huffed and snorted and her eyes became fiery little slits. Lyn thought she would explode with frustration, and exclaimed, "Oh, *merde!*" which caused Michel, Suzanne and Louise all to look at her in astonishment. "Stop playing games!" she snapped at Michel, not caring whether she sounded like Elisabeth or not. "If there is news, tell us."

Michel grinned. "I would like some rum in my coffee."

Muttering under her breath, Suzanne took a bottle from the back of a shelf in the cupboard. She poured a drop of liquid into Michel's mug, then corked it violently.

Michel decided not to push his luck. "There is word of the *Cantabre*." He took a swallow, his eyes bright over the rim of the mug. "And it is not good. *César* lost her in the fog and she was captured by the English early this month."

80

"No!" declared Suzanne. "That is not possible. I do not believe you. Marie-Claire Bonnard has a son on the *Cantabre* and she has said nothing. Captain Doloboratz is too clever to be taken by the English!"

Michel shrugged. "Do not believe me—*I* do not care. Go and ask the first person you meet on the quay. Everyone else in Louisbourg knows. Word came last night with Captain Beaubassin. The *Cantabre* was taken off Cape Cod."

"Cape Cod?" Lyn hadn't meant to say it aloud.

"It is near Boston," Michel explained for her benefit.

"Yes, I do know that." Last August she and Mike had taken the ferry from Boston to Provincetown, coming back through the warm, moist darkness under a fuzzy moon, after wandering hand in hand around the crowded town all day, stuffing themselves with fried clams and onion rings and soft ice cream. She tried to imagine all that gone. Instead, high-sided warships hung with flapping canvas firing cannons at one another across the empty sea. Fire and smoke, crashes and splintering and shouts and screams. She blinked and found Michel watching her, eyes calculating under the brown thatch.

"So?" said Suzanne irritably. "It is only one ship. What is one ship?"

"Aha, but how many do we have? Hmmm?" The reedy voice made Lyn jump. It was Florent, rocking back and forth on his stool. He didn't seem to expect an answer from anyone.

"There were eighty men on the *Cantabre*," Michel pointed out. "And I have heard as well"—he paused for effect—"I have heard that there are men in Louisbourg who have lost much money because of this."

"Ahhh." Florent rocked.

"They are the ones who can afford to lose money," declared Suzanne. "Monsieur Bigot and the governor. They can take such a loss and not notice."

"That is true perhaps. But there are others who cannot."

"Others?" said Lyn, and Suzanne demanded, "What are you saying?"

Michel shrugged again. He had told them all he was going to. "Only rumors. You would not believe them. You do not believe what I tell you, so I will save my breath. Listen for yourselves. I have much to do this morning.'' He put down his empty mug and went out, whistling, with Blaize trotting behind.

"He will go too far, that one—and soon," prophesied Suzanne darkly.

So Joseph had lost money on the *Cantabre*—that's what all of this was about. And whose money was it? Lyn glanced at Louise. The little girl's face was tight; she had been listening hard to Michel.

The *Cantabre* was not spoken of again that day, at least not in Lyn's hearing. If the family fortunes were well and truly smashed, Elisabeth was not told. Ever since Lyn could remember, she and Dorrie had dealt with crises by discussing them. There had been times, Lyn was forced to admit, when she had wished Dorrie would not be quite so forthcoming; when Lyn would have been happier not knowing that there wasn't enough money to pay the electricity bill *and* get a new muffler for the car, or that Dorrie was temporarily avoiding the landlord because the rent was overdue. But mostly she was proud to know that Dorrie considered them partners. There were, of course, areas of Dorrie's life that she didn't share, parts marked PRIVATE, but Lyn accepted that. The things that affected them both were always set out in the open. Not in this household, however, and Lyn resented it even though she told herself that it wasn't really *her* business; it didn't really affect her. . . .

Dinner was a grim, uncomfortable meal during which everyone avoided everyone else's eyes. Marguerite was absent, and Christophe looked even glummer than usual, and Joseph rose abruptly before they finished to return to the bakery. All afternoon he could be heard banging things around and shouting at Pierre and Thomas.

With the washing-up done, the afternoon stretched interminably ahead. Madame Pugnant went back to the shop, and as soon as she was gone, Suzanne snatched up her limp brown shawl and stumped out the back door, heading no doubt for the Widow Grandchamp and some serious gossip. Beyond the open door, sun trickled wanly into the yard, and Lyn could see a robin poking among the cabbages. When Florent roused from his afternoon nap and put on his sabots to work in the garden, in desperation, Lyn asked if she could help. He looked startled and doubtful. His lips twitched, but he didn't say no, so she spent a couple of hours grubbing about on her knees, getting dirt under her fingernails and learning the difference between weeds and vegetables. Florent watched her anxiously at first lest she pull up the wrong things, but she was careful to ask whenever she wasn't sure and he would answer with a nod or a shake of the head. Otherwise they did not communicate, and Lyn found it restful. Swallows were collecting in rows on the rooftrees of the house and sheds, preening and twittering, then launching themselves like darts across the garden to pick insects out of the air. They need not go short of food, Lyn reflected as she slapped and blew at the mosquitoes that whined around her.

One of the half-wild cats who lived in the cellar brought her litter of four kittens up the steps to play in the sunlight. They made Lyn think of dust bunnies; bits of fluff, scudding and tumbling over one another. She longed to pick one up and cuddle it, but knew she would only get a handful of claws and needle teeth if she tried. The cats were not pets; they were not fed or given names or allowed upstairs. They were tolerated because they kept the mice and rats out of the grain. When Lyn had once attempted to make friends with one, she had been scratched and sworn at for her pains. She missed Gilbert sorely and wondered how he was getting on with Philip.

Resignedly, Lyn surveyed the array of dirty lamps Suzanne set out on the table after dinner two days later for her to clean. She loathed the chore; usually it was Michel's, but he was off on some errand, and she knew that Suzanne was paying her back for her morning of freedom on Cap Noir with Marguerite.

It was a perfect August day, bright and warm, the horizon sharp between sky and sea, with breeze enough to keep the bugs away. Quite unexpectedly, Madame Pugnant had sent the two of them out to pick raspberries, refusing to listen to any of Marguerite's excuses for staying home. The old woman was adamant; Lyn guessed she had had enough of her daughter's tearful silence and pale, strained face.

All the way through the streets to the Queen's Gate, Marguerite fretted. She hated to leave the babies—they would bother Suzanne and Suzanne would scold them. She was behind with Monsieur Delort's waistcoat, and would never finish on time. The sun was so strong it would tire her eyes and she would not be able to work that afternoon. By the time they reached the walls, Lyn was ready to scream. But once through the gate, with the town behind them, Marguerite gave in, accepting the expedition.

Cap Noir lay on the ocean side of Louisbourg: a low, scrubby piece of land. In Lyn's time there was a visitors' viewpoint on it with charts and maps to show how the English had come ashore south of the fortress, at Gabarus Bay, to make their surprise attack. Farther down the coast was the wide sand beach at Kennington Cove where Lyn had picnicked several times with various staff members.

There were other people on the point that morning: figures scoured the rocky shore for driftwood and other bits of salvage, or sifted through the coarse, tussocky grass, gathering plants which Marguerite said were used for medicines and dyes. No one paid any attention to the two of them. The raspberry canes they were after grew in a thorny tangle at the bottom of a green hollow, protected from the wind and invisible, until they stood on its rim. From within it they too were invisible, severed from the rest of the world. Lyn pulled off her cap and felt the sun sink hot through her hair. The air was spiced with the sweet smell of wild roses, and bees thrummed around her. Perched in a bush overhead, a small stippled brown bird burst into ecstatic song. For a few minutes she closed her eyes and let herself drift, half believing that when she looked again she would find Sandy with her instead of Marguerite. Why not? It could happen that way—it was no more impossible than what had happened to her on the rue Royale. . . . She shivered and blinked, rubbing her arms against a sudden chill, and to distract herself she asked Marguerite about Joseph and the *Cantabre*.

At first Marguerite pretended to know nothing. Finally she admitted that, yes, Joseph had lost money on the privateer, but she didn't know how much. Lyn pressed her until, discouraged, she had to conclude that Marguerite truly did not know the amount. "But you *should* know—it is your business," she scolded. Marguerite shook her head stubbornly. "No, Elisabeth. It is Joseph's business, not mine."

It was no good arguing with her. "You let him bully you," said Lyn.

"Poor Joseph—it is very hard for him. He has had many disappointments. He was so certain that this would make his fortune. He said it could not fail."

"Well, he was wrong. He did it to himself. If he could not afford the money, he should not have risked it. None of it is your fault, and he has no right to shout at you as though it was."

Marguerite was silent for several minutes, then she said softly, "He wants sons—he wants them so very much and I do not give him any."

"But you have Anne and Marie, even if they aren't his."

"Ah, but it must be a son to inherit the business, Elisabeth."

"Pierre," said Lyn, understanding at last. "He is Jean Bernard's son and Joseph is jealous."

"He wants children of his own, that is all. And I do not conceive."

"That cannot be your fault either, not if you have tried. There are Anne and Marie to prove it."

"But it is the wife—"

In as reasonable a voice as she could manage, Lyn said, "It is not always the wife, Marguerite. If your first husband were still alive, you would have seven—eight—*nine* babies now."

Wordless, she shook her head.

"Why not? Why not a dozen?" said Lyn recklessly.

In spite of herself, Marguerite smiled. "But that is not possible, Elisabeth. It takes nine months."

Lyn grinned back at her. "Only six then. And you would be much happier."

Hesitantly, Marguerite told her about Antoine. He, too, had been a baker, and they had been very happy together. But Antoine died of a fever only a year after Marguerite's father, and suddenly there was no one in the family to run the bakery. Only Joseph Desforges, who had been working for Antoine for four months. His work was excellent—his cakes moist and rich, his bread good-textured, so when he made Madame Pugnant an offer for Marguerite's hand in marriage, she had agreed.

"But you," said Lyn, feeling something had been left out. "Did he ask you? Did you want to marry him? What if you had said no?"

"It was arranged." Marguerite sounded surprised. "And it was best for the family. Why should I say no?"

"Because you did not love him. Was there no one else? What about Christophe? Where was he? He is perhaps a little dull, but at least he does not get angry and shout. I would have thought—"

85

Catching sight of Marguerite's face, she broke off and asked, "What is it? What is the matter?" Suddenly another corner of the picture dropped into focus: the glances, the good mornings, the little awkwardnesses, the concern and attempts at indifference. "Why did you not marry Christophe then?"

Tears dripped silently down Marguerite's cheeks. "He was only a journeyman. He had not yet become a baker."

"But if he loves you—"

Marguerite looked down at her wet, clasped fingers. "I do not, know that he loves me, Elisabeth."

"Well, he does," said Lyn. "*I* know it. Has he never told you?"

"How could he? I am a married woman and he works for my husband."

"And Madame—your mother, does she know?"

Marguerite went pale. "*No one* knows! No one must ever know. You must promise me that you will never tell anyone about this—promise you will not. If Maman were to find out she would have to dismiss Christophe. He would lose his job and he would have to go away. He must not suffer because I am foolish, Elisabeth. And Joseph—it is not fair to him either. It must be our secret."

She was so distressed that Lyn could only reassure her, but she felt depression settle on her like a fog. The situation seemed intolerable, and yet they all put up with it. Marguerite sniffed and wiped her eyes. The morning was slipping past and they had almost no raspberries to show for it. They hardly spoke again, until, on the way back, they were in sight of the house and Marguerite said suddenly, "I would never have told you, Elisabeth, but I am glad that you have guessed."

"But there is nothing I can *do*," said Lyn almost crossly.

"There is nothing anyone can do. It is enough that you share the secret."

If Marguerite was comforted, Lyn supposed that was good. She herself felt burdened with a peculiar sadness—the responsibility that went with keeping someone else's unhappy secret.

Suzanne did not think much of the berries they brought back, but Madame Pugnant brushed aside her criticism. Watching the old woman during dinner, Lyn wondered how much she knew. Although not particularly sympathetic, Madame Pugnant was shrewd;

she missed very little that went on under her roof. Whatever her reasons for sending the two of them out that morning, the main one wasn't raspberries, Lyn was willing to bet. Unquestionably Marguerite looked happier, and if Joseph didn't notice, Christophe certainly did, and looked happier himself as a result.

So there she was, fiddling with charred wicks and getting soot all over herself when she would rather have been outside weeding again in the sunshine. The lamps were smelly, smoky, ineffectual devices—it was no wonder Marguerite's eyesight was so bad when she had such miserable light to work by. It was a miracle that everyone wasn't blind before the end of adolescence. . . .

"Grandmother wants to see you, Elisabeth."

Lyn looked up to find Louise at her elbow, regarding her with a wary expression. "Me?"

"You are Elisabeth," said the little girl, unsmiling.

"What does she want?"

"I do not know. She does not tell me what she wants with you. She is upstairs."

Marguerite jabbed herself with her needle, and Lyn knew what she was thinking. Why was it that when you had a guilty secret, no matter how deeply hidden, you were always sure you were on the verge of being discovered?

Suzanne said, "Do not worry, the lamps will be here when you come back."

Outside in the hall, Louise whispered, "What have you done?"

"Nothing," said Lyn, wondering herself.

"It must be serious to make her send for you."

"Perhaps she is lonely," suggested Lyn lightly.

"Will she send us away?" Louise's face was an indistinct oval in the darkness. "Papa has no room. If she does not keep us, where will we go? What will happen to us?"

"I do not think she will send us away," said Lyn.

"But there is no money. Suzanne says that Uncle Joseph has lost all his money."

"Suzanne likes to frighten people. You should not listen to her."

"But if you make Grandmother angry—"

"Why should I do that?"

"If you tell her—"

"Tell her what?" Lyn stood very still.

87

There was a long silence; Lyn found she was holding her breath and carefully let it go.

"That we do not want to leave," said Louise finally. "That we will do whatever she says if only we can stay."

"Louise—"

But she dodged away, leaving Lyn unsatisfied. For some time she'd been aware that Louise was deliberately avoiding her, refusing to let her close. Out of all the people in the household, Lyn knew that Louise was the one with doubts about her, but Louise would not admit it—not to Lyn, not even to herself. She was afraid, and Lyn couldn't really blame her.

⇛ 7 ⇚

MADAME PUGNANT AND JOSEPH WERE DISCUSSING SOMETHING. Lyn could hear them through the closed door; Joseph sounded angry as usual. She knocked and waited, then knocked again. The door was flung open.

"—only temporary!" Joseph exclaimed, his hand on the latch. "We are not destitute, for the love of heaven! We do not need his money, Madame. I will not accept it! You do not know where it comes from—you cannot be sure how he got it."

"By working for it, I am sure," said Madame Pugnant. "Whatever else you may say about Jean Bernard, Joseph, he is an honest man."

"Honest, is he? Look at his friends—do not deceive yourself. What about Martel? *He* is such an honest man the court would have been all too happy to send him packing."

"Nothing has ever been proved against Monsieur Martel, and he has a respectable job with Jean Bernard. It is well to be careful how you speak, Joseph. Monsieur Martel is said to have useful acquaintances."

"His acquaintances are rogues and scoundrels!" cried Joseph. "Why do you argue against me, Maman? I do not understand you!"

"No." She sighed. "That I think is true."

"I cannot waste my time. I have a wedding cake to bake this afternoon." He pushed past Lyn and stamped down the stairs.

Madame Pugnant sat, head bent, studying the columns on the page of the ledger open in front of her. The desk was strewn with papers. Lyn coughed discreetly and she looked up, staring at Lyn at first without seeing her. Then her eyes focused and the lines of tiredness in her face sharpened into irritability. "Elisabeth, look at you! What have you been doing?"

Lyn glanced at her apron. It was smudged with lampblack where she had wiped her hands. "Cleaning lamps," she said, then added, "Grandmother." She could call the old woman Grandmother if she thought of it as a proper name, like Marguerite or Louise.

"Hmmp. And your fingernails—they are a disgrace."

"It is very hard to get them clean." She had tried the point of a knife, but there wasn't one small enough to do a good job. Nail-brushes were a thing of the future.

"Well, you will have to get them clean. You cannot serve in the bakeshop with hands like that."

"In the bakeshop?"

"Do your ears need cleaning as well? Or are you merely as dull as Suzanne claims?"

Lyn felt her temper stir. "Suzanne is a—" She groped for the right word.

"Do not answer me back, Elisabeth. I have had quite enough argument for one day. You are here to listen, not to speak. I sent for you because you are the oldest." She stopped and Lyn could see her gathering her thoughts. "We have had some unfortunate news, your uncle and I. It has forced me to reconsider the arrangements I have made for you, and to make certain changes. I am not altogether satisfied—" She pressed her lips together tightly, then said, "That is no matter. I do what I must. So—tomorrow you will begin to work in the shop with me. Suzanne tells me you are clumsy and only half awake. That you do not know how to do the simplest of chores and must be shown everything. It is not encouraging to hear this, but it is my hope that this is merely because you are unfamiliar with the household, not because you are unable to learn."

Lyn's cheeks were hot; with the greatest restraint she held her tongue. If only you knew, she thought. If only you knew who I really am and where I come from and what I can do. You have no idea! You couldn't *begin* to understand! It was the truth of that that kept Lyn silent. Her whole life to this point consisted of knowing and doing things of which Madame Pugnant had no concept. It was a barrier she was unable to negotiate; she faced it in frustration.

"—is to be expected, but it cannot go on forever. There is too much to be done, and we must all be willing to work hard. That is the best thing for grief: hard work. Are you listening to me, Elisabeth?"

"Yes—Grandmother," Lyn muttered.

"You do not fill me with confidence." She frowned. "There is no question about Pierre—he will go on with his apprenticeship. Christophe tells me that he shows promise. Joseph says he is lazy and unreliable. We shall see. He will continue his lessons with me. As for Blaize—well, there is nothing to be done there."

"What do you mean, nothing?" said Lyn. "Why not give him lessons also?"

"Be sensible, Elisabeth! What good are lessons to him? I will not turn him out, if that is what you fear. He is my grandson and we will take care of him. That is an end to it."

"But Blaize is not stupid—he could learn. And Pierre—how can you put him to work? He is a little boy! He should be outdoors playing games, not shut up in the bakery all day!" cried Lyn passionately. "It is not fair—"

"*Elisabeth!*" Madame Pugnant cut across her like a razor. "Do you hear yourself? Pierre is learning the business of a baker. One day, if God is willing, the bakery will be his—but only if he is prepared. He is *fortunate* to have such a chance—there are many boys in the town who would jump at it."

Under her apron, Lyn knit her fingers tight together and counted to twenty, her eyes fixed on the floor. I am not Elisabeth, they are not my brothers, she is not my grandmother, this is not my business, she told herself over and over.

"Very well then," said Madame Pugnant. "Now. It is Jeanne who gives me cause for greatest concern. She has a good position with Lieutenant Duvernay, in spite of what your father may say to the contrary. Her work is satisfactory and Madame Duvernay is pleased with her. In two or three years she will marry. The connection with the Duvernays cannot help but improve her prospects—if she does nothing foolish. I wish I could be certain—" Her brows drew together. "Madame Duvernay has requested that Jeanne be allowed to live in the household. At first I said no, she is too young, but circumstances have altered and I have changed my mind. She will go to them on Wednesday. This evening I shall tell her.''

There was an uneasiness in her voice; Lyn looked up. ''Does her—does Jean Bernard know this?''

''Of course he knows. He objects, but he cannot suggest anything better. Madame Duvernay is expecting a child and she wants Jeanne for company. It is a good place—I have told him this again and again.'' It sounded to Lyn as if she was still telling him, or perhaps herself. Remembering the lieutenant's offensively appraising stare, Lyn agreed with Jean Bernard. If Jeanne were plain and sensible . . . ''Jeanne will come to us every Sunday after Mass. She is not going far away,'' Madame Pugnant continued irritably. ''It is agreed and there is nothing further to discuss.'' She picked up the quill that was lying among the papers and turned back to the ledger. ''You may go and finish cleaning your lamps, Elisabeth. That is all.''

''What about Louise?''

''Louise?'' Madame Pugnant looked for a moment as if she did not remember any Louise.

''You have arranged all our lives but hers. What is she to do?''

''She will help in the kitchen, as before.''

Kitchen maid and baby-sitter. ''Could she not have lessons, too?''

Madame Pugnant was surprised. ''In the kitchen she will learn all that is necessary for her to know. What else does she need?''

''To read and write,'' said Lyn feeling rash. ''If you teach Pierre, could you not teach Louise also?''

Throwing the quill down so it made a blot on the page, Madame Pugnant said, ''You are talking nonsense, Elisabeth! Reading and writing!''

''But *you* know how—''

''It is not enough—everything I have already given you? You want more! I do not ask your opinion, Elisabeth. I tell you what has been decided, do you understand?'' She stood up, her anger filling the room. ''As it is, you have said too much. Go now before I change my mind and send you all back to your father. It would serve you right—and him. If you have any sense at all, which I begin to doubt, you will learn to keep your mouth shut.''

In spite of herself, Lyn was unable to hold Madame Pugnant's eyes.

"Now, you will send Marie-Marthe to me, and while I speak to her, you will mind the shop."

Rebelliously, Lyn said, "I do not know anything about the shop."

"Let us hope that you have the wits to learn quickly, is it not," snapped the old woman. "For all of our sakes. In the meantime, you will ask customers to wait."

Marie-Marthe was leaning on the counter in the shop with her elbows, staring into space. As Lyn entered, she jumped and her arm hit a basket, knocking its contents to the floor. "Ah, *zut!*" she cried as the hard little rusks rolled about her feet. She scrambled awkwardly to catch them and Lyn heard one crunch under her.

"I will do that. Madame Pugnant wants to see you."

"Me?" Marie-Marthe's face appeared above the counter, stricken. "But I have done nothing," she wailed. "It was an accident. I am not to blame!"

"You had better hurry," Lyn told her unsympathetically.

"Ah, *sacredie!*"

Lyn retrieved the escaped rusks and brushed them off, sweeping up the crushed one. The floor was clean, so she simply put them back in the basket; no one would be any the wiser. There were no customers while she was there, so she amused herself by fiddling with the brass scales and weights on the counter, and the curious device next to them: a hinged frame with thin wires stretched across it, about a quarter of an inch apart.

When Marie-Marthe returned, her cheeks were blotchy and her mouth trembled at the corners. Lyn couldn't imagine what Madame Pugnant had said to upset her so.

"It is *your* fault, this! It would not have happened but for you!"

"What have I done?" asked Lyn, taken aback.

"You know! What shall I do now? I have no work! Where shall I go?"

She had been fired. Rather than pay her to work in the shop, Madame Pugnant would use Elisabeth and save money. Lyn sighed. "I am sorry. It was not my idea—I do not want to take your job."

"Sorry? What good is that to me? Go away!"

Thoroughly discouraged, Lyn returned to the kitchen. Where was Elisabeth? What would *she* have wanted? Was she ambitious or passive, assertive or timid? Did she meekly do as she was told, or argue if she didn't want to? Probably the former, Lyn thought

92

glumly; that's what everyone seemed to expect from her. She sat down at her lamps without a word, ignoring the way they all looked at her. If they wanted to know, let them ask.

Finally Marguerite said, "Elisabeth—there is nothing wrong, is there?"

"Oh, nothing," said Lyn. "Nothing at all, except that Louise is to be a kitchenmaid, and Jeanne is to go live with the Duvernays. And Marie-Marthe has lost her job because I am to take her place. That is all."

"Louise cannot be of less use than you," declared Suzanne.

"I will miss you," said Marguerite. "Maman is fair, although she is strict. She will treat you well if you do your best."

Lyn didn't bother to say that was the least of her worries. Instead, she said, "I do not like Lieutenant Duvernay."

"You do not need to, do you?" said Suzanne. "It is nothing to do with you. Have you not finished with those yet? How can it take so long?"

"I am being very careful," Lyn said.

When she had protested to Marie-Marthe that she didn't want her job, Lyn had meant it. On the face of it, working in a bakeshop didn't sound like much of a thrill. But after the first week, she would have put up a fight to stay there. She didn't have to; Madame Pugnant seemed satisfied with her work, and though she watched Lyn like a hawk and was not patient with mistakes, she did not constantly criticize as Suzanne did.

Lyn's day in the bakeshop made her even more aware of how claustrophobic Elisabeth's life was. Elisabeth's contact with the outside world—even the microcosmic world of Louisbourg—was minimal, and always buffered by other people.

The kitchen and the bakeshop existed cheek-by-jowl, they shared a common wall; they were only steps apart along the hall. But one was insular, and the other cosmopolitan. The kitchen looked out on the confined, private courtyard; the bakeshop's single window opened onto the quay. The life of the town was spread out, in full view. Ships were loaded, cargoes discharged, little boys fished off the wharves and chased through the traffic, dogs fought, people gossiped, argued and conducted business, soldiers marched past. The shop was connected to the world outside by the flow of cus-

93

tomers. After weeks of being shut up day after day with Marguerite and the babies and Suzanne, Lyn felt as if she had emerged from a dark little hole into the fresh air.

The job itself wasn't difficult. The hardest part was learning what all the goods were and how much they cost. Whatever his other faults, Joseph deserved his reputation as a fine baker. Lyn marveled at the astonishing variety of confections he was able to produce from the two primitive wood-fired ovens: light, moist sponge cakes, little marzipan tartlets, rich chocolate biscuits, honey-spice breads, elaborately decorated fruitcakes for weddings and christenings. These last were baked to order; most of their trade was in bread: braided, round, or long, thin loaves, hard discs like enormous crackers, rolls of all shapes. The cheapest—bought by fishermen, sailors, the wives and children of laborers—were dense and dark, made of coarse-ground rye and barley meal. The most expensive—bought by the servants of officers, merchants and town officials—were light and pale, made of white flour, many times sifted by Pierre and Thomas. Stale rolls were turned into rusks: sliced and dried and sold to the poorest customers, who couldn't afford real bread with their soup. The device with wires on one end of the counter was for slicing loaves into neat, even pieces.

Each loaf had Joseph's mark and its weight cut into the crust, but Madame Pugnant made Lyn weigh it again, in front of the customer. "They must be assured that we are honest, Elisabeth. This is a good business because we are trusted. We hide nothing." Lyn had lost count of the times she had heard Mike's father make the same kind of little speech about the hardware store. They were very similar, Mr. Hennessey and Madame Pugnant: strict, hard-working, scrupulous and shop-proud.

Every afternoon after dinner Madame Pugnant retired to her room for several hours with the accounts. While she was gone and the shop officially closed, Lyn was expected to clean it thoroughly: to sweep, dust, restack the shelves, polish the brass scales. Sometimes customers came in while Madame Pugnant was upstairs, in which case Lyn was required to take their money, or remember who they were and what they bought until the old woman came back. On fine days, if there was time and the shop was empty, she stole a few minutes to stand on the front steps where she could watch the constant activity and enjoy the sun on her face. She would close her eyes for a few seconds and feel that, when she opened them again, she'd find herself back where she belonged. It never happened, but there was always the chance that it might.

Best of all, she was sometimes allowed out by herself to deliver a special order somewhere in the town. Ordinarily Michel went, but he couldn't always be spared for such errands. Madame Pugnant invariably sent Lyn off with dire warnings and explicit instructions not to linger or speak to strangers, and Lyn, aware that if she wasn't careful she would lose this precious scrap of freedom, fought against the temptation to explore the streets. Females of a susceptible age and from respectable families did not go about in the town unaccompanied without very specific errands.

The one thing Lyn was never allowed to touch was the ledger in which Madame Pugnant kept the daily accounts. Transient customers—men off the ships, traders, other strangers—paid in cash, handing over coins that disappeared immediately into a little wooden box with a lock. But most people paid on account and Madame Pugnant scratched figures in the book beside their names each time they came. Once, left alone in the shop for a few minutes, Lyn had opened it to see if she could make any sense at all of the words and numbers. Madame Pugnant's writing was like black tangled thread across the pages. Before she could work any of it out, the old woman returned and snatched it away. Lyn protested that she had only been looking, but Madame Pugnant said sharply, ''It is *I* who keep the accounts—*no one else*. They are nothing to do with you. There must be no mistakes. Do not let me find you meddling again, is that clear?''

It was no use arguing that she was good at figures, or that it would be much safer to keep track of afternoon customers in writing than in her head; the old woman refused to discuss it. In that she was like Mike's father, too. Only in the last year and with the utmost reluctance had Mr. Hennessey allowed Mike to begin writing up bills and charges and help with the bookkeeping. He made it seem like a great privilege instead of merely additional work. Mike had been fifteen before Mr. Hennessey let him punch up sales on the electronic cash register, even though he was less comfortable with it than his son. He said customers were too valuable to alienate through carelessness and mistakes, but Lyn guessed shrewdly that it was really Mr. Hennessey's way of maintaining his authority. Adults were frequently guilty of withholding pieces of information, not because their children were incapable of understanding it, but because they needed to feel they were still in charge. Even Dorrie did it from time to time.

Watching Madame Pugnant guard her ledger, Lyn wondered if she ever feared becoming obsolete. Was it the old woman who supported the business, or the business that supported the old woman? The former, Lyn would have said, except that every now and then Madame Pugnant seemed to falter and for a moment Lyn caught a glimpse of someone small and frail and tired.

Thursday morning, when Thomas brought in the second tray heaped with fragrant four-pound wheaten loaves, Madame Pugnant said, "You will remind Joseph that we have business this morning." He rolled his eyes at Lyn, who was stacking the bread on the counter, but replied, "Yes, Madame."

There was quite a lot of banging and shouting in the bakery. Madame Pugnant ignored it as she waited on customers and made her ink scratches, but once, after a particularly audible curse, she remarked dryly, "I do not see why Joseph criticizes bad temper in others. It is clear he is deaf to himself."

"He shouts far too much at Pierre," said Lyn.

"Shouting will not hurt Pierre, Elisabeth. He must learn to pay attention to his work and do it well."

Before Lyn could reply, Joseph himself appeared in the shop, brushing the sleeves of his shirt. "You are determined to go through with this, are you?" he said crossly. "I can say nothing to change your mind, I suppose?"

"We have discussed it many times over, Joseph. You are a baker—you must bake bread in order to earn a living. In order to bake bread, you must have flour. You know for yourself that soon there will be none left in the cellar and none to buy in the warehouses. What will you do if we cannot get more?"

"I would rather go hungry than buy English flour!"

"But I would not. And I do not wish to see my family go hungry. We have agreed to nothing yet. We will listen to what Monsieur Martel has to say, that is all. But remember this—if we have no business, we have nothing."

"It is against the law, Maman." Joseph's tone was righteous. "What if we are found out? What will your family do then?"

96

"You know as well as I how many people in Louisbourg deal in English goods. The courts turn a blind eye to it—they must unless they wish to prosecute half the merchants in town. And flour from New England is of very high quality. As you are aware, Joseph, it is much better than most that comes to us from France. If we can get it, we will be fortunate."

"But to do business with rogues—"

"I do not like to owe favors," she snapped. "But I will do what is necessary to keep the business." She skewered him with her sharp stare.

There was an uncomfortable silence. Lyn kept still; she was afraid that if they remembered she was there they would stop talking.

"It is because of the *Cantabre,* is it not." Joseph sounded like a sulky little boy. "You are paying me back for that. How could I know what would happen? It was an honest mistake."

In exasperation, Madame Pugnant said, "It is because we need supplies. If it makes you feel happier, Joseph, consider this. Jean Bernard is beholden to us because we have taken in his children and given his son an apprenticeship. We do him a favor, and now he does us one. So. We are even."

"I do not like it."

"That is not important. Sometimes you must—" She broke off as two men entered the shop.

"Good day, Madame. Monsieur Desforges." They had not come to buy bread; Lyn recognized them as Jean Bernard and Mathieu Martel. "I believe you wanted to speak to us, is it not?"

"Good day, Jean. It is good of you to come," replied Madame Pugnant formally. Joseph said nothing, but the color rose in his face.

Mathieu Martel said nothing either, but his eyes came to rest on Lyn. He gave her a slight nod, perhaps in greeting, she wasn't sure. She looked back at him curiously. She guessed he was in his mid-twenties; he had an interesting, angular face, his features too rough to be handsome, and he was taller than Jean Bernard. She wondered about the connection between them. Jeanne and Louise had made Martel sound quite shady.

"—we conduct our business upstairs in private," said Madame Pugnant. "Elisabeth? Elisabeth, pay attention! You will look after

97

the shop while I am gone. If there is any difficulty you will fetch Christophe, or wait until I return, do you understand?''

''Yes, Grandmother,'' said Lyn with resignation.

''Monsieur Martel.'' Madame Pugnant turned to him. ''Jean tells us that you have—shall I say, useful—friends?''

''I have contacts among the traders, Madame. Whether they are useful—that must depend upon what it is you need. Mademoiselle.'' He nodded again at Lyn, and this time she smiled in return. He was, after all, the only person who had bothered to acknowledge her presence. She caught a flicker of interest in his eyes, before Madame Pugnant, with a repressive frown, said, ''I believe you have not met my son-in-law, Monsieur, Joseph Desforges.''

''Ah, no. But I have heard much about him,'' Martel replied pleasantly, extending his hand. Joseph gave it an awkward, grudging shake, and they all followed Madame Pugnant out. Their feet were heavy on the stairs.

Lyn was beginning to have trouble sleeping. Now that she no longer had to concentrate all her energies on functioning, she had time to brood. Down in the pit of her stomach, a cold place was starting to grow. She was still tired at the end of a day's work, when she and Louise went up to bed. She closed her eyes and sank into oblivion, only to find herself suddenly wide awake again an hour or two later, staring into the darkness. She listened to the even, regular breathing of the others in the room and her muscles pulled tighter and tighter, like elastic stretched to the snapping point. Her heart began to pound and her hands grew clammy. The clock on the citadel relentlessly picked off the quarter hours while she lay rigid, her eyes hot.

She had had attacks of anxiety before, in the middle of other nights—over something she hadn't done that she was supposed to have, or something she had done that she shouldn't have. The best remedy was to turn on her bedside light and read until her eyes closed, with Gilbert curled like a round fur cushion against her stomach. If she didn't distract herself, the night had a way of multiplying and exacerbating everything depressing, unpleasant and guilt-producing. Her mind would begin to ask questions that she had no way of being able to answer, and they would chase each other round and round inside her head, boring deep into those places

98

where she was most vulnerable. They almost always turned into questions about who she was, who Dorrie was, who her father was, how they fit into one another, and why. There were gaps she couldn't fill that upset and angered her in the middle of the night. So she would turn for refuge to one of the books she had known and loved since she was little, something familiar and comforting: *The Secret Garden,* or *Little Women,* or *Anne of Green Gables.* They were books she had read so often she knew she could trust them, and they didn't fail her.

But where she was now, in this bedroom of this house on the quay in Louisbourg, she couldn't do that. She tried telling the stories to herself—she knew them virtually by heart. It helped a little, but it wasn't nearly as effective as losing herself in someone else's words.

Nearly a month had gone by since she'd fallen into this place. Still there was no sign of the real Elisabeth Bernard. Reluctantly, Lyn had come to the conclusion that she was not in Louisbourg. The town was too small, ingrown, full of gossip; no one could disappear into it without a trace. The only other possibility was that she had run away—cleared out altogether. But from what Lyn surmised about Elisabeth, that seemed highly unlikely. Running away here was a far cry from running away in Lyn's own world—here you'd need help, you couldn't possibly do it by yourself. Where would you go? There was nothing for miles and miles outside the town, and no public transport to take you anywhere else.

It was the second half of August. In the normal course of events, she and Dorrie would be making plans to start home; they would be finishing up at Louisbourg, packing, beginning to say good-bye. Their thoughts would be stretching ahead to the next pieces of their lives: for Dorrie, putting her photographs into a coherent shape; for Lyn, beginning the semester at U. Mass.

What, she wondered in the middle of the night, would happen if the time came for them to leave *and she wasn't there*? What would Dorrie do? Would she stay on at Louisbourg, waiting for Lyn to suddenly appear, or would she go home? The longer Lyn was missing, the harder it would be for Dorrie to stay; the longer she was missing, the longer she might continue to be missing.

If she didn't show up in September to register, what would the college do? There were waiting lists, she knew. Would U. Mass give Lyn's place to someone else? When she finally arrived, would she be told, "Sorry, it's your own fault, Carolyn Paget. You've lost your chance. We can't be bothered with irresponsible people like you."

What would Mike think if she didn't come home at the end of the month? What did he think now, when she'd stopped answering his letters? Had he called Dorrie to ask about her, or had he simply assumed she was no longer interested in him, that she'd found someone else in Nova Scotia? He said he loved her and she didn't doubt him, but how long would he wait for someone who vanished without a word? Diane Sullivan had been looking for the chance to move in on him all year, and in the fall she and Mike would both be starting at B.U. . . .

Lyn had sworn to herself she would never be jealous—it was ugly and small-minded and it did terrible things to a relationship. She'd seen it happen. She couldn't understand the violence of her feelings about Mike now. It was like having her innards sandpapered; she felt raw and sore.

Night after night she lay awake, struggling under the weight of her thoughts, not moving for fear she would disturb Louise, resentful over Louise's ability to sleep so soundly. Renée never wiggled. It was Blaize who rescued her, with his bad dreams. He threw himself around his little bed and whimpered and cried. Even when he woke Louise, she refused to go to him or call out to reassure him. She simply wound herself in the bedclothes and shut her ears. Lyn went. Blaize reminded her of a stray puppy, pathetically eager to please someone—anyone—desperate for a person to pin his affections to. During the day it was Michel. In the middle of the night, it was Lyn.

During one of her sessions with Blaize, as she felt her right forearm going to sleep under his weight, the solution to the situation suddenly came to her. It was like having one of Dorrie's flash bulbs go off in her face. She couldn't imagine why she had been so obtuse for so long. All she had to do was go back to the rue Royale—back to the exact spot where she had fallen in July, and walk over it, stand on it, jump up and down, until she got back through again to her own time. It was so simple.

Gently she released Blaize's grip. He was breathing loudly and steadily through his mouth now. She wondered if anyone here had heard of adenoids as she brushed the hair off his forehead. She

100

would miss him. That was part of the trouble: the longer she stayed, the more involved with these people she became. What would happen to Louise? And Marguerite and Christophe? When she got back she resolved to go to the library in the compound and dig through the records to find them, to find out what became of them. Creeping into her side of the bed, she closed her eyes and sank at once into the pool of sleep that filled the room.

In the morning she felt better than she had for days: clear-headed and cheerful. As she dressed, her fingers touched the key over her breastbone and she smiled. Soon she'd be using it again to open a door. . . .

Louise was watching her. "You are happy this morning." She sounded suspicious.

"Yes," said Lyn.

"Why?"

"You would not understand."

No one but Louise noticed. Madame Pugnant could barely climb the stairs by herself; from the deep little lines around her eyes and the pinched look of her mouth, Lyn guessed she was in considerable pain although she did not say so. Joseph was wrapped in bad temper; it clung to him like a sea fog. He never sang in the bakery anymore; instead he shouted and swore and slammed doors.

About a week after Jean Bernard and Mathieu Martel had come, several cartloads of barrels appeared on the quayside next to the cellar door. Abandoning their other work, Thomas, Christophe, Michel and Pierre went to roll them inside, down a makeshift ramp. The labels on them were in English. No one mentioned any of it.

Anne was cutting another tooth. Marguerite did her best to keep the baby quiet—at the merest hint of a wail, she would snatch her up and croon to her, rocking back and forth. But whenever Joseph was in the room, he glared so fiercely at Anne it was as if he wanted to pick her up himself and hurl her out through the back door into the cabbages. Marguerite's eyes were purple-shadowed. Christophe watched her with such stoic misery Lyn couldn't bear to look at him in case she said something ill-considered. It was, she reflected crossly, the most unholy mess. She had to keep reminding herself that it was none of her business and she would soon be out of it, far away from all of them. In the meantime, she had to be patient and wait for her chance—it was bound to come.

101

Talk in the shop these days was mainly about the expedition against Annapolis Royal. Even though it was supposed to be secret, everyone knew about it. Captain Duvivier's five ships had left Louisbourg at the end of July, and news of their exact progress was vague, though the weather had been against them at first. It was common knowledge that he was heading for Chignecto first, to raise support among the Micmac Indians and Acadians. Complaints were getting louder and more vehement about the number of English prisoners being held in warehouses and outbuildings throughout the town. Nothing seemed to be happening about them, although the Governor claimed to be negotiating for an exchange with Governor Shirley in Boston. Instead, alarming news trickled in about the number of ships being lost to English privateers, and the word "blockade" came up with increasing frequency. Ominous references were made to the winter of 1742, when supplies had all but run out in Louisbourg and people had nearly starved.

In the kitchen, Michel and Suzanne sparred with one another; Michel darted and jabbed, Suzanne blundered forward, arms flailing. "Jacques Lamartine says we must win at Annapolis or we are finished," announced Michel.

"What does Lamartine know? He is only a stupid fisherman! Of course we will win," declared Suzanne. "God is on *our* side—we cannot lose to the English."

"Perhaps we should send you to them to tell them that," Michel suggested, a wicked gleam in his eye. "Then we would not need to waste our time in fighting, is it not. They would see it is pointless to oppose us. *Voilà!* We give you the keys to Annapolis Royal, Madame Labreche. You must win because God is on your side—"

"*Fou!*" cried Suzanne. "That is sacrilege! May you be struck down for it!"

And so it went.

Late on the Friday afternoon following Lyn's brainstorm, Christophe brought a batch of newly baked white rolls into the shop. They were for Madame de la Plagne in the big house at the end of the rue Toulouse, overlooking the Place Royale.

"Michel will take them," said Madame Pugnant. "Do not leave them here, Christophe." But it seemed that Joseph had sent Michel out for tobacco and Michel had not yet returned. Madame Pugnant said, "They can wait until he does, then."

Christophe nodded in agreement and said deferentially, "Madame de la Plagne has not given us such an order before, of course, and she did say promptly, but an hour or so cannot make any difference to her, Madame."

She scowled at him. "They are all the same, these people! They think only of their own convenience, that is all. Send Pierre, then."

"He is sieving flour for tomorrow's sponges, Madame."

"I could go—Grandmother," said Lyn, hardly daring to hope. "There are no customers and the shop is tidy."

"Mmmp."

Christophe withdrew, leaving the rolls and giving Lyn a morose nod. She waited. Madame Pugnant opened the ledger and scratched something in it, then she looked up. "Well? Why do you stand there? Did you not hear Christophe? Promptly, he said. Get your cloak—it is wet."

Lyn snatched it off the peg in the hall while Madame Pugnant wrapped the rolls and packed them in a basket. She gave it to Lyn, keeping her fingers on the handle for a moment. "You will go there and come straight back, is it not. You do not speak to anyone in the streets, Elisabeth." It was her customary warning.

"Yes, Grandmother." Lyn did not meet the old woman's eyes. She left quickly lest Michel suddenly turn up to be sent instead. As she pulled the door shut behind her, her heart shot upward. This was the chance she'd waited for—she was on her way home. Unable to keep from smiling, she ran down the steps feeling light and full of energy. She would deliver the rolls first—to assuage her conscience—then go straight to the rue Royale.

It was a murky afternoon, the streets full of damp, fishy fog. Outside the Hotel de la Marine, an untidy, off-duty clump of soldiers had collected. As Lyn approached them, they elbowed each other and made remarks. One whistled through his teeth, and another one suddenly stepped into her path, half pushed by his fellows, so they collided quite hard. With a mixture of bravado and embarrassment, he fumbled at her clothing, his face twisted in a silly grin.

"Well?" she said, shaking herself free. "Will you get out of my way?"

He hesitated, then with a shrug replied, "What will you give me?"

He reminded her so much of Rob Gowan, for a moment she thought she was already back where she belonged. But she smelled rum on his breath. "Shall I tell you what I will give you if you do not let me pass?" she retorted cheerfully.

Someone behind the soldier gave a nudge, but he stood his ground. There were rude comments and scraps of laughter. "Go on, Louis!" "Why do you hesitate? Why do you not seize your opportunity, man?"

"If you try, Louis, you will be sorry, I promise you," Lyn warned him.

"Oh-oh!" More laughter. "She has spirit, that one!"

"You have the spirits, I think. And they have made you foolish. Now, if you do not mind, I have an errand—" She gave Louis a hard stare. He turned an unflattering shade of red, mumbled something while looking at his feet, and backed into his friends. "Thank you." Lyn suppressed a smile.

As she continued up the street, she noticed another soldier standing at the edge of the group, not really part of it, staring at her with a peculiar expression. He was shabby and pinched-looking like most of the privates, but there was something about him that wasn't quite right. He opened his mouth, but she hurried past before he could speak to her. She had enjoyed her encounter with the others, it had made her feel like Carolyn Paget again for the first time in ages. But the man by himself made her vaguely uneasy. She thrust him out of her mind, reaching with her free hand to straighten her cloak. Her fingers touched the hard little shape of the key. It was still warm— it must have fallen out of her chemise in the scuffle. Carefully, she tucked it back out of sight.

The de la Plagne kitchen was full of savory smells. A small boy was turning an enormous crackling roast on the spit over the fire, and a girl about Louise's age was polishing pewter serving dishes. Madame de la Plagne's cook unwrapped the rolls and inspected them critically before she would let Lyn leave. She broke one apart and tasted it. "Yes," she said then, eyeing Lyn narrowly, "they will do, even if they are made with English flour."

Back on the street, Lyn wondered if anyone managed to keep anything secret in Louisbourg. The town was so small and isolated and ingrown, all people had to talk about was one another. She still marveled at the fact that no one except Louise suspected there was anything wrong with Elisabeth Bernard. She marveled, but was no longer incredulous. She realized sadly that Elisabeth was so un-important—even to her own family—that no one really bothered to look at her. So long as she was the right size and shape and filled the requisite space, it didn't matter who she was.

At the corner of the rue Royale, the hairs on the back of her neck stirred and her heart began to slam, beating in her ears like the sound of Michel's hatchet. The spot was about a dozen steps along the street, close to the wall of Monsieur Verrier's house. She took a deep breath, squared her shoulders, and slowly walked the length of the building: ten, eleven, *twelve,* thirteen, fourteen, fifteen. . . . At the end, she stopped and blinked. Nothing. Not the slightest flicker. She had missed it. Locking her fingers on the basket handle, she turned and started back. Left-right-left-right-left-right—slowly, de-liberately. Still nothing. The street was firm under her feet. There was no explosion of sunlight, no heart-stopping lurch. Just the same dirty, gray, smelly afternoon, and a little boy she hadn't noticed standing in a gateway, staring at her.

She snuffed the flare of panic in her chest—it had seemed so simple when she thought of it, so obvious. But of course she couldn't be certain of the exact spot; she would have to work at it. Back and forth she walked, quartering the ground. Overhead, dis-embodied by the fog, gulls chuckled and laughed humorlessly, and the little boy leaned against the gatepost and watched. She lost count of the number of times she tried; her ears were full of a thick, prickling silence and her mouth was sticky. It wasn't going to work—she was trapped. Either trapped in 1744, or—which was unimaginably worse—trapped in her own mind somehow. Like the woman Kathy had told them about—she lurked frighteningly in the shadows of Lyn's thoughts.

She forgot the boy; if there were other people on the street, she didn't see them. Her skin clammy, she chose what she thought was the precise spot and dropped self-consciously to her knees. The ground was muddy and unyielding. She picked herself up and tried again. The third time she wondered if she had the energy left to get up, and if she managed to, what she should do next.

Then, as if the whole thing were happening all over again from the beginning, a hand grasped her by the shoulder. ''Mademoiselle? That is what I thought—it is you. But why? Why are you here like this? What has happened? Are you hurt?''

Lyn shivered and blinked in an effort to focus. The face above her this time was one she recognized. She allowed its owner to pull her to her feet.

''What is the matter with you? Can you not speak?''

Getting her brain to function was like rousing a limb that had gone to sleep; it hurt. Little bubbles of pain burst behind her eyes. The face belonged to Mathieu Martel. Beside him, looking quizzical, was Michel. And behind Michel she glimpsed Blaize, his hair on end as usual, his eyes solemn. She gave a gulping little laugh— she couldn't help it.

Mathieu's face drew together. ''Mademoiselle!'' He shook her quite roughly and she bit her tongue. ''Now. You tell me what has happened, is it not.''

She pulled herself together. ''Nothing.''

''Nothing?'' His eyebrows quirked skeptically. ''I find you alone, on your knees in the mud, and you say nothing has happened?''

''I fell,'' said Lyn with some dignity. ''That is all, Monsieur. You did not need to shake me like that.''

He gave a half shrug. ''I am sorry.'' He didn't sound it. ''You are quite certain that no one has harmed you?''

There was a rusty taste on her tongue—blood. ''Only you, Monsieur.''

''Why are you here alone? Does your grandmother know?''

''She sent me. I delivered rolls to the de la Plagne house.''

He grunted. ''And so you are here, on the rue Royale. It is a roundabout route, I think. Perhaps you lost your way in the fog, Mademoiselle?''

She bent and brushed at the dirt on her apron, ignoring the note of mockery in his voice. ''I am all right now—as you see. You need not trouble yourself further.''

''It is as well that we were the ones to find you, not someone else.''

''Whatever you—or anyone else—may think, Monsieur, it was an accident.''

''It is not what people think''—he sounded impatient—''it is what they say, and to whom they say it. If they would only *think*, then it would not matter. But they will talk, and what they do not know they will make up. Who can say what your papa will hear? Or your grandmother? Or your very important uncle?''

"Why do they not mind their own business," said Lyn crossly.

"It is not so interesting as other people's," Mathieu said with a smile. "You see, even I ask myself what you are doing here and why, and if I do not like your answer, then perhaps I find another. That is your basket, is it not? Michel.''

Michel picked it up and handed it to her. In order to take it, she had to unclasp her fingers from the key. Unconsciously, all the time she had been walking up and down the street, she had been clutching it, so hard its edges had dug deep red lines on her palm. She slipped it under her chemise, but not before Michel saw it.

"I think it best if Michel takes you home—in case you suffer another fall.''

"But—'' Michel protested.

"You have been gone long enough," said Mathieu. Michel shrugged, accepting the decision. "You can walk, Mademoiselle?''

Lyn heaved a great sigh and surrendered her hope; it sailed out of reach like a helium balloon. "Yes.''

He nodded. "I am off then. I do not think I will mention this to your father. I would not want to distress him." He strode away into the fog.

"They will ask you what happened," said Michel, eyeing her with disapproval.

"I will tell them I fell," said Lyn flatly.

Michel grunted. "They will believe you. It is the kind of thing that happens often to you, I think.''

Blaize pushed his hand silently into Lyn's; his fingers were cold. He looked up at her with a worried frown, and in spite of herself, she gave him a rueful little smile. She didn't at all want to go back to the bakery—she'd been so sure she would never go there again. But at least it was somewhere to go. . . .

⋙ 8 ⋘

"**T**HERE IS SOMETHING WRONG WITH YOU, IS IT NOT."
Startled, Lyn glanced at Michel, who was lounging in
the doorway of the bakeshop. She was in the midst of her afternoon
cleaning, brushing crumbs off the shelves and counter into the crock
for the hens, concentrating very carefully on what she was doing
and trying not to think about her situation. Her failure in the rue
Royale the day before had been disappointing, but she was determined not to let it overwhelm her. It was the obvious answer—and
it had been wrong. There was a right one, and she would find it.

"Do you want something?" she asked.

Michel grinned. "I always want something. And usually I get
it."

"I have noticed," said Lyn dryly. In spite of the guerrilla warfare
that went on in the kitchen between Michel and Suzanne, several
times Lyn had noticed Suzanne slipping Michel a small bundle as he
left for the night. She gave it grudgingly and he snatched it without
a word of thanks and tucked it under his shirt. It was clearly not a
gift; she suspected it was food: cheese, dried beef, bacon. . . .

He pushed himself away from the doorframe and walked into the
room, regarding her shrewdly. "I have been wondering about you
for quite some time," he said. "I do not think you are who you
pretend to be."

Her heart gave a kick. "What do you mean?"

"As I say." He took one of the morning's rolls and began to tear
it into small pieces which he slowly ate. "You are not Mademoiselle Elisabeth Bernard," he said after a minute or two. "I can see
that I am right."

"You must know Elisabeth Bernard very well." It shouldn't have
surprised her—Michel seemed to know everything about everyone,
but her skin prickled.

"Me, I hardly know her at all," he replied with a shrug.

108

"Then how can you say this?"

"I watch you. For—what is it?—four? five weeks? What you say, what you do. I watch and I listen. And then yesterday, I am sure. You are different."

"But if you are not familiar with Elisabeth, I do not understand how you can claim to know. How am I different from her?"

"I did not say that. Not from Mademoiselle Elisabeth are you different—from *every*one you are different." As he spoke, he watched her closely. "I ask myself why. How do you come to be here, in this house? And where is Elisabeth Bernard?"

Slowly Lyn shook her head. "I do not know where she is. I wish I did."

"I do not believe you."

"It is true. I have never seen Elisabeth Bernard."

"Not possible," he declared. "But she is not in Louisbourg, *that* is true. I would know it if she were. You must have planned this with her."

"No," said Lyn. "I do not know what happened to her—or to me, for that matter. I do not belong here, you are right. But I do not know how to get home again. I am lost."

"Where is home?"

The enormity of the answer to that question loomed before her. Michel thought it could only be a matter of crossing space: an ocean, a state, a continent. But she could make her way south to Massachusetts from Louisbourg, to Belmont, to Waverley Street— the very spot where she and Dorrie lived—and if she couldn't somehow cross *time*, she would be no closer to where she belonged than she was now.

"It is a long way, is it not." His eyes gleamed under the uneven fringe of hair.

Bleakly, she agreed. "You do not know."

"Why do you not return as you came?"

"I have tried and it did not work. I do not know how to get back." Frustration made her angry. "Do you think I would stay if I did? I do not want to be here, pretending to be Elisabeth Bernard. It was not my idea!"

He grunted noncommittally. She could not tell what he was thinking.

109

"If you are so sure I am not Elisabeth, why have you not told anyone? Madame Pugnant, or Joseph?"

Again the characteristic, casual lift of the shoulders she was coming to expect. "Why should I? If they choose to look, they can see for themselves what I see. Otherwise? I do not tell people something unless it is useful to do so."

"Useful?"

"There is nothing to be gained by giving the answer before the question is even asked." He was scornful. "I am in no hurry. I wait and see how it goes."

Lyn nodded. "And what you can get."

"Of course. Why not?"

"You are an opportunist."

His eyes narrowed. "I do not know what that is."

"You collect information and use it to your advantage."

He thought about it, then grinned. "It is true. I am clever, is it not."

"Why have you told *me* this? I have nothing to give you."

"You have a secret. It is good to let people know when you guess their secrets, in case they want to keep them."

"It is only a secret because no one else cares. Elisabeth does not matter much to anyone, as far as I can see."

Michel continued to eat his roll, bit by bit, in a considering silence. "I know someone else like you," he said when he had finished.

"Like me how?"

"Different."

Lyn's mouth went dry. "Who?"

He shrugged dismissively. "You do not know her—she does not come here. She lives in the faubourg, near my aunt. Her husband is a fisherman."

His words were slippery—she had trouble grasping them. It had never occurred to her that she was not the only one—that what had happened to her could have happened to anyone else.

Gauging her reaction, Michel frowned. "You did not know this. I should not have told you. *Merde.*" He was annoyed with himself.

"But how do you know she is different, Michel—this other person?" asked Lyn urgently.

"It is not for certain. I could be mistaken. She is from away—Niganiche. It is only that which makes her strange."

"No." She caught him by the arm so suddenly he had no time to back away. "You would not have mentioned it if you believed that. Who is she? What is her name? I must know. I must talk to her."

He shook himself loose and stepped out of reach, his face angry. "I will not tell you—you will be stupid. You will get us both into trouble."

"There you are," said Christophe, putting his head around the door. "We need water and Suzanne is calling for firewood. What are you doing here? Are you bothering Mademoiselle Elisabeth?" He gave Lyn a questioning look.

"No," she said hastily. "It is my fault. I asked—"

"She asked me if I had heard anything about Captain Duvivier," said Michel smoothly. "Did you know that he has reached Baie Verte, Christophe?"

When they had gone, Lyn stood still, trying to untangle her thoughts. She had to find out who the other person was. She would make Michel tell her, and if he refused, she would go looking by herself. He had said the faubourg, the fishing settlement outside the Dauphin Gate, near his aunt. Her husband was a fisherman. Never mind that she didn't know Michel's aunt and that probably every woman's husband out there was a fisherman. If Michel was right and she really was "different" like Lyn, they would recognize each other.

She had all of Sunday to brood about what Michel had told her—and what he hadn't. On Monday he ignored her, going about his usual chores as if their conversation had never occurred. She watched him for a sign, any sign, but he gave her nothing. It was worse than waiting for college board scores; by the end of the day her nerves were raw.

That night she decided she could wait no longer. The next morning she caught him in the cowshed before breakfast. He was sitting on a stool, leaning against the cow, deftly pulling her teats while Blaize sat splay-legged in the straw, chin on hand, watching.

"Michel," she said.

"Mmmm." The milk continued to stream into the pail.

"I want to talk to you."

"Yes? About what?"

111

"You know." She kept her voice level.

Silence except for squirt-squirt.

"I have come to tell you that if you do not take me to the woman you told me about, I will go by myself."

"You cannot. You do not know who she is."

"I will find her. I will ask until I do. I will find your aunt and ask her."

He stopped milking. "You do not know my aunt."

"Not yet, but soon I will."

He stood up and looked at her across the cow's angular hips. "What did I say!" he exclaimed crossly. "You will have us both in trouble."

"It is your own fault," said Lyn. "Which is it? Will you take me, or do I go alone?"

"You will have to wait. Until I say it is the right time. And you must say nothing about this to anyone, do you understand?"

"Yes." It was an easy promise. She had no one to say anything to. He returned to his milking and she went back to the house.

Three days later, unaware, Madame Pugnant made her a present of the right time when she handed Lyn a small, heavy leather bag. "I have an errand for you, Elisabeth. It is *very* important. Listen carefully and do exactly what I tell you. I want you to take this to Monsieur Marcotte's tavern, outside the walls. You must deliver it *only* to him. You will wait for a written message in return and bring it to me. Do you understand?"

Lyn swallowed. "Yes, Grandmother. But—"

"But?" she snapped. "But what?"

"Only—I do not know where Monsieur Marcotte's tavern is," she said meekly, keeping the excitement out of her voice.

"Michel is taking the laundry, he will show you. If there were a choice—but Joseph has refused, and I cannot go—it is too far, and I would be noticed. You must speak to no one but Monseiur Marcotte, and you must not dawdle." She searched Lyn's face with her fierce eyes.

To distract her, Lyn asked, "What is it for?"

"That does not concern you. All you need worry about is doing as I have instructed."

"Yes, Grandmother." She turned to go.

"Elisabeth!"

She caught her breath and crossed her fingers.

"Carry the bag out of sight. It is safer if no one sees it."

"Yes, Grandmother."

Every week Michel trundled the handcart full of soiled bed linen, napkins, and the caps and aprons from the bakery out of town to his aunt, who washed them for a fee and sent them back. He was waiting impatiently by the back gate when Lyn emerged from the house.

"Is he coming too?" she asked, nodding at Blaize, who stood beside the cart.

"Yes. He is helping me. If you do not like it—"

"I only asked," said Lyn. She knew Michel was cross because he had lost control of the situation and there was nothing he could do about it.

The sun was rich and warm that afternoon, spreading itself like melted butter over the town and the harbor. The slate roofs gleamed like gunmetal and flecks of light danced between the ships. Gulls rode the air currents, swooping and lifting in great arabesques. The quay was full of traffic: a cart drawn by two oxen creaked past, piled with lumpy sacks; men were unloading a bargeful of salt cod near the Frederick Gate and a couple of small boys were fishing over the retaining wall. Two Indians stood nearby talking to an officer. Lyn looked at them curiously. They wore hide leggings and moccasins and grubby blanketlike cloaks, and had shapeless wool caps pulled down over their long black hair. A small foxy dog sat between them, scratching himself luxuriously. The Widow Grandchamp was filling her doorway, arms folded, calling out to people as they passed. She grinned and nodded at Lyn.

A part of Lyn's mind kept pace with her, noticing everything, enjoying the bright soft day, while the rest went leaping eagerly ahead, quivering with anticipation, like a dog on the end of its leash.

At last Michel decided to throw off his sulk. "So," he said. "You did not tell me where it is you are from. It is far away, I think?"

"What?" said Lyn, and then without considering, "Yes—far away. Belmont."

"Belmont?" He made it sound French. "I do not know of it. It cannot be very large."

She saw no reason to be evasive. "It is a city, Michel. It is larger than Louisbourg."

He stared at her in disbelief. "No. It cannot be. I would have heard of it."

"You have heard of everything, have you?" she teased. "It is in Massachusetts. Near Boston."

"Aha! You are not even French then!"

"No."

"And you speak English?"

"Like a native." There was an effervescent sensation in her chest; she felt almost light-headed.

Michel gave her a long, calculating look. "You can teach me?" he said at last.

"Teach you what?"

"English, of course."

"Why on earth—"

A shrug. "It could be useful to know. At least a little. You can do this?"

"Yes," she said in English.

"Yes?" he repeated, suspicious.

"*Oui.*" She turned to Blaize who had been trotting along with his hand on the cart. "And you—do you want to learn English, also?"

He studied her solemnly, then gave a careful imitation of one of Michel's shrugs. Michel grinned and Lyn laughed. "He is not stupid, that one," said Michel.

"No, he is not. I know." For a moment their eyes met over the little boy's head, and Lyn glimpsed something Michel ordinarily kept hidden, something that made her warm toward him.

They had no trouble leaving the town. There were soldiers on duty at the Dauphin Gate, others sitting in the sun outside the guardhouse, cleaning their muskets, talking, smoking clay pipes, picking their teeth. They looked bored and scruffy in the bright light, their uniforms ill-fitting and frayed, their faces spotty. Michel called to them and several called back, exchanging good-natured insults. The soldiers at the gate didn't even glance at the three of them as they crossed the drawbridge.

"You should not stare at them so," said Michel severely. "It is not proper."

"Things are different where I am from," she replied.

114

"But you are not there, are you?" he said unanswerably.

"Do you know this Monsieur Marcotte?" She changed the subject.

A shrug. "What of it?"

"I only wondered why he is so important to Madame—to Grandmother."

"It is not Georges Marcotte who is important. It is the English captain who visits him. If you want to know more, you must ask Mathieu."

"Mathieu? Michel, who *is* Mathieu?" She had wondered about him off and on since the first time she'd seen him. He appeared just often enough to make her curious.

"A friend of your father, is it not."

"And of you," she prodded.

"I know him."

It was like trying to pry open a clam. "Joseph does not like him." Michel snorted.

"Has he done something wrong?"

"Questions! All the time questions!" he cried. "Why do you ask me?"

"Because I thought you knew all the answers. But perhaps you do not."

He looked at her sideways. "Flattery! If you do not know, he is a trader. He came to Louisbourg early last spring—soon after the ice broke up—on a boat with three other men. They did their business and started north. The boat hit a rock. One drowned, the other two disappeared, the boat washed ashore not far up. So. That left Mathieu with no boat and no money. Jean Bernard gave him a job shingling roofs, and a place to stay. Now you know all the answers."

"What do you mean the other two men disappeared?"

"Poof! They were gone," he said unsatisfactorily. "They did not want to hang around."

"Why did Mathieu not disappear with them?"

"He lost them in the shipwreck. Perhaps they thought he had drowned also. And it was a week before he was well enough to get out of bed."

"Hmmm," said Lyn. "There is a lot you have left out, I think."

The faubourg was a clutter of little buildings, a fishing settlement

115

that had accumulated according to no plan in the lee of the town wall: cottages, inns, sheds, fish-drying racks called flakes and landing stages; it had the same feel Lyn had noticed in the modern town of Louisbourg: well used and hard-working. The flakes were covered with stiff gray cod fillets, salted down and curing in the sun. Packed into ships' holds and sent off to Europe, the stuff would last almost indefinitely. Lyn regarded it with interest and distaste. A few old men mended nets on the shore; babies and chickens scrabbled on the hard packed dirt; two women, their forearms bare, took turns stirring an immense cauldron full of pungent liquid. The flames under it were invisible in the sunlight, but Lyn could see waves of heat blurring the air, and the women's faces shone with sweat.

"This is what you want," said Michel, stopping outside one of the cottages. "Monsieur Marcotte." He knocked on the door, and after a moment a small, round-faced man opened it.

"Monsieur Marcotte?" said Lyn, and he nodded. "I have something from Madame Pugnant."

He nodded again and took the pouch from her. "I need—"

"Wait," he said, and disappeared inside. He was gone several minutes and when he returned he handed her a sealed, folded paper. That was all; the whole thing felt secretive, like a drug drop. She tucked the paper inside her chemise, wishing it weren't sealed, and turned to Michel. "Now."

"You are sure?"

"Of course I am. Why not?"

Telling Blaize to wait with the cart, he led her to a long, white-washed building. She started at it, puzzled for a moment until she realized that she was looking at the des Roches's fishing property—the one structure in the faubourg that had been rebuilt for the park. All day long tourists funneled through it on their way into the town. The buses from the visitors' center stopped beside it, and at night the staff collected there to be taken back to their ordinary lives.

"Here?" she asked. "The woman is *here?*"

Michel gave her a sharp look. "Do you know it?"

"I—yes, I think so."

"You stay outside. She may be away. I will see."

Lyn paced, unable to stand still. She had focused so hard on the extraordinary fact that this woman existed that she'd given no thought to what she was going to say to her. She glanced again at the house, wondering if it was significant, or merely a coincidence that it existed in both times.

Michel was gone for what seemed to Lyn like hours. Back and forth she fidgeted—suppose he was wrong after all? Suppose she wasn't there? The door finally opened and a woman came out, blinking in the sunlight. Lyn's heart sank like a brick. She was dressed like every other woman in the faubourg: over her lumpy skirt she wore a large apron of coarse striped material like mattress ticking, patched and stained and scorched in places. Her hair was hidden under the ubiquitous white cap. She hesitated, glancing furtively around. Her eyes slid past Lyn, then came back, but her expression did not change. There was nothing eager or welcoming or excited in it. In French she said, "Michel tells me you want to see me."

Sick with disappointment, Lyn nodded.

"Well? I am busy. I do not have time to waste."

"He said—he thinks we have something in common," said Lyn.

"That is not possible. You are from the town, is it not?"

"No," said Lyn. "Not really."

The woman stared out at the harbor, narrowing her eyes against the glitter. She held one hand underneath her apron; the other, red and rough, was knotted on a fold of her skirt. She looked much older than Dorrie, her face blunt-featured, lined and toughened from exposure to heat and salt wind. Despairing, Lyn searched it for something—whatever Michel had seen. She was sure he hadn't made it up, but the woman gave her no help. She had nothing to lose, she decided, and said in English, "I am not from Louisbourg, and I am not Elisabeth Bernard. I don't belong here."

The woman continued to stare over the water, giving no sign she understood. Defeated, Lyn turned away. There was nothing more she could do.

"Come," the woman said, still in French. "Walk with me. I cannot be gone long or they will send someone to look for me." When Lyn didn't move, she said sharply, "You came to find me, now do as I say."

They walked through the faubourg, away from the shore, not hurrying but purposeful, and climbed the low, bare rise above the harbor. To the east rose the walls of the town, and behind them the long dark roof of the King's Bastion barracks, surmounted by its

117

clock tower. Immediately below lay the harbor crowded with ships and ringed with fishing properties. Beyond this thin rind of civilization, stretching on all sides, flattened by the huge uninterrupted weight of sky, lay wilderness. No highways, towns, shopping centers. No airports, telephone poles or cars. Nothing but bears, moose, a few Indians, a cabin or two, for hundreds and hundreds of miles. The reality of it hit Lyn fully for the first time. Instead of creating a reassuring sense of security, the walls around Louisbourg only emphasized its insignificance and isolation. Its walls were built of stone and fear to give the illusion of safety and civilization where there was none.

"It is not there," said the woman, breathing hard. "What you look for is not there. I know. I have looked myself."

Hardly daring to hope, Lyn said, "Who are you?"

"I am Agathe Grimard and I work in Madame des Roches's tavern. I have a husband who is a fisherman on Georges des Roches's boat, and two children. That is who I am."

For a moment Lyn didn't understand, then her mind made the shift. The woman was speaking English. She felt giddy. "But why didn't you say? Down there—I thought—"

"You must be careful—everyone listens. Nothing is private in this place."

"I know," said Lyn with feeling. "I never thought—it never occurred to me that there was anyone else here. Did you think—"

"Listen." The woman interrupted her. "We will only talk about this once, that's all. There is nothing we can do for each other." Her face was hard and dark.

"But how can you say that? If we can work out what happened to us, we can figure out how to get back."

"I will tell you what happened to me, and I will tell you what I decided. If it helps you, that's good—I'm glad. But that's all. Then you must promise to go away and leave me alone."

"Go away? But why . . ." protested Lyn, at a loss.

"Do you want me to tell you, or not?" When Lyn nodded, the woman went on. "It was the ninth of July, late in the morning. I was in the des Roches's house, making fish stew. It was windy and the fire wouldn't draw and there was a busload of Japanese tourists, all of them talking and waving cameras. There was a flash. I was startled and I lost my balance. I fell and burned

118

myself. There. Look.'' She took her left hand from under her apron and thrust it at Lyn. The skin on the back and side was twisted and shiny. "I was lucky it wasn't worse. I had a fever for three days—I was delirious, they told me afterward. They couldn't understand what I was saying. I couldn't get out of bed. They thought the accident happened because I was sick, but I wasn't sick until it happened. I *know* that. And when I could get up—'' She paused, her eyes distant. "There was no one I knew, and everyone called me Agathe. I still get headaches, but they aren't as bad.''

Unable to look away from the hand, Lyn said, "Where did you burn yourself? There, or here?''

The woman tucked it under her apron again. "I don't know.''

"Were you—was Agathe your character name?''

The woman nodded.

"Do you look like her?''

"How should I know that? I've never seen her. She isn't here, if that's what you mean.''

"No,'' said Lyn, "neither's Elisabeth. All I know is she's my age, and nobody notices that I'm different.''

"Nobody?''

"Well, Michel,'' said Lyn, "and Louise, Elisabeth's little sister, but she won't admit it.''

"Have you asked her?''

"I've tried—but she's afraid. And there's nothing she can do.''

The woman nodded. "Have you told anyone?''

"I've thought of it—''

"But no one would believe you, so you haven't. That's the truth of it. And why should they? Would *you* believe such a story? It doesn't matter anyway—it would do no good. André—my husband—he's a decent sort of man, but he has no imagination. He would think I was mad—really crazy—and that would only make it all worse.''

"So you pretend to be Agathe.''

"What else? In this place, if I am not Agathe, who can I be? There is no room for—the other person.''

"How long have you been here?'' An uncomfortable suspicion was swelling in the back of Lyn's mind. She was thinking of Kathy's story again—about the woman who'd had a breakdown.

119

Her character name had been Agathe, and she had worked in the fishing property.

"I told you—since July ninth. It was six weeks yesterday."

"I don't remember you," said Lyn. "Did you work with Karen and Jane?"

The woman shook her head. "I told you, I was at the fishing property."

She forced herself to ask, "What—year was it?"

"Nineteen eighty-one, of course. What else?" Her face had grown hard again, closed.

"But my time is nineteen eighty-three."

"I must go back," said the woman abruptly. "I have been up here too long. There will be questions."

"Oh," begged Lyn, "wait! There's so much more—you haven't even told me your name!"

"As long as I am here, my name is Agathe," said the woman grimly. "It is the only name they know for me in this place. I don't want to talk to you anymore. There's no point. If you knew how to get back, you wouldn't be here. Neither would I. So what's the use?"

"Don't you want to understand—"

"How can you understand something that's not possible?" she demanded angrily. *"This* is where we are—*this* is where we have to live."

"But not forever!" cried Lyn. "You can't believe we're stuck here forever!"

"No, I don't. It happened once, it will happen again—and I will stay here and wait until it does, as long as that takes. I have thought and thought and there is nothing else to do. Right now I am Agathe Grimard—I do Agathe's work and I look after her family. At the end of the day I'm tired out and I sleep. I try hard not to think anymore because it does no good. I don't want to be reminded—it doesn't make life easier. That's why I don't want to see you again. Can you understand that?"

It was as if she had slammed a door in Lyn's face. She shut her out, firmly and deliberately, turned her back and walked quickly down the hill toward the faubourg. Left standing, alone and confused, Lyn felt cold in spite of the sunshine. She watched until the woman reached the settlement, where she vanished among the other people: an ordinary fisherman's wife, like all the rest.

Could she really be right, that there was nothing they could do except wait? Wait for lightning to strike a second time, with no warning? But suppose she was wrong, and they just went on and on, living out the lives of Agathe and Elisabeth, gradually forgetting who they really were and where they belonged? She had spent seventeen years becoming Lyn Paget, a lot of it had been hard work; now suddenly she was being forced into another person's shape. A hard, sharp-edged fragment of something lodged itself in her chest. It hurt when she swallowed, like a splinter of glass.

Her eyes, which had been staring at nothing since Agathe disappeared, suddenly focused on movement at the edge of the faubourg. Two small figures beside a cart, waving at her. Feeling dazed, she stumbled down the rough slope toward them.

"Why do you stand up there like a statue?" demanded Michel when she reached them. "Madame will be cross—we must hurry. She is waiting for the letter."

Lyn had forgotten all about the note. "You will think of an excuse."

Michel grunted. "What did you say to Agathe, eh? She would not speak to me. I do not think she was happy to see you."

"No," agreed Lyn.

"But I was right about her, no? That she is like you?"

Struck by a sudden thought, Lyn stopped and Blaize bumped into her. "Michel?"

"Did I not say hurry?"

"Michel, tell me. Do you know of *more* people like Agathe? Different?"

"*Sacredie!* I do not *want* to know more. Already it is too much!"

"But do you?"

"Why me?"

"Because it is the kind of thing you know, and it is very important to me."

"Well, I do not. And if I did, why should I tell you? It is only more trouble. If you do not come now I will leave you behind."

121

-»» 9 «-«

SHE COULD HAVE WALKED RIGHT PAST AGATHE GRIMARD ON THE rue Toulouse and never known about her. She didn't think she had—Lyn didn't think she had ever seen the woman before—but the knowledge that she *could* have was sobering. It had taken Michel to spot the connection between them. His persistence was inexhaustible; he kept after Lyn for information: why did you want to see Agathe? why is she angry with you? why does she never want to see you again? Although Lyn stubbornly refused to tell him, she kept her part of their bargain and began teaching him bits of English. He didn't want proper lessons, he made that clear. He wanted words, phrases, sentences that would be useful to him, according to his private purposes, and he grew annoyed with her when she didn't know what he asked: the parts of a musket, nautical terms. "But what good is this to me if you cannot give me the words I need?" he exploded.

"I can only teach you what I know!" she retorted. She wondered how much it would change the course of history if she taught him words like submarine and nuclear bomb and aircraft carrier, then decided against it. No one would have the faintest idea what he was talking about, and she would only harm herself if she alienated him; he was useful. Besides, he was the only other person in the household who had any time for Blaize, and for that she liked him.

Agathe was a painful disappointment to her. She had expected an ally, and found instead a brick wall. But inadvertently Agathe had given her something valuable: she had reminded Lyn of herself. By denying her own identity, Agathe made Lyn resolve to hang onto hers, no matter what. She was tired of always trying to be Elisabeth, of watching what she said and how she behaved. If she was going to be stuck here any longer, she was going to have to find a more satisfactory balance. Elisabeth was going to have

122

to step back and let Lyn breathe. Once she decided that, she felt much better.

She began to stare at people obsessively: the women who bought bread in the shop, the Récollet friars hidden in their brown robes, the sailors on the wharves, the girls who worked at the Hotel de la Marine. She scanned the faces of the people entering and leaving Mass, the crowds on the Place Royale. Now that she knew there was someone else from her time here, it seemed more and more likely to her that there were others. It could be anyone—anyone pretending to be what other people expected, instead of what he or she really was.

Then it occurred to her that there had to be a link somehow between the two times. She and Agathe had become the people they were impersonating, and the space they inhabited existed in both times: the bakery, the des Roches property. If that was important, then she could eliminate all those who existed only in 1744 and had no counterparts in the modern park: the friars, the Duvernays, the sailors off the big ships. . . .

It also occurred to her that the house key could be useful. So far she had kept it hidden where she could feel it but no one could see it and wonder about it, or try to take it away. Anyone from her own time would recognize it instantly: a common Yale house key. Whenever she was alone in the bakeshop, or out on an errand, she began to wear it outside her clothing.

The last days of August were warm and bright and very busy. Whenever Lyn could be spared from the shop, Madame Pugnant sent her to the kitchen to help Suzanne, Marguerite and Louise. They were deep in preparations for the winter: cooking preserves and relishes; turning ashes, lye and fat into soap over a fire in the courtyard; picking herbs and tying them in bunches to dry; dipping candles by the dozen. Careful stock was taken of everything in the cellar and cupboards: barrels and sacks of meal, dried peas and beans, salt, molasses, dried fish, beef and bacon.

To Lyn, an ordinary urban child of the late twentieth century, the idea of laying in supplies for an entire winter—six or seven months—was mind-boggling. She had learned from Dorrie how to plan a week at a time. They shopped together on Thursday evenings to avoid the weekend crowds, whipping around the supermarket with great efficiency, buying everything they needed until the following Thursday except a quart of milk, or a loaf of bread, small miscellaneous things like that. But this was planning on a scale that made Dorrie's look insignificant.

"We will need more beans," said Marguerite.

"That looks like a lot," said Lyn, eyeing the sacks. "How can you tell?"

"Because I know what we used last year, of course. And now there are more of us. It is important to keep a record, so you do not have to guess. Surely Françoise kept one?"

It was easiest to simply say, "Of course."

After a long, sweaty, sticky day in the kitchen Lyn found it most satisfying to see the results lined up on the table: crocks of wild cherry preserves, pickled cucumbers and onions, heaps of tallow candles, blocks of soap. It pleased her to realize that she could make such things by hand, from scratch, and that they were good and useful. As she sat darning stockings in the evenings, she found herself counting them over and over. Even her darning had improved; her heels were no longer poor, lumpy things that Marguerite, with a sad little headshake, had to pick out and redo.

The happiest times were those when Suzanne was out, either on her mysterious errands, or visiting with one of her cronies. Then Marguerite relaxed; she laughed and sang and told stories to the babies, letting them play with spoons and bowls all over the floor. Even Louise unbent a little, although she kept a watchful distance from Lyn. Once Marguerite confessed shyly that with Suzanne gone, she could pretend the kitchen was hers.

"But it *is* yours, isn't it?" said Lyn. "Suzanne is a servant."

"She has been here many years, Elisabeth. She came soon after Françoise was born."

"Suzanne is a miserable old crank," declared Lyn flatly. "You know I am right. Admit it."

Marguerite made a little gulping sound; she was laughing in spite of herself. "But you must not say such things, Elisabeth! It is very rude."

"I do not care." It was on the tip of Lyn's tongue to say, *and besides, I am sure she steals from you,* but she stopped. If she told anyone her suspicions it should be Madame Pugnant, not Marguerite. Marguerite would not know what to do with such information, it would only upset her. But Lyn had noticed discrepancies when she counted candles and crocks and sacks. There were fewer in the evenings than there had been in the afternoons. And several times she had found the sugar loaf appreciably smaller than it had been the day before, or the butter almost gone when there had been a lot left. Suzanne was the one with the best opportunities, and there was no doubt in her mind that Suzanne was capable.

"She is so fierce," said Marguerite. "She frightens me."

Everyone frightens you, Lyn thought sadly. "Stand up to her—that would surprise her."

"I cannot. She would be so angry and Maman would hear of it. Suppose Suzanne left us—what would we do?"

"We would do very well. You could run the house as you wish. But do not worry. Suzanne is too comfortable to leave."

It was no longer possible to pretend the French privateers were still having the best of things at sea. Very few supply ships were arriving in Louisbourg harbor. Trading and fishing vessels were being captured by the English practically within sight of the citadel tower. More and more, the talk in town was of blockades.

August twenty-fifth was the feast day of St. Louis, king of France. Ordinarily Louisbourg celebrated the occasion with parties, artillery salutes, parades, fireworks and a huge bonfire. It was the last opportunity of summer for a good time, the last chance to forget whatever worries there were, to drink too much and eat too well, to dance and sing in the parlors of the well-to-do, or the cabarets and taverns, or the streets, depending on your condition in the town.

But this year the approaching festivities were soured with apprehension and unease. The town was still full of several thousand sailors and fishermen who were more than willing to celebrate with the usual rowdy good spirits, but the citizens themselves were subdued. They, after all, were the people who stayed behind when the others departed for France, before bad weather set in. They were the ones who would have to make do during the hard, dark, cold winter months with whatever was left in the storehouses after the ships had been provisioned. While the seas were open, the French warships in harbor gave the townspeople a sense of security, but before they sailed with the other vessels, they, too, would need to be supplied.

"It is well enough for some to say that the Governor will look after us," said Madame Vanasse, in the bakeshop on the afternoon of the twenty-fourth. "How, I ask, will he do that when he has thousands of sailors to feed for the king?"

"It is the prisoners," declared Madame Pinot, a carpenter's wife. "They are a danger to us—they are eating our food but they do no work in return. Let the prisoners go without, I say. Why should we starve later so they may eat now?"

"And in France they do not care what happens to us," said a third woman, whom Lyn did not recognize. "In France they are safe. They sit on their backsides and do nothing while it is we who take all the risks."

"I have heard," Madame Vanasse said, "that the fishing this year has not been so good."

"What did I say?" asked Madame Pinot with gloomy satisfaction. "We will starve."

Clucking like the hens in the courtyard, they left together, and another person edged furtively into the shop past them. One of the soldiers from the barracks. Madame Pugnant always watched them carefully when they came in. She, like most people in town, had a low opinion of the privates in the Compagnies franches. "You do not let them *touch* anything," she instructed Lyn emphatically. "And they do not buy from us on credit. If you have trouble ever, call for Joseph or Christophe, do you understand?"

Lyn finished collecting the crumbs from the counter, sweeping them tidily into the crock below, and gave the man her attention. There was something vaguely familiar about him—in all likelihood it was only the ill-fitting uniform and seedy appearance. His hair was pulled back in a straggling queue, and his face under the tricorn was sallow. "Yes?" she said briskly, hoping he wouldn't come too close. She was quite sure he must smell.

He didn't answer immediately. His eyes slid from her face downward and fixed on her chest. He stared with such intensity that she became annoyed. She put a hand protectively to her breast and her fingers touched the key. They closed around it. He blinked, and his gaze shifted upward again. Lyn's heart began to thud.

"May I help you?" she asked.

"Oh, I hope so," he replied with fervor.

There was a long silence. He seemed incapable of saying anything else. Finally, to break the impasse, she said, "What is it you want?"

126

"Who are you?"

"Elisabeth Bernard."

"Do you speak English?"

"Do you?" She knew she was stalling, but she couldn't help herself. He was not at all what she expected. But neither had Agathe been. His eyes were stark with misery. Involuntarily she put out a hand to him and he seized it as if it would keep him from falling.

"Are you—are you—?"

"My name is Carolyn Paget," she said softly in English. "Who are you?"

For a moment he closed his eyes, his fingers tight on hers. "Donald Stewart. I saw you before—in the street. That." He nodded at the key. "I couldn't believe it. I didn't know where to find you, and then that woman—the old one who's in here so much—she scared the shit out of me!"

Lyn nodded sympathetically. "I know. She's my grandmother."

He looked startled.

"Elisabeth's grandmother," she amended. "You were with the soldiers who tried to pick me up on the street." She remembered him now, the one who had almost spoken to her.

"I thought I'd dreamed it. I never would have guessed—but you're *real!*"

There were footsteps in the hall. Lyn recognized the sound of Christophe's clogs and tried to pull her hand away, but the soldier wouldn't—or couldn't—let go. She managed to jerk herself free just as Christophe came in with a tray of rolls. She could tell from his expression that he had seen them, and she took a step back, distancing herself from Donald Stewart. He swallowed hard; his Adam's apple bobbed, and he straightened himself with an effort.

"Thank you, Christophe," said Lyn, her voice sounding brittle. "I will stack them."

He set the tray on the counter. "Everything is all right, Mademoiselle?"

She nodded and made herself smile. "Why would it not be?"

He scrutinized the soldier with a frown. "Do you wish to buy bread, Monsieur?"

"Yes." Lyn answered him quickly. "But he has no money. He was hoping I would give it to him on credit and I said no, I could not."

"Ah. Shall I call Monsieur Desforges?"

"No, do not bother him, Christophe. The soldier is going."

Christophe waited, looking from the soldier to Lyn and back. For a terrible moment, Lyn was afraid that Donald was going to burst into tears. He looked stricken, as if she had taken the big bread knife on the counter and plunged it into him. What did he think she could do, for heaven's sake? Introduce him to Christophe? Why didn't he take his cue from her and leave? She hurled brain waves at Donald, and after an endless minute he seemed to understand. He blinked rapidly, hunched his shoulders, and said, "Very well then," in a muffled voice, and shuffled toward the door.

"There," said Lyn, greatly relieved. "Thank you, Christophe."

"Mademoiselle," he said, giving her a melancholy nod, and went back to the bakery with one last suspicious look at the soldier as he passed him.

"Go on," she mouthed at Donald. "Go!"

"But—"

She glared at him ferociously and pointed at the window that faced the quay. After he'd gone, she waited a few minutes to give Christophe a chance to get back to work, then went to the window and opened it. Donald was there, in the street below. "I will meet you," she called softly.

"How? Where?"

She scowled, thinking hard. "Tomorrow night. I will try—I can't promise—but there's a dinner party. They're going out, and I think I can get away. Can you?"

"It's a holiday. Where?"

"The bonfire," she said with a sudden inspiration. It would be dark and there would be lots of people milling around—they would be inconspicuous.

He nodded, and she closed the window on him before he could keep her there any longer. A soldier—of course a soldier! Weren't there more of them than anything else? Lots of the animators were soldiers, taking their names off the garrison rolls. They existed in both times, as did the barracks and the guardhouses. Donald added credence to her theory about overlapping. Roll on tomorrow night, she thought fervently. Somehow she'd find a way to get out and meet him.

In honor of the holiday, the bakery and shop were closed and

Michel did not come. Joseph went out, and Madame Pugnant organized Lyn, Louise and Marguerite to turn out both rooms and clean them thoroughly. They scoured the floors, swept under and behind everything, dusted, washed all the shelves and windows. Pierre shoveled ashes out of the ovens and stacked firewood for the next baking, while Blaize, lost without Michel, trailed Lyn, trying to help and getting in the way.

Marguerite spent the day fretting over the dinner party she and Joseph and Madame Pugnant had been invited to attend at the house of one of the merchants on the rue d'Orleans. "I shall have nothing to say, Elisabeth, I never do. I know nothing of fashion and I cannot play cards. Joseph only gets cross with me when I try and I do not like to play. I would so much rather stay at home. If only *you* could go in my place."

"That is silly," said Lyn briskly. "You will have a pleasant evening once you are there. It will be good for you to go out." How many times had she said the same thing to Dorrie when her mother dragged her feet over going somewhere, she thought with a momentary pang.

Marguerite's forehead pleated anxiously. "I do not think—"

"If you do not know what to say, you can listen. Too many people talk and not enough listen." She pushed Dorrie firmly aside.

Pierre was sulking because Madame Pugnant had forbidden him to leave the house. He was longing to go up to the Place Royale at dusk to see the bonfire lit, even though Michel had informed them that the bonfire this year wouldn't amount to much. The governor and the ordonnateur refused to spend money for firewood. Various townspeople had contributed wood, but the pile was pitifully small compared to previous years. And there was to be no gunpowder wasted on salutes. The festivities, in Michel's opinion, were going to be extremely tame.

"The streets will not be safe. They will be full of drunken sailors," said Madame Pugnant, as she prepared to set out with Joseph and Marguerite in the evening. "You must bar the doors when we have gone, Elisabeth, and open them only to members of the household. And you," she told Pierre, "must promise to obey Elisabeth."

Lyn gave Marguerite an encouraging hug. "You look very pretty.

They will be glad to have you come," she whispered. Although pale, Marguerite managed a faint smile.

Then Lyn settled back to wait. To fill time, she hemmed a skirt that Marguerite was making over for Louise, and told Blaize and Pierre stories she dug out of her baby-sitting repertoire, adjusting them to fit the time and circumstances: Snow White and Sleeping Beauty, Little Red Riding Hood. She was much better at the stories than the hem: her stitches were long and uneven. Florent, in his corner, listened intently, rocking himself as usual, and even Louise paid attention. At one point she said, "I do not remember these stories. Where did you learn them? Not from Maman."

"No," agreed Lyn. It was true, no matter which time. Dorrie didn't like fairy tales; Lyn had read them to herself.

Even from the kitchen at the back of the house, they could hear the sounds of celebration outside: occasional explosions, singing and shouting, bursts of laughing and cheering. It was as if everyone else was in the streets. Finally, Lyn decided her moment had come. She had waited long enough. She folded the skirt and stood up. Blaize was curled near the fire asleep like a kitten, and Pierre's eyes were half-shut. "I am going out," she told Louise, who was knitting diligently.

Louise looked up startled. "Out? But Elisabeth, you cannot! It is not safe. Grandmother said—"

"I must," said Lyn firmly. "I have business. I will be back before they return, I promise. There will be no trouble. They will never know I have gone unless *you* tell them, Louise. You must do as we were told and keep the door locked."

"But what about Suzanne and Christophe?"

"Let them in, of course."

"You do not know when they will come back—*they* will know. Even if I do not tell, Suzanne might."

"I will take care of Suzanne. Do not worry."

"I do not see why *you* should go and not me," complained Pierre, rousing himself.

"Because you are too young and Grandmother told you to stay in. You promised."

Louise scowled. "I do not like it. Something bad will happen."

"Florent is here with you, nothing will happen." Florent was sound asleep on his stool, his head sunk forward on his thin chest.

She couldn't imagine him being much use in an emergency, but there would be no emergency, she assured herself.

"You could take me with you, Elisabeth," said Pierre hopefully. "I will stay right beside you."

"You must stay here with Louise and Blaize and the babies. They need you for company." She hardened her heart to the unfairness of the situation and Pierre's disappointment. Never mind that he had a rotten kind of life for a kid not yet ten years old. She could not afford to distract herself. He glowered, but did not argue further.

Outside the kitchen door, she waited until she heard Louise slide the bolt home. With the streets full of rowdies she didn't like leaving the courtyard gate unlatched, but it couldn't be helped; she would have to get back through it later, and by wedging a piece of kindling under the bottom, she made it seem locked. It was easy to merge with the disorganized throngs beyond the fence. She was wearing an old dark cloak with its hood pulled forward to shroud her face, and she had tucked the key securely under her chemise. She knew for whom she was searching this time, and she didn't want to attract attention. As inconspicuously as possible, she made her way through the town, eyes watchful, not wanting to risk appearing hesitant. Several times she side-stepped invitations to "come and have a drink, sweetheart!" and shrugged off friendly arms.

She began to wonder uncomfortably if she remembered what Donald Stewart looked like well enough—could she really pick him out of the milling crowds in the confusion of darkness and firelight? There were so many people in the narrow streets, spilling out of doorways, leaning against walls, weaving back and forth. If only she had asked him for his French name, she could make inquiries. She doubted that anyone else here knew him as Donald Stewart.

Still, there was no point in despairing yet; she had told him the bonfire on the Place Royale, and she hadn't reached it. This was the first time she'd been out in the town at night; it seemed very different. Although after nine, there was still light in the sky, but darkness gathered below in the maze of streets, oozing out of alleyways and courtyards and down from under the wide eaves. It was made denser by lamp- and candle- and firelight. She had to be careful where she put her feet—people threw all kinds of unsavory things into the streets, and there had not been a good rain for several days to wash the garbage into the harbor. All the darkest corners seemed to be occupied, mostly by couples, but also by small groups of men clenched together in low-voiced conversation. Lyn wondered what the equivalent of drug-dealing was—what kind of illegal activities did they get up to? Selling contraband or stolen goods, most likely—liquor, tobacco, that kind of thing. Mathieu Martel's business. Michel said there was a brisk trade in black market government supplies, if you knew the right people and had the resources. She gave an involuntary yelp as someone grabbed her around the waist from behind, but a firmly placed elbow in the assailant's ribs got prompt results and a curse. It reminded her that she had to keep her mind on her errand.

Once she glimpsed Michel, with a couple of fishermen, near the foot of the rue d'Orleans; she stayed away from him. He would be most interested in what she was doing out by herself at night on the Feast of St. Louis. Carefully, she made her way along the edge of the Place Royale. The bonfire had been lit and people were dancing and singing in the open space around it. In spite of Ordonnateur Bigot's lack of support, it seemed enormous to Lyn. Men kept heaving chunks of wood onto it, sending blizzards of sparks into the air, swirling upward. The crowd cheered raggedly each time.

She began to feel slightly panicky at the passage of time, and afraid she would have to go back before finding Donald. This had seemed such a perfect chance to meet him, but she had reckoned without the difficulties. She stopped and scanned the firelit faces and felt an unexpected stab of loneliness. There were very few people in the place by themselves; almost everyone was with friends or sweethearts or husbands or wives.

Last Fourth of July, she and Mike had taken a huge basket of food—enough to last all day—and staked out a blanket space on the Charles River Esplanade. They'd spent the warm lazy morning and afternoon sprawled in the sun with Mike's transistor, listening to the ball game. Then in the evening there had been the Boston Pops concert and fireworks—the 1812 Overture lit by great glittering sunbursts over the river, while thousands of people oh'ed and ah'ed appreciatively and little kids grimaced and held their ears and shrieked with delight and overtiredness. She and Mike wandered home afterward, sunburned and content, surrounded by the soft night. She remembered the physical sensation of being close to Mike, of leaning against his shoulder, holding his hand, touching

132

him, and she ached for it. The flames blurred and swam in front of her eyes for a moment, then she gave her head a determined shake. Self-pity was loathsome; she had learned that from Dorrie. It did nothing but incapacitate you and make other people steer clear. Pulling herself together, she continued her search, glancing at faces—and then she found him.

He was alone, standing a little apart in the shadows outside the festivities. She knew him instantly, without even seeing his face, and approached cautiously. Even though she was certain he was the right one, she couldn't quite let herself believe it. Just beside him, she whispered, "Donald," and he jerked convulsively as if she'd given him an electric shock.

"I couldn't find you!" he exclaimed, his voice choked. "I thought you hadn't come. I'd almost given up."

"I told you I'd be here. I'd forgotten everyone else would be, too," she said ruefully.

"But you found me, that's all that matters." He gripped her arm. "I prayed to God you'd come," he said quite seriously. "We really are here, aren't we?"

"Well, *I* am," said Lyn, "and I'll be able to prove by these bruises that you are too."

"Sorry." He loosened his fingers but didn't let go. "It's just— I mean, I really thought I was going crazy. I thought my mind had gone."

"It hasn't. Come on, let's get out of the way, where we aren't so visible. We have a lot to talk about."

They wove through the crowd to the empty, dark space near the Governor's garden on the east side of the place, where they would not be overlooked, and Lyn said, "Tell me how you got here."

"I don't know."

"No, but what were you *doing*?" She tried not to sound impatient.

He took a long, unsteady breath. "I was splitting wood. Is that what you mean? Right over there, by the guardhouse. It was damp and cold and we had a fire going inside—you know, authenticity. I wasn't very good at it—I'd never used an axe before." There was a note of defensiveness in his voice. She nodded encouragingly. "Anyhow, it slipped. Almost took my leg off, but I jumped back and dropped the axe. I must have fallen over a log—my head hit the wall. I had a lump the size of a tennis ball.'' He felt his head, then scratched it vigorously. ''I bet I have lice—I just bet I do!'' he said miserably.

''Then what?''

''I guess I knocked myself out. I don't know what happened. Except when I opened my eyes again I didn't recognize anybody, and they were all speaking this bastard French, and they smelled, and—well, *you* know. I really thought I must have lost my marbles. I mean, who would believe—how *could* you believe—'' His voice trailed away. ''But then you turned up. If you're here too, then I'm not mad. We can't both be—not in exactly the same way, can we?''

Lyn shook her head. ''Actually, there are three of us that I know of so far.''

''Three? Who else?'' He glanced around as if expecting the third to materialize.

''An older woman,'' she said evasively, thinking of the unwelcoming reception Agathe had given her. Instead she told him what she had been doing when she found herself in 1744. ''I've been here four and a half weeks now,'' she finished. ''What about you?''

''I don't know.'' He sounded bleak.

''Haven't you kept track?''

He shook his head. ''I did at first—then I stopped. I couldn't bear to any longer. Day after day and nothing changes. It just gets worse. This is a *terrible* place! I never realized—I mean, we were just *playing*. I read all the stuff in the library, sure—I'm writing my dissertation on French soldiers in eighteenth-century Nova Scotia. I thought I knew what it was like for them, but I never imagined this. Did you?''

''I hadn't thought a whole lot about it,'' Lyn admitted. ''I knew life was different—''

''Different?'' His voice rose. ''It's cold and wet and filthy. The barracks are a pit. The floors are rotten, the walls are never dry and there are *rats*. I lie awake and listen to them fighting. You can die from ratbite, you know. And nobody here could save you. They feed us garbage—I can't eat most of it. The bread has bugs in it and the water stinks. I had a pair of decent boots when I came, but someone stole them. They're all like that—thieves and villains, they'd cut your throat for a couple of lousy coins or some tobacco.

134

There's no one I can even *talk* to—most of them won't have anything to do with me. Not that I want anything to do with them, either, but just to talk—I'm covered with fleabites, I haven't washed in ages and my scalp itches something fierce. The first week I was so sick I thought I was dying. I couldn't stop throwing up and my head pounded all the time. I saw double. I still do sometimes. The truth is, I almost wish I had.''

"Had what?'' She was shaken by the depths of his misery. Her own situation seemed luxurious by comparison.

"Died. I've got to get out of here. I have to. I can't last a lot longer—I mean it!''

He did, too, she was convinced. "Have you tried to get back?''

"How? I've gone over it and over it and I can't think of anything. If you know, tell me. I don't care what I have to do, I'll do it. I've been all around this hellhole looking for something—anything. If I hadn't found you, I swear I'd have—I don't know what, but—'' He broke off. "What about you?''

She shook her head. "I tried going back to the spot where it happened, and nothing. There's got to be a way, though. If we just hang on, we'll find it.''

"You really think so?'' She could see in his face how desperately he wanted to believe her.

"I'm sure of it,'' she declared. His desperation touched things inside her she didn't want disturbed. To distract him, she said, "You must have known an animator named Rob Gowan—he was— is a soldier, too.''

"Gowan? No, not that I—no, I'm sure I didn't.''

A terrible suspicion struck her. She remembered Agathe. "Before—before you got here, what year was it?''

"Nineteen eighty-four, of course. Why?''

"I just wondered.'' She gave an involuntary shiver. None of the three of them had come out of the same year, although they had ended up in the same time. But then *all* summers were 1744 in the park—year after year, they went back to the same one. She felt the beginnings of a headache behind her eyes as she realized that in her own life she would never have met either of these people. The clock on the citadel struck the half hour. Half-past ten. "Look, Donald, I have to go back or they'll miss me. If they find out, I'll never get away again.''

"No!" he cried with genuine alarm. "Please don't! Just a little longer."

"I'll see you again. You know where I am—just be careful. We can't afford to make people suspicious."

"Soldiers make everyone suspicious," he said bitterly. "They're the lowest form of life around here. Good-for-nothing scum."

"Are you really hungry?" She was afraid of the answer, but she had to ask.

"Starving. I've lost weight."

"Can't you buy extra food?"

"You're joking! With what? I haven't got any money."

"The soldiers get paid, don't they?"

"Oh, yes. Then they take it all away again—for clothing they don't give us and food that's inedible. Besides what I'm wearing, I've got one shirt and a moth-eaten overcoat. My socks have holes in them."

"You could darn them," Lyn suggested.

He snorted.

"I *have* to go," she said again. "There's nothing we can do right now except get into trouble, and that'll make everything worse. We'll work out a way to meet and maybe I can get some food to you—I don't know. I'll try. All right?"

"At least let me walk back with you."

"If someone recognizes me—"

"It's dark."

She sighed. "As far as Ordonnateur Bigot's house, that's all. It's too risky."

He linked arms with her, attaching himself close to her side. It wasn't what she had been thinking of earlier when she'd been longing for Mike. She steered them carefully away from other people and patches of light, and with her free hand kept the hood around her face.

"I'm supposed to be back at McGill the second week in September," he said dismally. "What'll they think when I don't show up? What will Judith think?"

"Who's Judith?"

"My fiancée. We're supposed to get married next summer. What do you do when someone you know disappears? It's the kind of thing you read about in newspapers."

"My mother knew someone who disappeared," said Lyn reflectively. "Years ago. They were tellers at the same bank."

"She absconded with embezzled funds, no doubt."

"No. She didn't take anything. She just didn't turn up for work one day. She left her husband and three children. Dorrie said no one ever heard from her again."

"What did they do?"

She was sorry she'd started the story. "The police searched, and I think the husband hired a private investigator."

"Maybe she's somewhere here," he suggested with a humorless laugh. "Are there any bank tellers in Louisbourg?"

"She *wanted* to disappear, Donald. We'll get back."

They reached Monsieur Bigot's handsome, well-appointed house on the corner of the rue St. Louis and the place du Port. The end of the building overlooking the quay, where the ordonnateur conducted his business, was dark, but lights and music splashed through the unshuttered windows of his residence into the night. Monsieur Bigot was having a party. There was a scattering of applause, a strident male voice lifted over the simmer of conversation, followed by a gust of laughter. Lyn halted in the shadows and turned to Donald. "Tell me your French name, so I can ask for you if I need to."

"Gerard Grossin. They call me La Grenade. My *nom de guerre*, heaven help me."

"And I'm Elisabeth Bernard."

"You're Carolyn Paget and I'm Donald Stewart," he said with sudden ferocity.

She nodded. A rowdy group of sailors tacked past them, weaving from side to side of the street as if beating against the wind. Once they had gone, Lyn gave Donald's hand a brief squeeze and said, "Good night." Before he could protest, she left him. The sailors had turned right on the quay, Lyn turned left, glancing over her shoulder. Donald was still there, looking after her.

⇢⟫ 10 ⟪⇠

THE THIRD TIME SHE RAPPED ON THE DOOR, LYN HEARD SCUF-fling sounds. After a minute, the bolt was pulled back and Louise's small, suspicious face appeared in the crack. "You have been away for a very long time," she said accusingly. "Christophe has come in and gone upstairs, and Suzanne is back."

"The others? Grandmother?"

"Any minute they will come. You would have made me lie for you, Elisabeth."

"Now you do not have to," said Lyn, slipping inside. The kitchen was dim and close after the night air. Suzanne was heaped untidily at one end of the settle, like a pile of used laundry, her head back, snoring loudly.

"She asked about you. I said you had gone out back. But that was half an hour ago," said Louise.

"Go up to bed," said Lyn. "I will wait until the others come home." She sat down again with her sewing. The fire made tiny rustling noises as it settled at the back of the fireplace and Lyn suddenly felt very tired. She wasn't sure what she thought about Donald, but she hadn't the energy to work it out. He would be better left until morning; she didn't want to make hasty judgments. She was roused from a half sleep sometime later by banging on the front door and Joseph calling, "Come! Let us in! Let us in!" Suzanne jumped and snorted. Her bleary little eyes found Lyn and narrowed speculatively, but she said nothing, and Lyn ignored her, going to answer Joseph's impatient summons.

"Why were you so slow? Where is Florent?"

"He has gone to bed, Uncle Joseph," she said, hoping it was true. His corner in the kitchen had been empty. "Did you have a good time?" she asked Marguerite.

Marguerite gave a tiny nod; she looked exhausted. "The babies? They are all right, Elisabeth?"

Fingers crossed, Lyn assured her they were sleeping soundly.

"Marguerite, you are silly," snapped Madame Pugnant. "Of course they are fine! Elisabeth, you will give me your arm." She hung onto Lyn as she climbed the stairs, and her breath came in short audible puffs between her lips. At her door she disengaged herself. Lyn hesitated. "Do you want help, Grandmother?"

"No, I do not. It is late and I am weary. Go to bed. We will be up as usual in the morning."

Louise was not yet asleep. She waited until Lyn had undressed and climbed into the bed, and then she said, "Why did you go out tonight? Where did you go?"

"To see the bonfire," answered Lyn, hoping to shut her up.

"Was that all? Did you meet anyone?"

"Whom should I meet?"

"That is what I asked you."

"I do not think," said Lyn deliberately, "that it is any of your business."

"But it *is* my business if you do something foolish. You do not want anyone to know, so I think you should not have gone. You did not go only to see the bonfire, is it. You went to meet a man."

"Why do you think that?" Startled, she wondered if Louise had dared to follow her.

"Ah, *zut!* And if you are caught—you will ruin everything for us all, Elisabeth!"

"Louise—"

"Grandmother has already made plans for you. You are to marry Christophe."

"What?" Lyn felt as if she had been punched in the stomach.

"It is being arranged. I have heard her discussing this with Marguerite."

"Marguerite?" Lyn repeated stupidly.

"Shhh! You will wake Blaize. I had so much trouble getting him to sleep. He is such a baby," said Louise with disgust.

"Are you sure she has discussed this with Marguerite?" whispered Lyn, appalled.

"That is what I told you! Why do you not listen?"

"But—she has said nothing to me—"

"She will when it is time."

"I do not want to marry Christophe."

139

"Why not? He is a good man—what is the matter with him?"

Lyn swallowed wrong and choked. She couldn't believe that she was lying there in bed in the middle of the night, listening to a ten year old telling her about the marriage that was being arranged for her. Louise sounded so *old* somehow.

"Well?"

"And Marguerite," said Lyn after a minute. "Did she agree?"

"Of course. It is good for the family. But you will spoil it if you are not careful. Christophe will not have you if you are seeing another man, is it not. I warn you. I do not want to suffer because you make a mistake." With that, Louise rolled over on her side away from Lyn and pulled the blanket over her ear.

This was something that had not occurred to Lyn. Louise's revelation blew poor Donald Stewart right out of her mind. At seventeen, Elisabeth was marriageable; Madame Pugnant talked about a husband for Jeanne, and Jeanne was at least a year younger. Bemused, Lyn wondered how long she had—how long did engagements last in the eighteenth century? And had Christophe been told the happy news? He showed no sign of it, but Christophe didn't hang his feelings out like laundry on a line, the way Thomas did. What about Marguerite? And what on earth would Dorrie say if she knew all this?

Then, with a sinking feeling, she remembered Agathe Grimard. That woman, whoever she was, had found herself in this place with a husband and children. At night, when she went to bed, it wasn't with a younger sister, it was with a man she had never laid eyes on before, a man who thought she was someone else. . . .

She was astonished suddenly to find Louise shaking her by the shoulder, and the sky outside the window filling with light. She had not thought it possible that she could go to sleep, but she had.

As she sat in the privy, she decided the best thing to do about Christophe was nothing. Nothing could happen until it was announced, and in the meantime, assuming Louise was right, Madame Pugnant could change her mind or Marguerite would argue against it, or Christophe himself might refuse. With luck, it would never come up at all while she was there. In the light of day it seemed so preposterous that Lyn had little trouble pushing the whole thing out of sight underneath the matter that required her immediate attention: what to do about Donald.

140

It was unfair of her, but she couldn't help wishing she felt more confidence in him—that he was someone a bit more solid, more adaptable and optimistic somehow. Like Rob Gowan. Donald didn't seem very *tough*. But, she told herself firmly, she barely knew the man, and he was in a lousy situation. It was well known in both times that the ordinary soldiers in Louisbourg had little to be grateful for. Lyn had been through the reconstructed barracks and seen the tiny, dark rooms stacked with narrow bunk beds. The animators who played soldiers were given a free hand, within the bounds of decency, to be unkempt, surly and ill-mannered among themselves; most of them played their parts with enthusiasm. But here—as Donald said—it wasn't a game; you couldn't get away from it. On the whole, Lyn had been very lucky to turn up as Elisabeth Bernard: she had clothes, food, a decent place to sleep and she was not ill-treated. Life was not so easy for either Gerard Grossin or Agathe Grimard.

And perhaps Donald had hit a particularly bad patch. Everyone had low periods from time to time. Lyn herself could always count on feeling dull, slow and depressed the week before her period, and since she had arrived in 1744 it had gotten worse. Part of the reason was discovering how awkward it was to cope with only wads of clean rag, wrapped and tied in uncomfortable ways, disguised under layers of clothing. But it was also the uncertainty: of not knowing when she would get home, of being unable to do anything except wait, without being sure for what, as time passed.

At any rate, she and Donald were going to have to be careful. In a town the size of Louisbourg, it was inevitable that if they saw one another regularly, they would be found out. The inhabitants took an avid interest in one another's affairs and *affaires;* someone was bound to notice. But perhaps they could keep their meetings secret for a while, buy a little time to work things out, and find the way back.

Lyn was fairly sure of Louise; Louise would only tell on her if she thought it would do more harm not to. Right now it wouldn't. And she knew how to handle Suzanne; the same way, she supposed, Michel did. When Suzanne asked her in an insinuating undertone, "And where did you go to last night, I would like to know?" Lyn met her gaze blandly and replied, "And I wonder what has become of the eggs this morning. I thought there were ten in the bowl last

141

night. Can I have miscounted?'' There was a long fraught moment of silence. Lyn held her eyes steady and Suzanne was first to look away, her face coming out in red blotches. "You were mistaken," she snapped. "You should be careful—*very* careful."

When Lyn turned away, she found Michel watching her with a speculative expression. "You are learning," he murmured. "But now you must watch your back, I think."

He was right. Lyn had forced Suzanne to reassess Elisabeth: not quite so slow and biddable after all, perhaps even dangerous. Suzanne stopped making contemptuous remarks about Elisabeth's upbringing and stupidity; instead she muttered evil things under her breath, and scowled, and ignored Lyn blatantly as often as possible. Their relationship solidified into the same hostile neutrality that existed between Suzanne and Michel. While Lyn found a certain satisfaction in altering Suzanne's opinion, now she had to be on her guard. Suzanne would use anything she could find against her.

Even though it was still summer, sunny and warm, September was the month Lyn had always considered the beginning of fall. Nearly all her conscious life she had lived by the school calendar. Now every morning she woke to the sound of feet overhead, the smell of woodsmoke and fish, the thin predawn light washing the window, the wailing of gulls. At night she flung herself wearily onto the straw mattress and slept with Louise curled beside her. Nothing changed, but somewhere, she was uncomfortably aware, Lyn Paget's world must be going on as usual, just as Elisabeth Bernard's was. She was missing part of her own life.

She managed to see Donald several times after the bonfire, but never for very long. Donald seemed content just to reassure himself that Lyn really existed and was still there. When he was off duty he often glimpsed him hanging around on the quay outside the bakery. Once or twice he actually dared to come into the shop—she told him it was safest in the early afternoon, when Madame Pugnant was upstairs. Even so, they only managed to exchange a few words, always in fear of being walked in on. They stole ten minutes together behind the empty lot next to the Récollet friars' house. She thought she had run into Donald by accident, but he told her he had been following her through the streets as she delivered loaves of bread. It was a gray, wet afternoon and there were few people around, so Lyn decided they were reasonably safe.

"Do you know what I dreamed about last night?" said Donald, the brim of his tricorn dripping like a gutter. "Hamburgers." He groaned softly.

Lyn, who'd never given a whole lot of thought to food, felt her mouth water.

"Not *coq au vin* or *boeuf bourguignon* or *coquilles St. Jacques*—fat, greasy hamburgers with onion, ketchup and dill pickles." His voice was filled with yearning.

"Don't," said Lyn.

"French fries. Coleslaw oozing with mayonnaise. Hot fudge sundaes. Cinnamon doughnuts."

Lyn put her hands over her ears. "You're only making it worse! Listen, if we can find a place to meet, where no one else goes—somewhere we can leave things—I'll sneak you some food. I promise. If Suzanne can do it, *I* can do it."

"Who's Suzanne?"

"The cook. She steals stuff and sells it."

"You know this? You haven't told anyone?"

Lyn shook her head. "It's more useful not to." She gave him a wry smile. "It's the way people live. Actually, they do it in our time, too. The woman in the drugstore where I worked briefly used to *borrow* lipsticks and eye shadow."

"If you could really get me something to eat—something without bugs—"

"What about a job? Don't the soldiers get jobs and earn extra money? Then you'd be able to buy some decent food for yourself."

"The only thing they'll hire me for is unskilled labor." He sounded resentful. "Chucking lumps of stone around or chopping wood or carting lime."

"Well? It wouldn't hurt you, would it? I spend quite a lot of time scrubbing floors and washing dishes," Lyn retorted. "Besides, it would keep you warm."

He stared moodily at his feet. "Why couldn't I have been the secretary to the governor, or the engineer's assistant?"

"Probably because you couldn't walk right," said Lyn, remembering Sandy with a pang. "Never mind. But there must be ways

143

you can help yourself more. What did you used to do? Besides write your dissertation?''

To her astonishment, he raised his head and sang, '' 'I am the very model of a modern major-general/I've information animal and vegetable and mineral/I know the kings of England and I quote the fights historical/From Marathon to Waterloo in order categorical.' ''

She burst out laughing in spite of herself and he grinned a little defensively. ''There isn't much call for patter songs around here, and you won't find a soul who's ever heard of Gilbert and Sullivan. I'll bet you ready money, even though I don't have any.''

''Neither do I, but I don't bet.''

''Everyone else in this place does. On *any*thing. How much gunpowder's left in the warehouse, whether the next baby born will be a boy or a girl, how many pounds of cod were caught this season—you name it. I suppose there's not much else to do except get drunk.'' His tone was gloomy, but she saw he'd cheered up.

''We'll work something out,'' she told him. ''Just be patient.''

''I'll hang by my fingernails,'' he replied, only half joking.

One morning the second week in September, Michel brought news of the long-awaited prisoner exchange: English hostages for French. ''It is all over town,'' he told them, enjoying himself. ''I am surprised that you do not know already. You must be the last to hear. Perhaps, Madame Labreche, you are getting deaf?''

''When will the English be sent back?'' asked Marguerite quickly, before Suzanne could explode.

''Within the month. The ships are being outfitted now.''

''Thank God.'' Marguerite crossed herself.

''And I know something else.''

''I know that you will not live to see old age the way you are going,'' declared Suzanne.

In his corner, Florent gave a dry, wheezy chuckle and Lyn jumped. She had forgotten, as usual, that he was there. ''What is it? Tell us,'' she demanded.

Michel shrugged. ''But you can find out for yourselves, I am sure.''

''Why are you not all working?'' Madame Pugnant suddenly appeared in the doorway. ''Elisabeth, to the shop. Michel, there is water to be drawn.''

"Michel was telling us that the English prisoners are to be sent back to Boston, Maman," said Marguerite. "Is it not good news?"

"It would be better news if Michel were doing what he is paid to do."

"Indeed, that is what I say, Madame," agreed Suzanne righteously.

"Elisabeth, I am going out this morning, but I will return within the hour. While I am gone, you will sweep the floor of the shop—it is covered in mud from yesterday. I expect to find everything in order."

On Saturday afternoon, Sister Saint-Joseph and Sister Saint-Benoît of the Congregation of Notre Dame sailed from Louisbourg. For eleven years Sister Saint-Joseph had struggled to maintain the school for girls in the town. Now, old and tired, she was returning to the mother house in Montreal. A small, solemn crowd, mostly women, gathered on the quay near the bakery to say good-bye, and Lyn came out on the steps to watch. The four sisters staying behind stood in a black knot surrounded by their pupils. Père Athanase asked a blessing and even Ordonnateur Bigot emerged from his offices to wish the nuns Godspeed, while the sailors jigged up and down with impatience to catch the tide that would set them on their way to the St. Lawrence River.

As Lyn turned to go back inside, a voice at her elbow said, "I must talk to you. *Please.*" Donald stood just below her, close against the house. Lyn glanced apprehensively around; no one was looking.

"Just for a few minutes, that's all," he begged. "I haven't seen you to talk in *days*. You don't know—isn't there *some*where—?"

On the other side of the steps the cellar door was open, letting fresh air into the dank, earth-smelling darkness. Lyn made up her mind quickly—it was better than being seen to stand on the steps arguing with a soldier. "Does it really matter so much if someone sees us?" said Donald, reading her thoughts. "I only want to talk."

"Use your head—of course it does. It isn't done. If we deliberately break their rules, I don't know what they'll do, but they won't make life easier, I'm sure."

He leaned against the cellar wall by the doorway and slowly let

145

himself sink down it, onto the floor, his knees up. A strip of pale hairy calf showed between his sagging stockings and his breeches. "Why does everything have to be so hard?" he complained. "Sometimes I think you don't want to see me."

"Don't be stupid. It just isn't always possible." She couldn't help sounding annoyed.

"I have a nightmare now," he said in a calmer voice. "I dream that I come to see you and you're gone."

"Gone where?"

"Back. You know. You wouldn't do that, would you? You wouldn't just leave without saying?"

"You make it sound as if I had a choice. Of course I wouldn't, not if I could help it."

He was silent.

"I've been thinking," she began after a bit.

"Oh, Lord. I try not to anymore," he groaned, then with a touch of anger, "I got a job."

"A job?"

"You told me to, remember? To earn some money. If you have a job they pay you. If you live long enough to collect it. Look." He held his hands in the light from the doorway so she could see them. They were scraped and blistered and very dirty. "I was so stiff the second day I could hardly move."

"What are you doing?"

"Digging stinking ditches, that's what I'm doing! I couldn't get anything else. This whole rotten place was built with slave labor." He was sinking into a swamp of self-pity.

"You'll get used to it," she said briskly. "Other people have. It ought to help you to sleep."

"I'm digging my own grave, that's what I'm doing. I can't stick this much longer."

"So what are you going to do about it?" Lyn challenged. "What are your choices? Have you thought of anything else? Listen, Donald, if this is all you have to talk about, I don't need it. I'm not going to stay and listen to you moan."

"I only want a little sympathy, that's all. No—don't go, Lyn. Please. Actually, I did think of something, only I'm not sure—"

She stood waiting, not helping him.

Finally, he said, "Have you ever thought about going away from here?"

"Donald—"

"No, I mean leaving the fortress. Walking out of it. Now."

"I have been out of it," she said, not understanding. "Several times."

"Where?"

"Once out on Cap Noir and once to the faubourg."

"Were you still in sight of it?"

"Yes, but—"

"Well, that's what I mean!" He was excited now. He stood up to face her. "Suppose it's just this place—*here*. If we got away from it, really away from it, maybe we'd leave it behind."

She thought hard. "You mean if we went north we'd find Sydney?" she said doubtfully.

He gave an eager nod. "Didn't the whole setup feel peculiar to you when you first came to work at Louisbourg? Didn't you think it was odd—this business of pretending to be real people? When they gave me the uniform—I thought I'd simply be a generic eighteenth-century soldier. But no. I had to be a *particular* soldier— Gerard Grossin, someone who actually existed. I didn't really like that, but no one else seemed to mind, so I went along with it. I should have trusted my instincts."

"It didn't bother me," said Lyn. "I was only a waitress in the coffeehouse—I didn't *have* to be anyone. I found Elisabeth myself, in fact."

But he wasn't listening to her, he was too involved in his theory. "We could try it, couldn't we? See what happens, and if I'm right—"

"And what if you're *wrong?* Suppose we climb over those hills and don't find anything except more hills. Then what?"

"We'd have to go far enough," he said impatiently, "give it a chance. Anyway, it's an idea. Have you got one?"

She had to admit she hadn't thought of anything since the day she'd tried walking up and down the rue Royale.

"Will you at least consider it? Don't say anything more now— but consider it."

"If we leave the fortress," she said slowly, "we're leaving the place we fell through."

"Maybe that's got nothing to do with it. You don't know it has. Are you afraid to try?"

She considered. "Yes, I guess I am a bit. Think about what happens if you're wrong, Donald. What would we do? Do you know how to survive in the wilderness? That's what's out there—at least now, in this time. I've never even been camping before, with all the proper stuff. We wouldn't have *anything*. Besides, you're a soldier. If you leave you'll be deserting—you can't come back. Heaven knows what they'd do to you."

"All right." He straightened his shoulders defiantly. "So *you* think of something better. But it's September already. Have you stopped to wonder what winter's going to be like? I don't think my chances are any better in the barracks than they would be out there somewhere. If I have to stay here I'm not going to make it, I *know* that. If we haven't come up with anything else by the end of October, that's it. I'm leaving." He sounded suddenly sure of himself.

Lyn shivered. "You won't do anything without telling me first, will you? Promise, Donald."

"That's only in my nightmares," he said. "Of course not. But"—he was serious again—"I won't be here this winter—one way or another—I promise you that, too."

⇥ 11 ⇤

"THERE IS SOMETHING WRONG WITH JEANNE," SAID LOUISE without preamble. "I have thought so for some time and today it is obvious. You must have noticed, Elisabeth."

"Hmm?" It was Sunday night, a little over a week since the nuns had sailed. Lyn had come to bed expecting Louise to be asleep, or pretending to be. The little girl hardly ever spoke to her when they were alone; Lyn's overtures met with stony silence, so she'd pretty much given up. And that night she had a lot on her mind: Donald was becoming a problem. He had began to turn up everywhere. That morning after Mass, she had seen him loitering on the Place Royale, throwing her significant glances, obviously eager to speak to her. But it was impossible with everyone around, surely he knew that. She did her best to ignore him.

To his credit, he persevered with his job, although he continued to complain about it. The drawback she hadn't foreseen was that now he was earning a little money—very little, it was true—he felt he could legitimately come almost daily into the bakeshop. Lyn usually found ways to slip him an extra roll or some rusks or broken pan bread because he made her feel guilty, and she hoped that no one else in the household took any special notice of him.

He told her all about himself, in eager little snatches: his father was a postmaster in a little town in Ontario; his mother was active in the church. He had two younger brothers, one of whom had gotten in with a bunch of wild kids and run away twice. The second time he was gone for months, turning up finally in Chicago. Now he worked freighters on the Great Lakes. Malcolm was still in elementary school. Sheila, his older sister, was married to an English professor at McGill. Lyn heard all about Donald's two nieces, and he talked endlessly about Judith Bailey, his fiancée. Lyn rapidly concluded that she was almost too perfect to live. Still, Donald telling her about his own life was infinitely preferable to Donald complaining about Gerard Grossin's.

"Look at my boots," he'd say, "they're wearing through. My feet get soaked every time it rains. What'll I do when they fall apart? Do you know how much new ones cost?"

Lyn shook her head, but it was a rhetorical question.

"And I have a rash all over my chest. Red lumps. Look, I'll show you—"

"No—for heaven's sake, Donald! Not here—button your tunic!"

"It's like fire. I can't sleep because of it."

"Here's a customer. You'd better leave."

Later she described the rash to Marguerite, and Marguerite produced a small pot containing a thick, strong-smelling, tarlike substance. "It must be rubbed in at night before bed, three times," she told Lyn. "But if it is not for you, Elisabeth—" "For a friend," said Lyn evasively, as aware as Marguerite how unlikely it was that Elisabeth would have a friend with a chest rash. Marguerite gave her a concerned look, but questioned her no further.

"Phew, it stinks!" exclaimed Donald, making a face.

"That doesn't matter if it works," said Lyn tartly. "Thank you very much, Lyn."

He was instantly contrite. "Yes, of course. Thank you."

"She said you need to keep your clothes clean."

149

"Did she suggest how? The water's like raw sewage and I haven't got any soap."

So she pilfered a lump of soap for him, from the kitchen when Suzanne was out. And that didn't please him much either. She suspected he would prefer it if she offered to do his laundry for him, but she had no intention of that. Over one evening she did darn his socks, doing the best she could with the ragged holes in the heels, glad that Marguerite's eyesight wasn't good enough for her to see what Lyn was working on.

Reluctantly she concluded that Donald simply wasn't very resourceful. She couldn't blame him for being unsuited to Gerard Grossin's miserable existence, but she wished he was better able to fend for himself, to improvise a little. It seemed unfair that she should have to worry about him as well as herself. Once or twice he raised the subject of leaving again, but she always steered him away from it. The notion that the twentieth century lay just over the horizon was very seductive, but she couldn't escape nagging little doubts. Something else was bound to turn up long before the end of October.

The weather remained calm and sunny. For days on end the navy blue sea glittered benignly under a bright sky, and the fish flakes all around the harbor were covered with drying cod. The town simmered with activity. Four ships had been commissioned to return the English prisoners: three bound for Boston, one for Placentia in Newfoundland. At last the townspeople could see the end of their enforced hospitality, and it made them light-hearted in spite of the looming winter and the long period of isolation that lay ahead.

At the same time, a rumor was spreading through Louisbourg that the six Compagnie des Indes ships at anchor in the harbor would be sailing for France in a few weeks. Michel said flatly that it wasn't true, but Suzanne was contemptuous. "All you need do is to look out of the window and you can see for yourself, if you use your eyes! Why else are they provisioning them? You are so smart you are stupid, Michel Jacques!"

Michel only shrugged. "Remember it was I who told you," he said. "If the prisoners are as easy to fool as you, then all will be well. That is what they are supposed to believe—so they can tell them in Boston what is not true."

It certainly looked as if Suzanne was right. Men swarmed all over the ships, up the rigging, over the sides on ropes, on the decks and in the holds. Flocks of rowboats and barges ferried enormous loads out from the quay. The wharves were crowded with men, barrels, crates and sacks, and small boys getting underfoot. Blaize watched from a safe distance—through a window, or sitting on the front steps, his chin on his fists, but Pierre yearned to be out in the midst of the action, and sometimes when Joseph was away, Christophe let him join the other boys for a little while.

With all the busyness and confusion, Lyn hoped that Donald would escape attention, but the afternoon he came to collect his mended stockings, she found he hadn't altogether. About five minutes after he left with a five-pound loaf which he had only fractionally paid for under his arm, Christophe appeared in the shop, his expression lugubrious. "Mademoiselle," he said. "I cannot help noticing that soldier. He comes often, is it not?"

Lyn made a job of polishing the scales. After a silence, Christophe said, "Forgive me for asking, but does he bother you?"

She made herself meet his eyes. There was no suspicion in them; they were brown and steady. He did not seem to be accusing her of anything improper. Did he know he was looking at his bride-to-be, she wondered suddenly? If so, he gave no indication. She swallowed the wrong way and gave a choking cough. "No. No, he comes to buy bread, that is all. He is lonely and he talks to me. He means no harm."

"You must be careful of such people," he cautioned her gravely. "They will take advantage of you. They are not honorable men, Mademoiselle. It is best not to encourage them."

"Do not worry on my account."

"Madame Desforges worries. She is very fond of you."

Did he mean that Marguerite knew about Donald? Lyn was about to ask, when Joseph came thundering through the door, hauling Pierre by one arm. His face was red and his eyes glittered angrily. "What is this? Who allowed this?"

Christophe winced and muttered some kind of oath under his breath. "I did, Monsieur," he said aloud. "Do not be angry with the boy, I said he could go out until the oven is cool enough to clean. There was nothing for him to do and the sun is shining, so I thought—"

"Nothing for him to do? Nonsense! There is always something!

Why is he not bringing in wood? Why does he not sweep the floor or clean the tables? Is the flour for tomorrow sieved? Who are you to say he can go out?''

''I am sorry, Monsieur. It was for a very short time. He promised to return within a few minutes.''

''And you are fool enough to trust him?'' Joseph's voice rose in disbelief. He gave Pierre a shake. ''This good for nothing boy! He would as soon run away for the rest of the day!''

''I do not think so,'' said Christophe mildly.

''In my bakery he will be treated like any other apprentice. He is not to have special privileges! Do you understand me, Christophe?''

Christophe nodded.

Joseph released Pierre and aimed a swat at him which he managed to duck. ''And you!'' He turned on Lyn. ''What are you staring at, eh?'' She set her teeth against telling him, and began to dust the clean counter. If she answered him back it would only provoke him further and he would take out his temper on Pierre or Marguerite. That was the trouble with bullies—they chose their victims carefully: the small, the meek or weak, those who couldn't fight back.

Off and on all week she brooded about what Christophe had said to her. It was essential that she and Donald find another way to meet—another place. Somewhere in all of the town there had to be an out-of-the-way corner. Maybe if she asked Donald to search for one it would give him something constructive to do with himself.

''Do you not agree?'' Louise gave her a nudge with a sharp little elbow. ''Elisabeth! You are not listening to me!''

''Agree?'' Lyn dragged her thoughts away from Donald.

''About *Jeanne*. All is not well with her, I am sure.''

''Why?''

''Are you deaf? That is what I have been telling you! Did you not notice how quiet she was today? She did not want to go walking, and when Aunt Marguerite asked about Madame Duvernay, she almost burst into tears. You must have seen!''

''Perhaps she is ill.'' Lyn hadn't noticed anything wrong with Jeanne.

''Ah, *zut!*'' Louise was disgusted with her. ''Jeanne tells *every*-one when she is ill. It cannot be that.''

''Why do you ask me? Why do you not simply ask Jeanne?''

"Because she will not tell me. I am too young, that is what she says. But she will have to tell you—you can make her."

Lyn almost said, but you're her sister, *I'm* not, but thought better of it. "There is nothing to be done now, Louise. Next Sunday, if you are still worried, I will speak to her."

"That is a whole week."

"So it is." Lyn agreed, and this time she was the one to roll over and shut Louise out. She was certain that by Sunday Jeanne would be fully recovered from whatever Louise imagined ailed her.

"Well? What is it, Elisabeth?" Madame Pugnant sounded preoccupied. She had barely glanced up from her ledgers when Lyn entered her room.

"It is important, Grandmother."

"It had better be. I am busy."

"Jeanne is in trouble."

At that, Madame Pugnant looked directly at her, fixing Lyn with those penetrating eyes. "What do you mean, trouble?" she asked in an ominous voice. "Lieutenant Duvernay has said nothing to me."

"Lieutenant Duvernay would be the last person to tell you," said Lyn.

It was Monday afternoon, a little over a week since Louise had goaded her into the promise to speak to Jeanne. She had been forced to make good on it, much to her dismay. Even she could see there was something wrong. After dinner, when they went out walking with Joseph and Marguerite and the babies, Louise arranged things so that Lyn could walk alone with Jeanne, lagging behind the others, unencumbered by Renée or even Blaize.

For a long time Jeanne paid no attention to Lyn; she was silent, her eyes not seeming to focus on anything around her, her face clouded. Getting her to open up and admit that she was troubled required almost more patience than Lyn could scrape together. But she persisted, aware that Louise kept glaring at them over her shoulder, and knowing she would get no peace unless she could convince Louise that she had learned the truth.

At last Jeanne crumbled and falteringly confessed that Lieutenant Duvernay had propositioned her. His wife was pregnant and frail, unable to satisfy him. Jeanne was almost sixteen, living under his roof and very pretty. The temptation was great.

153

"I do not know what to do, Elisabeth. I am frightened," Jeanne said in a small voice.

"Why are you frightened? Of what?" demanded Lyn.

"He will be very angry if he knows I have told anyone. He said he would turn me out and that I would never find another position in Louisbourg. He said Grandmother would not have me back. What would become of me?"

"But *he* is the one—" Lyn felt her temper rising. Grimly she remembered her first Sunday and the impression she had gotten of the lieutenant. It had been all too accurate. "How far has he gone? You must tell me, Jeanne."

The girl looked away. "He keeps after me. Again and again he asks. He is very impatient. He will not let me say no. I am afraid of what he might do."

"And so you should be! You must not stay in his house."

Jeanne gave her a horrified look. "But I cannot just leave! He will say terrible things about me—he will ruin my reputation. He will tell everyone that I made advances to him, and that he sent me away."

"Would you rather have him say terrible things, or do them?"

"He has promised he will take care of me."

"You cannot believe him!" But she could see from Jeanne's face that she had almost let herself, that she was almost willing. Exasperated, Lyn said, "He has only spoken to you about this, nothing more—is that right?"

"How can you ask me such a question, Elisabeth?" Jeanne's eyes were very wide.

"You must tell Grandmother at once—this afternoon."

"*Mon dieu,* Elisabeth!" Jeanne turned pale. "I could not!"

"She will *help* you," said Lyn, wanting to shake her. But Jeanne would not be persuaded. At last, very much against her better judgment, Lyn declared that she would go to Madame Pugnant herself and tell her. "But not today. Not until I have gone," said Jeanne.

"You should not go at all," argued Lyn. "It is foolish!"

"But I must. I cannot abandon Madame Duvernay in such a manner. It would be wrong, Elisabeth. I have a duty to her and she is not well."

Nothing Lyn could say would change her mind.

"So," said Madame Pugnant. "Has she told anyone else about this, do you know?"

"She says she has not."

"She has not spoken to Madame Duvernay?"

Lyn shook her head.

The old woman pursed her lips tightly. "I think," she said at length, "that Jeanne must be mistaken. She is very young and frivolous. She has misunderstood the lieutenant. I had hoped that she would learn responsibility, but she has not."

"No!" protested Lyn. "I am quite certain that she is *not* mistaken! She is old enough to understand a man's intentions toward her. She is frightened—I could see it. She must not stay in his house any longer, Grandmother."

"Why did she not come to me?"

"She was afraid that you would be angry. She did not want to tell anyone."

"But she told you. She was right, I am angry. It is a serious matter to make such an accusation against a person like Lieutenant Duvernay."

"Yes." Lyn felt her temper beginning to bubble. "It *is* serious."

"Listen to me, Elisabeth. Lieutenant Duvernay is a respected officer in the garrison. He has a position to maintain. He has a wife and he is soon to have a child. He would hardly embarrass himself with a servant girl."

"Then you do not believe Jeanne." Lyn kept his voice level with an effort. "Does that mean you will do nothing?"

"I shall consider very carefully what you have told me, Elisabeth. And, if I decide, I shall discuss it with Joseph. It was right for you to come to me with this, but now you need concern yourself no further with it. Is that clear?"

"But you cannot leave her there! She is only fifteen years old! Did you not hear what I have been saying to you?"

"That is enough, Elisabeth! You do not speak to me in this manner. I will not have it!" More calmly, she said, "I am sure you have exaggerated the perils of Jeanne's situation, as she herself has to you. We will determine what is best to be done and we will do it. I do not want to discuss this any longer. Go and see if Madame Jodouin's meat pie is ready. She will be coming for it very soon."

The important thing was that Madame Pugnant knew of Jeanne's predicament. Although Lyn felt that Madame Pugnant would have been entirely justified in marching straight to the Duvernay house to confront the lieutenant with his lecherous behavior and embarrass him publicly before his neighbors, she reminded herself that Madame Pugnant did not operate that way. She was a shrewd woman—tough and unsentimental, but just. Lyn didn't believe she would sit back and do nothing.

She was certain that Jeanne had told her the truth, and that Jeanne had understood very well what Lieutenant Duvernay wanted from her. But at the back of her mind was a tiny nagging voice. Jeanne had told her the truth—but had she told her the *whole* truth, or had she held something back? There were questions that hadn't quite been answered.

Monday passed, and then Tuesday, and no one said a word. Wednesday morning Marguerite asked Lyn, "Whatever have you said to Maman, Elisabeth? Joseph is very annoyed with you."

"Joseph? Is annoyed with me?"

"He says you are nothing but trouble, and that Maman should send you back to Jean Bernard without delay. She will not do that, of course, but oh, Elisabeth, I could not bear it if you were not here."

"Did he mention Jeanne?"

"No. Why should he speak to me of Jeanne?" Marguerite sounded surprised. "Is there something wrong?"

"I hope not," said Lyn grimly. "It will be his fault if there is."

"But what has Joseph to do with Jeanne? I do not understand."

"She must not stay with the Duvernays, Marguerite. She is not safe there. Lieutenant Duvernay has propositioned her."

"Propositioned?" said Marguerite faintly.

Lyn wondered how to explain, but there was comprehension in Marguerite's eyes. "I do not like that man."

Impulsively Lyn gave her a hug. "Then you believe it. You must help to convince them to bring Jeanne back."

"But Elisabeth, if they know this, they will do what is best. There is nothing more I can say."

"That is just it! They have done nothing at all!"

"You do not know that. You must be patient. It is a very difficult matter, this. Lieutenant Duvernay has business with Joseph, so it must be handled with care. Do not worry, Joseph will do what is right.''

It was a waste of breath to argue, Lyn could see. She had no confidence whatsoever in Joseph. She thought it all too likely that he valued his business connection with Lieutenant Duvernay more than his niece's well-being.

It was her own fault; she should never have left it entirely up to Madame Pugnant. Instead, she should have told Jeanne flatly not to return to the Duvernays on Sunday evening, or forced her to tell her story at once to Madame Pugnant. How could they be so blind and stubborn?

That afternoon she could stand it no longer. She waylaid Joseph in the front hall as he was going out. At the sight of her, his eyes hardened and the color rose in his cheeks. He would have pushed past her without speaking, but she stood squarely in front of the door.

''You are in my way.''

''I want to talk to you, Uncle Joseph,'' she said. ''It is about Jeanne. Grandmother has told you—''

''She has told me that you are making trouble, Elisabeth. As usual.''

Underneath her apron, Lyn's fingers tightened. ''Lieutenant Duvernay—''

''You are in my way,'' he repeated. ''I am late. I do not have time to waste listening to your ridiculous stories.''

Anger swelled in her chest like an inflating balloon, pushing against her breastbone. ''You intend to do nothing.'' Her voice had trouble getting around it.

''I intend to warn you, Elisabeth, that I will not have you causing trouble in my household. I will not allow you to spread malicious rumors about Lieutenant Duvernay. He is a man of importance in the town. He is respected and influential. If you do not cease this immediately, I will turn you out of the house—make no mistake, I will do it. You will not mention this again, do you understand? Or are you incapable of understanding, like that witless brother of yours!'' He had worked himself into a fury. ''Now stand aside, at once!''

By sheer force of will, she kept her hands down, but the effort made her tremble. "If you will do nothing," she said, her voice icy, "then I shall."

He gave a harsh little bark of laughter. "You? What can *you* do? No one will listen to you! I will not waste any more of my time." He thrust her roughly to one side and strode out, banging the door behind him.

She stood still, blinking rapidly, her mind full of a furious, whirling blackness. Gradually it cleared a little, and she found Thomas studying her curiously from the bakery doorway. Behind him, Christophe said, "You have not finished your kneading, Thomas."

"It is near enough," he replied carelessly. "It will not matter. The dough will rise. Joseph is gone."

"But I am still here, is it not, and I say you must do it in the proper way."

"You are as bad as he, Christophe," grumbled Thomas, giving in.

By the time Donald appeared to buy his meager loaf, Lyn was much calmer, but extremely preoccupied. She barely heard anything he said to her, and answered in monosyllables when she caught the sound of a question mark.

"What is wrong with you?" he demanded at last in English.

"What?"

"You haven't been listening to me—you're miles away." He was reproachful. "I came to tell you about my discovery. I was sure you'd be pleased."

"I'm sorry," said Lyn. "It's just—there's a family crisis. I'm not sure what I should do about it."

"Why should you do anything? It's not *your* family, for heaven's sake."

She sighed. "But I'm in the middle of it, Donald. I can't help it. I can't ignore what's going on."

"The main thing you've got to think about is getting back. Don't be distracted, Lyn. Don't let them suck you in," he said urgently.

She changed the subject. "What did you come to tell me?"

He had found a place where they could meet, out of public view. He was so pleased with his own ingenuity that she began to feel better herself. It was an outbuilding that had been used to house English prisoners, and now that they had been shipped back to

158

Boston, it stood empty behind Jacques Talon's warehouse off the rue d'Orleans. "It's pretty ramshackle," he said, "but that's good. I doubt they'll use it for anything now. You can get in through the back gate, which doesn't have a lock. See what you think. We can leave messages there, behind one of the beams. And if you can ever get extra food—" He looked at her hopefully.

"I'll do what I can," she promised.

"I wish you'd come with me now so I could show you."

"Donald, I can't. There'd be a terrible fuss if I just left the shop, and besides—" She paused. She'd been going to say, "I've been warned about being seen with you."

"Besides what?"

"Besides they're all cross enough with me—I'd never be able to get out on my own again."

"Why should they *matter*? They aren't your people, I keep telling you."

"Yes, but I live with them. There isn't anywhere to go if I don't stay here. I keep telling *you*."

He gazed at her unhappily. "I suppose you're right. It's just that sometimes I think if I have to stay here another week—another *day* even—if I wake up again in this place—I will go stark staring mad. If it weren't for you, Lyn, I would have by now. I'd never have lasted this long. I've got to get out of here. September's practically gone—I should have been back at college two weeks ago. It isn't just my classes—I'm a research assistant. What am I going to do?"

"Hang on," she told him firmly. "We are both going to hang on."

"But—"

"As long as it takes."

He hesitated, then gave a little nod. "Keep telling me that. And promise you'll keep thinking. Don't get sidetracked, Lyn, for heaven's sake."

But she couldn't help it. After he'd gone, his pockets full of day-old rolls, her thoughts reverted to Jeanne, and she was filled all over again with fury at Joseph's response. Or lack of response. He was going to do nothing at all, leave Jeanne where she was and pretend nothing had ever been said. Jeanne might be silly and vain, but she didn't deserve to be sacrificed. Lyn wouldn't let it happen; her determination set like cement.

The answer came to her in the privy, as she sat staring at the wall, gritty-eyed with anger and worry and lack of sleep. There was somebody else in town intimately concerned with Jeanne's welfare: her father. Lyn didn't relish the idea of seeking him out—he rented a room over one of the taverns on the east side of Louisbourg, somewhere behind the hospital, she thought—but she'd run out of alternatives. And she knew that he shared her dislike of Lieutenant Duvernay; he had not been happy with Madame Pugnant's arrangements for Jeanne. Now all she had to do was find out precisely where and when she could talk to him. She knew who could tell her.

That afternoon, as she waited on two women who could not make up their minds about what they wanted—was it *really* worth the money to spend extra for white rolls?—a man strolled into the shop. She glanced at him as he entered, then looked again, harder. It was Mathieu Martel. Michel had been noncommittal when she'd told him she needed to talk to Jean Bernard. He wouldn't give her a straight answer, and she had wanted to shake him like a dust mop. If, by the end of the day, he produced no results, she resolved crossly that she would go out looking by herself. But here, in the shop, were the results.

He seemed casual and detached, waiting unconcernedly for the women to make their purchases and leave, but his eyes were watchful. They missed nothing, and he grinned a little when Lyn fumbled with the rolls and dropped one on the floor. He enjoyed making her awkward, she realized resentfully, but she didn't dare keep him waiting too long in case he decided to leave before she could speak to him. While she finished weighing the bread, he pretended to be interested in the view out the window, which was of furry, enveloping sea fog. He was playing a game with her for his own amusement. At last the women paid her and departed. "Monsieur?" She couldn't keep the edge out of her voice.

"Ah, yes. Good afternoon, Mademoiselle." He turned with a bland smile.

"Good afternoon," she replied stiffly.

The smile deepened. She stifled an urge to throw a five-pound loaf at it.

"Michel spoke to you?"

He nodded. "He said you wished to see me, so I have come."

"It is not you I wish to see." She hadn't meant it to sound quite so curt, but there was no point in beating around the bush; they could be interrupted at any moment. "I must see Jean Bernard. It is very important. Can you arrange it?"

The smile disappeared. "Perhaps. Why?"

"It is a family matter."

"Does she know?" with a nod toward the stairs.

"Madame Pugnant is aware of the matter, yes. She does not know that I want to talk to Jean Bernard about it."

He considered her for a moment. "You do not wish to tell me."

"No."

"But you need my help."

"If I must I will do without it. But I cannot afford to waste time. I thought—"

"Jean Bernard is my friend, Mademoiselle, but as you know, he has a temper."

"So?"

"He does not always think before he acts, and the results can sometimes be—difficult."

"No one else will act at all. Will you arrange for me to see him?"

He grunted. "Not here. It is best if you go to him, is it not."

"Yes. That is why I am standing here talking to you."

The smile was back, lurking at the corners of his mouth. "For no other reason, Mademoiselle?"

"None," said Lyn flatly.

"I see."

But she wasn't at all convinced that he saw only what she intended him to. "I must talk to him today. When the shop is closed, later."

"It might be done. Watch for me."

⇢⇢ 12 ⇠⇠

LYN LOST COUNT OF THE NUMBER OF TIMES SHE WENT TO THE window or out onto the doorstep to peer through the fog, ostensibly for a breath of air. She strained her eyes trying to make out the ambiguous figures on the quay, afraid she would miss Mathieu among the other men walking past. But when he appeared, she knew him.

She left the house quickly, her cloak around her shoulders and a basket on her arm, as if she had a late errand—which in fact she had, although not one that would meet with approval in the household. Mathieu had been watching for her; by the time she reached the street he'd walked ahead to Ordonnateur Bigot's house. She set off after him, keeping his lanky shape in sight. The streets were no longer unfamiliar to her; she could negotiate the hazards with skill: things shaken out of upstairs windows, pails emptied through doorways, heaps of dung and garbage, barrels, handcarts, chickens and children, suspicious dogs, sailors and fishermen at every corner. It always gave her a flicker of pure delight to be outside on her own in the town. For Lyn Paget it had been commonplace, she hardly ever gave it a thought: wandering around Belmont or Boston or Cambridge, poking into shops, having lunch at Friendly's, riding the subway or taking a bus somewhere—anywhere she pleased. Alone if she chose, or with Mike or Dorrie or another friend, but basically *free*. For Elisabeth Bernard, even this short walk was a privilege, although Lyn doubted that Elisabeth herself would have thought so. Like Marguerite, she was probably too timid to enjoy venturing out alone. As Elisabeth, Lyn felt stifled, as if she was wearing a corset that was laced too tight.

At the high, impassive wall that surrounded the hospital, she turned left after Mathieu, and walked straight into him. "Mademoiselle, you do not look where you are going, is it," he said, amused.

"Why did you stop? I did not expect—should you be seen with me?"

"I thought you did not care about such things."

"I thought you did."

He smiled again, quite a nice smile. Although she examined it suspiciously, she could find nothing offensive in it. "I thought perhaps I could risk it. It is only a matter of time anyway before everyone in Louisbourg knows that Mademoiselle Elisabeth Bernard has paid a visit to her father, and that Mathieu Martel took her to see him. They will hear of it in your house before nightfall, you understand."

Lyn nodded, chewing her lip.

"Then it is better if I take you."

The tavern on the rue Dauphine was small and seedy-looking outside, dim and smoky inside. As Mathieu ushered her through the door, Lyn looked around with interest, having never been allowed

162

to set foot in such an establishment before. It was quite unremarkable. It smelled of stale beer and tobacco and unwashed, damp bodies, the floor was covered with sand. There was a hearth on one wall, and the room was furnished with an assortment of scarred wooden tables and stools, and a few chairs. Four men sat playing cards together near the fire, and a plump, youngish woman, overflowing her chemise, was scrubbing tabletops while conversing in a loud cheerful voice with them. The only other person in the room was a man sitting by himself with a tankard in his hand. Lyn gave Mathieu a reproachful glance; she needed Jean Bernard sober.

"I have brought someone to see you, Jean," said Mathieu.

The man turned his head and stared at Lyn, then got heavily to his feet. "Elisabeth." His voice was rough-edged. "It is indeed a pleasure."

"I had to come. I need your help."

"Oh? I thought this to be a social call."

She knew she was being got at and was cross with herself for feeling nervous.

"She thinks that you are drunk," said Mathieu helpfully.

"Mmmp. She has not learned the difference between having a drink and being drunk then, has she. Her mother knew." He gave a little snort of laughter. "So. If this is not a social visit we need not waste time being polite. We will go upstairs."

He thinks he is my father, Lyn reminded herself. "All three of us?"

"But of course," said Jean Bernard.

Everyone else in the tavern had given up all pretence of minding his or her own business; Lyn could feel their disappointment as Jean Bernard led the way up a narrow dark staircase. His room was much like the one Lyn shared with Elisabeth's brother and sisters: it too looked out on a back courtyard. This one was much smaller and cluttered with barrels and crates. There were two beds, both obviously slept in, an old chest, and two battered trunks.

"Welcome," said Jean Bernard. "I do not think you have been here before. Will you sit down?"

In the absence of chairs, Lyn sat carefully on the nearest bed.

"I am sure that Mathieu does not mind, do you Mathieu? It is his."

"Not at all," said Mathieu, leaning against the doorframe.

163

"Do you not want to know why I have come?" asked Lyn sharply, feeling the conversation needed redirecting. "Will you be serious?"

"Is it serious?" Jean Bernard peered at her from under his untidy eyebrows.

"I would not have bothered you otherwise."

"I am listening."

Plunging straight in, she told him what she had told Madame Pugnant, and he did listen, in silence. "She cannot stay there any longer—it may be too late now, I do not know," she finished. "It is all so—so *stupid*!"

"Stupid?"

"That no one does anything!"

"Who is no one? Who knows what you have just told me?"

"Madame—Grandmother. Joseph. Marguerite. They have done nothing."

"And you are sure," said Mathieu. "It is true, what Jeanne says? She has not made it up for some reason."

"Of course I am sure." Lyn glared at him. "And so are they. Even though they pretend not to believe it, they do. Jeanne is afraid of Lieutenant Duvernay. I should have kept her from going back, but I thought—" She stood up. "And you are just like the others! You will do nothing! *I* will go myself and confront him, then."

But she found that Mathieu had shifted slightly and was blocking the door. Jean Bernard said harshly, "Sit down, Elisabeth!" He began to pace back and forth, four steps one way, four steps the other, his feet thumping the floor. "This is not for you to handle. You are right to tell me—you should have come at once. So this is the way Madame Pugnant looks after my children! She says to me, I can do it better than you, Jean Bernard. I will tell her what I think of that, once I have settled with that bastard Duvernay! If he has done harm to Jeanne, he will pay for it, I swear! Do not worry—I will find him and he will wish he had never heard of Jean Bernard." He stopped abruptly in front of Mathieu. "You take Elisabeth back while I deal with this business."

"Jean, I do not think—" began Mathieu.

"Just do it! Do not argue with me—I do not want to be argued with, Mathieu."

164

"It would be better perhaps to wait," Mathieu persisted. "Consider a little longer, is it not. Go first to Monsieur Delort. Or perhaps—"

"Get out of my way!"

Mathieu stood his ground. "It is not—"

"Enough!" It was an explosion. Suddenly Mathieu staggered to one side, clutching his jaw. Jean Bernard flung open the door so hard it yelped on its hinges and cracked against the wall, and thundered down the stairs. In slow motion, Mathieu slid to the floor, leaning back, cradling the right side of his face in his hands, his eyes shut.

"Mathieu?" Lyn's voice was a ridiculous squeak. Her brain felt choked, as if it were trying to swallow something it hadn't chewed. There was no response. "Mathieu!" She threw herself down beside him, sure he was unconscious. There was a groan.

"Mathieu, are you all right?" What an inane question.

Another, louder groan, and a muffled mutter. His eyes opened; there were tears in them. He blinked hard. Gingerly he felt his jaw with his fingers. There was blood running from the corner of his mouth. He winced.

"Is it broken?" she whispered, horrified, wondering what on earth you did for a broken jaw.

He thought about it for a minute, then said, "No." Frowning, he felt around inside his mouth with his tongue, then spat something bloody into his hand. *"Merde."* He held it out for her to see. It was a tooth. "Get me something to drink," he said thickly.

"Water?" She glanced around the room for a pitcher.

"No! Go ask Marie for rum. Tell her to put it on Bernard's account. Go on."

Not knowing what else to do, Lyn ran downstairs. Marie was plainly avid to know what had happened overhead. "It was an argument," said Lyn. "Ah, he has a temper, Jean Bernard." Marie nodded wisely, inviting further details. She sounded admiring. Lyn took the tankard and went back to Mathieu, leaving her disappointed.

He was still sitting on the floor, his head tipped back. He took the rum from her without thanks and swallowed, then coughed and winced again. "It is just what I told you," he said crossly. "And it is your fault, this."

Lyn was stung by the injustice. "Suppose it was *your* sister—you would do nothing?"

"I have no sister, thank God."

"You could have ducked! You knew about his temper. Or even hit him back."

He gave a half shrug. "I am not a fighter, me. Besides, he is my friend."

"Some friend!"

Mathieu grinned crookedly, then gasped. He took another swig. "If it were in front, I could whistle through it."

"What should we do?"

"Do?" He sounded surprised. "It is done. That is why you came, is it not?"

"What will happen now?"

"Lieutenant Duvernay will be fortunate indeed to get off as lightly as I have. And then—he will go to jail, most likely."

"So he should," declared Lyn with feeling.

"Not the lieutenant, Mademoiselle. Your father, Jean Bernard. For attacking an officer. Lieutenant Duvernay will throw your sister out of his household in disgrace. There will be something exciting for the citizens to talk about on Sunday. Your uncle will be furious, and your grandmother also. And for all this, you are responsible."

"That is not true. Lieutenant Duvernay is responsible. He is to blame, not Jeanne, or Jean Bernard, or me. He should be punished for what he has done."

Mathieu studied her with a slight frown. "Mademoiselle, I do not believe that you can be as stupid as you seem," he said at last.

"Well, thank you!" she said indignantly. She couldn't understand why she felt suddenly on the verge of tears; she turned away quickly, not wanting him to see. She was overwhelmed with a sense of isolation. There was no one here she could talk to, no one who spoke her language, who knew who she was and where she came from. No one except Donald, and he was so full of his own miseries he had no room for hers. She could hear Mathieu struggling to his feet. She didn't want him to say anything more—her hold was too precarious at that moment—she just wanted to get out, into the air, away. Perhaps Donald was right—perhaps it *was* the place.

"Mademoiselle." Mathieu was standing right behind her; Donald receded. She gulped and said, her own voice sounding muffled this time, "I must get back. They will miss me."

"It is what you wanted," he said gently. "He will do what you wanted. He will see that she does not stay in that house any longer."

"But nobody cares!" she cried. "Nobody cares that it is wrong—it should not be allowed to happen!" She swung on him. "Why?"

"I do not understand you."

They faced one another in silence, then Lyn said bleakly, "No. No one does." It was true; the tears were unstoppable.

"Sacredie!" he exclaimed in horror. "What are you doing?"

"What does it look like?" Furious with herself and with him, she groped blindly for the door. He caught her arm. "Let go of me! I do not want you to come—I want to be left alone." She tried to pull loose.

"You cannot leave like this. Everyone will think—"

"I do not care! Let them think what they want!" She was working herself into a passion, unscrewing the lid she had kept down tight for so long. She was both frightened and exhilarated by it. "I do not care what anyone in this place thinks! You can all go to hell!" She fought against him, but he grasped her firmly by both arms and shook her.

"Elisabeth!"

"And I am *not* Elisabeth! I am not. I am Carolyn. That is my name. Carolyn." she shouted into his face.

He shook her so hard her teeth chattered. "Stop it. You are hysterical."

"Yes!"

Poor Mathieu, she thought afterward when it was all over. She supposed it was simply the release of everything that had been building up inside her since the very first moment. Even when she'd felt perfectly calm and in control, all of this must have been seething underneath, like a volcano, waiting to find a vent. It was Mathieu's misfortune to have been standing smack in the way of the eruption. When she dissolved weeping against him, he put his arms around her and sat her down beside him on the bed. He let her cry—there wasn't anything else he could do; she couldn't stop until her tears at last ran out, leaving her exhausted and hiccupping, but curiously peaceful.

He did what Donald couldn't: he put his arms around her and held her quietly. She felt him touching her, comforting, real, physical, and she hung onto him, not caring for the time being what he thought behind the sympathetic facade. Finally calm, she leaned against him, wrung out like a washcloth, her mind empty. She had no idea how long they sat there.

At last he stirred, then gently disengaged himself. He got up and went out of the room, and she just watched, too limp to move, afraid she would fall over if she tried. In a few minutes he was back with a basin and a rag. He crouched in front of her as if she were one of the babies—Anne or Renée—and washed her face for her and she let him do it without protest. It occurred to her that a short time before it was what she should have thought to do for him. There was a streak of dried blood on his chin. She pulled herself together with a long, shuddering breath, took the rag from him, scrubbed her eyes hard, then dabbed at the blood. He flinched backward and she managed a watery smile. "Do not worry. I do not hit as hard as Jean Bernard."

"No. Sometimes it would be useful, I think. I could perhaps have laid him out until he cooled off a little," said Mathieu. "But come. It must be all over by now. Whatever has happened. They will wonder where you are, and if they find you here then I will be joining Jean at the barracks."

"If they do not mind about Jeanne, they won't mind about me."

"I am not Lieutenant Duvernay," he replied ironically.

There were more people in the tavern when they left, and at the sound of their feet on the stairs all conversation stopped. Lyn looked around defiantly, meeting stares of undisguised curiosity and speculation, but Mathieu hurried her out into the street. Sighing, he said, "It will be long before this is forgotten, I am afraid. What a blessing it is to have no family."

"You have none at all?"

"In France perhaps. Perhaps not. It has been years since I was there, and I do not know anymore."

"You do not mind being alone?"

"Ah no, Mademoiselle," he said with feeling. "Life is so much simpler. I need only think of myself, no one else."

"You think of Jean Bernard."

"I share his roof. He has done me a favor which I am working to repay, but I am not responsible for him, thank God. I do not like trouble.''

At Ordonnateur Bigot's house she stopped and told him she would go on alone. When he protested that Jean Bernard had told him to take her home, she reminded him, ''You do not like trouble, so you said. I am sure there will be trouble.''

With a shrug he gave in, but when she got to the steps of the bakery, she looked back and saw him, a vague shape at the corner, waiting. The feeling of peace that had followed her crying jag was gone, but it left behind a reservoir of calm. There was no point in trying to sneak into the house unobtrusively; they must all know by this time she'd been out.

The household was in uproar. Thomas, hovering in the bakery door, was the first to see Lyn. He shook his head at her and made a tutting sound, but said nothing.

Marguerite and Louise were across the hall, in the shop. Louise came darting out. ''Elisabeth! Where have you been? It is terrible— so terrible. Uncle Joseph has been summoned to the Duvernay house and Grandmother is full of anger.''

''Do you know what has happened?'' asked Lyn cautiously.

''It is Father. He has attacked Lieutenant Duvernay and they have arrested him. Why should he *do* such a thing?''

It occurred to Lyn that actually, if anyone were to blame for starting this, it was Louise. It was she who had brought it to Lyn's attention and then agitated until Lyn did something. She had noticed Jeanne when everyone else was too preoccupied. She had noticed Elisabeth, too, although she refused to admit it. Looking at her now, Lyn felt very tired. More than anything, she would have liked to go upstairs, fall onto the bed, and sleep off the whole day.

''What have you done, Elisabeth?'' asked Marguerite, behind Louise. ''Maman says you are to go to her at once.''

''I did the only thing I could think of,'' said Lyn wearily. ''No one in this house would help Jeanne, so I went to Jean Bernard. Whatever he has done, Marguerite, you know as well as I, Lieutenant Duvernay deserved it.''

Marguerite nodded unhappily. ''Why must such things happen?''

Madame Pugnant was seated as usual at her desk by the window. First came the lecture: about interfering with things that did

169

not concern Elisabeth, about leaving the house without permission, about going out alone to find Jean Bernard, about being seen entering a tavern in the company of a man with a questionable reputation. Lyn waited in silence for the old woman to finish so that they could get to the heart of the matter. Behind the hard lines of anger, Madame Pugnant's face was pulled and puckered like tired crepe paper. Her eyes were shadowed with worry and something else Lyn couldn't read. She was unexpectedly touched. Madame Pugnant was alone, too. Lyn felt a treacherous sympathy for her.

"You have behaved very foolishly," she said finally. "We will all suffer for what you have done. Poor Joseph has gone to try and make amends as best he can, but it is very difficult for him—"

"Poor Joseph?" The sympathy vanished in an instant. "He is to blame as much as anyone. It did not need to happen like this—it would not have—if he had acted at once. He is too worried about what people will think of him."

"And you are not worried enough."

"That is what everyone tells me," Lyn retorted. "What about Jeanne? Is she not important? At least Jean Bernard thinks so."

Madame Pugnant gave her an odd, sharp look. "Your uncle," she said, "would like to be quit of all of you. And now you have provided him with another good reason."

"I am well aware that he does not want us here. But if Jean Bernard is in prison, then he cannot take us, can he? And Louise told me that he has been arrested for doing what Joseph had not the courage to do."

"I will not have you speak of your uncle that way." Madame Pugnant's tone was suprisingly mild, as if she were saying something she felt she ought to say. "He has so much violence, that man. He does not *think* first," she continued crossly. "At least when Françoise was alive, she knew how to control him." She sighed. "Now Jeanne *must* return to us—there is no other choice. I will not be able to find her another place, not for some time. Whatever chances she had are as good as lost. It is too bad."

"Would she not have lost her chances if she had stayed with Lieutenant Duvernay?" asked Lyn. "Suppose she became pregnant?"

170

Choosing to ignore the question, the old woman said, "Go down to the kitchen. I still have work to finish. I have no doubt that Joseph will have words for you later, Elisabeth."

"What about Jean Bernard? What will happen to him now?"

"You have said—he is arrested. He is a dangerous man. Prison would seem to be the best place for him. Perhaps it will teach him to control his temper, is it not."

"It does not matter to you that he is your son-in-law? And Joseph—will he not mind having a relative in the town jail? What will people think of that?"

Madame Pugnant's eyes flicked her faced, and Lyn did not look away. A spark jumped between them. "The townspeople have much to talk about concerning our family today," she said dryly. "This is only one more thing that Joseph will hold againt Jean Bernard. And the rest of you."

"Is it not possible to persuade Lieutenant Duvernay not to bring charges?"

"That, I think, is highly unlikely."

"It must be very distressing for his wife. Especially at this time, in her condition. Jeanne says that she is not strong. Even if they are not true, rumors spread quickly. . . ."

"That is enough, Elisabeth. Do not go any further. You would be well advised to stay out of Joseph's way for now. The sight of you is bound to provoke him sorely."

"Yes, Grandmother," said Lyn meekly.

The old woman gave her a narrow look. "There is more of Françoise in you than I had thought. She could be stubborn and devious when there was something she desired. Sometimes she got more than she expected. Be very careful, Elisabeth."

Joseph brought Jeanne back from the Duvernay house with him, and deposited her in the kitchen like something with a bad smell. She sat on a corner of the settle, tragic and tearful, twisting a damp lace handkerchief in her fingers, and allowing Marguerite to fuss over and comfort her. This was rich stuff to Suzanne, who soaked it up like a sponge and muttered knowingly under her breath.

The evening was strained and difficult. Joseph was in a vile temper, complaining over and over of the disgrace Jean Bernard

171

had brought down on his family. Madame Pugnant was so remote as to hardly be present in the room. Lyn, watching her, knew she was thinking and wished she could read her thoughts, but the old woman gave nothing away. Jeanne wept softly, making just enough noise to be noticed, and Louise looked like a small black stormcloud.

Lyn found the relief of escaping to bed short-lived, because once in their room with the door shut, Jeanne dropped her weepy silence, and described to Louise and Lyn in lurid detail precisely what had happened at the Duvernays': the way Jean Bernard had come bursting into the house, pushing past the servants, shouting for the lieutenant, who was having coffee with his wife in the parlor. "Oh, it was terrible! He was like a bear—you cannot imagine!" she exclaimed breathlessly. "He said that if Lieutenant Duvernay did not wish to come outside with him, they could discuss the matter there, in the parlor. And *poor* madame! She was *terrified*. He said dreadful things—oh, I *cannot* repeat them, the things he said! I was so ashamed!"

"Why can you not tell us what he said?" asked Louise.

"You are too young, Louise. You are only a child," said Jeanne. "It was a tragic misunderstanding. There was no time to explain— Papa *attacked* him! He is a savage."

Irritated beyond endurance, Lyn said, "Suppose he had not come?"

There was a pause. "I do not know what you mean, Elisabeth." Jeanne's voice was prim.

"What would have happened to you if Jean Bernard had not come?"

"But he did. I have just been telling you what it was like, did you not listen? I cannot imagine what you told him to make him so angry, Elisabeth." She sighed dramatically. "I do not see how I shall face Madame Duvernay again."

"Why would you want to?"

"She has been my *friend*. It will be very difficult for me to live this down. I do not know how I shall."

"You sound just like Joseph!" exclaimed Lyn in disgust. She lay down and closed her ears. It was pointless to argue with Jeanne. Now that the incident was over and she was safe, her view of the situation had shifted completely. It was far too convenient for her to

172

hold Jean Bernard responsible for everything that had gone wrong. He was hot-tempered and disreputable, and associated with shady characters like Mathieu Martel. Lyn went to sleep thinking about Mathieu.

⇢⟫ 13 ⟪⇠

JOSEPH STALKED ABOUT IN A STATE OF PERPETUAL BAD HUMOR, his face frozen in a scowl. Lyn found it was unnecessary to stay out of his way; he ignored her. Madame Pugnant, wearing her Sunday clothes, went out several times during the next few days without telling anyone where she was going, or why, and it was impossible to guess anything about her errands from her face, although Lyn studied her expression intently, searching for clues.

Marguerite was no help. She merely shook her head and told Lyn not to ask what was going on. "It is a difficult time of year, this. It will soon be St. Michael's Day. Joseph and Maman are busy reckoning the accounts, Elisabeth. You must do nothing to upset them."

St. Michael's Day came at the end of September. People had been preoccupied with it for weeks. The fishing season was ended mid-month to allow everyone to settle his annual accounts and figure his profits and losses. Rumors about the poor fishing that summer were gaining strength and substance; many faces were drawn with worry. Lyn knew that the loss of the *Cantabre* in July had hurt Joseph's finances, and other merchants and officers and some of the artisans in town had suffered similar setbacks because of the increasing aggression of the English privateers. An alarming number of ships and cargoes had been lost. Adding everything up, people were beginning to realize the extent of the damage caused that summer by the war between England and France, even though it seemed so distant from Louisbourg.

It wasn't St. Michael's Day that Lyn was concerned about, how-ever. It was Jean Bernard. She hated the thought of him shut up in the barracks' prison, while Lieutenant Duvernay walked around free and unrepentant.

"You *must* know something, Marguerite! I cannot believe that Joseph has said no word to you about Jean Bernard. Whatever it is, tell me."

173

Marguerite only shook her head. "We do not talk of such matters, Elisabeth."

Then what on earth *do* you talk about, Lyn nearly asked in exasperation. But she was afraid she already knew the answer: Marguerite and Joseph didn't really talk to each other at all. They lived together because they were married, and they shared a bed and meals, but that was all. Sometimes she would watch Christophe watching Marguerite and think how dismal it was that none of them could be happy: not Marguerite, not Christophe, not even Joseph. They were trapped by a set of rules Lyn saw no sense in, but that none of them would break.

It was common knowledge that Jean Bernard was being held in the barracks, waiting—no one was quite sure for what. There were rumors that Madame Duvernay had collapsed, that she had lost her child and was deathly ill; that Lieutenant Duvernay was at her bedside so distraught he could think of nothing else. Lyn found it beyond her imaginative powers to picture Lieutenant Duvernay distraught, however, and Michel said he had heard the lieutenant had a black eye which he preferred people not to see. Remembering Mathieu's bloody tooth, Lyn suspected he was nursing more than a black eye.

With grisly relish, Suzanne recalled all the criminals she had seen punished during the course of her years in Louisbourg. Men flogged through the streets, branded as thieves, pilloried in the place du Port, deported in chains, sentenced to life as oarsmen on government ships, executed. Four years earlier, the town executioner had broken the bones of a Basque fisherman who had been bound to a rack on the quay, then, after several hours of torture, had strangled him. It was, she declared righteously, only what offenders deserved for disturbing the order of the town. They should be made to serve as examples of what happened to those who transgressed. Unfortunately there was no executioner in Louisbourg at present. Although such men were necessary, they tended to be shunned socially, and it was impossible to find anyone to accept the position.

Lyn was sickened by her stories; she found it impossible to reconcile such bloodthirsty punishments with people who said their prayers daily and attended Mass every Sunday—people who were

174

supposedly civilized. Their idea of justice seemed to have no connection with mercy, or even rehabilitation.

Finally, in desperation, she waylaid Michel in the courtyard and asked him what she could do to help Jean Bernard. *"Sacredie!"* he exclaimed. "Have you not already done enough?"

"But I *had* to tell him. There was no one else."

Michel shrugged. "It was Jeanne's problem, why not let her solve it?"

Because Jeanne wasn't even sixteen, Lyn argued. She wasn't old enough or strong enough to stand up to a man like Lieutenant Duvernay. And she was silly enough to let him approach her in the first place, Michel returned, unsympathetic.

"But can I not go to the ordonnateur or the governor and explain?"

"Explain what? That your father attacked an officer in the Compagnies franches? What good is that? They know already. Anyway, you would not get inside the door."

"But now again no one is doing anything!"

"You do not know that. You do not understand how these things work."

"No, I do not," she agreed hotly.

"Then leave it to those who do," he retorted, and would say nothing more.

Although she would never have admitted it, her greatest disappointment was Mathieu. Daily she expected him to appear, to tell her what was happening. Each time a man entered the shop, her breath would catch for an instant, then she would look up and find it wasn't Mathieu. Didn't he know that she cared? Or like Michel, did he feel she'd already meddled too much? Had his kindness toward her been only surface deep, the easiest way for him to deal with an awkward situation? Every day he didn't come, her doubts and depression increased.

To distract herself on one of her errands, she went in search of the shed Donald had found as a place for them to meet. It was small and weather-beaten, dirt-floored, uninviting. She felt sorry for the English prisoners who'd been cooped up in it. One had carved his initials—G.M.—in the door brace, and a series of vertical scratches, as if he'd been counting the days of his confinement. In one corner was a heap of musty straw, and a wooden tub had been turned upside down to make a stool. Donald was right: it would do for their purposes. It looked and smelled as if no one had been in it since the Englishmen had been removed.

Donald was impatient to put it to use. Finally, to prevent him from coming almost daily to the shop, she agreed to meet him there, when she delivered bread, Saturday afternoon. She was surprised at how much she really didn't want to talk to him just then, and felt guilty because of it. When he arrived, soon after she got there, he wouldn't stand still, but fidgeted around the little room. His face seemed to have gotten thinner and his eyes looked feverishly bright. "I thought you would meet me here before this. I was sure—"

"Oh, Donald." Her helplessness on so many fronts frustrated her. "There's been so much going on, I haven't had time—"

"Time?" He gave a humorless laugh. "That's a joke, isn't it? We've got time, both of us, but it's the *wrong* time. What's going to happen to us, Lyn? Seriously. No pretending."

"We'll figure it out and get back."

"That's what you keep saying. It's the end of September. The wrong time keeps going by and we're still stuck in it. Pretty soon it'll be winter—suppose we're still here? And next spring? Have you thought about that? There's going to be a *war* here. Cannons and muskets—people getting killed—"

"I know, I know. But that's not for months, Donald. We can't worry—"

"Can't you? I do. All the time."

He was wearing down. She felt a pang of guilt. It wasn't his fault he was who he was. He hadn't asked for this, any more than she had. "I'm sorry," she said, impulsively reaching for his hand.

"For what?"

She shook her head. "I don't know. That things are so rotten for you."

He managed a lopsided smile. "I'm hanging on." His fingers closed tightly around hers. "It's just—I don't even speak the language, Lyn."

She knew he didn't mean French. "I know. Look, can you come again Monday? I'll have an order to deliver in the late morning. I'll bring you some food."

He took a deep breath and squared his shoulders. "All right. Monday." As he was leaving, he paused. "You've never told me who she is."

"Who?"

"The third person. You said it was a woman, but that's all."

Agathe, she almost said, but something stopped her.

"I thought—maybe I could go and see her. It might help if I could talk to her."

Slowly Lyn shook her head. "I don't think so."

"Why?"

"When I went, she told me not to come back again. She doesn't want to be reminded."

"What did she say exactly?" He sounded disbelieving.

Unwillingly, Lyn dug up her conversation with Agathe. "She's convinced that what she has to do is wait. She has to stay in the same place, where it happened the first time, and it'll happen to her again. She'd never leave Louisbourg. In the meantime she doesn't want to think about who she was—she wouldn't even tell me her real name."

"But suppose she's changed her mind since you saw her? How long has it been—a month? More?"

"No. She knows who I am and where to find me. If she'd changed her mind, she'd let me know."

"You aren't going to tell me who she is." It was a statement.

"It won't do any good."

"You don't trust me," he said in an injured tone.

"It isn't that, Donald." But Lyn couldn't tell him what it was: that she was afraid talking to Agathe would only make things worse for him. He was desperate enough now.

As if reading her mind, he said, "I've considered alternatives—throwing myself in the harbor, shooting myself with my musket—things like that."

Her scalp prickled. "Then you would never get back," she said matter-of-factly.

"I thought of that, too. I've decided against it—at least for the time being." He made a face. "I'm a terrible coward, anyway. I can't stand blood, and I can swim, so I wouldn't drown."

"Good," said Lyn.

Since Jeanne had lost her job with the Duvernays, Madame Pugnant decided that she should work in the bakeshop. For Lyn that meant spending hours every day in Jeanne's company, which Lyn found tiresome in the extreme. Jeanne made no effort to learn anything; she did what she was told by Madame Pugnant in a kind of slow motion, then forgot what it was so she had to be told precisely the same things again and again. When Madame Pugnant was not there, she sat behind the counter staring at nothing for hours, and complained constantly of being tired. Lyn gave up on her. It was far easier to ignore her and get on with the work than to nag and chivvy and cajole. It was clear that Jeanne considered herself too good to be an ordinary shop clerk.

On Sunday, Jeanne announced that she did not feel well enough to go to Mass with the family. Had it been up to Joseph, he would have gladly left her behind, but Madame Pugnant would not hear of it. "It will only be worse for you if you do not go. People will say that you have cause to hide. You must show them you do not." So Jeanne went, her head high, and looked at and spoke to no one. And Joseph went, looking as sour as if he'd eaten a lemon, but he didn't argue with his mother-in-law because she was right, as usual. "Perhaps she really is ill," Marguerite murmured to Lyn. "Ill at losing what she wanted," said Lyn. The Duvernays were not in the chapel.

A week after Jean Bernard was arrested, he was released. Lyn found out from Jean Bernard himself. He appeared without warning in the bakeshop, looking more presentable and subdued than she had seen him. His wild hair had been forced into a sort of queue, his mustache trimmed, and his clothes, though limp with use, had been brushed and tucked in where appropriate. He hesitated awkwardly in the doorway, turning his hat round and round in his hands, and cleared his throat. Jeanne let out a little gasp, and rushed out past him, down the hall to the safety of the kitchen.

Caught by surprise, Lyn said, "You are not in prison," unable to think of anything more sensible with which to break the difficult silence.

"No," he agreed. "I have come to see your grandmother, Elisabeth."

"She is upstairs with Joseph."

178

His face pulled together threateningly. "I do not want to see Desforges, only Madame Pugnant. Why did Jeanne run away?"

"She is upset." Lyn was dismissive. "Could you not have spoken to Lieutenant Duvernay first? Before you attacked him? If you had talked—"

"Talk? Talk!" He snorted. "I cannot talk to a scoundrel like that! His words have no meaning. I only wish that I had had longer with him before that goat of a sergeant stopped me. I am not certain that Duvernay understood me well enough." His fingers tightened convulsively.

"I will go and tell Grandmother that you are here," said Lyn quickly. She was afraid he was about to pull his hat to pieces.

Madame Pugnant and Joseph were both bent over the desk, a pile of ledgers strewn open between them. Joseph's face was flushed and Madame Pugnant's lips were so thin they were barely visible. It did not seem a propitious moment to announce Jean Bernard, and Lyn was very glad he'd stayed downstairs.

"What is it?" snapped Madame Pugnant in answer to her knock.

"There is someone to see you, Grandmother."

"So?" said Joseph. "If he is looking for money, go and tell him she cannot be disturbed. She is occupied. Go on."

"I do not think he will leave."

"Well, tell him he must!" Joseph's face got redder.

Madame Pugnant gave Lyn a sharp look, then said, "I will see what he wants, Joseph. In the meantime, you think about what I have said. We have been lucky to see any money at all from the fishermen this year. Others have not." She rose stiffly.

Joseph glowered over the books. "It cannot be that bad. You always think the worst."

"I do not think, Joseph. It is there, in the figures. Look at them yourself. See if you can find the money to pay Monsieur Delort."

"He will give me credit then," said Joseph. "If it were not for all the extra mouths we are forced to feed—"

"Jean Bernard pays for them. And if they were not here we would still be paying Marie-Marthe in the shop and there would be no one to help in the kitchen, so Marguerite would have no time for her needlework and you would have to find a boy for the bakery. Consider all of this."

Jean Bernard was standing in the hall, his stocky legs apart as if braced. Madame Pugnant stopped on the stairs so that she was slightly taller than he. "I thought it might be you, Jean," she remarked. "You are not welcome here, you know."

"I have never been welcome here. Not even when my wife was alive. Only when you need something from me, Madame."

"You have caused us much trouble."

"Tell me about Jeanne."

"She is here."

"This I know. I have seen her. That is not what I mean."

"She will stay here. All of them will stay. Jeanne will have to be content with less than I—and she—had hoped, but that cannot be helped. You did not act with finesse, Jean."

"A man like that cannot understand finesse, as you call it." His brows were a thick dark line. "Nor a man like me, Madame."

"That is certainly true," she agreed dryly.

"You should never have sent Jeanne to that house. I warned you."

"It is done. It does no good to discuss it now. She is safe and I will do the best I can for her, be sure of that. We must let people forget, is it not. And you—you will have lost work by all of this."

"There are many roofs to mend before winter. People do not mind who does the mending so long as the shingles are tight enough to keep out the rain. In the meantime, Martel has been working for us both. He is not so good as I, of course, but he does well enough."

"You might have been deported."

"I was lucky."

Madame Pugnant sniffed. "It was not luck, Monsieur."

"It was on account then, not done for love, I think. I did only what someone else should have done sooner, as you know."

She made no reply. After a moment, Jean Bernard gave an abrupt nod and left, closing the front door decisively behind him. Lyn started down the stairs, expecting Madame Pugnant to scold her for standing idle, but she put out a hand and stopped her. "Elisabeth, you would tell me if all were not well with Jeanne?"

Several possible replies jostled in Lyn's mouth; she held them in with an effort and nodded.

"Mmmp." Turning, Madame Pugnant slowly climbed the steps.

*   *   *

180

In fact, all was not well with Jeanne, and Lyn was annoyed with herself for not having guessed right away. She was not ignorant. Carol Sherman had finished her senior year with the rest of them, in spite of being six months' pregnant; several other girls Lyn had known only distantly had dropped out; one had gotten married when she was barely older than Jeanne. And that was just the senior class. Early on, Dorrie had made sure that Lyn had all the right information about birth control, proving how open-minded and practical she was; and at the same time, Lyn could see how keenly Dorrie didn't want her to have to use it.

She and Mike had long talks about sex. It was Mike who was so adamant about not being ready, not rushing things. He was cautious and conventional; he believed in saving himself for marriage which, Lyn had suddenly realized one evening in February in the middle of a loving embrace, meant for someone other than her. She thought it entirely likely that she would one day get married, but not to Mike. It made her a little sad, but only to think that they would outgrow one another, drift away, lose touch.

She never told Dorrie any of this. They had stopped discussing sex when Dorrie felt that Lyn was well-enough educated to make informed, sensible choices. That was several years ago.

But waking early in the morning, Lyn realized with a sinking feeling that it wasn't the usual footsteps that had roused her this time, it was the sound of someone retching into the chamber pot. Lyn lay perfectly still, wondering what would happen next, and thinking the whole thing was like a French-colonial soap opera. What did people do about unmarried mothers and illegitimate children in 1744? It would be a fascinating subject for a dissertation—she would tell Donald. She wondered if there was a footnoted report on it already in a leatherette binder in the park's library: "Pregnancy Out of Wedlock in Eighteenth-Century Louisbourg."

She waited to confront Jeanne until they were alone in the shop, then she waded straight in, wasting no time on tact. "Why have you told no one you are pregnant?"

Jeanne gave her a horrified, stricken look.

"You must know it yourself," Lyn went on relentlessly. "You told me only that Lieutenant Duvernay had propositioned you, not that he had gone further."

"I did not think—it was not—it was only twice." Jeanne whispered.

"Twice? *Once* can be enough!" Lyn heard Dorrie's voice echo weirdly in her head.

"But if Papa had known, Elisabeth, he would have killed him."

"Probably," Lyn agreed grimly. "It is just as well he did not, I suppose, but not for Lieutenant Duvernay's sake. You have said nothing to anyone?"

"No." Jeanne gazed at her hands which were clasped tightly in her lap. "You will not tell Grandmother, will you?"

"What good will it do not to tell? If you wait long enough everyone will be able to see. It is not something you can keep secret forever. You will only make it worse if you try."

"I had thought—I kept hoping that it might not be true, Elisabeth. Perhaps it is not. Perhaps it was the shock—"

"It is *not* shock. The best thing is to go to Grandmother at once."

"But what will she do?" wailed Jeanne. "I cannot bear to be sent away from here, too. She might send me to Papa. Oh, Elisabeth, I would rather *die!* Can I not get rid of it? There are ways—I know this. There is a woman—"

"No." Lyn was emphatic. "It is much too dangerous." The idea of arranging an abortion in this place was truly horrifying; she refused to think about it.

"Pardon," said Thomas, interrupting. He brought in a savory-smelling golden-brown pie. "It is for Madame Deshaies. She is sending a boy for it, Christophe says." He gave Jeanne an interested glance.

She sniffed. Her cheeks were wet, her eyelashes becomingly webbed with tears. When Lyn cried, her eyelids swelled and her face got blotchy.

"Well?" said Lyn to Thomas. "Is that all?"

"Yes, Mademoiselle." He withdrew.

"You must tell Grandmother today. This afternoon. It will do no good to put it off," she told Jeanne mercilessly.

"Could you not tell her, Elisabeth? She would not be so angry with you, I know." Jeanne gave another sniff.

"No, I could not. You must do it yourself when the shop is closed."

"But you will come with me?"

At the end of the day, when Lyn carried the cash and accounts upstairs for Madame Pugnant, she made Jeanne come with them. In her room Madame Pugnant listened to Jeanne's faltering confused story in silence, her lips pressed flat, her eyes on the desktop. Jeanne's voice ran down to a whisper, like a transistor radio left on too long. When she had done, the room was very still. "And when did this happen?" said the old woman at last.

"Grandmother, I do not remember when it was, I—"

"Think! It is important."

"It was—it was the end of August. Before the sisters sailed for Montreal. Believe me, Grandmother, I could do nothing—he insisted—"

"Be still! You are a very foolish girl, Jeanne Bernard. I am very deeply dismayed by this, although"—she glared at Jeanne—"I am not altogether surprised. I had hoped you had more sense. Now we must decide what is to be done."

"Please do not make me leave, Grandmother."

"Leave?" said the old woman irritably. "Where would you go?"

"I am afraid—I had thought—to Papa . . ."

"Ah, *mon dieu!* There is no place for you with him! I doubt that he would have you in this condition, not when it was I—no. I will think of something. But I cannot have you in the shop any longer. You will help Suzanne after today. And we will have to manage by ourselves again."

"What about Louise?" asked Lyn. "Could she not help me if Jeanne is to work in the kitchen?"

"Louise? She is only a child."

"She is clever. She will learn fast." Louise was bound to be more use in the shop than Jeanne, and it would give her a chance to learn a little.

"Mmmp. I will consider it. This is not at all what I had intended—for any of you. It will change everything. And I do not look forward to telling your father."

"Does Papa need to know?" ventured Jeanne.

"Do not be stupid! A baby is not something you can hide, you silly girl. We must act at once if we are to avoid a scandal. I will not be surprised at all to find that others know already."

"How could they?"

"They are clearly more experienced in such things than you."

183

The next day after breakfast, Jeanne stayed in the kitchen, and Louise, reluctant but obedient, was sent to the bakeshop with Lyn. Madame Pugnant offered no explanation for this and no one asked her for one. Louise spent the day dusting and sweeping, cleaning every crack and corner. She was quiet and unobtrusive and she watched everything intently.

In the middle of the morning there was a sudden explosion of angry voices from the bakery: Joseph's was loudest, although Lyn could not make out the words. It was Thomas shouting back at him, and underneath them both, she heard Christophe. Monsieur Verrier's cook, who happened to be in the shop at that moment, gave Lyn a startled look and cocked her head. Lyn could almost see her ears turning under her white coife, like satellite dishes. Madame Pugnant excused herself and hurried out, just as the argument moved into the hall.

"That is it!" they heard Thomas declare. "I will stay no longer! I have better things to do with my life than spend my days being abused in this manner! Find someone else to shout at, Joseph Desforges, I am off!"

"Then do not ever come back, do you hear? Do not set foot in my house again!"

"Thomas—" began Christophe.

"Do not worry, Monsieur! As soon as I have collected my belongings, you will not see me again. That is a promise!" There was the clatter of feet on the stairs.

Louise looked at Lyn wide-eyed. Monsieur Verrier's cook sidled toward the door, clutching her two white loaves to her bosom.

"Joseph, what is this?" said Madame Pugnant, her voice like ice.

"He is leaving, that is what. I have thrown him out! Good riddance, I say. I will not tolerate his insolence any longer. He is—"

But whatever Thomas was, they did not find out—the bakery door closed on it, and only moments later Thomas came thumping back down from the attic and went out, slamming the door behind him. Monsieur Verrier's cook gave Lyn a conspiratorial look. "What was *that* about, eh?" But Lyn only shook her head. "I do not know."

Officially, Thomas's work had been less than satisfactory for several months, and he was no loss to the bakery. Joseph made it

184

sound as if he had fired Thomas, but Michel said Thomas had been planning to leave for a long time, just waiting for the right moment. "He has signed on with Captain Amiot and will sail for France before the end of the month."

"I never trusted that one," declared Suzanne. "I daresay he will be sorry, when he is in the middle of the ocean, tossing around."

"I doubt it," Michel said. "It is a life of adventure."

"Who is Captain Amiot?" asked Lyn.

"He is a trader from Marseilles."

Although Lyn had had very little to do with Thomas, she noticed that his departure made the house much quieter. Christophe's long face was gloomier, presumably because there were fewer hands to work, and there was no mention of finding anyone to take Thomas's place. It was money, of course. Everyone in Louisbourg seemed to be concerned about money. Just around the corner, in the rue de l'Estang, Monsieur Morand was losing his shop. Young and ambitious, he had managed to build himself a respectable dry-goods business in only three years, but he had overextended himself at the beginning of the summer, buying more than he could pay for, and his creditors had decided he was a bad risk. His shop had closed, and his stock was to be auctioned in a few weeks. He himself had decided to go on to Quebec and start again. Nor was he the only one in trouble.

⇨⇨ 14 ⇦⇦

"ELISABETH, PUT ON YOUR CLOAK. WE ARE GOING OUT." Madame Pugnant stood in the bakeshop doorway, dressed in her good clothes.

"Out?" Lyn was astonished. Never before had Madame Pugnant taken her anywhere in town alone. "But the shop—"

"Marguerite will look after it, with Louise. We shall not be long, and Joseph is close by. Hurry—I do not wish to be late."

As they set out, Lyn asked, "Where are we going?"

"You do not need to know. Do not waste breath."

Ragged webs of fog blew across the harbor, heavy with moisture. The streets were wet and muddy and scattered with puddles, and the houses were closed against the chill. The few people abroad that

185

Friday afternoon moved purposefully through the town, intent on their business and disinclined to loiter in the raw gray air. Woodsmoke hung low over the roofs, thickening the afternoon dusk.

It was midautumn. By this time her mother must have gone back to Belmont. College had started without Lyn—all the other freshmen would be learning their way around the campus and the town, making friends, writing papers, getting used to dorm life. When she arrived she would be the only stranger. . . . Shivering, Lyn pulled the cloak tighter.

"It will soon be winter," observed Madame Pugnant. "Another winter. The harbor will be empty."

"The town will be strange without the sailors." Lyn shut off thoughts of home like a faucet.

"It will be peaceful again. That is what I want. I do not want this war. I want life to be settled. At my age I should not have to worry about such things at all. It is too hard." Madame Pugnant sounded fretful. "Nicolas should not have left me alone."

They walked up the rue St. Louis to the Place Royale and turned left. Abruptly Madame Pugnant said, "We are going to see Père Athanase. And your father."

"Jean Bernard? But why?" Lyn asked, startled.

"Why do you think?"

"I do not—is it about Jeanne? Does he know about Jeanne?"

"He is about to learn."

"Now?"

"It could serve no purpose to tell him until I had made arrangements for her, but now it is best that he know so he will make no trouble later. He will be angry, but I will not allow him to ruin what I have planned. All he must do is give his consent." She was talking more to herself than to Lyn, but Lyn could not help asking, "Consent to what, Grandmother?"

"You ask too many questions. I did not bring you to ask questions. Keep your ears open and you will learn."

Then why did you bring me, Lyn wanted to ask. She could feel Madame Pugnant drawn tight as a bowstring beside her. The answer was simple: she had brought Elisabeth with her to help defuse Jean Bernard's explosive temper. It would be easier to deal with him if there were other people present.

The Récollet friars were housed in an unpretentious pole-

and-plaster building next to the weedy, open piece of land set aside for the Louisbourg parish church. At the door, Madame Pugnant said, "Elisabeth, I wish to speak alone to the curé. Your father will come soon. You wait here for him."

The clock on the citadel chimed the quarter hour, sounding muffled and dull in the heavy, damp air. Quarter to four. Resigned, Lyn stood under the eaves, watching the fog condense on the roof and drip past her nose, wondering if Jean Bernard had any suspicion of why he'd been summoned here to meet his mother-in-law. Wondering, too, why Madame Pugnant had chosen the friars' house—in hope of avoiding a scene, perhaps? Believing that Père Athanase would be able to prevent Jean Bernard from storming off again after Lieutenant Duvernay when he heard the news? Lyn was doubtful. Jean Bernard never went to Mass, so why would he listen to the curé? He hadn't listened to Mathieu. . . .

Down the street two men appeared, growing out of the gloom: one short and square, the other tall and angular. Even thinking of Mathieu, it hadn't occurred to Lyn that he would come too. He and she were like seconds for a duel, she thought wryly.

"You?" Jean Bernard's eyebrows were like dark thatch above his eyes. "Your grandmother is inside already? She is conspiring against me with that priest, is it not. What does she want?"

"I cannot tell you," said Lyn. "She has not discussed anything with me. But I think she expects you alone." She had glanced at Mathieu and found him watching her.

"I do not care what that woman expects. This can only be trouble—she only sees me when there is trouble. Aha! In your face I can see that I am right, Elisabeth. Well, then let us get on with it. I have roofs to mend." He thumped on the door with his fist and went in without waiting for an answer. Mathieu stood aside for Lyn, his face quizzical. She didn't know why she was so glad he'd come—he had not been very effective the last time.

"How is your tooth, Monsieur?"

"It will never trouble me again, Mademoiselle," he replied.

They entered a room that was small and plain and sparsely furnished. Several benches were pushed against the walls. A large crucifix hung over one, and over another was a large, dark painting of a man with a hooded, shadowy face, standing in a wilderness of rock against a stormy sky. A saint, no doubt. Madame Pugnant sat

187

squarely beneath him, her hands knotted on the head of her cane, and beside her stood the curé. Lyn had only seen him from a distance, at the front of the chapel; she had no real sense of what he was like, just one among the brown-robed figures. He had the tough, weathered look of someone who had spent his life meeting trouble head-on instead of ducking it. His nose appeared to have been broken in the past, and there were deep lines on either side of his mouth. He looked at each of them as they came in, and Lyn, meeting his eyes, was surprised by their intensity.

"Good afternoon, Jean Bernard," he said. "I do not see much of you these days."

"You are punctual. That is good," said Madame Pugnant. "Père Athanase and I have finished our discussion and it is best that we get this settled quickly."

Jean Bernard grunted, eyeing the two of them with suspicion, ready to be provoked.

"This is a family matter," she went on. "It does not concern other people."

There was an uncomfortable silence, then Mathieu suggested, "I should perhaps wait outside for you, Jean?"

"You will stay where you are," Jean Bernard declared. "I need you to protect me from this holy father. Whatever you have to say, Madame, can be said now."

"Very well. It is your choice." Clearly she disapproved of it. "It concerns your daughter."

"Elisabeth?" He turned to Lyn in surprise. "What has Elisabeth done? *Sacredie,* woman, can you not—"

"No, not Elisabeth," she cut in, holding up a twisted hand for silence. "You do not need to curse, Jean, only to listen and then to agree. It is Jeanne I am talking about, and I have made the best that I can from a sorry situation."

"What did I say? Trouble!" Jean Bernard said to Mathieu. Mathieu said nothing.

"I shall not waste time with explanations. Jeanne is pregnant."

"She is *what*?" Anger broke over his face like a great wave. "You told me—you *assured* me that she was untouched! That nothing had happened! It is that bastard Duvernay! I will kill him— with my hands, I will kill him!" He was bunched together, ready to explode. Mathieu shifted apprehensively on the balls of his feet—whether to leap out of range or to restrain his friend, Lyn wasn't sure.

"Peace, Monsieur!" commanded the curé. "Violence is no answer. It can change nothing for your daughter, except that she will once again have a father who is in prison. And this time, no amount of persuasion will release him."

"But is it Duvernay?"

"It does not matter who is the father," said Madame Pugnant crisply.

"Does not matter? You would let him get away with this? None of it would have happened if you had not meddled with my family, Madame! If you had left us alone! You are so certain that everything you do is right. Pah! You are willing to trust your own granddaughter to a scoundrel like Duvernay for the sake of your son-in-law's connections. Desforges *has* no connections. He is deceiving himself if he thinks he does. This is your fault, Madame, and still you do nothing."

"Monsieur," said Père Athanase warningly.

"Let him shout," Madame Pugnant said. "Then, when he is out of breath, we can get to our business. He knows the foolishness of what he says."

"Do not deceive yourself, Madame. I know why you took my children in—it is because of Pierre. You have no sons of your own, no other grandsons, so you have taken mine. I should never have agreed."

"But you did. You could not look after them when Françoise died. Look at you. You do not attend Mass, you drink too much, you do not always go home at night, you have a wild temper. At least while Françoise was alive you behaved better."

"Do not speak to me about Françoise," he said in a low, dangerous voice.

They glared at each other, and Madame Pugnant was first to look away. "Very well," she said stiffly. "I am sorry this had to happen, Jean, I did not want it. Jeanne is very young and foolish—I overestimated her good sense. That no longer matters. Now we must decide what is to be done, and instead of acting like a savage, it would be well if you listened to me."

Jean Bernard stood still, his chest heaving like a bellows, his hands clenched at his sides. Mathieu, ignored by everyone but Lyn, never took his eyes from him.

"Good," said Madame Pugnant. "At Mass Sunday Père Athanase will announce the marriage of Jeanne Bernard and Christophe Rigault. They will marry before Advent. The curé has agreed it is best."

Christophe Rigault, thought Lyn, who on earth—? And then, Christophe! She means *our* Christophe—she must.

"Rigault!" exclaimed Jean Bernard.

Madame Pugnant gave a decisive nod. "I have thought much about this. Christophe works hard. He is steady. He has a good trade and good prospects. In two more years he will be a master baker. Jeanne could do far worse."

"What about Christophe?" said Lyn. "Has *he* agreed?"

"We would not be here if he had not. He would be foolish to refuse and he knows this. He is marrying into a respectable family and a prospering business."

"But Jeanne—she is so *young*—"

"She is old enough to have a child, Elisabeth. Christophe is thirty-one, so there is no problem with consent. And Jean Bernard will give his consent, I am certain."

"I do not like it," he growled.

"I did not expect you to like it. But what have you to offer instead, eh? Nothing, except to kill Lieutenant Duvernay." She snorted. "There is no need for you to like it, only to agree."

"She is fourteen."

"Jeanne will be sixteen in January," she snapped.

"Have you told her? What does she say?"

"She will do as she is told. She is in no position to object. They will live with us. There is a room upstairs that is empty. Jeanne has much to learn before she is ready to keep her own house, but"—she glared around—"she will learn it."

The curé, who had said very little thus far, expressed his opinion that the marriage was a good one, that Christophe was an honest, decent man and he would treat Jeanne well and provide for her. "I suggest you do not argue further, Jean," he said.

"I suppose I must be grateful that he is not a man like Desforges," grumbled Jean Bernard, giving in.

"I will not ask what you mean by that," said Madame Pugnant.

"I think you do not need to ask," he replied.

Lyn felt overwhelmed. She kept thinking of Christophe and Marguerite, and wondering how much of this Marguerite knew. How could Christophe allow himself to be railroaded into a marriage with a silly, frivolous girl—a girl half his age, who was carrying another man's child? He could not possibly *love* Jeanne. Nor she him, for that matter. She had her heart set on marrying an officer and living in style like Madame Duvernay, not over her husband's bakery!

Why did she have to marry at all? She had a family to look after her—why was it essential that she have a husband? Dorrie had managed perfectly well on her own for seventeen years. She had made a choice: better to struggle a bit than to tie herself to someone who didn't want the relationship.

It wasn't until Lyn and Madame Pugnant were halfway home that Lyn remembered what Louise had told her. *Elisabeth* had been intended for Christophe, not Jeanne. In a roundabout way, she supposed she ought to feel grateful to Jeanne for spoiling her grandmother's plans, eliminating a complication Lyn hadn't wanted to face. But in fact what she felt was an angry, inarticulate sadness.

At the bottom of the rue St. Louis, Madame Pugnant stumbled on a loose cobble and gasped. A spasm of pain twisted her face, and she dropped her cane, clutching convulsively for Lyn, who reached out to steady her. "Grandmother?"

"I—am—all right," said the old woman between her teeth. "Stand still." Slowly she recovered herself. "These streets are not safe," she complained querulously. "They do not care, these men. It is all falling to pieces, and they do nothing. What will become of us, I wonder? What is it all for?" Her voice was thin and discouraged. The afternoon had taken all her stamina, she was exhausted. "If only he were not so—so—if he were calmer. If he did not *shout*. I wish—" She broke off.

"What do you wish?" Lyn asked gently.

But the crack closed over as suddenly as it had opened. "Wishing is useless, Elisabeth. It only brings dissatisfaction. It is what we have that we must deal with. That is Jeanne's greatest shortcoming—she does not understand. Joseph's also. They wish too much. Pick up my cane—we have been gone too long."

* * *

191

At Mass on Sunday, Père Athanase read the first banns for Jeanne and Christophe. It was another gray, lowering morning, punctuated with sudden sharp showers of cold rain that sent people hurrying home from the chapel. A few stopped outside the gate to offer their congratulations and look with kindling speculation at Jeanne, who did not seem in the least embarrassed by their attention. In fact she basked in it. Christophe was less comfortable, although he made an effort to be sociable. He was not accustomed to being noticed. Watching them together, Lyn couldn't help thinking they were remarkably ill-suited. Thomas would have made a better match; he was younger and livelier, good-looking under the flour. But Thomas had gone, cleared out. Once or twice Lyn had caught sight of him on the quay, though he never seemed to see her. It was as if he were already miles away from Louisbourg. Marguerite, on Joseph's arm, looked pale and unhappy, but she had looked pale and unhappy for weeks. The banns did not seem to be a surprise to her.

"Of course," Jeanne said to Lyn and Louise in their room that night, "it is not at all as I had imagined. A baker is not what I expected." She sighed. "Christophe is the smallest bit dull, I think."

"You are lucky that he will marry you," declared Louise. "He is better than you deserve."

"Do not speak to me that way—you know nothing about it, Louise. I wish I did not have to stay here. I do not want to be like Aunt Marguerite and live in someone else's house all my life. I will encourage Christophe to find us another place."

Poor Christophe, thought Lyn. He would need all his patience.

Louise had taken the news of her sister's marriage calmly when Lyn told her. "She is going to have a baby, is it not," she said matter-of-factly.

"How did you know?" Lyn was curious.

"She is like Maman. Each time before Maman would have a baby she was ill in the same way."

Lyn was amazed at the way in which everyone accepted the situation, even Christophe himself. When she caught him alone in the hall and asked him outright if it was what he wanted, he answered with surprise that it was a good marriage for him. "You need not worry, Mademoiselle," he said, misinterpreting her concern, "I will take good care of your sister, that I promise. And she will give me a child."

"Someone else's child!"

He shook his head slowly. "No. When we are married it will be my child."

She couldn't explain to Christophe why she was upset, not so that he could understand. She doubted very much that he could make Jeanne happy, although she knew he would try, but it wasn't Jeanne she was afraid for. Madame Pugnant was right about her: she wished too much. Like Joseph. Like Dorrie.

Suddenly Lyn remembered Dorrie sitting at the chipped yellow kitchen table with two piles of bills and the checkbook in front of her, saying in a tense voice, "We can't buy you sneakers this month if we pay the phone bill," and the heavy feeling that grew inside her, not because of the unattainable sneakers, but because Dorrie was so grim about them. Dorrie was always having to prove things: that they could have the telephone *and* new sneakers, and if the postponement of the sneakers was not exactly evidence of failure, it was at least an indication of the limits of her success.

Lyn was like Madame Pugnant. She chose not to wish. Instead she looked at what there was and determined to make the best use of it. Her mother's bouts of depression seemed so pointless, but Lyn had always rather envied Dorrie her sudden explosions of euphoria, when she was charged with energy and joy. When she had sold her first photographs, for instance, she had blown all the money and more on dinner for the two of them at Locke Ober, and Lyn, even while she was horrified at the extravagance, had loved every minute, infected by Dorrie's excitement. It had begun to occur to her then that perhaps you didn't have the euphoria without the despair, although she hadn't wanted to think so.

"You will see," Christophe told her gravely, "it is God's will."

But it wasn't; it was Madame Pugnant's will. If only a year or so ago God and Madame Pugnant had willed that Marguerite marry Christophe instead of Joseph . . .

Whatever Madame Pugnant was thinking, it was obvious she felt the strain of these events. She moved stiffly and with economy, as if always in pain, her mouth tight. Somewhat to her dismay, Lyn found she was worried about the old woman, but Madame Pugnant

193

was not a person to welcome concern; she did not wish to acknowledge that she needed it, so Lyn left her alone.

One morning, as she set off to deliver orders, she found Blaize sitting on the doorstep. Michel had been sent off somewhere by Joseph and had left him behind, so Lyn offered him her hand and he took it with an audible sigh of gratitude. She tried very hard not to think of what kind of future lay ahead of Blaize. There was nothing wrong with his mind, she was sure. It lay bright and alert behind his eyes, absorbing all that went on around him, making connections, working things out. Firmly she reminded herself, he is Elisabeth's brother, not mine. I can't let myself feel responsible for him—I won't *be* here. There is nothing I can do.

The rain of the day before had blown out to sea, driven by a boisterous fresh wind, leaving behind a vast sweep of blue sky. The harbor danced and gleamed and the masts filling it swayed like a field of wheat. Underneath the ubiquitous odor of fish came the damp, sharp scent of evergreens: spruces and pines far inland, beyond the reach of the firewood parties that had decimated the woods surrounding the harbor. Lyn sucked in great lungfuls of air, relieved to untangle herself temporarily from the emotional snarls of the household.

Anne, one of the Widow Grandchamp's servants next door, was sweeping out the tavern, sending little explosions of dirt through the open door. "Good morning, Elisabeth," she called. She was a pleasant, sloppy-looking young woman with a good-humored grin. "It is a fine morning, no?"

"Yes," agreed Lyn.

"So, your sister is to marry Christophe Rigault, is it! Suzanne says that they will have a late wedding present—in six or seven months. Ah *bien*!" She winked. "I did not think it of Christophe. He is a dark horse, that one. I could not get him to look at me."

Lyn gave a creditable imitation of Michel's off-hand shrug. "And has Suzanne told you whether it will be a boy or a girl?"

"But how?"

"Suzanne knows everything, is it not?"

Anne laughed. "Indeed! So she says."

Lyn walked on, gently swinging Blaize's hand and wondering whether anyone in Louisbourg had what could be termed a private life. At least Anne did not seem to be aware of Lieutenant Duvernay's role in the wedding, not yet at any rate. She made her deliveries, feeling no sense of urgency. In the bottom of the basket was a small parcel wrapped in an old bread cloth which she would leave for Donald, tucking it into the space between two supports in their shed.

Monsieur Verrier's kitchen was full of savory smells and bustle. There was an impressive array of pots on the hearth, and a turkey on a spit, turning slowly by means of an elaborate system of ratchets and pulleys. The engineer was having a dinner party that evening and his cook, Marie Brulé, had ordered white rolls for it. She was up to her elbows in a huge bowl of pale, sticky dough, her hair curling damply around her pink face, directing a sulky-looking girl who tended the pots.

"Ah, you have come with the rolls," she greeted Lyn. "Etienne, clear a space on the table there. Yes, that is good. No, not that cloth—it must be *clean,* you donkey! Now cover them. *Bien.*"

Lyn recognized the man who took the rolls from her, just as she recognized Marie Brulé—she had seen them often in the last few months. But they had also been among the very first people she had seen at the beginning, when she had burst into this kitchen expecting to find the people she knew from her own time. She never entered it without remembering, without feeling the hairs stir on the back of her neck. The cook was too busy to stop and gossip, but she offered Blaize a piece of candied orange peel which he accepted with a shy smile, and Lyn thanked her.

Outside again, she saw that Monsieur Verrier's garden was brown. The vegetables had been harvested against frost, and the beds were forlorn and empty. There were no sparrows taking dust baths, no swallows speckling the sky, no doves cooing from the rooftrees. Summer was gone and the wind had changed . . . and she was still here. She had never dreamed she would still be here.

Blaize tugged at her hand and she blinked. He opened his fist, and grinned, and there in it, rather gummy from the heat, was a second piece of orange peel which he was offering to her. "She only gave you one," said Lyn. He shrugged and she grinned back at him, taking the sticky little gift. Small as it was, it raised her spirits.

She had reason to be glad when they reached the shed; Donald was there, waiting for her, pacing back and forth in the cramped space. "I can't keep still," he told her. "Where have you been? Why is he here? Why did you bring him?"

"Because I wanted to," said Lyn. "This is Blaize—he's one of Elisabeth's brothers—"

"But we can't talk, not with him here."

"In the first place, he doesn't understand English, Donald. And in the second, he's very good at keeping secrets. You can keep a secret, Blaize, is it not?" she asked him in French, and the little boy nodded vigorously. "*Bien*. This is Gerard Grossin, he is a special friend." Blaize looked hard at Donald.

Donald sighed. "But why bring him at *all,* Lyn? What is he to you? Never mind. Have you thought any more about leaving?"

Reluctantly she nodded. "A little."

"You still don't want to try it, do you? Look, I *know* it's a chance—of course it is. The thing is, time's running out. It's almost *November*. If we're going to go, we've got to do it before winter sets in, otherwise we really don't have a chance. It's almost too late now." He rubbed his hands together nervously. "You still haven't thought of anything, have you? Think, Lyn—just imagine it— *home!*"

For a moment Louisbourg disappeared, and Donald's eager, feverish face was replaced by Dorrie's. Lyn could see the perplexed little V between her neat dark eyebrows; she was saying something Lyn couldn't quite hear. Lyn wanted home so much in that instant she could hardly breathe. That was why Donald was always desperate and miserable: He lived constantly in his thoughts of home. For the most part, she pushed hers to the back of her mind and got on with Elisabeth's life.

"Well? Will you? Will you go with me?"

"What if I say no," asked Lyn cautiously. "What would you do then?"

He shook his head. "I don't know."

"You wouldn't go by yourself, would you? Not alone, Donald. Promise me you wouldn't."

For a long time he didn't answer; he stood staring at the floor, motionless for a change. Then he raised his head and looked straight at her. "I'll give you to mid-November," he said slowly. "You have to decide by then, or think of something better. I can't face the winter here, it's that simple. Anything's preferable. The barracks

196

are a nightmare now—in January—'' He shook his head. "I'd rather die all at once than bit by bit up there.''

"But you won't do anything drastic—not without telling me?'' She couldn't see his face, he had turned away from her, and he took his time before answering. At last he said, "No. Not without telling you.''·

She was relieved. "I've brought you some bread and cheese and an apple. Here—I've got to get back to the shop—''

"You *always* have to get back!'' He sounded angry. "Sometimes I think it's just an excuse to get away from me.''

"Stop feeling sorry for yourself,'' she said briskly.

With a sudden flash of humor, he replied, "It's a dirty job, but someone has to do it. You're much better at this than I am, Lyn.''

"Flattery will get you nowhere.'' But it did; it disarmed her and made her feel guilty by reminding her how much she owed to luck. She honestly didn't know whether she could do any better than Donald if she were stuck as an ordinary soldier. "I really do have to get back,'' she said.

He followed her to the door. "Let me walk with you—just part way. It won't hurt anything.''

She opened her mouth to argue, then gave in, although she knew it was unwise. "Just to the quay then.'' It shouldn't matter—they were doing nothing wrong, just walking together.

On the rue d'Orleans, in the shadow of the hospital wall, Donald told her about his favorite bookstore in Montreal. "I don't think I've ever been without something to read for so long in my entire life. I'm afraid I'll forget how. I'm sure Grossin is illiterate. What about Elisabeth?''

"I don't know. But her mother could read and write—perhaps she taught Elisabeth. People don't expect her to be very clever. When we get back, Donald, what's the best thing for me to read about Louisbourg?'' She was happy to distract him.

"I would think you'd have had enough of Louisbourg by this time!'' he said with a wry face. "The standard work is McLennan's history—it was out of print for a while, but there's a reprint for sale now. McLennan's the one who agitated to save the place—his stuff's a bit dated but still sound. There's a new book called *Louisbourg Portraits* by Christopher Moore that's quite fascinating. Or I'll tell you what.'' He grinned suddenly. "Wait a few years and you can read the definitive work on life in Louisbourg by Donald H. Stewart.''

Lyn grinned back. "Sounds good to me. I'll wait."

"Elisabeth? Elisabeth!"

She started and turned her head, her fingers tightening on Blaize's hand.

"Who is this man?" demanded Mathieu, standing in their path, his face sharp with suspicion. "He is bothering you?"

Oh, *merde!* thought Lyn, her heart sinking. Some people got away with things, other people didn't. "No, he is not. We have been talking, Monsieur."

Donald had stopped dead in his tracks and was eyeing Mathieu with apprehension.

"About what?"

"That does not concern you," she said, and Mathieu's eyes narrowed. "It is nothing—he is a customer at the bake shop," she added, trying to mollify him.

He looked from Donald to Lyn and back. "It would be better if I accompanied you home, perhaps."

"There is no need to inconvenience yourself. Thank you," said Lyn firmly. "Monsieur Grossin will see me home. And I have Blaize to keep me safe."

"Umm—" Donald sounded uncertain. "It is not—I mean, I ought—"

Mathieu folded his arms; he was not about to leave them together.

"This has nothing to do with you." Lyn glared at him, wishing Donald would stand up for himself, but he seemed to shrink beside her.

"It is time I got back," said Donald apologetically. "I do not want to cause trouble—"

Hot bright anger flared in Lyn's head. "Trouble? It is not you who cause the trouble!"

Mathieu said calmly, "I am certain that your father would not be pleased with the company you keep, Mademoiselle."

"Then let him tell me that!"

"Is that really what you want, Mademoiselle?" There was a glint in Mathieu's eye.

"Well," said Donald, "good-bye. I must go."

"An excellent idea." Mathieu nodded.

Lyn stifled an urge to knock their heads together. "Tomorrow then, Gerard," she said pointedly. "I will see you."

"I would not count on that. Come with me, Mademoiselle. I will take you as far as the quay. It is not safe for you to be out on your own, that is clear." Mathieu sounded so sure of himself. Donald opened his mouth, then shut it. He glanced miserably at Lyn, then hurried awkwardly up the street, as if his feet hurt.

→»» 15 «««

NOT SURE WITH WHOM SHE WAS MORE FURIOUS, LYN TURNED ON Mathieu. "You had no right to speak that way! Why did you do it?"

"I told you, he is bad company for you to be seen with. Your father would be very angry if he heard of it. You know his temper. And he would be right—that kind of man is after one thing only."

"And what is that Monsieur?"

"If you do not know, ask Lieutenant Duvernay," replied Mathieu with the glimmer of a smile.

"How can you say that? You know nothing about him. He is a friend of mine."

"You do not choose your friends with care then. Such men are all alike."

"But of course *you* are different."

"Of course." The smile caught hold briefly. "Even if I were not, I am not so foolish as to risk your father's anger."

"Good," said Lyn. "Then you will leave me alone. I can take care of myself."

"I am glad to hear it. I will sleep much better now that you have told me. All the same, this time I will walk with you."

"You will not! Why should I trust you any more than you think I should trust a soldier? I do not believe your reputation is above suspicion, Monsieur."

He studied her for a minute with an odd expression, then gave a shrug. "Very well then, go."

She hesitated. "You will not—mention this to anyone?" In spite of herself, she made it a question.

"Ah," he said. "You wish to buy my silence, is it not."

"I have nothing to buy it with," she said, hating him.

"You can buy it with a promise. Promise that you will not see the soldier again."

"You—why do you *care* who I see? I am nothing to do with you!"

"Your father is my friend, Mademoiselle. I owe him much."

Helpless with frustration, she cried, "You do not understand!"

"No," he agreed.

"I cannot explain."

"Why not? If you have done nothing wrong. . . ."

"Because you would not believe me, that is why not."

"You are very mysterious, Mademoiselle." He was mocking.

Without warning, she was flooded with an intense desire that he *should* understand. A chasm yawned at her feet; it was a very long way across it to where he stood looking at her, his eyes skeptical. She didn't think anyone could leap that far. She bit her lip.

"Alas, I cannot stand on the rue d'Orleans all day with you, Mademoiselle. I have business out beyond the faubourg."

"I will not keep you," she said, her throat tight with disappointment. "Now that you have rescued my reputation."

"I do not believe that you are entirely grateful."

"And I did not believe that you were that perceptive," she retorted.

"Why did you say that I would not understand?" he asked unexpectedly. "You have not tried to explain."

She swallowed hard. "It is because—"

A stocky, brown-robed figure rounded the corner and strode purposefully toward them. Père Athanase. "Damn, damn, damn," she swore under her breath.

"Because?"

"I cannot—never *mind*!" She grabbed Blaize's hand and pushed past Mathieu. "Good morning, Mademoiselle Bernard," said the curé. She gave him a stiff little nod and hurried on before he could read anything in her face.

Mathieu caught her arm. "Wait. Where are you going?"

"Home—just as you told me!" She was wound so tight she was trembling.

He took a deep breath, looked down the street after the curé, his eyes distant as if he were debating something with himself, then let it out in a sigh. "Come with me."

"Did you not hear—?"

Impatiently he cut her off. "I am going to see a man about a boat, Mademoiselle. We must walk there, but perhaps I can borrow a boat to bring us back."

Lyn stared at him.

"Yes, fool that I am. And on the way you can explain yourself to me."

Something warm and reckless burst inside her. "Blaize, too?"

"Are you good at walking?" Mathieu asked the little boy and Blaize nodded shyly. "And Blaize, too, God help me." Blaize smiled his rare, transforming smile, his fingers secure in Lyn's. "I was right," said Mathieu as they set off, "you have no sense at all, Mademoiselle. If you had, you would have refused me. Jean tells me that his daughter Elisabeth is very sensible. 'At least *Elisabeth* has sense,' he says to me. I begin to wonder how well he knows her."

She gave him a sideways look. "And how well do you know Jean Bernard? Would he be happier to see me with you than with a soldier?"

"I doubt it."

For the second time Lyn passed beneath the original Dauphin Gate, out of the town walls, leaving behind the bored-looking sentries. She suffered a momentary qualm. "Will we be gone long?"

"Long enough. It is very likely that you will be missed," he replied equably. "But it is too late to go back, if that is what you are thinking. You have made your choice. Resign yourself to the consequences."

If they were found out, there would be the devil to pay. But the day was beautiful, and so was the feeling that she was doing what Lyn Paget wanted to do instead of what Elisabeth Bernard was supposed to do.

With the fishing season over, the faubourg was much busier. Above the high tide line, the shore was littered with upturned boats, bleaching in the weather like half clamshells. Men were working on them: scraping and tarring, replacing planks. Others sorted through great drifts of blackened net, mending holes, untangling snarls and spreading it to dry. Most of the fish flakes were empty, but here and there one was still covered with stiff gray triangles—a late catch. A number of men nodded and spoke to Mathieu. All the women they passed looked at Lyn.

"Mathieu, do you know Agathe Grimard?" asked Lyn, seeing the des Roches' tavern.

"Grimard? He is a fisherman for des Roches, is it not? I do not know the wife. Why is it you ask?"

"I only wondered—if you had seen her lately."

He shook his head. "I cannot say. But how do *you* know her?"

"She is—an acquaintance of Michel's," said Lyn vaguely.

The road ran through the faubourg, rutted with wheel tracks and well-traveled, following the edge of the harbor. It crossed the streams that wandered out of the boggy interior on rough plank bridges. Above it on the left, the land rose dun-colored and lumpy, like oatmeal, patched here and there with dark green where stunted little evergreens were struggling to hold on, warped and twisted by the prevailing winds. They hadn't a chance; as soon as they were big enough for firewood they'd be chopped off and hauled away. The stumps of their predecessors gave the land a raw, ill-used look. Between the road and the water, the shore was strewn with fishing properties, their landing stages so skeletal and frail they looked as if they'd never survive the next high tide, let alone a winter of storms. Here and there Lyn saw a cow tethered on a threadbare patch of turf, and around each cottage scraggly, tough-looking chickens dithered about in their half-witted fashion. Down at the water's edge, children collected things from the tide wrack in sacks, and a woman spread wet grayish sheets on the scrubby bushes to dry.

"Do they live out here all winter?" asked Lyn, watching her.

"But of course." Mathieu sounded surprised. "Where else?"

She wondered how it felt, in the middle of frozen January, to be stranded on the edge of the harbor, squeezed between the empty hills and the bitter sea. But if it was all you knew . . .

"Where does this road go?"

Mathieu's eyebrows quirked. "To the Royal Battery, there"—he pointed to the gray shape looming ahead—"then around to the careening cove, and to the lighthouse."

"Nowhere else? Are there no other roads?"

His frown deepened. "There is one leading to the Mira River—to the farms. Another north to Lorembec, but it is easier to go by boat. Why are you asking me?"

202

She felt him watching her. Pretending she had dust in her throat, she coughed self-consciously as an oxcart lumbered past, loaded with seaweed. It was overtaken by a detachment of soldiers, marching unevenly toward the town. "I only wondered," she said at last.

"You should know these things better than I. You have lived here all your life, is it not."

Her heart began to thump.

"I think it is time for you to explain a little. You told me that I would not believe you. Why?"

"Because," she said, nerving herself, "because you believe that I am Elisabeth Bernard and I am not."

His eyes narrowed. "Then who are you, Mademoiselle?"

It was like the moment of opening an exam: No matter how well-prepared she knew she was, her first reaction was shock. It was gone within the space of a breath as she wrote her name carefully on the paper, but there was always that instant of paralysis. For the last hour she had known this was coming, but she hadn't known exactly when, or how it would happen. She pulled herself together, aware that Blaize was watching her closely. "My name is Carolyn Paget. I do not belong here, I do not know how I came here, and I do not know how to get home." She spoke slowly and deliberately, as if that would make him understand what she was saying. There was a long silence; she could not tell what he was thinking.

"Paget," he said finally, giving it the French pronunciation.

"Paget," she corrected him firmly, sounding the *t*.

"Then where is Elisabeth Bernard?"

"I do not know that either. I have never seen her. When I came she was gone."

Mathieu's stare shifted to Blaize. "He is not your brother?"

"No. I have no brothers."

"And Jean Bernard—he is not your father?"

"No." She hoped he wasn't going to go through the entire family.

Deep in thought, he watched a raven row steadily north on black ragged wings just above the crest of the land, turning his head to follow it until it disappeared over the hills. Then he said, "Forgive me, Mademoiselle, but we must hurry. I have work to be done once I have seen Lepine. Blaize, are you tired?"

His eyes troubled, the little boy looked hard at Lyn before he shook his head.

"Good." Mathieu set off again, his stride long and easy.

"Mathieu—" But he didn't stop or turn; he expected them to follow. It was as if she had said nothing. She looked after him incredulously; he was going to ignore the whole thing—not even try to understand. She had known it would be difficult for him, perhaps even impossible, but she had expected him to make an attempt. Instead he just kept walking. Blinded with disappointment, feeling raw and exposed, she started after him, searching her brain for something that would stop him. But he stopped of his own accord, without warning, and she ran into him.

Angrily he swung on her. "You make this up—you think I am a fool! Everyone calls you Elisabeth. Jean Bernard says to me, 'My daughter, Elisabeth—' and it is of you he speaks. No one says, who is this person? She does not belong with us. No. It is not possible! You are mad."

She gulped for words, but he was off again, not waiting for her to speak. The next time he halted she was ready and caught herself several paces back. "How can you expect me to believe this? Eh? Such a thing—it cannot happen! Do you think I have no brain? You tell me this to pay me back. You are angry because of the soldier, that is it."

"No."

"You!" He glared at Blaize, who tightened his grip on Lyn's hand. "*You* must know. Who is she? Is she Elisabeth—your sister? Is she?"

"He cannot speak!" said Lyn between her teeth. "You know that."

"But he hears, does he not?" Mathieu was equally furious. "Michel says that he understands what people say. He is not stupid. So—he can nod his head." He took a step toward them. "Well? Is this your sister?"

Blaize looked up at Lyn with round, fearful eyes. "It is all right," she told him fiercely. "He is not angry with you. He will not hurt you."

"Hurt? What is this—hurt? What do you think? That I would hit him?" Mathieu's voice rose. He gave off anger like coals throwing heat.

"You want to hit *me*," Lyn retorted.

He flexed his fingers involuntarily and dropped his hands to his sides. "I will take you back to Louisbourg," he growled. "It was a mistake, this. I will see Lepine another day."

"Go and see him now! We can find our own way back. If this is how you behave, I do not want your company."

"I do not care what you want. I brought you this far—I will see that you get home. I do not *hit* people—not children or women." She had offended him. "It is pointless to stand all day in the middle of the road." He grunted. "We will finish the errand and *then* I will take you back and be done with you. I do not care if you see *fifty* soldiers—the entire garrison!"

The glory had gone from the day. What had seemed adventurous when they started out, now seemed merely stupid: to walk miles along a dusty road for something that didn't concern her, with the prospect of an unpleasant scene at the end.

"Well? Are you coming?"

"I do not want to go any farther." She knew she sounded like an eight-year-old, stubborn and sulky. Mathieu glowered at her, his face all hard, sharp edges. Out of the corner of her eye, Lyn saw Blaize give his head a small, determined shake. "He does not want to either." Blaize shook his head harder, his fingers locked on hers.

Mathieu's expression altered subtly, from anger to something else. "Blaize?"

The little boy faced him squarely, chewing his lip.

"Is this your sister? Is she Elisabeth?"

Decisively, Blaize shook his head again, then looked up at Lyn. Her mouth opened, but it was empty of words. He knew. Of all the people in the household who ought to know, or at least suspect, Blaize was the only one willing to admit it. She had recognized the doubt and fear in Louise's eyes; but Louise could only allow herself to think, "Elisabeth is acting peculiarly." She could not comprehend the truth: *this is not Elisabeth*—it was beyond her imagining. Even Michel, with his suspicions, could not go that far. Only Blaize. The crippling weight of desolation lifted from Lyn; she felt immense relief. At that moment it didn't matter that Blaize was only six, trapped in silence, and regarded by most people as deficient. It was enough that he knew.

After a long silence, Mathieu said, "You are right. I do *not*

205

understand. I was certain that I would. Unless Blaize—but no, I do not think he is lying.''

There was a burr caught in Lyn's throat; it hurt to swallow. ''I cannot really blame you,'' she said at last. ''I do not understand it myself—only that I am here, so it does not matter if it is possible or not. At first—in the beginning—I was sure that everyone would see right away that I am not Elisabeth. I thought she would come back—but she has vanished, and I am where they expect to find her. I do not think anyone really *looks* at Elisabeth anyway. I do not think they bother,'' she added with an edge of bitterness.

''I have heard of witches,'' said Mathieu slowly, ''but I do not believe that I have ever met one.''

''I am not a witch,'' Lyn said with conviction. ''More like a ghost—from the future.''

''Future?'' He looked wary.

They began to walk again, Blaize between them, no longer alarmed now that they were not shouting at one another.

''More than two hundred years in the future,'' said Lyn.

Mathieu stopped. ''No. I cannot—you try to trick me.'' His face tightened dangerously.

Resigned, Lyn said, ''You asked me. I am telling you. It is not a trick. Not on you, anyway. I am not French at all. I come from Massachusetts—do you know where that is?''

''Of course I know! What do you take me for? I have been many times to Massachusetts—to Boston, to Salem, trading. That is where the flour comes from for Desforges's bread—Massachusetts. So you are English.''

''I am American.''

''What is that?'' He was belligerent.

She sighed. ''In seventeen seventy-six there will be a war between the English colonists and England, and the colonists will win and become independent. They will establish their own government. I come from the United States of America.''

''That is a fine story,'' he told her derisively. ''But this is seventeen forty-four. In seventeen seventy-six I will be sixty years old. An old man! If I live that long.''

''If you live that long,'' she retorted, ''you will see that it is not a story. But it will be too late then for you to be sorry that you did not believe me. At least Blaize believes me." She smiled at him and he smiled back, aware that he had pleased her.

"Why have you told no one else this? Why only me?"

"I should have thought by this time it would be obvious to you."

"Do you truly expect me to believe you?"

It was a genuine question; he meant it seriously. "I would like you to," she replied honestly, "but I know it is very hard."

He grunted but said nothing. He was troubled by her, unsettled and anxious for the time being to let the matter drop, she sensed. She would have to be very careful with Mathieu or she would frighten him away altogether, and she did not want to do that. She was surprised at how much she did not want to do it. Somehow, before the day was over, she would have to raise again the subject of Donald. Even if Mathieu were not completely convinced about her, she had to make him agree not to interfere.

Later, she told herself. For the present she resolved to enjoy the rest of the expedition. The harbor was as calm as a giant's wading pool, scattered with toy boats of all kinds, and the air had a snap and freshness to it. It was wonderful to be outdoors away from the cramped town, simply walking. For a short time she was truly outside Elisabeth's life.

"You mentioned a boat," she said after a while. "What boat? Who is Lepine?"

He shook himself out of his silence and glanced at her as if surprised to find she was still there. "She is my boat. Lepine has been repairing her. She should be ready by this time."

"I thought your boat sank. Michel said you were shipwrecked."

"That is half true. The boat ran onto rocks near here, but she did not sink. The others, they abandoned her and cleared out—except for Sedilot, poor beggar. Talon, Gaspard, they did not hang around to see what happened. They were afraid people would ask questions. They went to Port Toulouse, and then—?"

"Questions about what?"

Mathieu shrugged. "Where they had been. What they had been doing."

"What *had* they been doing?"

"How should I know? I did not ask. Before we met up, that is no business of mine, is it. Anyhow, now they are gone and the boat is mine. We salvaged her, Lepine and I, and he has been working on her. He knows boats. In the meantime I am working for your—for Jean Bernard—so I can pay Lepine. It is almost done, and then I am free.''

She thought about that. ''When you are—free—what will you do?''

''I thought to go to Isle St. Jacques, or up the St. Lawrence before winter. Then in the spring, south. There is money to be made trading along the coast.''

''Mathieu, is what you do illegal?'' she asked, curious.

He frowned. ''Illegal? What is illegal? I do not steal, I do not rob anyone. I make a living for myself, me. I do no one harm.''

''But it is against the law, trading with the English. It is dangerous. You could be arrested, is it not?''

''They wanted to arrest me.'' He nodded. ''But only because I was a stranger and they do not like strangers. Do you know how many people in Louisbourg break the laws? I am in the best of company, Mademoiselle. And when Jean Bernard agreed to give me work they could not arrest me. I do an honest job. And now your grandmother has flour in her cellar for the winter—fine New England flour, and''—he grinned—''Monsieur Desforges must swallow his displeasure. I do not think he likes the taste.''

''No.'' Lyn smiled back, then grew serious. ''Will you—then you plan to leave before winter?''

''There will be no work for me when the weather turns. Jean himself will have little to do but repairs. What is there to keep me? It is too close here—I do not take to life in this town and I have no family to pull on me. I am alone—I can go where and when I like.''

She nodded. The sun, still bright overhead, wasn't as warm as she had thought. Anyway, there was nothing Mathieu could do for her, and she'd be gone before he was. . . .

They were near the Royal Battery by this time. As they approached the massive fortification, Lyn saw that its walls were badly weathered and much less substantial than they appeared from a distance. There were alarming cracks in the masonry, and in places great chunks of mortar had crumbled away leaving jagged cavities. Knowing what she did about the future of Louisbourg, she found the decay very depressing.

She and Donald had only six months left: the siege began in May. Louisbourg lay peaceful under the spread of sky across the harbor, its chimneys smoking, its inhabitants pursuing their ordinary lives, not dreaming of the violence and disruption to come. What was going to happen to Blaize—to the rest of his family? She shivered. Dorrie said that meant someone had walked over your grave.

"What is the matter with you then?"

"It is nothing," she said quickly, and struggled to pull herself out of the future.

Jacques Lepine's property lay on an inlet, practically in the shadow of the battery: a snug little house sheltered from the sea winds by a fold of land. The fish shacks, the landing stage, the flakes, looked worn but well cared for. Behind the house was a small garden plot, and four white ducks rested companionably beside a marshy trickle of water that ran out of the hills. Several small boats were pulled up on the mud, and a large one was heeled over on its side, having its bottom scraped by a stolid, dark-faced man with a knit cap pulled down over his ears.

An older man sat on a bench outside one of the sheds, a clay pipe between his teeth, his lap full of fishnet. It lay in heaps around him; his fingers sorted deftly through it, weaving a wooden bobbin in and out of the mesh. They worked by themselves, by feel, so quickly Lyn couldn't follow their movements. The old man paid no attention to his hands; he watched Mathieu approach.

"Monsieur Lepine."

"Martel," he shouted around the pipestem. "I wondered when we would see you. The boat, she is finished. She is good." He glanced from Mathieu to Lyn and Blaize. Mathieu made no attempt to introduce or explain them. "You have walked from the city, is it not. That is a long way for the boy—he will be hungry. Marie-Josephte!" He raised his loud voice to a bellow, and after a moment a woman appeared in the cottage doorway. She had a plain, leathery face and her forearms were very brown against the white of her chemise. "We have company, woman!"

"I can see that," she shouted back. She squinted at Lyn and Blaize and smiled, showing a gap in her teeth. "Leave the men to their business," she said in a normal voice. "Come in and tell me the news."

Although reluctant to leave the sunshine for the stuffy half darkness of the house, Lyn was also curious to see what it was like inside, and the woman, whom she took to be Jacques Lepine's wife, was obviously eager to be hospitable. She towed Blaize behind her through the open door.

The cottage was only one room with a ladder to the loft above; it was plainly furnished and meant to serve all purposes: a double bed in the corner near the hearth and a *cabane,* like Suzanne's, against the back wall. At one end of the long plank table in the middle of the floor sat a younger woman, peeling apples, and beside her in a beautiful carved wood cradle lay a baby wrapped tight in a blanket. Long curls of apple skin unwound smoothly from the white flesh as she turned the fruit to her knife.

Lyn watched admiringly. "I wish I could do that."

The young woman glanced up and almost smiled.

Madame Lepine gave them cornbread and cheese and some very tough dried, salted beef, and a mug of cider between them. And she talked. Long before Mathieu and Jacques Lepine were finished outside, Lyn had heard all about how the Lepine family had come to Louisbourg twelve years earlier from Placentia. They had lost a daughter and two sons, one son only last spring. He had drowned near Scatarie and his body had never been recovered. The woman paring apples was his widow. She worked on impassively, as if she did not hear her mother-in-law, and the baby slept in its cradle.

Fishing had been poor for them again that summer, and with the loss of their second son, the Lepines had decided to sell what they could and find passage on a ship bound for France. Madame Lepine was from Brittany herself and longed to see the country where she had been a little girl. "I was only eighteen when I left. I want to go back before I die. Lepine, he does not care so much. He says it will have changed, but I will know it. He does not want to go, but he has now no reason to stay. He has no sons to work with him and to inherit the property. I say we are better off to go now, while we have something left, than to wait and lose it all. We will be safer in France with this war." She clicked her tongue disparagingly. "But look at him. He is out there mending his nets as always. He will not use them again, but he cannot stop. What do I do with myself if I do not work, he asks me." For a moment she was silent, staring at the blinding sunlight in the doorway, then she gave her head a shake. "But listen to me! I talk too much—and *she* does not talk at all." Lyn could see why. "Now you. You tell us the news from the city, eh? What about the funeral? It must have been splendid."

She composed herself to listen, and Lyn was filled with a sense of inadequacy. What she knew of the governor's funeral had come filtering down to her through layers of other people—Suzanne, Michel, customers in the shop—and she had paid very little attention. She had known long ago that he was going to die in October; he had died. They'd buried him under the floor of the chapel, and lit a hundred candles. It made no difference to Lyn; she had nothing to do with Jean-Baptiste-Louis le Prévost Duquesnel, alive or dead, though it had given her an odd feeling when she caught glimpses of him in the congregation at Mass. Madame Lepine was clearly disappointed in her, so out of desperation Lyn described instead the embarkation of the English prisoners for Boston. She had actually seen this herself, through the bakeshop window, and could make quite a good story of it: the shouting and milling, the families separated then reunited, the children lost, the calling of good-byes— complete confusion up and down the quay for hours as three hundred and forty men, women and children, and whatever possessions they had managed to hang onto, were loaded onto the ships to be sent home.

Although the Lepines lived within sight of Louisbourg, it was a strange and distant place to them. Their world was so much larger than the one Lyn was used to, and at the same time their horizons were so much narrower.

Jacques Lepine came shouting into the house with Mathieu, filling the room. "Give us some beer, woman! We have concluded our business—it is dry work! Will you have a pipe, Martel?"

The young woman—Lyn still did not know her name—kept peeling apples, and Madame Lepine brought the men tankards. Mathieu drained his as speedily as was polite, then rose. "Thank you for your hospitality, Monsieur. We must get back. I will come next week for the boat and move her to a mooring off the quay." He raised his voice to match Lepine's and Lyn realized the man was deaf.

"Ah, well," roared Lepine. "I am glad you are pleased, Martel. She is sound."

"Monsieur Lepine has agreed to send his man with us in the rowboat, to bring it back. It will be much quicker to go across the harbor, if you are not afraid?"

"Of course not," said Lyn. "I have been in boats before this.

211

Blaize can be lookout. But," she cautioned the little boy, "you must sit very still and not lean over the side." She wished they had a life jacket for him; then suddenly wondered if Mathieu himself could swim. Prudently she decided not to ask. In her heavy, enveloping skirts she was as likely as the rest of them to drown, so it was just as well not to admit the possibility.

Jacques Lepine's man was the one who had been scraping the boat. Mathieu spoke briefly to him in a language that was utterly foreign to Lyn, and together they pushed one of the small boats down to the water. Gathering up great handfuls of skirt, Lyn clambered aboard, cursing as she caught her foot in the hem and heard it rip. She sat down hard in the stern, and a moment later the other man joined her. He had a strong cheesy smell which she decided was better left unconsidered. Mathieu sat amidships, facing them, and picked up the oars. Jacques Lepine lifted Blaize into the bow and shoved them out, splashing into the water up to his knees. He lifted his hand in farewell, and from the house, Madame Lepine fluttered her apron. Lyn waved back, glad to know they were soon to leave; they would be well away from Louisbourg before the trouble started. She settled back to enjoy the trip.

Lyn had been fifteen before she had discovered that her mother was a competent sailor. All those years Dorrie had never mentioned it. Then in the summer of 1981, on a beautiful warm blue day, she had casually—too casually—suggested they rent a sailboat on the Charles River. "But shouldn't one of us know *how*?" asked Lyn doubtfully. "I mean, it isn't something you just do, is it?" "Maybe I'll remember. I used to sail a little. Once." "You did?" Lyn stared at her in amazement, but that was all Dorrie would own to.

"You never told me," accused Lyn as they slid back and forth across the wide brown river. "Why? When did you learn?" "Oh, long ago," said Dorrie, noncommittal. In the hardly-ever land of her childhood, of which she hardly ever spoke. "I used to sail sometimes with my father and brothers. But they raced." "We could have been doing this all along." Lyn thought of the wasted time. "You're good." But Dorrie shook her head. "Only all right—never good enough. So I quit. Ready about!" she called, ending the conversation. The boom swung over, the *rainbow* changed course, the wind pushed it sideways, the velvety water gurgled past and smoothed out behind them. Lyn had to change the shape of her mother, rearranging her collection of pieces to accommodate this new one.

"What are you thinking?" asked Mathieu, pulling steadily at the oars.

The Charles River vanished in a blink. "You would not—" she broke off.

"Understand," he supplied, his eyes on her face.

He reminded her that she still had not told him about Donald. And now it was too late. She could hardly try to explain Donald out here in a boat with a strange man listening.

As if reading her thoughts, Mathieu said, "He will not know what you say. He speaks only Basque."

Startled, Lyn glanced at the man, then away. She nodded. "There is something I must say to you, Mathieu."

"Yes?" He was on his guard.

"It is about the soldier."

"I do not like him." It was a flat statement. He saw nothing to discuss. "You should stay away from him."

"I cannot."

Mathieu's eyes grew chilly. "I had thought we were finished with this."

"We are. It is finished if you will leave it alone. It is really none of your business if I see him."

"It is a secret because you are ashamed, because you know it is wrong. You know it would make Jean Bernard very angry, so you sneak behind his back."

She struggled to control her temper. "Please do not ruin it, Mathieu."

"You are in love with him, is it."

"No. He is a friend, a special friend. He is like me—another ghost. We are both of us lost—we need each other."

He shipped his oars and leaned on them, regarding her intently for what seemed like a very long time. The Basque frowned and said something. Mathieu shook his head, and the man hunched his shoulders resignedly. Finally Mathieu said to Lyn, "I have tried. Truly I have, Mademoiselle. But—" He shook his head again. "If you persist, Jean Bernard will hear of it. There is no doubt. If not from me, then from someone else. It can only bring you grief. I

213

have told you what I think—a man like that cannot be a friend. Do you believe that I am simple-minded?"

"That is not—I never—"

"I will not tell your father. It is what I should do, but I will not. When he learns about your soldier, you will please remember that it was not from me." He returned to his oars.

She could think of nothing else to say, and Mathieu did not speak again until they reached a little wharf at the end of the place du Port. He steered them skillfully between two heavy-laden dorries and an obliging sailor caught their painter and helped Blaize out. Impersonally, Mathieu handed Lyn up, and the Basque shifted to take the oars. As soon as Mathieu stepped ashore, he rowed away and was quickly lost in the crowd of ships. Mathieu walked with them as far as Monsieur Delort's house on the place, then said a brusque good-bye and left them to make their own way from there. Lyn watched him go with a dull sense of failure, and asked herself crossly why it should matter.

⇻⟫ 16 ⟪⇺

CHRISTOPHE BOUGHT A SECONDHAND SUIT FOR HIS WEDDING. IT fit him well and had been worn very little; it was being sold by a gentleman who had had a difficult year and was being pressed by his creditors. Jeanne was critical. She thought he ought to have ordered a new one, made specially for the occasion. It did not seem right to get married in someone else's clothing, she complained. Her own dress was less elegant than she would have liked, but at least it was new, and Marguerite had laid aside her other work to do the fine sewing on it. She was patient with Jeanne's fussing over the fit and drape of material. But when Jeanne criticized Christophe, Marguerite actually became angry. Lyn, who happened to be in the kitchen at the time, could hardly believe her ears. She had never heard Marguerite angry before.

"For what? It is one day—not even that—this wedding! You should be grateful that your husband-to-be is frugal, that he saves his money for more important things. The clothes are not important, Jeanne. It is the man inside them. You if anyone should know this. Christophe is a good man, and you are very lucky. Never forget it, and do not be so foolish." Marguerite was quite

214

pink in the face and her eyes very bright. She should get angry more often, Lyn thought. It gave an animation to her features that made her beautiful. But as soon as she had scolded Jeanne, she subsided again, bending to her work as if ashamed of her outburst.

"I should not lose my temper," she told Lyn apologetically later.

"Why not? If you are angry, why should you hide it? Especially when you are right and Jeanne is being silly."

But Marguerite was not convinced. "Elisabeth, it is never right to be angry. Besides—"

But she was interrupted by Marie, who bumped her head on the table leg and let out an indignant wail, and she never returned to the subject. Whatever Marguerite felt in those days before the wedding, as she watched Christophe and worked with Jeanne, she never spoke of it, nor did she invite questions. Instead she talked of other, ordinary things: the herbs she was drying, the state of the larder, the babies, that Louise was growing out of her skirts and would need new shoes. . . .

At this last, Lyn reflected glumly that she would need them too. Ever since she arrived she had been wearing the boots she had come in. Recently, to her dismay, she had discovered that the sole of one was paper-thin and there was an actual hole in the other. It let in water when the weather was wet, which these days it usually was. The trouble was that her feet were too big for eighteenth-century women's shoes; she would need a pair of men's boots and they looked dreadfully uncomfortable. She wondered if her own could somehow be mended, but they were so badly scuffed and worn it hardly seemed worthwhile, and she was reluctant to draw attention either to the shoes or to the size of her feet. As a temporary measure, she made a pad of grain sacking to cover the hole from inside, which helped a little.

When she and Blaize had returned after their day out with Mathieu, there had been surprisingly little fuss. They had found Louise and Marguerite in the bakeshop, and Marguerite hugged them both with great relief. "Oh, Elisabeth! I was so worried about you! Where have you been?" she cried.

"There were many deliveries," said Lyn cautiously, "and we stopped to visit."

"But all these *hours*—! When you did not come home to dinner—"

"Did—has Grandmother asked about us?" Over Marguerite's shoulder, Lyn could see Louise watching her narrowly.

"Ah, no. Maman is not feeling well. Soon after you left, Elisabeth, she went upstairs and has not been down since. So I have been in the shop with Louise."

"What is the matter with her?"

Marguerite shook her head. "It is only the usual—her legs give her much pain. I am only glad you are back safely."

Under the circumstances, it was nothing short of a miraculous escape. Joseph had been out at noon, so the two people who would have caused her real trouble didn't know that Lyn had been missing for so long. And they never would, unless Louise told them, which was unlikely. Louise might not trust Lyn, but she had no intention of upsetting their precarious balance in the household. If only, Lyn thought dismally, the afternoon had been a success. But she had misjudged—either Mathieu or herself or both. In spite of her best efforts to make him believe her, she was convinced that he did not. And mention of Donald had only driven him further away. At least he had promised to say nothing.

Among her other chores in the days before the wedding, Jeanne was given the task of cleaning out the little room on the second floor behind Madame Pugnant's. It was used to store odds and ends: broken chairs, old trunks, pieces of lumber, a table with a short leg, an armoire missing its hinges, anything that needed mending but was still too good to throw out. All of it had to be hauled up the ladder to the attic, where soon only Pierre and Florent would sleep. Then the room had to be swept and scrubbed and scoured and furnished with necessities for Jeanne and Christophe. Jean Bernard contributed the money for a secondhand bed which he and Christophe had to maneuver up the narrow, dark stairs in sections and reassemble once they got it through the door.

"I do wish I was to have my own house," Jeanne fretted. "When I am married I should not have other people always telling me what to do. I should be in charge."

"First you had better learn how to be," said Lyn dryly. "Marguerite says—"

216

"Aunt Marguerite is so critical." Jeanne pouted.

"You are lucky to have a place to live in at all."

"Everyone keeps saying that I am lucky. I do not *feel* lucky! I am treated like a child."

"You are not very old."

"Old enough to be a wife and to have a baby of my own. I am old enough to run a house of my own too, is it not."

"You would do well to listen to Marguerite," said Lyn, feeling a pang for Christophe.

The wedding date was set for mid-November, on an unfashionable Thursday. It was to be a very small wedding: only the bride's family and two of Christophe's friends, because he had no family in the town. Lyn was rather surprised to learn that he had friends; she had never laid eyes on them or thought about what Christophe did during his time off. One was a butcher, and the other a clerk for one of the merchants on the quay. They seemed perfectly nice, but not in the least fashionable. Jeanne was torn between her delight at being the center of attention, and her longing for the wedding she dreamed of: to an officer in the garrison, with the Duvernays and their friends as guests, and an elaborate party afterward. She fussed and preened and posed until Lyn wanted to slap her. But it wasn't really Jeanne's fault, not most of it. She was silly and vain and childish, but she was only fifteen. Lieutenant Duvernay had taken advantage of her inexperience and saddled everyone else with the consequences. It was Jeanne's good fortune that her family had accepted the responsibility instead of washing their hands of her.

Dorrie had been twenty-two when she got pregnant; she must have realized what she was doing. Or had she? When did you become aware of consequences, of cause and effect? Did it actually have anything to do with age? Had Dorrie woken up one morning to the same fright as Jeanne, not knowing what to do, hoping that if she did nothing she could pretend it hadn't happened?

On the morning of the wedding, a businesslike November wind drove shoals of clouds across the sky, here and there pierced by a bolt of light. Gulls planed overhead, igniting when the sun touched them. The sea was heavy and opaque. Lyn and Marguerite went out onto the front steps to watch the wedding party set off, skirts and ribbons and capes fluttering bravely, hats held down.

With uncharacteristic stubbornness, Marguerite had insisted that she stay behind to watch the babies and prepare the wedding lunch. Joseph had argued halfheartedly—he didn't like to be seen on a social occasion without his wife—but Madame Pugnant had taken her daughter's side, and he gave in with rather poor grace. And at the last moment, when she knew it was too late for anyone to waste time objecting, Lyn declared that there was too much for Marguerite to do alone, so she would stay and help. After a brief probing glance, Madame Pugnant agreed. Suzanne had been given the day off, to her annoyance; she had been counting on being able to tell widow Grandchamp all the details of the party firsthand.

"She is your sister, Elisabeth. You should have gone," said Marguerite as the wedding party turned the corner.

"They will not miss me."

"It is so peaceful without Suzanne, is it not?" Marguerite gave Lyn a guilty smile.

"I do not know why you put up with her."

"She is a part of the household, Elisabeth. Now she is getting old, like Florent. He came to work for Papa when they first arrived from France. He cannot do much now, but Maman will not turn him out. He has nowhere to go."

Together, Lyn and Marguerite set the table in the kitchen and spread on it all the food Suzanne and Marguerite had been preparing for days: a ham and a roast goose stuffed with apple and sausage, little marzipan tarts decorated with sugared violets, oranges glazed with caramel, spiced nuts, white bread and plum preserves with brandy, beans pickled in vinegar and a bowl of very sweet mulled wine. Joseph's cake was the centerpiece, iced with white sugar and rich with raisins and cherries and nuts; he had worked on it for days. Even Lyn had to admit it was beautiful—as fine a cake as anyone in Louisbourg could have ordered.

After a while, Marguerite said, "It is because of me you stayed, is it not, Elisabeth?"

"Yes," said Lyn honestly.

"You need not worry. I have made my peace with this marriage. I am glad for Christophe. He should have a wife and children."

Just not that wife, thought Lyn. Aloud she said, "It was not his choice to marry Jeanne."

"He did not have to agree. Maman would not have held it against

218

him, Elisabeth. He will be a good husband to your sister, have no fear of that.''

''I do not worry about Jeanne, Marguerite. It is Christophe—I do not think Jeanne will make him a very good wife.''

''You are wrong.'' Marguerite's voice was confident. Lyn glanced at her in surprise. ''Jeanne is young and inexperienced. She complains and is sulky because she does not yet understand what it is to be married. That will take time, but she will learn. I will teach her everything she must know to keep Christophe's house and to make him happy. I promise this to you and to myself.''

There was a strength and determination in Marguerite that Lyn had never seen before; she felt somehow chastened by it. She watched Marguerite set out the best china. But could she teach Jeanne to love Christophe?

''He had thought we would have parties.'' Marguerite held up one of the elegant blue and white plates. ''Joseph bought these when we were married. He wanted so much—more than just to be a good baker. What is it that makes people happy, Elisabeth? I do not think it is love. So often it makes us unhappy. But life is both and we must accept and trust God.''

Dorrie didn't think so. She didn't believe for a minute that she couldn't alter circumstances if she tried hard enough. She believed you had to take charge of your own life, take responsibility for your mistakes and credit for your triumphs. You persevered, you struggled, you kept reaching. ''God gives you life,'' she said, ''and then you get on with it. He has much too much else to do to guide you every step of the way.'' Were you shaped by your beliefs, or did you shape them to your need, Lyn wondered.

Jean Bernard came back with the wedding party, looking ill-at-ease and slightly raffish in his version of good clothes. He did not stay long, and to Lyn's relief he made no attempt to talk to her other than to say good day. So Mathieu, who had not been invited, had kept his word about Donald. All she had seen of Mathieu since their expedition was his boat, which Michel pointed out to her, lying at anchor off the Place du Port. Michel told her it was a shallop. It looked very small surrounded by the warships, merchantmen and the enormous Compagnie des Indes vessels, but Michel was impressed with it. He said Mathieu had promised to take him aboard, and Lyn felt a mean little pinch of envy.

Christophe looked unfamiliar in his new suit: it was neat, not fancy, a serviceable dark green broadcloth under which he wore an embroidered waistcoat that looked suspiciously like one Lyn had seen Marguerite working on earlier that fall. Jeanne was radiant in pale blue. Marguerite had decorated the neckline and wrists of her dress with a froth of delicate lace which set off her pretty face and slim hands to perfection, and the voluminous skirt disguised her condition. Joseph himself toasted the bride and groom and wished them many years of happiness. Then, overcome by the occasion, he put his arm around Marguerite and hugged her while she blushed and smiled.

Much too quickly for Jeanne's taste, her life returned to normal. She spent her days under Marguerite's supervision in the kitchen, and her nights in the little back bedroom with Christophe. Lyn and Louise had the bed to themselves, but otherwise nothing seemed to change. Lyn wondered how Pierre managed in the attic with only Florent for company, but if he missed Thomas and Christophe he didn't say. The days grew shorter and wilder: the household rose in darkness and went to bed earlier in the evenings. Candles and oil lamps were romantic only if you did not actually need them to work by. As the days got colder, Lyn was increasingly grateful for the big ovens in the bakery; they kept the whole house relatively warm.

A succession of autumn storms blew in off the Atlantic, gusting up and down the streets, rattling shutters and dislodging shingles, dashing rain and salt spray against the houses. Even in the shelter of the harbor, the water roiled and seethed and threw itself against the quay, sending up plumes of white. The front windows of the house were blurred with salt. At night, when the wind was particularly loud, Blaize crept into bed with Lyn and Louise, and Lyn told him stories: Hansel and Gretel, or Jacques and Marie as she called them, and Little Red Riding Hood. In Lyn's version, Granny lived in the faubourg, and Blaize, although he had never seen one, knew about the wolves that prowled the forests of Nova Scotia. Louise pretended to be asleep, but Lyn knew she wasn't. Several times she overheard the younger girl repeating her stories to Renée, Marie and Anne, almost word for word as Lyn had told them to Blaize.

Outside the confines of the house, Louisbourg had been working itself steadily into a frenzy of activity. The quay and the harbor swarmed with men; little boats and barges crowded the wharves and clustered around the ships, ferrying tons of provisions from the quayside where carts and wagons dumped them. It seemed as if all the warehouses in the town were being emptied simultaneously. On board the ships, hundreds of sailors hoisted crates and barrels and bales up and down into cavernous holds. All day long, from first gray light until darkness, traffic rumbled past the bakery, and the wind was ragged with shouts and curses, creaking, grunting, splashes and thuds. Customers to the bakeshop watched with misgiving, expressing sour doubts about whether there would be anything left in the town, and asking each other rhetorically how the king expected them to survive the winter after supplying all his ships. At least they would have bread, Lyn thought, aware that the cellar beneath her feet was full of barrels of New England flour thanks to Jean Bernard's money and Mathieu Martel's connections.

On the last day of November, with a flint-hard wind blowing out of the northwest, the fleet left the harbor, bound for France: more than fifty ships of all sizes. Somewhere on one of the merchantmen was Thomas, and on another the Lepine family, setting their futures on the wind, with the sails that carried them east. Most of Louisbourg turned out to watch them go, flocking onto Rochefort Point—men, women and children, waving hats and handkerchiefs as the ships filed between the rocky jaws of land, past the lighthouse and the Island Battery, to spread across the waves. Tiny figures on their decks waved back, and flags and pennants cracked overhead as the sails bellied and began to pull. Gulls lifted and fell, crying plaintively down the wind. From the island at the harbor mouth came the dull thud of cannon, fired in salute. Then from behind, the cannon of the Bastion, then the Royal Battery. The guns on the warships answered back, spitting flames and blots of dirty smoke.

People stayed on the point, watching, until the sails disappeared through the distant crack between the ragged sea and the sky. Then they began to drift, reluctant, through the Maurepas Gate, back to chores and jobs and ordinary life, filled with the shapeless unrest left behind by a departure.

Lyn had argued to Madame Pugnant that since there was no one left in town to buy bread, they should all be allowed to watch the fleet sail. She, Louise, Blaize and Pierre had joined the crowds beyond the cemetery and the lime kilns, where they had found

221

Michel, who had somehow managed to get away by himself. He knew the names and destinations of all the ships and gave them a running commentary. "That is a fisherman going back to Saint-Malo for the winter. That one—there—that is the *Caribou,* the warship, is it not."

"How long will it take them to reach France?" asked Lyn, watching as the sea was scattered with sails. The fleet was like a flock of geese beginning its migration. She thought of the miles of empty, churning water ahead, and the ships which had seemed so large in the harbor shrank alarmingly. "How will they stay together?"

"They will not," replied Michel. "There will be winds and storms to separate them. They will sail at different speeds. If they are lucky, two months? But because of the war they are late leaving—it will be hard."

"I would like to be on one," said Pierre with longing. "Like Thomas."

"Do not be silly," Louise said. "You would be ill. Besides, his ship may sink, or be captured by the English. You are lucky to be here, learning a trade."

Pierre kicked irritably at a pebble. "I do not like to be shouted at always by Uncle Joseph," he said mutinously.

Lyn could hardly blame him. "Christophe does not shout," she reminded him.

He nodded. "Christophe is nice. I do not mind working for him, Elisabeth. When Uncle Joseph is out he lets me make rolls and he says they are good."

They walked slowly toward the gate. There were a number of soldiers among the stragglers, but although Lyn looked for Donald she did not see him. With a twinge of anxiety, she realized that it had been several days since she had glimpsed him last. He couldn't—she swung round and stared out to sea, her heart contracting. No, of course not. He would never leave Louisbourg that way, on a ship; there could be no hope at all for him out there. Surely he'd know that.

"What is it?" asked Michel, ever alert.

She shook her head. "Nothing." But she couldn't entirely rid herself of a feeling of unease.

Ahead, Pierre, Louise and Blaize were playing some kind of

222

game with each other, dodging in and out of the crowd. Lyn was glad to see Blaize actually joining in, diffident but eager, and Louise accepting him. Usually she had no patience with her brother, and little with playing. She expected to work, to be useful, as did Pierre, in spite of his complaints. And Michel was earning the money for his own keep. Life was already serious business to them—they weren't children as Lyn was used to thinking of children. They were apprentice adults. They didn't seem to mind, but why should they— it was what they knew. Lyn was the one who knew different, and she was out of time.

"We should be going too. With them." Michel interrupted her thoughts.

"We? What do you mean?"

"Not you." He scowled at her. "Mathieu and me. He has promised me that I am to go with him when he takes his boat."

"I did not realize—I had not thought—when will he leave, do you know?" Mathieu had told her he would go, but she had buried the fact under other things.

Michel shrugged. "It must be soon or the gales will stop us. There will be ice in the sea and it would be too dangerous. Then we would have to wait for spring."

"What about your family, Michel? Your aunt?"

"What of them? They will not miss me. The money, perhaps, but it is not so much and I have been saving some for myself. It is mine, so why not. I know English"—he gave her a sideways look—"that will be useful if we go south. There is no reason for me to spend my life here. I want to see other places. He says he is not ready yet, but I do not know why. Soon it will be too late and still he delays."

Talk of leaving made her think again of Donald. She had begun to worry about him. Since the day with Mathieu, she had seen him only once to speak to and had told him what Mathieu said about the roads, that they led only into the wilderness, to tiny settlements and isolated farms. But of course, Donald countered, Mathieu *belonged* in 1744. When he went away from Louisbourg he remained in his own time. They did *not* belong, and when they went away they would find themselves.

"But suppose it doesn't work, Donald. Suppose we just get lost?"

223

"We are lost *now*. How could it be worse? I can't go on doing nothing, Lyn. It's killing me."

Someone like Rob would have learned how to get by very quickly in Donald's situation. Rob had knocked about. He played the angles. But all Donald knew, everything he was good at, was of no value to him here. It didn't help to be well-educated; you had to be resilient.

"It could kill you to walk away from here," said Lyn.

"What're your chances if you stay? Smallpox, typhoid, childbirth. People are going to die in the siege—and if you survive that, you'll be crammed into the stinking hold of a boat and sent to heaven knows what in France. The only chance *I* have is to get out. The end of November, Lyn. That's it."

On the first of December she woke with a feeling of dread; she didn't know where Donald was. The last three food parcels were still where she had left them, between the posts in the derelict shed. All day, as she went about her ordinary chores, she hoped she would find them gone. When she didn't, she was swept with a desolation and despair greater than any she had known since finding herself in this place. If he had given up on her and gone, she realized she would never know what happened to him—whether he got back to their world, or whether he didn't. She spent the night lying awake, staring blindly into the bed curtains, alone and bone cold.

In the morning she thawed out enough to think constructively. If Donald had actually left the garrison, someone would know. A soldier couldn't simply disappear unnoticed. Even though he seemed to have no friends, he had a commanding officer and barracks mates; they'd have missed him.

"What do you want?" asked Michel, instantly suspicious, when she waylaid him in the courtyard where he was splitting kindling.

"I want you to find out something for me."

He grunted. "Tell me what it is and I will tell you what it will cost."

"Do you know what a favor is?" He didn't bother to answer. She sighed and went on. "There is a man who used to come into the shop. A soldier. He has not been for many days now and I want to know where he is."

"Aha," said Michel with a knowing grin. "You have had a quarrel with him, is it, and he does not come to see you?"

"There was no quarrel," said Lyn shortly. "He is a friend and I am worried about him. I want to be sure that he is all right. Can you find out?"

"A friend, eh?" The shrug. "Maybe."

She controlled her irritation with an effort. "I will tell you his name and—"

"Gerard Grossin, is it not?" Michel enjoyed disconcerting her.

Before she could stop herself, she asked, "How do you know?" It was a foolish question.

"Why is it you come to me to find out these things? I must go or Joseph will begin to shout. He is in a good temper this morning. It would be too bad to ruin it so early, I think."

Later, when Lyn was alone in the bakeshop, he came and told her the information she wanted would cost her a pair of woolen stockings.

"What? But I am knitting them for Pierre."

"I know. They will fit me quite well."

"Your price is very high."

"You need not pay it."

She looked down at his legs. His brown stockings were shapeless and lumpy with careless darns, and showed pale crescents where the heels of his shoes rubbed. Why didn't his aunt knit him some, she thought crossly. Pierre's were nowhere near as bad, but how was she going to explain the sudden disappearance of his new ones? That was a problem for the future. "All right," she agreed grumpily.

"Good." He grinned at her. "Is good," he repeated in English.

His vocabulary was patchy, but surprisingly extensive. He had developed his own pidgin English which he practiced relentlessly on Ordonnateur Bigot's Irish stableman, Andrew McSweeney, an amiable, rather simple soul. The first time Michel attempted a conversation with him, he had come storming back to Lyn full of fury. "You said you would teach me *English*!" he cried. "And so I have been," she replied. "You have not! I could not understand anything that he said—he does not sound like you. I could not talk to him. You have *cheated* me!" Lyn had never seen Michel furious before. At last she had sorted it out. "But Andrew McSweeney is *Irish*," she told him. "I am not Irish. *I* cannot always understand him. He is from a different country—of course he does not sound like me." And a different century, she might have added. "Do not trick me,"

Michel warned, giving her a fierce look. "I would be foolish to try," she said, and he nodded, satisfied, knowing it was true.

"When will you know about Gerard Grossin?" she asked him.

"How can I tell? You have not finished my stockings yet."

"And I will not, until you have news for me."

He accepted that—it was the kind of bargain he understood—and the next morning he brought her word of Donald that was both good and bad. On balance, she decided the good outweighed the bad. At least he was still in Louisbourg; he was in the hospital, where he'd been taken almost a week earlier with fever and cramps. He had collapsed while on duty.

"What is wrong with him? What does he have?" she asked Michel, but he couldn't tell her.

"That was not in the bargain. If he is in the hospital he must be very ill. Only men who are very ill go there."

"Can I visit him?"

Michel gave her a surprised look. "Visit? Why? Anyway, they will not let you in."

"It is not allowed?"

"It is stupid to go where people are ill. Me, I would not enter the gate. That is why the walls are so high, is it not—to keep in the sickness. And what can you do for him? If he recovers he will come out and you can see him. If he does not—" Shrug.

"Will you go and ask about him?"

An emphatic shake of the head. "At least he is not yet dead. I would know that."

His words sent a shiver down her spine. Already Donald had been in the hospital six days and she had not known. When he said it would kill him to stay in Louisbourg she had taken it as an exaggeration. She had never truly believed—but these people got all kinds of horrifying diseases: diphtheria, yellow fever, things that were all but unknown by the 1980s. They did die. What did anyone know about medicine in 1744? What was it like in the hospital, behind that twelve-foot wall? The idea of Donald, shut away inside, alone and sick, possibly even dying— Her stomach clenched.

"Michel—"

But he was backing out the door. "No. I have done what you asked. That is all. You owe me the stockings."

She had to go. Even though Michel had told her she wouldn't get

226

in, she had to try to see Donald. She wrapped herself in Elisabeth's old brown cloak against the rainy afternoon, and without even bothering to give Louise an excuse for her absence, she set off for the hospital. It wasn't far through the smoky streets. The double wooden gate was securely closed; in the left-hand panel there was a little door with a bellpull beside it, which she tugged. After what seemed like hours, the little door opened part way. Beyond she glimpsed a dark, bedraggled garden and the forbidding bulk of the hospital itself, its barred windows blank and impassive. It made her think of a prison. The monk who had opened the door wore a harried, preoccupied expression. "Yes, Mademoiselle? What is it?"

"I want—I have come to see a patient," she said, unsure how to address him.

"But no, Mademoiselle, that is not possible." He began to close the door, muttering something under his breath. Inside somewhere another bell rang.

"Wait—" protested Lyn, catching the small door before it slammed. "Is there someone I can talk to? Please—it is very important!"

"Brother Boniface is busy. We are all busy. If you want to see him, you must come back." The bell jangled again, impatiently. "I must go—that is for me. God be with you," he added hastily, as an afterthought, and vanished. Lyn heard the sound of a bolt being shot into place.

"But when should I come?" she asked the solid gate in dismay. She did not know what to do next. Her mind was blank. Automatically, her feet began to move; without any real purpose they carried her along the streets, stepping carelessly into puddles and worse, until she found herself on the edge of the Place Royale, staring across the sodden open space at the King's Bastion. There was only one thing she could think of, and no reason at all why it should work, but it was all she had. She turned back, into the town.

⇶ 17 ⇷

THE TAVERN WAS THICK WITH THE SMELLS OF TOBACCO AND damp things: wool, leather, fur and hair. It was like walking into a roomful of sour, lukewarm soup. Lyn stopped just over the threshold, peering through the fog. The draft from the open door made smoke billow back down the chimney; faces turned toward her in curiosity and annoyance. Someone uttered a curse and cried, "*Sacredie!* Will you shut the door!" Lyn pulled it to behind her, keeping her fingers on the latch, and the atmosphere cleared slightly. There were many more people occupying the benches and chairs this time, seeking refuge from the weather: a couple of women, but mostly men, playing cards, or talking, one sprawled on a bench against the back wall, snoring audibly. Bemused, Lyn searched among them for the right face, and a man suddenly sprang up and came over to her in a couple of long strides. She sighed with relief. It was Mathieu.

"I was afraid you would not be here," she said, pushing back her hood.

Without answering, he seized her by the arm and thrust her back out the door into the dank street.

"But I must talk to you—"

"Not *here*," he said through his teeth. "Why have you come here? Jean Bernard is out. He will not be back until evening."

"I came to see *you*. It is important."

"But I do not want to see you. Every time I see you it means trouble. I am happy to live without trouble—I do not need it." He glowered at her. When she did not speak, he said, "What is it then? You are here, so tell me. I will listen."

If she hadn't needed him, she would have derived great satisfaction from turning her back on him and walking away, but as hard as she had tried she could think of no alternative. Exerting all her control, she said, "I have just been to the hospital. They would not

228

let me in. There is someone there I must see, and I hoped—I thought you might help me.''

"How?"

"I thought that you could talk to the man at the gate, tell him I must be allowed inside. Convince him for me.''

"Who is this person you must see?"

"That does not matter.''

He regarded her steadily for a minute. "So. It is someone you should not be seeing then.''

"You do not know that.''

"Why else would you come to me, eh? Why not to your uncle or your father? You come to me because you cannot ask them. I am right, is it not.'' She glared at him and he gave a nod. "I can do nothing for you, Mademoiselle, if you do not tell me who this man is.''

"I did not say it was a man.''

His eyebrows shot upward. "You said the hospital, is it not? So it must be a man.'' The lines sharpened suddenly in his face. "Tell me who it is.''

If she wanted to see Donald, she would have to tell him. "Gerard Grossin. I know from Michel that he has been taken there, but that is all. Michel would not go to find out—''

"Michel is smart. It is a place to stay away from, and Grossin is a man to stay away from. I told you that. Now, you will excuse me—I left my rum and my card game.''

"You will not help me.'' In spite of herself, Lyn heard her voice tremble.

"Mademoiselle, they will not let you in, even if I go with you,'' he said exasperated. "It is pointless. Go home and forget about this. It is not worth your bother.''

"I cannot. I must find a way to do it. I cannot leave him there alone.''

"*Sacredie!* Why me? Why do you come to *me?* You should have nothing to do with this man! Why do you plague me with this?''

"Because I do not know anyone else to ask. And because I tried to tell you—I wanted you to understand.'' Beneath his words there was something that gave her a glimmer of hope: he was angry with her. He would not be angry if none of it mattered to him.

"You *are* a witch—I am convinced of it,'' he growled. He turned

229

his head away, staring down the gloomy street, and she waited, hardly breathing. His dark hair was frosted with drops of rain, like cobwebs, his jaw was tight. Finally he said, "You will wait here. I will not take you with me."

"Oh, but I must—"

"That is my offer. I make the conditions, not you. If you do not like them, you can try to find some other fool to do your errands for you."

She took a deep, long breath. "In the tavern?"

"No. You will have to wait upstairs. In the room."

"Suppose Jean Bernard—"

"Did you not hear me? I said he would not be back until evening. That is several hours. And if he is early you can use your magic on him. You will think of something—you are good at telling stories. I will take you to the room, then I will finish my drink. *Then* I will go and see what I can learn."

She put a hand on his arm. "Mathieu, you will *see* him? Please. Tell him I wanted to come—I tried. He must know that I tried."

"I make you no promise," he said crossly. "I will do what I can. I do not know why I am agreeing to this at all. If you are wise, you will say nothing more until I come back."

She waited alone in the dark little room for what seemed like a very long time. She could hear voices from below, now and then raised in argument or laughter or snatches of unfamiliar song, and the thump of boots on floorboards, or the scrape of chair legs. If she could just have sat in a corner down there, unobtrusive, without saying a word to anyone, she would not have felt so utterly lonely. But Mathieu had made her pull her hood around her face and had hurried her up the stairs, then left her. For something to do, she picked up and folded the few articles of clothing she found scattered on the floor: trousers, several pairs of stockings, a coarse linen shirt. She noticed the shirt was pulling apart at the shoulder seam and looked about for needle and thread, but saw none. Was it Mathieu's shirt, or Jean Bernard's? She didn't know. It was obvious that neither of them had many possessions, only the clothing and whatever the trunks and the wardrobe contained. Lyn noticed that the wardrobe door was ajar and after a brief internal debate, she pulled it open to see what was inside. Only a small collection of eating utensils and crockery, a couple of shirts and a leather vest, and two bottles. She uncorked one and sniffed it. Experimentally she tipped it to her lips and took a cautious swallow. It was sharp and strong and made her think of charcoal lighter as it tracked down her throat. She put it back, rejecting the idea of getting swacked to pass the time. On another shelf, hidden behind a pile of stockings, she discovered a small cloth-wrapped bundle and was reminded of her own, back at the Pugnant house—the relics of her real self. To open the parcel would be deliberately prying, something she ordinarily would not allow herself to do.

But there were so few clues in this place, and the circumstances were unlike any she had ever encountered—the rules were different. Chewing her lip, she carefully opened the bundle. The cloth was a fine-woven woman's handkerchief, embroidered all around the edge with a delicate pattern in white silk. With the grudging help of the window light, Lyn saw that an *F* had been worked in one corner. Inside were a comb, a silver-backed hairbrush and a rosary of dark beads, that was all. Lyn looked at the little collection for a long time, thinking, then gently wrapped it up again and put it back where she had found it. They were Elisabeth's mother's things, she knew. Jean Bernard had kept them. She closed and latched the wardrobe, not wanting to pry any further. Suddenly she did not want to know anything more about anyone in this place.

She went and sat on one of the beds, hugging herself, while the afternoon grew cold and thin and shadows crept out of the corners of the room. Why was it taking so long? Had something terrible happened to Donald? Was Mathieu reluctant to come and tell her? Was he hoping she'd give up and go away? Was he still sitting downstairs, playing cards? Suppose he didn't come, suppose she waited all evening for him? Suppose Donald had died? Ice formed in the pit of her stomach and spread through her body, freezing out rational thought, leaving her numb and immobile.

There were footsteps outside; firm, deliberate, quick. She heard them without comprehending. The door opened and Mathieu came in, but she could not look at him. She kept hugging herself, unable to move for fear of shattering.

"I hope you are satisfied," he was saying. "I had to kick my heels for an hour before they let me see Brother Boniface. And then—Elisabeth?'' He stopped. "What is this? Why do you sit in the dark this way? Did you not see the candle?''

"No,'' said Lyn, her voice brittle. "Do not light it.''

"What?''

"Just tell me.'' Her teeth were chattering. "Just say it.''

"Say what?''

"That he is dead.''

"Dead?''

"Why?'' she cried. "Why do you do this? Why did you not just come and tell me? Why did you make me wait so long?''

"I have just said—it was an hour before I could talk to anyone.'' He was standing over her. "You are cold—you are shivering.'' He pulled a blanket off the bed and put it around her shoulders. "He is not dead. Why do you think he is dead?''

"No?'' The word was hardly a breath.

"Of course not.'' He sat down close beside her, wrapping the blanket tighter, holding it there with his arm. He sounded annoyed. "Your soldier has dysentery. He was never much to look at, if you ask me, but now—he is lucky that you cannot see him. Every soldier has dysentery. They recover. *I* have had dysentery. It is unpleasant, but—you do not need to worry. Already he is better. He will be back at the barracks before the week is out. He is more likely to die from the treatment than the disease.''

"You saw him? You actually saw him?''

"It is what you wanted. He had little to say for himself, but I told him you had sent me.''

A flooding of heat—painful—circulation restoring itself to her arms and legs—her heart beginning to pump again. How stupid! How stupid to sit here imagining the worst, a thing she never allowed herself to do. Scaring herself witless and for no reason. She pushed off the blanket and Mathieu's arm and threw her own around him, holding onto him tight. "Oh, thank you! Thank you!''

There was a fractional hesitation, then he thrust her away and stood up abruptly. "Go home,'' he said in a rough voice. "I have done what you asked. I have told you all I can. That is what you came for. Go home.''

She looked up at him; his face was hard to see in the gloom.

232

"Mathieu—" She was uncertain. She had thought that was all she had come for, but suddenly she wasn't sure. She remembered with intense clarity the last time he had held her, there in the same room. She had needed comfort and sympathy, and he gave them, and was relieved when she pulled herself together again. Mathieu had simply been there, in the way when she let go. But this time she had come to find him, not just because she couldn't think of anyone else, but because it was Mathieu she wanted. The knowledge pierced her, made her hot and cold, shut out everything else. She got shakily to her feet and stood in front of him. "Mathieu, I cannot go home. Do not make me leave now."

He kissed her hard and angrily, trapping her fiercely against him, as if to teach her a lesson. If he hoped to frighten her, he failed. She simply held onto him and kissed him back, then felt the anger in him diminish. When he looked at her, his face was lined with doubt. "I do not think—"

She smiled. "That is good. Do not think."

"I am right. You are trouble."

"Mathieu, I do not love Donald. It is the truth. You asked me."

"I did not ask. It is what I saw."

"You must look again."

She didn't really know Mathieu at all. She hadn't consciously thought about liking him, much less being in love with him. The fact remained that she had noticed him, and he her, and that somehow their paths kept interweaving. But such an awareness was hardly love.

More than anything for her it was need: in this alien place the need to be as close to another person as she could get; to be touched and caressed and held, to be part of someone else, not a self-contained entity any longer. And Mathieu made her part of him. For a blissful space he made her lose time altogether. She was contented in a way she had not been since she came, her body relaxed, her mind still. For a long time she was happy just to lie against him on the lumpy straw mattress, breathing the smell of him, his arm under her head. His chest rose and fell so steadily she thought he was asleep.

Suddenly she was attacked by doubt. She wondered if she had simply used him because he was accessible. She had always be-

233

lieved she would be certain of her feelings when the time came, and now they were in such chaos she couldn't begin to sort them out. She lifted herself on her elbow and looked at him.

"That is better," he said. "My arm is numb. I was afraid you had gone to sleep."

"I have never done that before," said Lyn.

"I thought as much."

"But of course *you* have."

"I am a number of years older than you." He smiled lazily at her.

"How many? How old are you?"

"Twenty-eight."

"I am seventeen."

He nodded. "Yes, I know that."

"Mathieu—"

He interrupted her. "Soon you must leave. If your father were to find us—"

"He is not my father."

Mathieu sighed. "Perhaps. But he thinks that he is. I do not want to bet my life that you can convince him otherwise."

"Oh, God, what is going to happen to me?" she asked softly.

"Not, I hope, what has happened to your sister, Jeanne."

She rolled over and sat up, her toes curling on the bare floor. The air was chilly and damp against her skin. She shook her hair back and felt the key on its cord around her neck. It was no good. The problems were still there, still the same. The respite was temporary; nothing had been solved.

"Caroline." Her named sounded tentative on his tongue.

"Caro*lyn*!" She was losing her grip; she never used to feel close to tears all the time, she thought, furious with herself. "I am called Lyn."

"Lyn?" he repeated. "What is that?"

"My name!"

He brushed the hair off her neck and kissed her there. "No," she said, shaking him away. "Do not do that."

"I thought you liked it."

"You do not believe me."

"Ah, that." He shifted away from her. "It is so very difficult, you know. You must be fair—"

"Why?" she cried passionately. "Why should I be fair? What is

234

fair about any of this? I do not know why I am here, I do not know how I will get back where I belong, I do not know what is happening to my life—my real life—or what my mother thinks. For all I know your Elisabeth is *there,* in *my* place, with *my* mother, while I am stuck here.'' She stopped, wide-eyed, unfocused. Suppose it were true—she really was? In the twentieth century, with Dorrie. Dorrie would *never* have mistaken Elisabeth for Lyn, not for a minute. But what difference would that make? It wouldn't change them back. The enormity of it hit her between the eyes like a mallet. Elisabeth, catapulted out of 1744 into 1983. At least Lyn had some idea of 1744—she could find herself in it. Elisabeth wouldn't have had a clue about Lyn's world. She couldn't have dreamed what life would be like in 1983—no one had lived it yet. And she thought of Agathe, a fisherman's wife, and Gerard, an illiterate foot soldier. It was mind-shattering.

"Carolyn? Carolyn—"

She swallowed and blinked and found Mathieu watching her with a frown. "I do not want to believe you," he said honestly. "When I am away from you I do not believe you, and it is easy. But when I see you—"

"It does not really matter. Even if you did believe me, there is nothing you can do," she told him sadly.

"I will help you, whenever I can," he said. "You must tell me."

She put her hand up against his cheek and traced the line from his nose to the corner of his mouth. He turned his head and kissed her fingers. "I am trouble, remember?"

He smiled and her heart contracted, as it did when Blaize smiled. It warmed his eyes and melted the sharp angles of his face. "I do not think that I will be allowed to forget. But against a witch, what can I do?"

She woke in the depths of the night, clammy with the grasp of a dream. Louise was shaking her hard. "Elisabeth! Elisabeth! You cried out but I could not understand you! You will wake the others!" Like a slug, the dream slid away from her, leaving a slimy, thick trail behind—no substance, just a heavy, nasty sensation she could not throw off. For a moment she was terrified that it had to do with Mathieu, but at the thought of him it vanished, and she went to sleep again comforted.

It had been late in the afternoon when she came back from Mathieu, hurrying through streets that were almost deserted. Overhead, clouds flew like smoke across the sky, driven by the wind. Mathieu had helped her to dress. When he saw her shoes, he said, "You must have new ones, before it snows. Will your grandmother not buy you new ones?"

"I have not asked. It is my feet—they are too big." She held one up for him to see. "Elisabeth has shoes, but I cannot wear them."

He examined the worn ones more closely, fingering the soles and stitching, and the angles came back into his face. He said nothing more about them, but gave her a strange, wary look, and wrapped her in her cloak. He bundled her down the stairs and out as if he couldn't wait to be rid of her, but once outside, he kissed her again. "Go quickly," he commanded and gave her a little push, and she knew that he didn't want her to go at all, so she went buoyant and happy through the dusk.

When she got in, Marguerite was alone in the bakeshop, tidying the shelves, her eyes worried. "Where have you been all this time?" she asked. "You did not tell Louise where you were going. She came to me. I have been so afraid that something had happened to you." Lyn only just stopped herself from saying, "But it has!" Instead, she smiled and said, "Do not worry about me. Where is Louise?"

"With the babies. Maman was cross that you left her alone—she is only a child. She asked where you had gone, Elisabeth."

"What did you say?"

"I told her that I had sent you to buy green silk for me from Monsieur Gaspard so that I might finish the waistcoat. She said that I should have gone myself."

Marguerite looked so distressed that Lyn knew she ought to feel contrite, but she was too filled with other things. "Shall I go and see her?"

"No. She is upstairs and does not want to be disturbed. Elisabeth—you would not do anything—foolish?" There was a note of pleading in her voice. "It is not good that you go out alone like this. I worry—"

Lyn began to fold dustcloths. "I told you, you must not, Marguerite," she said firmly, closing the conversation.

Two days later, Michel told her that Gerard Grossin had been released from the hospital. When she asked how he knew, he hesitated, debating with himself, then admitted grudgingly that Mathieu had sent the information. "Though why it is you care, I do not see. What good is this soldier to you? He can do nothing for you."

"Does that always matter?"

He gave her a pitying look. He was, she noticed, wearing the stockings he had extorted from her. She had wondered when she gave them to him whether he would keep them himself or sell them.

"Will you give the soldier a message?"

Michel took one of the fresh white rolls out of the tray Pierre had just brought in and put it casually in his pocket. "Perhaps."

"Tell him to meet me—he will know where. This afternoon, I will come."

He shook his head disparagingly and went out.

Donald was waiting for her in the shed, and he looked awful: gaunt and yellow, the skin around his eyes bruised. His voice rasped uncomfortably in his throat and his hands shook. Lyn had been prepared for him to look ill, but his appearance was a shock. Her first reaction was, how could they let him out of the hospital in such condition, but when he began to tell her about it, she remembered Mathieu's remark that the treatment could be worse than the disease.

Donald talked and talked in that hoarse, painful voice as if he could not hold the words in any longer, as if by letting them out he could rid himself of the experience. And as a kind of penance, she made herself listen to him. He had been in a ward with some twenty other men. He had no idea what they were all suffering from: some were delirious and moaned continually, some coughed, some shouted and gabbled. There was a soldier whose hand had been crushed under a block of granite he was helping to position in the wall behind the Bastion. Another had suffered extensive powder burns when his cannon had misfired during practice. His face was pulled and blackened like melted candle wax and he had lost the sight in his right eye.

"I was lucky," Donald told Lyn harshly. "They didn't operate on me. They have never heard of anesthesia, you know. When they cut you, they just do it. If you're fortunate, you're unconscious, otherwise they hold you down. I could hear them—the victims—shouting and crying. Oh, God. It was like being in hell. They bled me—twice. I thought I was going to die. The first time I fainted. I wanted to the second time, but I couldn't. One of them held me, and the other took a knife—'' He pushed back his sleeve and she saw a narrow red line across the vein on his wrist. Her stomach convulsed. ''I just watched—as if it was someone else. But it was my blood, running out of me into a basin. I felt as if I was floating around somewhere overhead.'' He closed his eyes and shivered.

''Donald—'' But she didn't know what to say.

''One of them died, you know. He was two beds away from me. I don't know what he had. I might have it myself now. I don't know. I saw it. I thought he was asleep, then he gave this funny little cry, as if he was surprised, and lifted his head up and that was it. He was gone. Have you ever seen anyone die?''

Wordless, she shook her head.

''No. Well, I hadn't either, but now I have.'' He swallowed several times; his Adam's apple bobbed violently. ''I dreamed about it. About dying. I dreamed about dying here—being buried. I was at the bottom of this pit, looking up. There was sky—then there was nothing. No one will ever know. They'll never know what happened to me.'' He stared at her, his eyes vacant, his mind lost somewhere behind them.

''Donald, listen.'' She was desperate to drag him back. ''I figured something out while you were—sick. I know what happened to the others—the ones who should be here. Elisabeth and Gerard and Agathe. We've swapped places—I'm sure that's it. They must be where we were.''

His face showed the merest flicker of interest; he thought it over. Then he gave a rasping little laugh. ''It's a joke—a practical joke, isn't it? So he's at McGill now—this minute. Writing my dissertation about life in the eighteenth-century army. Better than I could—he can do it from experience! Who would know better than Gerard Grossin, poor bastard. But they won't believe him—they'll think he made it up. Where are your sources, they'll ask, and he won't be able to tell them. Of course, I'm forgetting. He can't write anyway. He can't even sign his name.''

She was losing him and it scared her more than she had ever been scared before. She didn't know what to do. He must have seen it in

238

her expression; the laughter that had nothing to do with amusement vanished. He shrank down inside himself and she saw Donald again, so pale he was almost a ghost, but Donald.

"Thank heaven," she said.

"I never liked it here." He shook his head. "Never. I was uncomfortable from the beginning, pretending to be someone else. The rest of them didn't seem to mind—only me. They all thought it was great sport—they didn't know. . . ."

"You didn't either," said Lyn. "If you had—" A bizarre thought struck her. "If you'd known, you could have found out what happened to *me*." The hair prickled on the back of her neck and she rubbed her arms. As soon as she'd said it, she was filled with thankfulness that he hadn't. She didn't want to know. It was better to have it simply happen, no matter what it was.

But Donald seemed not to have been following her. "Well?" he said suddenly. "What is it?"

"What is what?"

"What you worked out. It's cold standing here—I'm freezing."

"But I told you—that we changed places. That because we're in their time, they must be in ours. And it must be even worse for them—they can't know where they are. Everything's unimaginable."

"That's it?"

"Well, yes—I mean—"

"What good does *that* do us?" he demanded. "So what?"

Stung by his tone, she said, "Well, if I'm right, then I don't see how leaving Louisbourg will help. We can't all be in the same place at the same time, so we can't just walk out of this one and into our own. They have to change back, too."

He gave her a long, bleak, unbelieving look. "Who is he, anyway?"

"Who?"

"The guy who came to see me. He said you sent him. He's the one who told me to get lost before—you know. He looked as if he'd like to slit my throat."

"He's a friend of my—of Elisabeth's father. That's all." She didn't look at him.

"You never wanted to try my idea. You told me to wait, and I did, and now it's too late. There was a sailor next to me when I got there—an Irishman with two of his fingers gone—off one of those big boats. Came round the Cape of Good Hope. He kept me sane that first day, talking to me—when he wasn't out of his head with fever. He said he had to be on his feet again before November thirtieth or he'd get left behind. Have to stay here all winter. I guess he made it. I didn't.''

"Until you're better," said Lyn, "you wouldn't get out of sight of the walls.''

"No," he agreed. "But I'll get better. I'm not going to die in this place. Before May—before the siege, I'm going to be gone, Lyn. So help me. And you've got to keep bringing me food.''

"I'll do what I can, but it isn't easy. I have to steal it.'' She knew he was telling her it was her fault that he hadn't gotten away. He was laying on her a large part of the burden of his survival, and she felt guilty enough to accept it.

⇢》 18 《⇠

"YOU ARE TO BLAME," SAID MICHEL SOURLY. "I am? For what?" Lyn had paused in the doorway of the cowshed to watch him milking. Blaize leaned against the cow's solid, warm shoulder.

"For keeping us here. We should have sailed with the others. We would be well away by this time, but he will not go. And—it is because of you.''

"Did he tell you that?''asked Lyn. Michel's words struck sparks inside her, little fountains of light. It was dangerous to believe them.

"Of course not. It would shame him to admit such a thing. But I know. If he does not leave soon—''

But he did not go. From the front steps of the bakery, first thing each morning, she looked across to where Mathieu's little boat rode at anchor; she did it automatically, for good luck. And seeing the shallop, she knew that somewhere in the town was Mathieu, and that there was a chance that sometime during the day she would see him—perhaps only a glimpse, out on the quay or turning a corner in the street ahead of her. Even when she did not see him, she knew he was there. In the middle of her chest there was a small warm bubbling, as if there were a secret spring inside her, a source of well-being.

Michel's irritability fed it. She felt a strength and a power she had not known before. At first the boat made her afraid because it reminded her that Mathieu meant to leave Louisbourg. He had told her so the day they had gone to see the Lepines. Already he had stayed longer than he had intended. Jean Bernard had much work to do mending roofs before winter settled in, and Mathieu stayed to help him, because he owed Jean Bernard a favor for taking him in and giving him a legitimate job, Lyn knew that. But now—if she believed Michel—she knew he also stayed because of her. Every day the boat was still there was another day he delayed, another day further into winter and the bad weather that would postpone his departure until spring.

She had not gone to his room again—there was never the chance—but she saw Mathieu often. He simply appeared, at the end of a street, behind a knot of customers in the shop, walking beside her when she was out on deliveries. She knew he was there even before her eyes confirmed it, and knew instantly where to look. They never had more than a few minutes together.

About a week after Donald's release, Mathieu met her on the rue Royale and handed her a parcel wrapped in sacking.

"What is it?"

"An Indian gave it to me," he said mysteriously.

She opened it, and right there in the street, where anyone could see, she had been audacious enough to kiss him. Even as he protested, he kissed her back, laughing at her delight. Inside the sacking was a pair of soft leather moccasins. "They are for large feet," he said.

She was happy. Under the circumstances she knew she should not have been, but she couldn't help herself. Whenever she talked to Donald, she did her best to hide it; he was morose and pinched and feeling the weather badly. Their meeting place offered little more than shelter from the full force of the wind. Its roof leaked like a colander, and there were gaps in the walls where plaster had crumbled and fallen out. The dirt floor was always damp and there was a depression near the door which was usually full of water. But it was private, and inside they could talk without fear of being seen or overheard.

She did her best too to provide him with extra food. Once when

241

Suzanne caught her cutting a slab of cheese, Lyn had faced her down. "What are you doing?" Suzanne demanded, and Lyn retorted, "You know exactly what I am doing. You have done it yourself often enough." Suzanne's mouth snapped shut like a coin purse and her eyes narrowed to glittering slits, but she said nothing more.

Lyn wished she could get Donald some warmer clothes: a better shirt, some new stockings, a scarf—but that was much harder. She had no money of her own, so buying anything was out of the question, and no one in the household had anything to spare; there were no extras. Things got used until they fell apart. If they became too small, they were passed on to someone else, or even sold if they were good enough. She would have taken something from Joseph— he had most, but she was afraid that Marguerite would be blamed for its disappearance. Florent had only the clothes on his back, and she couldn't take from Christophe. If only Donald would do something for himself.

With the sailing of the fleet, the atmosphere in town changed drastically. Suddenly the streets and taverns and cabarets were deserted; the empty harbor seemed vast. Some four thousand people had departed from Louisbourg all at once, leaving an immense void. The sailors took with them their rowdy laughter, songs, the exotic stories and jumbled accents. Many others, like Thomas, vanished as well: servants, apprentices and journeymen; fishermen like the Lepines, who had decided it was time to cut their losses and go elsewhere, before cold weather trapped them. The war and the bad fishing season had blasted their enthusiasm for life in the colonies.

Those left behind were suddenly face to face with the long, dark tunnel of winter. For all practical purposes, the world beyond the town walls ceased to exist for them; they pulled inward and barred their doors. Like a hungry cat, the wind unsheathed its claws and hunted up and down the narrow streets, moaning and growling, raking at houses, howling down chimneys. Shutters were latched in the early afternoon dusk against something they couldn't keep out. People piled firewood close to their doors and huddled beside their hearths. When they ventured out, they swathed themselves in heavy cloaks and shawls and pulled their hats down low and hurried through the bitter streets, bowed against the slicing rain and sleet.

Everything was cold and damp, inside as well as out: bedsheets, clothing, feet, hair, fingers.

The first big gale of the winter came roaring out of the northeast the third week of December, driving torrents of freezing rain. Great bursts of seawater exploded like mortars all along the rocky shore of Rochefort Point and the wind drenched the town with salt spray, so that it was impossible to tell which water came down and which up. All morning the storm built. Michel left for the faubourg early, and Lyn, watching him disappear into the howling gray, wondered if they'd ever see him again, or if he'd be blown off the face of Isle Royale. That morning Mathieu's boat had been gone from its mooring, and for a moment her heart had stopped. But when she asked Michel, he gave her a baleful look and said, "Do you think I would be here still? He has only moved her to where she will be safer. There is a storm coming."

He and Florent, with Blaize trying to help, had secured all the loose bits and pieces in the courtyard and carried armfuls of firewood into the cellar. They had fastened the shutters, and the house was filled with shifting, restless dark. The family moved into the kitchen while the storm battered the walls and roof. Drafts swirled around the room, teasing the candle flames, making shadows leap and shrink in the corners. Marguerite set aside her embroidery because she couldn't see it and worked instead at hemming a sheet, which her fingers could do by themselves. The babies were very quiet. Lyn tried knitting to distract herself, but when the storm was finally over, Marguerite had to rip most of it out again.

She fell back on her stories to keep her mind off what was happening outside; the one she found herself telling was The Three Pigs. The pig with the house of stone had survived—and the Pugnants' was a house of stone.

"I did not realize you knew so many stories, Elisabeth," said Marguerite. "Where did you learn them all?"

"Oh," said Lyn vaguely, listening to the crashing and booming beyond the door, "here and there. How long will this last?"

"Days," said Suzanne with gloomy relish.

"Days?" Lyn jumped as something large and solid hit the house. "What is that?"

"A water barrel, by the sound," said Christophe. Periodically he and Joseph went to the cellar to make sure the flour stayed dry.

Every now and then they could be heard shifting things. Lyn hoped the cats were all safe below, but she supposed they were experienced in looking after themselves.

They went to bed early that night, and again the next, for the gale showed no signs of letting up. The house groaned and rattled as if a giant were shaking it like a piggy bank. Renée slept stolidly through it all in her trundle bed, and although Blaize crept in with Lyn for comfort, both he and Louise fell sound asleep almost at once. Lyn longed for oblivion herself, but it would not come. Never before could she remember being worried about the weather. Sometimes it was inconvenient, sometimes uncomfortable, sometimes exciting, but never really threatening. When disasters occurred—tornadoes, earthquakes, blizzards, hurricanes—they were always somewhere else: pictures of tragedy and destruction on television or in the papers. Then the Red Cross was there; teams of doctors flew in to help; school gyms opened for refuges; fire departments and civil defense dispatched ambulances and rescue crews; there were instant floods of food and clothing and money to help the victims. India, South America, Africa—the remotest parts of the world.

But here, in this tiny settlement on the edge of the ocean, they were on their own. Not only would no one rush to help if they needed it, no one would even know for weeks—or months—if Louisbourg was completely wiped away in such a storm. It hadn't been—she *knew* it hadn't been. It had taken the English to destroy Louisbourg finally, years later, so it was silly to allow the storm to bother her, but she couldn't help it.

For the first time she began to really think about the English—the siege that she knew was coming in the spring. It would be very much like the storm: violent and loud, only less random and more deadly, aimed entirely at the town. She wondered how Donald was surviving up in the barracks—whether he was warm and dry; she hoped so, but she was very much afraid he wasn't. Like pinballs, thoughts kept shooting around inside her head, making sleep impossible.

Sometime during the second night, the storm finally blew itself out; rain continued to fall in great, heavy drops, as if exhausted by its struggle with the wind. Lyn's eyes ached from the hours she had lain awake in the furious dark. She was dull and heavy herself, like the day, and wished she could roll up in the bedclothes and sink into

244

unconsciousness now that she need no longer worry about the roof being torn off and the windows bursting inward, or the walls cracking on their foundations. But life was back to normal again: Christophe, Joseph and Pierre rose as usual to fire the ovens in the bakery and stir the flour into the sponges for the second batch of bread.

Michel returned, coming in from the courtyard dripping wet to report that there was a hole in the back fence and one of the hens was missing. Lyn's relief at the sight of him seemed disproportionate to her until she realized it meant Mathieu was still in Louisbourg. She hoped he'd bring his boat back soon for confirmation.

The men took the shutters down, and although there was little light in the day, at least they were no longer sealed blindly inside the house. Customers began to arrive as the first baking came hot from the ovens. They grumbled and complained and exchanged glum news of damage, but no one seemed surprised that they had all survived. They took the storm in stride.

The weather was still raw and gray when Lyn looked out the following day, but her spirits rose irrepressibly, for there was the shallop, riding at her moorings in the familiar place, among the other boats that were overwintering in the harbor. She thought that Mathieu would come by to make sure that all was well, but he didn't. Every time someone came into the shop she looked up, hoping, and was disappointed. As the day wore on she became increasingly preoccupied and made careless mistakes. Madame Pugnant scolded her irritably and Louise scowled in disapproval. Finally, her patience tried beyond enduring, Madame Pugnant sent Lyn out with a meat pie and three loaves of bread for customers in the street behind the hospital. "Get out," she said. "Get out from under my feet, Elisabeth! You are useless today! Go straight to Madame Jodouin and the Mingot tavern and come straight back, is it, and take deep breaths of air while you are out. When you return, I will expect you to settle down, do you understand?"

"Yes, Grandmother," said Lyn meekly. She could make a detour past the tavern where Mathieu lived—it was almost on the way—and perhaps he'd be there. Though serve him right if she ignored him altogether.

When she had made the deliveries, peering up and down the streets to no avail as she went, she walked past Lopintot's tavern, still without a glimpse of him. Feeling dismal, she was heading back to the shop when he came up behind her and caught her unaware. "I thought you might be out today."

Her heart gave a kick and she swung on him accusingly. "You startled me! Where did you come from?"

"I have been following you since the rue de l'Estang." He sounded amused.

"It has been days since I have seen you. Where have you been?"

He raised his eyebrows enquiringly. "Are you angry?"

"I had thought—suppose something had happened to us in the storm?"

"Michel assured me that you were all safe."

"You could have come to find out for yourself," she replied grumpily.

"What—to the house? Be sensible! I would have come if there had been trouble. Jean would have heard."

She hunched her shoulders and began to walk. "I am not used to such storms."

"No? There will be many before the winter is finished. Snow instead of rain," he said, keeping step with her. "Does the sun always shine where you come from?"

She knew he still had doubts about her; usually she didn't blame him—it required a tremendous act of faith to believe the story she had told him—but at that moment she was bone tired and edgy. She walked faster.

"It has been good to Jean Bernard, this storm," he went on conversationally. "There are many roofs to mend."

"How fortunate."

He paid no attention to the sarcasm in her voice. "And my boat rode the storm well. She is tight and dry. Lepine has done his work."

Lyn didn't want to hear about the boat. "It is foolish to stay out here in the wet," she said shortly.

"Yes," Mathieu agreed.

"I must go back." On the rue de l'Estang she paused and gazed drearily down the wet cobbles to the harbor. Her cloak was heavy with rain and her shoulders were damp.

"Yes."

"But I do not *want* to go back!" she cried in frustration. "Oh God, I am so sick of this life! I want to go somewhere with *you*. Just

246

to sit and talk, that is all. I do not ever see you to *talk!* There is nowhere in this town to be private.'' No Pizza Hut or Friendly's, no library, bookstore, museum, MBTA bus, back porch, park bench . . . how did people ever get to know one another? When Mathieu didn't respond, she turned away from him in despair.

"Wait. I do not understand—what do you mean, talk? About what?'' He sounded genuinely puzzled.

"Anything! Everything. I do not care. About you—there is so little I know about you—''

"Like what?'' he asked suspiciously.

"Your family—who they are. Where they are. What you did before you came here. What you will do when you leave. If you are married even. I do not know.''

"*Sacredie!* Why do you think I am married?'' he demanded.

She had merely said what came into her head; at least she had his full attention. "Many of the men here are married, but their wives are in France. The old governor, Monsieur Verrier—''

"But not me!'' he declared. "I am *not* married. Why do you care about my family? Why do you want to know these things. What is the reason?''

"The reason is—is only that I like you. I want to know who you are. That is all. In my time—''

"Mmmp.'' Suddenly he took her by the arm and began to walk.

"Where are we going?''

"We are going to talk.''

"But—''

"But first you will be still.''

He marched her briskly through the streets. She took little notice of where they were going; she really didn't care. The rain and her wet feet no longer bothered her. They wound down through the town, to a cabaret behind the place du Port that Lyn had not seen before. It was small and plain, furnished with the usual assortment of benches, stools and tables. Two men in coarse working clothes were playing a game with dice at one of the tables; another smoked a pipe before the fire, a small black dog with a gray muzzle stretched at his feet. The players looked up as Lyn and Mathieu entered, exchanged a glance, then went on playing. The man with the pipe nodded. "I had thought you left with the others, Monsieur,'' he said. "I have not seen you in some weeks.''

247

"I was not ready to sail," Mathieu replied.

"It is late in the season to go now, I think."

"The ice is not yet bad. There is time." Mathieu changed the subject. "You have lost most of your custom, Antoine. It has gone to France."

The proprietor shrugged. "Every year it happens the same. The winters are quiet, but they will return in the spring."

"You do not think the war will stop them next year?"

"I am too old to worry about wars, Monsieur. The sailors and the fishermen will be back—they always are. Like geese. You would like something to warm you? And the lady?" He gave Lyn an interested glance.

Mathieu nodded. He ordered rum for himself, and for Lyn a hot sweet wine drink. Antoine heated a poker in the fire and plunged it into her cup with a hiss of steam. She and Mathieu sat in a corner, away from the other men. Mathieu's expression was quite forbidding, but she sensed he wasn't angry with her, rather he was uncertain. When they had their drinks and he had paid Antoine, he said, "Now, who has been talking to you? What have you heard about me, eh?"

"Nothing. That is the point. Except that you came as a trader, and that you have a boat, and that Jean Bernard has given you work, and that you knew how to find flour for the bakery."

"Then what is this about a wife?"

"Do you have one?" For an awful moment she was afraid that her random shot had been a bull's eye.

"I do not. I told you." He scowled at her.

"I only said that for all I knew you might be married."

He took a swig of rum. "I do not want a wife, or children. I do not want a family. I do not want to have to think about other people. Not like Jean Bernard. He is not free. Even though you do not live with him you cause him worry and trouble just the same. He cannot forget that he has children." He sat brooding into his tankard for several minutes. "I do not think it was a lucky day for me when I came ashore at Louisbourg."

"What about me?" Lyn remembered her first view of the town, the modern town, not the reconstruction. "It was worse for me. At least you are where you belong."

248

"I do not understand, Mademoiselle." Mathieu leaned toward her across the table, his face intense. "How did you come here?"

Lyn took a deep breath as it all crowded in on her. The temptation was too strong; she couldn't hold it back. "I came here in a car—automobile," she said defiantly. "I came with my mother—it has always been the two of us. I do not know my father. I have never seen him—he left us before I was born. I have no brothers and no sisters, and no other family, only Dorrie. Last spring I graduated from Belmont High School, and in September I was supposed to go to college. I like baseball and music and children." She thought perhaps she was telling him all this because of the wine—it made her feel slightly fuzzy. Many of the words she used he could not know, could never have heard: car, graduated, college. . . . She told him about Gilbert, how she had found him one day on her way home from school: a tiny gray-and-white kitten, arched like a croquet hoop, tail stiff as a pipe cleaner, spitting curses at an enormous bumbling golden retriever that kept making hopeful little dashes at him under a barberry bush. Lyn just scooped Gilbert up, right there out of someone's front hedge, and took him home. Dorrie made her put an ad in the paper, but they were neither of them surprised when no one answered; Gilbert was Lyn's. She told Mathieu about Mike, and his father's hardware store, and Mathieu listened, frowning, without comprehension. On and on she talked, unable to stop herself: about Dorrie and her jobs and her struggle to become a photographer—he couldn't possibly know what a photographer was. But the words kept coming. I'm just like Donald, she thought, hearing herself. I am telling him who I am to keep from being swallowed by Elisabeth. Perhaps it means that I'm losing my grip.

Mathieu said nothing. She could feel his eyes on her face, grave and steady, as the words rushed out of her. Every now and then she would glance at him, but she couldn't tell what he was thinking. When at last she ran down, she became aware of another conversation going on in the room. The two men who had been playing dice had left, and three other men were sitting by the fire, talking together. She had not noticed them come in, or the others leave. She took another sip of wine—it was cold—to calm herself, and said, with an attempt at a smile, "So. Now you know everything about *me*."

But Mathieu shook his head. "No. I think I do not begin to know about you. Most of what you say I do not understand. It is another language."

"Yes. But I needed to tell someone—to tell you."

"What can I do? What is it you expect from me?" he asked fiercely. "If I could help you to get back to where you come from, I would do that. But I do not know how."

Stay with me, she wanted to say. Don't go away. I don't want to be alone. But she couldn't ask him to do that, because she knew that if *she* had the chance to go, she would seize it. She would leave him and return to her own time without hesitation. She looked at his strong, blunt fingers resting on the table and remembered him loving her—and knew that she would ache for him, but that would not stop her.

Behind her, the door was flung open, admitting a gust of damp, chilly air. The men stopped talking. Mathieu's hands tensed. She glanced up. "Mathieu?"

Ignoring her, he rose to his feet. She turned and saw Jean Bernard in the doorway, his face knotted with anger, hair springing wildly around it. He filled the space, massive and threatening, like a goaded bull. "What is this?" he demanded. "You—what are you doing here, in this place, with my daughter?"

Lyn stared at him, open-mouthed.

"It is all right, Jean," said Mathieu, placating. "We do nothing but sit. We have come out of the rain."

"Out of the rain, is it? Out of the rain?" With a snort, he lumbered across the room at them. Lyn, who had managed to get to her feet, was directly in his path.

"It is true! We have done nothing—we have been talking." He made her feel defensive without any cause.

Giving her no more notice than he would a mosquito, Jean Bernard thrust her aside with one powerful arm and she stumbled against the table.

"Jean, listen—" said Mathieu.

"Listen to what?" he roared. "There is nothing to be said! You—after what I have done for you—this is how you repay me! Villain! You will be sorry you set eyes on Louisbourg before I am through with you!"

The proprietor came hurrying out of the back room and stopped short, just out of range. "Now, now, gentlemen—" he said in alarm. "Can you not discuss this—"

But Jean Bernard was in no mood for discussion. He went straight at Mathieu, arms swinging. Lyn heard a dull, sickening thud as one of his fists connected and Mathieu staggered back. Jean Bernard was on him at once, and Mathieu had no choice but to try to defend himself. This time he was the object of Jean Bernard's rage, rather than an obstacle to be removed from his path. The table skidded out from under them and collided with a bench, and the tankards scattered, spraying what was left in them. Lyn got the rum down the front of her chemise as she made a desperate grab for Jean Bernard, shouting at him, "No! Stop it! Wait!" Her fingers hooked the sleeve of his shirt and she heard it tear as he threw himself at Mathieu.

The three men by the fire had risen and were watching the proceedings with great interest and not the slightest inclination to get involved. Antoine jigged helplessly on the sidelines, his face a study in anguish, his hands flapping like sheets on a washline, as the two men crashed around the room, falling into furniture, sending it flying. There was the sound of splintering as Mathieu landed heavily on a stool. He was clearly getting the worst, using his arms more for protection than defense. The air was ragged with curses and grunts, harsh, rasping groans, muffled cries. There was a lot of blood, though it was impossible to tell whose or from where it came.

"Stop it! Stop it! Can no one stop it?" cried Lyn in a frenzy.

Antoine grasped her by the shoulder. "You! You are the cause of this. Get out—go home! If you go, we can separate them."

"But Mathieu—"

"For the love of heaven, Mademoiselle! Before my inn is destroyed and the guard comes!" He shoved her toward the door, thrusting her damp cloak into her arms. "As long as you are here, he will not listen. You can do nothing!"

Despairingly she looked at the heaving tangle of bodies. Jean Bernard had Mathieu against the wall, hands at his throat, and was pounding him so hard his head jerked back and forth, while Mathieu struggled to break his grip. He stamped his boot on Jean Bernard's instep, and Jean Bernard howled and pounded even harder.

Lyn threw her cloak over her head and fled, out into the cold gray air. She ran away from the inn, her heart throbbing so violently in her throat she could scarcely breathe. At the edge of the deserted

251

place du Port she stumbled to a halt. The rain had stopped. The sky was a solid sheet of hard, dark cloud, spread from horizon to horizon; the wind was jagged. She clutched at the rough stone wall of a warehouse for support. Gradually she stopped shaking and the wordless tumult in her head quieted a little. If he had caught them in Mathieu's bed—but all they had been doing was sitting together, in public, where everyone could *see* they were doing nothing wrong. The inn was seedy, but not disreputable. How had he known where to find them? Who could have told him? Why wouldn't he listen? What was happening now?

She was wracked with such violent longing for her own familiar world she began to shake again, frightened and utterly alone. She didn't understand the rules here; she had not grown up knowing what they were, understanding the consequences for breaking them. Mathieu knew, but this was her fault—she had forced him to disregard what he knew and he was paying the price. Never before had she seen two men actually fighting, attacking one another with the single-minded intention to do as much damage as possible: smashing, gouging, tearing, trying to break each other apart. The wine shot bitter into her mouth and she was sick, grasping the building with icy fingers to keep from falling as she bent retching over the ground.

There was nowhere for her to go—nowhere but the Pugnant house; she had nothing else. Shakily, she straightened and made her way slowly along the quay toward it.

Louise had been watching for her. As soon as Lyn entered the hall, she darted out of the shop. "Where have you been? What have you done? Grandmother wants to see you, and I could not tell her when you would be back. It has been almost two hours, Elisabeth—!" Her eyes widened as she took in Lyn's appearance.

Lyn didn't bother to answer. She hung her cloak carefully on one of the empty pegs and started up the stairs.

"No—she is in the kitchen with Aunt Marguerite. She wants to see you at *once*. She said—"

Lyn paid no attention. She did not want to talk to anyone. She especially did not want to talk to Madame Pugnant. She wanted to be alone, to try to sort things out. She had no answers for anyone. She went into the empty bedroom and shut the door, then lay down on the bed, staring hard at nothing. The horror that gripped her now

252

was nothing like the anxiety that had robbed her of sleep during the storm; that had been fear of something definite, something real and immediate with edges she could feel. She could deal with it because she understood it. But this was like sea fog: cold and clammy and limitless, erasing all the landmarks she lived by. She had believed that she could survive by being herself; she had rejected Agathe's way of coping. She refused to merge indistinguishably with the eighteenth century, becoming Elisabeth Bernard as long as necessary. She was *not* Elisabeth—she would not *be* Elisabeth. But it was Elisabeth's world she was living in, that was the trouble.

Time drifted. There were voices downstairs in the hall, and beneath her in the kitchen. Noises. Doors opening and shutting. Footsteps. Feet on the stairs, going past her door to another room. Still she lay, letting the sound wash over her without sinking in.

Then the silence in the room was broken; someone opened the door and came in. Marguerite's pale, anxious face appeared like a moon above her in the twilight; her voice called Lyn back to Elisabeth's present. "Why did you do such a thing, Elisabeth? Your papa has arrived in such a rage—and covered in blood! We did not know—Maman would not let him see you until he grew calmer. He shouted so, did you not hear him?"

Lyn sat up, the pulse heavy behind her eyes. "Is he still here?" Her tongue felt thick and furry.

Marguerite nodded. "He is with Maman—they have gone to her room."

"What did he say? Did he say what happened?"

"That he found you in Lacroix's tavern—alone with a *man*, Elisabeth!" she said in a horrified whisper.

"With Mathieu Martel, his friend," said Lyn bitterly.

"Elisabeth, how could you?"

"What? I did *nothing*! Why is it not allowed simply to *talk* to someone, Marguerite? Why does everyone think the worst? Why do you?"

"But in a place like that—and with such a man—you will be ruined, Elisabeth. And Maman, she trusted you. She is very upset. Why did you not refuse him?"

"You have it wrong," said Lyn. "He should have refused me. I asked *him*—I am to blame, not Mathieu."

But Marguerite did not believe her; she saw it plainly in the blue eyes. "When you see Maman, Elisabeth, do not answer her back. Do not say such things. It will only be worse if you do. Please promise me."

Lyn stared at her helplessly, feeling grim. She could do nothing for Mathieu.

It was like facing a court of inquisition: Madame Pugnant at her desk, Joseph inflated with righteous indignation, and Jean Bernard only slightly less wild-looking than when she had last seen him. He had washed the gore off his face and hands, but the knuckles of his right fist were bandaged and his left eye was puffed nearly shut, the skin around it stained purple. Mathieu had landed at least one good blow. They all glared at Lyn as she entered, pinning her to the floor. Behind her, she heard Marguerite withdraw, softly closing the door, cutting off retreat, and she set her chin.

"I see no need to go through this with you, Elisabeth," said Madame Pugnant in a voice like splintered glass. "We all know what has happened. I do not ask you to explain yourself because you cannot. I had believed you to be sensible—more sensible surely than your sister. I am sorely distressed to find that I have been wrong. It is clear that you have been foolish enough to allow this man Martel to take advantage of you."

"And whose fault is that, I would like to know?" broke in Joseph. "Who is it that encouraged this? Her own father!"

"I did nothing to encourage it, Desforges," declared Jean Bernard. "He deceived me! I gave him my help and he went behind my back! She is under your roof—why did you not see this happening?"

"*I* am not father to your sluts!" retorted Joseph.

"You are father to no one!" Jean Bernard looked ready to spring at him.

"It is not true," said Lyn. "Mathieu did not deceive you. If you must blame someone, it is my fault."

They all stared at her in amazement, as if she were a chair that had just risen on its two back legs and spoken aloud.

Jean Bernard sprang, but at her instead of Joseph. Before she could see it coming, he delivered her a stinging slap with his left hand. She put her hands to her face; never in all her life had she been hit in anger. Dorrie had spanked her only twice: when she was seven and had exposed three rolls of film which Dorrie had shot of some-

254

one's wedding, thinking she could see the pictures that way; and when she was nine and had decided to go on her own to Logan Airport for the day to watch the airplanes. Both times, Lyn was forced to acknowledge, Dorrie had been justified. But being spanked was different from being struck. "Is that the only answer you have for everything?" she asked Jean Bernard, her voice shaky.

His face grew black and his hand twitched.

"Enough!" Madame Pugnant stood, leaning her weight on the desktop. "Elisabeth, you will be silent. And you—if you cannot control your temper, you will leave my house."

"Why do you not send him away?" said Joseph. "He can take his brats with him. They bring us nothing but disgrace."

"She—" Jean Bernard pointed to his mother-in-law. "She will not do that. No, she does not want to lose Pierre."

Joseph looked apoplectic. Distracted, Lyn wondered if he might have a heart attack. He looked like an excellent candidate. But perhaps these people didn't have heart attacks. Without knowing how, she felt suddenly that she had lost.

"We are not here to discuss Pierre," snapped Madame Pugnant. "It is Elisabeth we are concerned with."

"I say throw her out," declared Joseph. "If she behaves like a slut she has no place here."

"Yes, Joseph, you have made your opinion very clear," said Madame Pugnant wearily. "That will serve no purpose."

"Then she must be sent away."

"And that is not possible, not until spring, as you know. Jean?"

"I cannot take her. Even if I wanted to." He gave Lyn a furious glance.

Madame Pugnant nodded. "So. She must stay." To Lyn she said, "You will no longer be allowed to leave this house by yourself. It will make life more difficult for everyone else, but you cannot be trusted."

"But to deliver bread—" Lyn's heart plunged. She saw her only shreds of freedom snatched from her.

"Michel must do it. You will serve only in the shop and that because there is no choice. Jeanne cannot, and Marguerite makes too many mistakes."

"And what about Martel?" demanded Joseph. "What about him, eh?"

"Do not worry about Martel," said Jean Bernard with grim satisfaction. "He is leaving Louisbourg."

"When?" asked Lyn, struck cold.

"As soon as he is able to pick himself up. I do not think he will wait to be told twice."

Mathieu did not. The next morning, when Lyn looked out the bakeshop window, his boat was gone again from its mooring place. And Michel, they discovered as the day wore on, was not simply late. He too was gone.

⇢⟫ 19 ⟪⇠

IT SURPRISED HER THAT IT HURT SO MUCH. IT WAS LIKE HAVING A broken rib—a pain in the side whenever she breathed deeply or moved suddenly. When she had left Mike in June, he had been tender and properly despondent at the prospect of Lyn's departure. Their last evening together had been full of romantic melancholy. She had felt a twinge of guilt in fact because he seemed to mind more than she. But that was natural: she was going away, to a new place and new people, while he stayed behind in the old one. He would miss her because he was used to having her be there. The space she normally occupied in Belmont would be empty all summer. There was no such space for him in Nova Scotia—she didn't expect to find him there, so she didn't really mind his absence.

And it wasn't permanent anyway. Their parting was only temporary, a sadness to be indulged with a certain pleasure. Even now, though the separation was longer than either of them had anticipated and things might have changed between them, she knew she would see Mike again. Mathieu was gone from her life. When she thought of him she ached. He had not even tried to say good-bye to her, he had just gone. He could have attempted to see her. He could have at least sent Michel with one last message. He could have done *some*thing, instead of just creeping off in defeat. She felt abandoned, and she longed for someone sympathetic she could talk to, but there was no one. Since the moment on the place du Port when she had fully realized how different she was from everyone around her, Lyn had also realized how impossible it would be for her to

256

make herself truly understood. The gulf was not language; it was perception, expectation, meaning. She had tried to cross it with Mathieu, and although he too had tried, in the end it hadn't worked. Only Donald understood who she was, but he was so mired in his own miseries, he had no time to spare for hers.

Everyone was preoccupied and irritable. With Michel gone, the rhythm of the household was upset. His chores were all the kind that were never finished: splitting, stacking and carrying firewood, hauling water, feeding the hens and the cow, cleaning boots, sieving flour; they needed to be done over and over and over. Florent could do things like boots, but he was useless for heavy work; no one dared to suggest that Suzanne might bring in water. Pierre did it, and fetched wood, and Christophe split kindling, but that left the bakery very short-handed and Joseph more short-tempered than ever.

To everyone's surprise, Lyn volunteered to look after the animals. Ever since the first morning, when she had found the cow instead of the privy, she had been fascinated by her. She was such a placid, undemanding creature; she stood in her stall, grinding away on her cud and turning it miraculously into milk, unbothered by the people who came and went around her. Lyn had never been close to a cow before, never actually touched one, seen her breath make steam in the cold air, leaned against the warm flank and felt the ropy tail, or listened to her teeth working hollowly inside her skull. Unlike the cats, the cow was quite friendly in a passive sort of way. Lyn often found an excuse to be present when Michel milked her. Watching his small deft fingers pulling away at her rubbery teats, she asked one day, "Is it hard? Can I do it?" Michel shrugged and said, "Can you?" But he got up from the little stool and let Lyn try, grinning at her lack of success. She pulled and squeezed, and the cow turned her head, rolling her enormous eyes so the whites showed, as if to say, what's going on? But no milk came. Lyn was sure it must be gone, but when Michel resumed his place, the cow began to chew again and milk ran into the bucket in strong, steady spurts.

Lyn watched him closely, and the next time she tried she was rewarded with a thin, uneven stream. "Now," said Michel, grinning still, "the idea is to get it into the bucket instead of onto the

257

ground, is it not?'' She learned. She practiced until she could milk the cow as well as he, and the cow no longer seemed to notice the difference between them. That was the real test.

Now she was glad she had learned. The others looked at her with doubt and skepticism when she went out the first time with the empty bucket, but she came back with it full in the same amount of time it had taken Michel, and from then on the job was hers, along with mucking out the cow stall, cleaning the henhouse, feeding the chickens and gathering the eggs. Louise went to the bakeshop with Madame Pugnant right after breakfast, to prepare for opening, while Lyn went into the courtyard.

Being outside with the animals gave Lyn a much-needed respite from Elisabeth's family. It gave her a chance to be quiet for a little while, away from the muddle of human relationships and demands and emotions. It was soothing to shovel cow manure and scatter grain.

"Well, *I* would not do it,'' Jeanne declared. "It is not proper work for a woman.''

"If the cow does not mind, why should I?'' said Lyn. "She is better company than many.''

Jeanne sniffed, unsure of the insult.

But Lyn was not the only person to find refuge with the cow. Every morning Blaize slipped out the back door, too. While Lyn worked, he stroked the cow's broad concave nose and picked choice bits out of the straw to hand feed her. Blaize had been Michel's shadow. Without the older boy, Blaize retreated further into his private hole. He became almost invisible, locked in silence. People tended to forget about him; he was easier to overlook than to worry about: He did not complain or cause trouble, and there were too many things in need of attention.

It was several days after Michel's disappearance before Lyn could look outside herself far enough to notice the little boy. One morning as she watched him resting his cheek against the cow's smooth, steadily moving one, in a flash of insight she realized that he was as abandoned as she. They had both lost people they counted on. Tentatively at first, she began to talk to him—about little things: the cow and the hens, not sure he was listening to her. She asked him if he could find the eggs and gave him the basket, and was amused and chagrined to discover that he could find more than she. He knew about the hen that nested in the cow's loft, and the one that laid in the darkest far corner of the henhouse.

Once he found a mouse nest behind the manger: a globe of sheep's wool and shreds of sacking, all woven together, and in it four small toast-colored mice with tiny white feet and long pink tails. Blaize watched Lyn anxiously to see how she would react to this treasure, and when she smiled, his face relaxed. "We must keep the cats out," she said, and he nodded solemnly. She laid her fingers across her lips and then across his; it was their secret.

When she milked, she drew him in between her arms and he let her curl his fingers under hers, around the cow's teats, and they pulled together. Or sometimes he sat in the straw beside her with his mouth open and she would attempt to squirt milk into it, and he would grin and grin at the joke. She was glad to see him happy, but it made her heart ache for Mathieu's smile. She talked to Blaize about Michel, and gradually about Mathieu: where they might have gone, what they might be doing. Although he could only listen, she found it helped. There was much a six-year-old boy could not understand, but he did understand about missing someone. They formed a peculiar alliance, each comforting the other. When she looked into Blaize's homely little face, Lyn saw the bright, intelligent being behind his eyes and she was filled with a longing to free it. If only she knew about dysfunctions like his. If only she could take him with her back to her own world, where people knew how to help him.

In the meantime, there was Donald to worry about as well. Two days after the fight in Lacroix's tavern he came into the bakeshop. Lyn and Louise were there alone; Madame Pugnant was upstairs with the accounts. It was a cold day, and he wore a heavy gray overcoat that hung off his shoulders and the end of his nose was red and wet. Louise eyed him with undisguised suspicion, and behind her, Lyn made faces at him, hoping desperately that he would not say the wrong thing. He looked around uncertainly, and Louise said in a sharp voice, "Good day, Monsieur. You have come to buy bread, is it?" as if doubting that he had.

"I—um—yes—" He fumbled under the skirt of his overcoat, searching his pocket for a coin.

Fortunately, at that moment the wife of the apothecary, Madame Biron, and two of her friends came in, shaking off the chilly air and discussing the scandalous behavior of Angélique Beaudin, who had taken up quarters with the shoemaker in the rue de France. They glanced at Lyn and at one another with significant expressions, and Louise turned quickly from Donald to wait upon them.

Under cover of their business, Lyn managed to convince Donald to return in an hour or so, when Louise made the deliveries. With Michel gone and Lyn grounded, that had fallen to her. Louise had no sooner taken the basket and left than he reappeared.

"Donald, you must be careful. She knows you look familiar."

"Me? I should be careful? What about *you*?" he said accusingly.

"What do you mean?"

"Where were you yesterday? I waited until I nearly froze to the ground and you never came. And there wasn't any food."

"I couldn't get out. I can't—they won't let me leave the house by myself."

"So it *was* you! Dammit, Lyn—I was sure it couldn't be, until I heard who was mixed up in it—Jean Bernard and that man—the one who came to the hospital. Martel. What were you doing?"

"Nothing," she snapped. "I keep telling everyone. It was raining and we went to the tavern to talk, that's all. And anyway, why should I answer to you?"

"Because we're in this together—that's why. If you get yourself into trouble what'll happen to me? What will I do if I can't see you again? You told me to wait, don't forget. Hang on, you said, we'll get back all right. Well, I'm hanging on, Lyn, but it takes everything I've got to do it. I'm desperate. If I didn't know that I could talk to you, I'd go off the deep end."

She didn't want his dependence. "Suppose I weren't here, Donald."

"Then I wouldn't be, either," he said simply. "I'd never have made it this long. During that storm I thought we'd be blown clear off the face of the earth. It was dark as a pit in the barracks and all the rats came out." He shuddered. "One of the others had a bottle—they all got drunk. Someone was sick on the floor and no one cleaned it up, they just left it."

She almost asked him why he hadn't gotten drunk too, to take his

260

mind off the storm. But it was no good trying to start an argument with Donald; he was ill-equipped for a fight and too easy to wound.

"Anyway," he said, "he's gone now. I heard he'd been run out of town."

"He always meant to go," said Lyn, keenly aware of the loss.

He gave her a sharp look. "You miss him," he said with disbelief.

She would not meet his eyes. "He was a friend." She desperately did not want to talk to Donald about Mathieu. She wished he would let the matter drop.

There was an awkward silence between them. Then, to her surprise, Donald said roughly, "I'm sorry."

"Why? Why should you be sorry?" she cried. "Look at me— I'm so much better off than you are! I live in a house with proper floors, I have decent food to eat, and clothes, water to wash in—it's warm here and there are people I can talk to at least a little. You make me feel guilty!"

"But that does neither of us any good, does it?" he said sadly. "Listen, Lyn. I've got to *do* something. If I don't, I really will lose my marbles."

"You're not going to start in again about leaving, are you?"

He shook his head. "It wasn't your fault I got sick—I know that. It's the other woman—the one you mentioned, in the faubourg. I know you told me she didn't want to talk, but that was months ago. It was August when you saw her, wasn't it? Now it's the middle of December. I'll bet she's changed her mind after all this time. Or maybe she's thought of something that would help us." He was talking quickly, suddenly animated. "You can't go see her, but *I* can. Just tell me who she is—I'll find her. I'll be careful, I promise, Lyn. I won't frighten her."

Looking at his eager face, Lyn thought it was far more likely that Agathe would frighten Donald. The idea of his going to find her filled Lyn with foreboding. "Donald, I'm not sure it's a good idea. I don't think—"

"But things have changed since you went. The ships have sailed and there was the storm—it's different now. Unless"—he paused— "unless you've been back to see her without telling me. Have you?"

261

"No, of course not. But has it occurred to you"—the words came reluctantly—"that she might not be there anymore?"

He shivered. "Yes, I've thought of that. But if she isn't—then she's got back. We'll know we can do it."

"Donald—"

"It would help to know there really is a way. And you'll be right about not leaving. I'll have to believe you."

Her heart was like a lead sinker. She gazed at him helplessly.

"Is it because you don't trust me? Why? Do you think I'll blow it somehow? Or don't you want me to know?"

"Oh, Donald! Don't be stupid—it isn't that! I just don't think—she can help."

"Then tell me—I don't care. I have a right to know."

It was instinct, not reason—the certainty that sending Donald to Agathe was a mistake. She couldn't put it into words and she hadn't the energy to try. She could feel him waiting, pushing, willing her to relent, and with a sigh she gave in.

"The des Roches's fishing property—of course. I should have guessed!" he exclaimed, light dawning in his eyes. "Because it's in both times!"

Oh, God, thought Lyn, meaning it as a prayer, don't let anything happen to him, *please*. The thought of losing Donald, too. . . . She made him promise to come back and tell her right away, whatever he found out.

"Don't worry—I won't leave you here. I wouldn't do that. I told you, we're in this together. I'll go see her as soon as I can get away long enough—not for a couple of days. But I'll find a way to talk to you." He stood straighter, his shoulders squared, and he actually smiled at her. "Don't look so grim. At least it's something to do. It'll be all right."

Lyn made herself smile back, wanting to believe him. "I'm sorry about the food. I can't get to the shed for a while anyway, but in the mornings I go out to milk the cow. If you come by the back gate just after seven—"

He nodded. "We'll work it out. We'll manage." He was the confident one now. He buttoned his overcoat and set his hat squarely on his head. She watched him walk up the quay. A fine powder of snow was sifting down the wind, across the harbor. He left dark footprints in it.

262

The courtyard gate became their meeting place. It wasn't as satisfactory as the shed, but it was better than nothing. They couldn't linger because there was the constant threat of discovery—by Pierre or Christophe coming out for wood, or anyone else to use the privy. But Lyn could pass Donald a little food: a cupful of warm-from-the-cow milk—he questioned her about typhoid and she pointed out tartly that everyone in the household was quite healthy—a raw egg or two, whatever else she could sneak from the larder without being noticed.

Blaize had to be in on the secret. At first Donald was distrustful. "Does he know who I am?" "You're a soldier." "You know what I mean. Will he tell?" Lyn smiled at Blaize and said in French, "No. He can keep secrets." Blaize nodded gravely and put his finger to his lips.

In fact he became an accomplice. He was quite willing to wait by the gate while Lyn did chores, and fetch her when he heard Donald knock. He seemed to regard this as a kind of game they were playing and relished his part in it. Lyn told him how helpful he was and his eyes shone with pride.

Every time Donald came, she felt relief. She was afraid to mention Agathe to him, afraid to remind him, even though she knew it was useless to hope he might have forgotten. The conviction had grown within her that she had made a terrible mistake by caving in. But what else could she have done? If she had refused he would have been hurt and angry, convinced she was holding back on him, that she didn't trust him. She couldn't tell him she was afraid he wasn't strong enough, and that talking to Agathe would damage him in some mortal way. So instead she gave him food, bribing him to come back so she could see that he was all right. But she knew in the end it wouldn't be enough, and it wasn't.

About a week after Lyn told him about Agathe he went to look for her, and when he appeared the next morning, one glance at him confirmed all her fears. The bravado was gone; his eyes were stark. She couldn't shut the gate on him, so she pulled him into the cowshed with her, made him sit on a pile of straw, and tried to get him to tell her what had happened. She thought perhaps if he could talk about it he might revive a little. But he was uncommunicative. He answered her questions in monosyllables, licking his lips uneasily, rubbing his hands together as if to warm them. Yes, he had

263

gone. Yes, he had found Agathe. No, she knew nothing that could help them.

"Is that all?" pressed Lyn. "She must have said something else."

But he shook his head. "Only what you told me."

"Did she believe you? Who you are?"

"Oh, yes."

As gently as she could, she reminded him that she had warned him about Agathe. "I know, I know!" he interrupted her angrily. "I *had* to go. Now I have to think. I can't think when you ask questions."

"Think about what?" She was filled with apprehension.

"There you go again. I can't *think,* I tell you! I need to think!" he shouted at her. Then seeing her alarm, he calmed down again. "She's no good to us, that's all. She's no use. But it doesn't matter. There's a way—there's still a way. I just—have—to think," he said deliberately. "It's all right. Don't look at me like that. Really. It's all right. But I had to know, didn't I? I had to find out. I couldn't just—"

"Elisabeth? Elisabeth!" It was Suzanne, bellowing from the kitchen door.

"Oh, *merde!* She wants the milk." The bucket was too heavy and full for Blaize to carry through the snow; Lyn would have to take it herself. "Donald, wait for me. Just stay here for a few minutes and I'll come back. Blaize, stay with him."

Blaize looked at her doubtfully, then went and sat next to Donald. He hardly seemed to notice, just keep rubbing his hands and chewing his bottom lip. Blaize was still sitting there when she came back, his face screwed up with worry. Donald was gone, and the court-yard gate was half open.

All day she agonized. If only she knew what Agathe had actually said to him, what questions Donald had asked her. He was upset, but of course he would be—he had pinned so much hope on Agathe's help. He was probably annoyed with Lyn for being right about her. He didn't want to admit his own failure. At least he had come to tell her about it—that had to be a good sign. He could have simply stayed away, sulking. She had to have patience and wait for him to return, treat him normally and not demand to know why he'd gone off like that. She had to demonstrate her belief in him, show him she wasn't worried, even though she was.

Over and over she replayed their conversation, picking it apart for some hint of reassurance and finding only causes for alarm. Somehow she made herself function well enough to get through the day. The only person who was aware there was something wrong was Blaize. He avoided her, and at night he did not come creeping into the big bed as he always did now. She noticed but was too preoccupied with Donald to think much about it.

But when she wrapped herself up the next morning to go out and Blaize made no move to go with her, something clicked in her head. Anxious as she was to see if Donald would be there, she hesitated. "Are you not coming with me?" she asked Blaize. "You are much better at finding the eggs than I. And the cow will miss you."

Suzanne gave a great impatient sniff. "It is time he learned something useful, that one. There are too many people in this house who do nothing, if you ask me."

"I do not believe anyone has," said Lyn curtly.

"You watch your step, girl. You are not so clever as you think."

"Who is not clever?" asked Marguerite, coming in and setting Anne on the floor to play with Renée and Marie.

Lyn held out her hand to Blaize, and after a moment's indecision, he took it. Marguerite gave her head a sad shake. "It is such a pity."

Once they were outside, Lyn said, "I am not angry with you because he went away, Blaize. Did you think I was?" His fingers gripped hers. "It was not your fault."

She was certain that Donald would not come. But he was there already, waiting, hunched outside the gate. He seized the little bundle she had for him and pulled it open.

"Why didn't you wait for me yesterday?" she asked, keeping the reproach out of her voice.

"I couldn't. I couldn't sit still any longer. I'm *starving*—is this all you could get?"

"I do my best."

"I know, I know. It's the cold. It makes me ravenous. You

couldn't get me a blanket, could you? The wind howls through the barracks and the snow comes in the cracks—the floor's drifted with it in the mornings.''

"How would I get you a blanket?''

"They'd only steal it from me anyway,'' he said morosely. "Hypothermia's not such a bad way to die, actually. Quite peaceful. Not like the hellish hospital.''

"Don't joke about it,'' snapped Lyn. "It isn't funny.''

"Who's joking? I've thought a lot about dying. It's going to happen—to both of us if we stay here. Sooner rather than later. I'm only being practical.''

"You're being morbid. Blankets are *big,* Donald, not like cheese and dried beef.'' But she was already thinking about how to get him one. She was sure there were no "extra'' blankets in the house; People had either just enough or too few of things like that. "Sacks, maybe,'' she said.

"Better than nothing.'' He was grudging.

She managed to acquire two empty grain sacks from the cellar. They were musty-smelling and full of grain dust, but they were sound and heavy and would do for insulation. As Donald so graciously put it, they were better than nothing.

➥➥ 20 ⬅⬅

IN THE SECOND HALF OF DECEMBER, THE WEATHER RELENTED. Overnight the wind swept away the threatening banks of cloud that had oppressed Isle Royale for weeks, and by morning the sun rose in a brilliant sky, splashing blue shadows on the snow drifted in the lee of walls and fences, melting it to slush, then churning it to mud on the roadways. Icicles dripped from all the eaves and the slate roofs shone wetly. The harbor turned to rough navy blue within its white shores, and the air lost its frosty edge and tasted fresh. People opened up under the sun and stopped to talk to one another; it was only temporary, but it felt good.

Only Suzanne remained resolutely bad-tempered, and that because someone was always tracking mud into her kitchen. Lyn, coming in with the milk, having sent Blaize ahead with the eggs, found Suzanne scolding him furiously for a set of enormous gritty bootprints across the floor.

"—take your sabots off at the door, like everyone else! I cannot spend my time cleaning up after your carelessness, you wicked boy!"

Blaize stood head bowed and mute under the barrage of angry words.

Lyn, instantly roused, demanded, "How can it be his fault? Look at the size of his feet! He has only just come in the door. Why do you not scold the person who actually *made* the tracks? You know it must be Christophe or Joseph—it cannot be Blaize. But you dare not bully them, is it!"

Pierre, who slipped in after Lyn with a load of firewood, listened to her with undisguised delight. He had felt the rasp of Suzanne's tongue all too often himself. Marguerite was horrified. "Elisabeth—"

"*I* will clean the floor, if that is what troubles you so much!" Lyn seized the broom from its corner and began to beat vigorously at the mud. Suzanne stumped over to the hearth, where she rattled her pots and muttered evil things into them. It was a wonder that any of the food she cooked was edible.

"You must not speak to her that way, Elisabeth," Marguerite murmured.

"Why not?" Lyn didn't bother to lower her voice. "It is only what she deserves. She is a bad-tempered old woman and I do not see why she should be allowed to make everyone else suffer because she is so sour."

"You will provoke her too far and she will leave."

"No, she will not. She is too well off where she is to think of leaving."

Marguerite peered nearsightedly at Lyn, on the verge of saying something, when Louise burst into the room, white and breathless. "Aunt Marguerite! Aunt Marguerite, you must come! It is Grandmother! Something terrible has happened!"

"Maman?" Marguerite dropped her mending and hurried out. Lyn dropped the broom and followed.

At first sight, the bakeshop looked empty; it was too early for customers and Madame Pugnant was nowhere to be seen. She lay in a wilted heap on the floor behind the counter. At once Marguerite was beside her, feeling for a pulse, and Lyn steeled herself for the worst.

"She gave a little cry and fell, and she would not answer me," said Louise.

"God is merciful," said Marguerite, "she is breathing. Louise, run and fetch Christophe and Joseph. Elisabeth, you make up the fire in her room and open her bed."

Joseph carried his mother-in-law up the stairs, and Marguerite, pale but collected, settled her in bed with Lyn's help. Her breathing was shallow and the blue vein in her temple throbbed visibly. Lyn was surprised at how tiny Madame Pugnant actually was; it was her conscious presence that filled so much space.

"Now," said Marguerite, "I will wait with Maman. Christophe has gone to fetch Monsieur Bertin. You and Louise must look after the shop, and Jeanne will mind the babies."

"Will you be all right alone?" asked Lyn.

"But of course, Elisabeth. There is nothing you can do here and it would upset Maman to know the shop was not open on time, is it not."

Downstairs in the bakery, Joseph and Pierre were taking the first batch of bread from the ovens. Very soon Christophe returned with a severe, neatly dressed man who carried a leather bag. Without a word to any of them, he gave Christophe his cloak and ascended the stairs with an authoritative step. He was impressive, but not very reassuring. Joseph hastily dusted his hands on his apron before removing it and went after Monsieur Bertin. In less than an hour they came down again. Monsieur Bertin rearranged his cloak and left. Late in the morning Père Athanase came. Louise, in the shop, crossed herself when she saw him. "Grandmother is dying," she said in a tight little voice.

"You do not know that," said Lyn, although she felt far from optimistic.

But Madame Pugnant did not die. For three days everyone crept around the house and spoke in whispers. The women who came to buy bread wore solemn faces and asked about Madame Pugnant. Some even brought little gifts: herbs, a pot of salve, a bottle of thick, bitter brown liquid. Monsieur Bertin came twice a day, but whatever he said and whatever he did were a mystery to those of them who remained downstairs. Lyn decided on the whole she would rather not know anyway, not after Donald's descriptions of what went on in the hospital. She didn't see how Madame Pugnant could survive a cure like being bled. Most likely the old woman had suffered a stroke, but Lyn had no idea what people knew of such things in the eighteenth century.

The household rearranged itself. Lyn was once more in charge of the bakeshop, while Louise ran messages from the kitchen to the sickroom. Jeanne, looking rebellious but not daring to complain outright, took care of the babies while Marguerite spent her days beside Madame Pugnant. Suzanne boiled up an endless series of potions and tisanes, her mouth tight and her eyes grim. Even Joseph, Lyn realized, was deeply worried. He was so preoccupied he forgot to yell at Pierre, and prowled the house relentlessly, unable to settle to his work, leaving it to Christophe to run the bakery.

On the fourth day, Madame Pugnant opened her eyes, looked Monsieur Bertin in the face, and asked him what he was doing there. Louise reported it to them in the kitchen later. Marguerite had said, "He is here because you are ill, Maman," and Madame Pugnant replied, her voice faint but distinct, "Now I am better, he can go. Monsieur Bertin charges too much," and went off to sleep, snoring gently.

She was not going to die, Louise told them jubilantly. The crisis has passed. But although that might be true, Madame Pugnant was far from recovered. She was too weak to sit up and she spent most of the day sleeping. When she was awake and herself, she demanded to see the accounts and to hear about the bakery, but when Joseph brought her one of the ledgers, she hadn't the strength to open it, and she drifted away as he answered her questions.

When, to her surprise, she was summoned upstairs, Lyn was dismayed by the change she saw. Madame Pugnant was old and shrunken; her jaw and cheekbones were sharp under the creased tissue-paper skin, and her mouth was stitched with tiny lines.

Marguerite sat near the bed, hemming a square of linen. "Maman, Elisabeth is here to see you, as you asked." She touched her mother's arm. To Lyn she said, "She has little strength, Elisabeth, you must be careful. . . ."

And not upset her, Lyn finished mentally and nodded. "Grandmother?"

The old woman's eyelids flickered open. Underneath them Lyn caught a glimpse of the Madame Pugnant she was used to, deep inside the eyes, like live coals under the banked ash of a fire. The spirit was still there; Lyn was relieved.

"Elisabeth." Her voice was as thin as porcelain.

"Yes, Grandmother."

"You—must look after—the books."

"But I thought—"

"You have watched me. You know what to do. Joseph—Joseph will do the rest. But not the figures."

Marguerite frowned at Lyn. "Tell her you will do it," she said softly.

"I will try—I will do my best, of course, but—yes."

"Good." It was barely a breath. The eyelids fell, the thin lips parted. For an instant Lyn's heart stopped. Then she heard the faint, puffing snores and saw that the covers rose and fell almost imperceptibly on the old woman's chest.

"She must sleep now. You will do what she wants, Elisabeth?"

Ultimately it seemed as if everyone did what Madame Pugnant wanted, even when they didn't like it. Lyn went to the desk and opened one of the ledgers: painstaking columns of names and figures. She remembered helping Mike with inventory in the hardware store after Christmas—counting fuses and light bulbs and switchplates. It was only bearable because they could do it together, and Mike made his father pay her. But that meant he was entitled to keep a steely eye on them to see that they didn't have too much fun. Mike was better at all the fiddly record-keeping than she; she counted and he wrote. She sighed and sat down to see if she could make any sense out of the bakery records.

Everything was there, of course. Every sol paid out and every sol taken in, money owed and money owing. Madame Pugnant was meticulous—more so even than Mike. In one ledger were the names of everyone who bought from them, or who brought pies, cakes and loaves to be baked in the ovens. Each day Madame Pugnant had entered the latest figures in her thready, knotted hand. The second ledger contained a record of bills paid and money owed to various merchants for supplies: different kinds of flours, salt, sugar, honey, molasses, suet, butter, eggs, raisins, fruit, and many, many items Lyn did not recognize. It would take time and concentration to understand all of it, she realized with quickening interest. This was a part of her life that had been entirely missing since she left her own time: reading and writing, solving mental problems, playing with figures. The books represented a challenge she was going to enjoy, at least for a while. She shut the ledger with a snap and found Marguerite watching her anxiously.

"Can you do it?" she asked.

"I expect so. It will take time to learn."

"I would never be able to understand. Never."

Donald had never come daily to the back gate; sometimes he couldn't get away from the barracks early enough, or he was sent out to chop wood, or given sentry duty. But about a week after Madame Pugnant's collapse, Lyn suddenly realized that she hadn't seen him for four days in a row, and he had never before let four days pass without contact. The mild spell was over, and once again there was snow on the wind: tiny, sharp needles that swarmed and stung like black flies. The muddy ground had frozen into uneven ruts and ridges that tripped the unwary, and the town had retreated behind its doors again.

Lyn woke that fourth day with her head clogged and her throat dry, sure signs of a cold, and when Donald didn't appear, she was suddenly, horribly, afraid that he had been taken sick again. She didn't think he could survive another siege in the hospital. With both Mathieu and Michel gone, she didn't know how she was going to find out about him unless she went up to the barracks herself and asked. If he had ever told her what company he was in, she couldn't remember; nor could she remember him mentioning the name of any other soldier with him. She wished she didn't feel so heavy and thick-skulled.

Finally, after brooding over the problem all morning, she decided to talk to Christophe. Even if he would not help her, she was sure he wouldn't give her away. His relationship with Joseph was almost exclusively professional, and he would do nothing to upset either Marguerite or Madame Pugnant. When she knew he was alone in the bakery, she went across the hall. He was cleaning out the kneading troughs, scraping fragments of crusted dough from the insides with a broad-bladed knife.

She came straight to the point. "Christophe, I need help."

"Yes, Mademoiselle?" He sounded cautious.

Her nose prickled explosively; she caught the sneeze in her handkerchief. "I have a friend who may be in trouble. I do not know. I have not seen him for five days now."

"Him?"

She nodded. "He is a soldier. You have seen him in the bake-shop, I know."

"Do we not have trouble enough, Mademoiselle?"

For a split second she saw Mathieu's face instead of Christophe's; she blinked it fiercely away. "I must know that he is all right, this friend. He has been ill before and I am worried about him."

Christophe continued to scrape. "So what is it you want?"

"Just to know where he is, that is all. Can you—would you find that out for me—please? I would not ask if it were not important."

He said nothing, his attention focused on the knife he was using. At last he finished the spot to his satisfaction. "And if I tell you that I cannot do this?"

"Then I must go myself." Her nose was running. She blew it irritably.

"What is his name?"

"Gerard Grossin. He is a private."

"Yes, that I know. As you say, I have seen him, Mademoiselle. He comes to the back gate in the mornings, I think."

It was her turn to say nothing. She had tried to be so careful.

"It is bad for you to be involved with this person, Mademoiselle."

Stubbornly she said, "He is a friend, Christophe." But in Louis-bourg, decent young women did not have such friends, she knew that all too well by now. "Have you told anyone else that he comes?"

"No." His expression was sorrowful. "I had hoped that he would stop and that there would be no need. It is a difficult time— I did not want to make it harder. If I agree—to do this thing for you—will you tell him not to come here?"

She shook her head. "I cannot do that. I am sorry, Christophe. I should not have asked you."

He ran a finger thoughtfully along the knife blade. "If you go asking questions at the barracks everyone will hear of it."

"Yes, I know. But I cannot help that."

"Very well. I promise nothing, but I will ask one or two people."

"Thank you."

"Do not thank me, Mademoiselle. I do not do it for you, but to protect the family."

She nodded, knowing it was true, and sneezed.

By the next day Christophe could tell her that Donald was not in the hospital, for which she thanked God devoutly. Her cold had settled down on her like a broody hen, muffling her ears and filling her nose. She could count on one cold a winter and knew there was nothing to be done but wait it out. Two mornings later, Christophe followed her to the cowshed, and she could see at once that the news he had for her was not good. His long face was very long and his eyes were worried. He had learned that Gerard Grossin was not in Louisbourg.

She stared at him blankly. "Not in Louisbourg? But then—where is he?"

"No one knows, Mademoiselle. He is gone."

"Gone?"

"There is a rumor," he said, not looking at her. "It is said that he has deserted. He went out with a party of soldiers to gather firewood. They separated. All returned but Grossin. It is not uncommon here—desertion. It is a hard life and the winter is very long. Since the end of summer, a number have gone."

"But *now*? There is snow on the ground! There are no ships—" She stopped.

"He is in the company of Captain Duhaget, no? He has been gone for a week now. When they found him missing, they sent out three men to look, but they found nothing—no trace. Mademoiselle? Elisabeth?"

She had closed her eyes, suddenly dizzy. How could Donald have done this to her. He had *promised*. How could he go without saying anything? A week! An entire week—

"Elisabeth?"

She opened her eyes and saw Christophe hovering awkwardly. She gave her head a shake to clear it and tried to think how Donald had looked and what he had said the last time she'd seen him, but there was too much clutter. The words "deserted," "a week," "gone—*gone*" kept echoing in her ears as if trapped there. A cold little hand clasped hers. There was Blaize, his face lumpy with concern. She took a deep breath and very slowly counted to ten. "It

273

is all right," she said steadily. "I am not feeling very well. And the news is—a surprise."

Christophe's relief was palpable; she could tell he had been wondering what to do if she fainted again, as she had that first afternoon. "It is likely that he will come back, Mademoiselle. As you say, there is snow and there will be no ships until the spring. He has probably found shelter with some fisherman not far from here. When he has thought about it, he will return."

"Yes," she agreed, but she did not believe it, any more than Christophe himself. Deserters were dealt with harshly if they were caught—that knowledge kept many soldiers from trying it.

There was one other person in Louisbourg who knew what Lyn knew about Donald. One other person who had seen him and talked to him. After the initial numbing shock wore off, Lyn was able to make some order out of the muddle in her head and she remembered Agathe. When Donald had returned to her after visiting Agathe—and then kept coming back—Lyn had worked very hard to convince herself that no lasting harm had been done. He'd been discouraged, but at least he knew the truth about Agathe and was coping with it.

But ever since then, something had altered between them. Lyn hadn't wanted to admit it. She had begun to feel uncomfortably responsible for Donald, as if she had failed him in some fundamental way and she had to make up for it. Instead of being grateful for whatever she could give him, he was critical, always making her aware that it wasn't enough, expecting more from her. She buried her resentment as well as she could, reminding herself again and again that his lot was so much worse than hers. Once or twice his whining had goaded her past endurance and she had snapped at him. Then the wounded look he gave her smothered her with remorse, and she would spend the morning flat and depressed.

He had never told her exactly what had passed between himself and Agathe. Whenever she raised the subject, he deflected her with something else. He talked a lot about making choices, about being able to shape the course of one's own life.

But Agathe knew what she had told Donald, and Lyn began to be obsessed with finding out. It ruined her concentration. When she worked on the books, the words and figures on the pages wriggled into meaningless lines. She forgot how to add. To her horror, she discovered that she had actually written "Agathe Grimard" at the end of the day's accounts, although she didn't remember doing it. There was the name, black and inescapable, in her own slightly awkward penmanship. Without thinking, she had dipped her quill in ink and put those particular letters together, and when she saw them, she knew she would have to go and find Agathe again. And the sooner the better.

These days with Madame Pugnant in bed and the men busy in the bakery, Lyn could leave the house with little difficulty if she was careful. She was even permitted to deliver orders again when Louise could not be spared. So, after making up her mind to see Agathe, Lyn simply put on her cloak and let herself out into the cold afternoon as soon as the shop was closed.

She had not seen the faubourg since winter had clamped down. Except for the ribbons of smoke fraying from the chimneys, it looked deserted: a derelict huddle of buildings and upturned boats on the frozen shore. The fish flakes stood empty in the snow, frames collapsing, poles missing. A boy was pulling a broken barrel apart for the wood. A man sheltering against the wall of one of the cottages watched Lyn go past, his face remote and cold, offering no greeting. She scarcely noticed him. Her eyes kept straying beyond the settlement, to the great blank wastes spreading out on every side. Snow had erased all traces of life out there; she could not imagine plunging off into that emptiness alone, turning one's back on the only known vestige of civilization for hundreds of miles. A person would have to be crazy—or desperate—to do that; would have to be convinced there was no other choice.

She banged on the door of des Roches's tavern. When no one answered, she opened it. The room inside was dim and smelled of fish and smoke and unwashed clothing. Two men and two women were playing cards at a table; three more men were sitting near the fire, two whittled wooden pegs, the third spliced lengths of rope, while a couple of women bent over kettles hung in the flames. A girl about Louise's age, carrying three tankards to the cardplayers, paused and looked at Lyn. "What do you want?"

"Madame Grimard," said Lyn. "Is she here?"

"Angélique?" One of the men got up from the table and came over. "What is it?" He was young and very dark, and had a shrewd, narrow face. He looked Lyn over carefully. "I do not know you, Mademoiselle."

"I have come to see Agathe Grimard." Lyn spoke with determination.

There was an exclamation from the hearth. One of the women stepped quickly backward, brushing at her skirt and speaking angrily to the other. At the movement, Lyn turned her head and met the second woman's eyes. They were bleary from the fire, her face reddened; her hair escaped in grizzled wisps from her limp cap. Lyn hardly recognized her.

The man looked from Lyn to Agathe, then back. "She is busy."

"I will wait."

"I do not think that is a good idea, Mademoiselle."

"Monsieur, I do not care what you think," said Lyn loudly enough for the woman to hear. "If I cannot wait here, then I will wait outside—as long as I must."

The man gave a little shrug in Agathe's direction, as if to say, I tried. "Suit yourself, but it is cold out there."

She pulled her cloak tight around her and stepped through the door. She was certain the woman would follow, and in a couple of minutes she did, a shawl hastily thrown over her shoulders.

"You! Why have you come back? Did I not tell you? What is it you want from me?" Her breath made smoke in the gray air.

Lyn's fingers unclenched themselves. As she had closed the door, Lyn had been gripped by a sudden horror: suppose she was wrong, suppose the woman she had seen *was* Agathe Grimard—the real Agathe Grimard? And somehow the woman from Lyn's world had found a way back—what if Donald had discovered that? But it hadn't happened.

"I had to come. I had to talk to you," said Lyn, a little breathless. "It is about Donald—the soldier. He came here."

"You had no right to send him. You had no right to tell anyone else."

Lyn said, "I do not want to argue with you. I must know what you told him."

"Only what I told you—that I want to be left alone. That is all."

"He's gone," said Lyn, in English.

"I do not understand you," replied the woman angrily in French.

Lyn gave her a long, considering look. "I said he is gone."

"So? What is that to me?"

Lyn was strangely calm; it was the calm of disaster, not of well-being. "What did you talk about when he came? Did he tell you his idea—about leaving?"

"He is a fool!" said the woman bitterly. "I told him so. I told him that to leave would be suicide. He said he would die if he stayed. That is his choice—it is nothing to do with me. He went on and on—he argued with me. I told him to get out and not to come back again. He is crazy, that one. Life is hard enough. I was afraid he would be noticed and there would be trouble. That is all."

"No," said Lyn. "What else?" She caught the woman's arm as Agathe turned to go back inside.

Agathe glared at her. "Let go of me!"

Lyn shook her head.

"If he was so sure, I told him to go. To leave then. Why did he delay? Because he was afraid?"

Lyn waited, holding herself together.

"Then he said he would—that no one could stop him. But I did not think—I could not believe that he had the courage. And you—you did not believe him either, did you? Well, if he is gone, good riddance."

Lyn stared at her bleakly. "He was frightened, could you not see?"

"So? So? *I* am frightened! I wake sometimes in the night and I wonder who I am and what will become of me. And then, in the morning, I get up and I do what I must in order to live. It is not all bad. The children—her children—need me, and I am mother to them, as someone must be to mine. André Grimard is not a bad man. I work hard and I forget about the rest. It does no good to remember. I must live here, now. He refused to listen to me. What could I do?"

"Poor Donald," whispered Lyn. She was tired out. She ached all over.

"There is no hope out there. Only *here*. On this spot. I will go nowhere." She was adamant.

"But we don't know how it happened in the first place," said Lyn. "I've always believed we'd get back—I never thought I'd be here this long. But now—what happens in the spring, when the English come? They send everyone away—to France. How can you stay?"

277

"Madame des Roches will stay. I know this. And there are others. They hang on. I will stay as long as it takes."

"Just waiting?"

The woman nodded grimly, her face hard as the frozen ground. "It is the only thing to do. I told him that. It is not my fault that he would not understand. If he is gone and you have any sense you will forget about him."

→≫ 21 ≪←

LYN'S COLD HUNG ON GRIMLY, HOOKING ITSELF INTO HER NOSE and throat. She longed for aspirin, orange juice and an enormous box of Kleenex. Few things were truly as disgusting as cloth handkerchiefs put to serious use. Marguerite concocted horrible drinks for her made with various herbs and ground bark and dried leaves, and then watched to make sure Lyn drank them after catching her as she poured one into the dishwater. "Elisabeth, it is for your own good, is it not," she said in a hurt voice. So Lyn held her breath and swallowed, feeling wretched.

Everyone in town now knew that a private from the barracks was missing. Joseph brought the news back with him shortly after Lyn's visit to Agathe. "The man must have been crazy," he declared at dinner. "To desert at this time of the year? Pah! He is insane. Clearly."

"But," said Christophe, "they do say that conditions for the soldiers are insupportable. And the officers have cut their firewood ration."

"Soldiers are always complaining," said Joseph. "One cannot take them seriously. They are a miserable lot. Pray God we never have to entrust our safety to them."

"Perhaps it is because their complaints have merit," suggested Lyn, stifling a sneeze.

Joseph gave her a frosty stare. "You do not know what you are talking about, Elisabeth. You would do well not to speak of what you cannot understand."

Behind his back she stuck out her tongue and crossed her eyes. Louise, who happened to see her, gaped. But Christophe said, "If we do have need of soldiers, Joseph, surely they must be healthy."

"As far as I can see, all they do is sit about on their backsides all day. Let them prove their value—it is past time they did something to earn their keep. Let them drive the English out of Isle Royale, once and for all, instead of only talking about it. Then—perhaps—they would deserve better treatment.''

"I have heard,'' said Christophe, "that the English are planning to mount an attack against Louisbourg in the spring. Captain Duvivier has said this, and Doloboratz, back from New England.''

"Only gossip. I do not believe the English are that stupid. And even if they are, we have supplies laid by. We can hold out against them well into the summer. By then France will have sent warships to defeat them.''

"I do not—'' began Christophe, then noticed Marguerite's face. "Still, it is winter now and we need not worry about such things. It will be months before the sea is open.''

"What have I been saying? You worry too much, Christophe. The king will never put us at risk, we are too important.''

But Christophe had not been speaking to Joseph, he had been speaking to ease the tightness around Marguerite's mouth. He said nothing more.

Dark and cold, the year closed on Louisbourg. Christmas was celebrated only as a feast day: the bakery and the shop were shut, and the family, bundled against the raw salt wind, struggled up the hill to Mass in the drafty chapel. Although she tried hard not to, Lyn couldn't help feeling bleak. Home seemed extremely far away.

But on the twenty-seventh of December something happened to distract the whole town: the soldiers mutinied. Lyn, having forgotten what little she had learned about this, was as surprised as anyone when, early in the morning, she heard the drummers march through the streets, sounding the alarm. People dropped what they were doing and came to see what was happening; faces appeared at windows and in doorways, dogs barked, children shouted. With the drummers came a company of thirty fusiliers, their bayonets fixed at the ready. No one knew what was going on, but word came round like a brush fire that all the officers had gone up to the citadel, that something was happening among the soldiers—they were mutinying. The soldiers were going to take over the town. People closed their shutters and barred their doors, and men flung on their coats and hurried out into the raw morning to see what they could learn

279

about the disturbance. Joseph went, leaving Christophe to look after the bakery and the women and children. It was only discovered too late that Pierre had managed to eel out somehow as well. In the confusion, no one had thought to forbid him from going.

Marguerite went up to sit with Madame Pugnant, who demanded querulously what was going on, and as soon as Joseph returned he must come and tell her, even before he removed his coat. So when Joseph did return, more than an hour later, Lyn contrived to be present in the old woman's room.

He reported that almost all the troops had assembled on the parade ground, under the ringleadership of three Swiss soldiers. There they had presented their demands to the officers and to Messieurs Duchambon and Bigot. They wanted firewood and the rations they claimed had been withheld from them; they wanted decent vegetables to eat instead of the rotten ones they'd been given; they wanted proper uniforms for the newest recruits, the uniforms they had been promised three years ago and never been given.

"So?" Madame Pugnant, propped sharp-eyed on her pillows, drew her mouth tight.

"They have agreed. Bigot has appeased them for the sake of our safety. They will give the miscreants what they want. And the soldiers have accepted de la Perelle as their major. It is a bad business," he said darkly. "It is the Swiss who have stirred this up—they should be sent back."

"Were all the soldiers involved?"

"Everyone but the sergeants and a company of artillerymen."

Pierre described a different view of the same scene when he reappeared in the kitchen. He told his sisters and Suzanne that the soldiers had actually forced many of the officers to lie on their bellies in the snow, had threatened them with bayonets, "even Lieutenant Duvernay," he said with a sideways glance at Jeanne, who pretended not to hear.

"But what will happen now?" asked Louise.

Pierre made a face. "They all went in again. I do not know. There was much shouting and waving of arms. Ordonnateur Bigot seemed very angry—so did lots of others. But it is over."

The next day, many of the soldiers roamed through the town carrying their muskets and bayonets, approaching various of the merchants with threats and insults, forcing them to sell goods at whatever prices the soldiers chose to pay, boasting of their power and success. The townspeople, who had never thought very highly of the soldiers to begin with, now actively disliked and feared them. Rumors began to circulate that the soldiers were in collusion with the English and this was all part of a plot to hand Louisbourg over to the enemy if they came north in the spring, as some predicted. No one wanted to be seen being friendly with any of the soldiers, but neither did anyone want to arouse their anger.

Donald was well out of it, Lyn thought. She knew that Christophe would never have helped her after the mutiny; he would have felt obliged, for the family's sake and her own as well, to inform them of her undesirable liaison. Her friendship with Gerard Grossin would have been extremely suspect, and if anyone had heard them speaking English together the consequences would have been grave indeed.

But Donald was gone and Christophe knew it, so her secret was safe. He did not come back, as Christophe had unconvincingly predicted, nor did anyone report finding any trace of him. He had vanished into the overwhelming vastness that surrounded the town walls as if he had never existed. Depressed and lonely, Lyn couldn't help wondering if he had been right—if he had found his way back to his own place in his own time. She had no way of knowing.

Except that the real Gerard did not reappear in Louisbourg. If *she* was right, and somehow, with each of the three of them, a swap had taken place, then Donald and Gerard could not both inhabit the same space. The law of physics that Mrs. Lambert had dinned into her physics classes kept rattling around her head: matter can neither be created nor destroyed. If Elisabeth, Gerard, and Agathe were not here where they belonged, they must be somewhere else. And if she and Donald and that woman *were* here, then their counterparts must be stuck in the 1980s. It made as much sense as any of the rest of it.

But if Donald had *not* gotten back, then where was he? Time after time she came to the question and turned away from it.

Daily Madame Pugnant grew a little stronger, though she still did not get out of her bed. Her brain was sharp and alert inside her white bed cap, and every afternoon after dinner she went over the bakery accounts with Lyn, seizing on the smallest mistakes and berating her for them. At first resentful because she was doing the best she could under trying circumstances—deciphering Madame Pugnant's tangled handwriting was enough to give anyone a headache, in addition to which her spelling was remarkably inconsistent even on proper names, and many items were still mysterious to Lyn—she gradually came to realize how important it was to the old woman to find the inaccuracies Lyn committed. She did not want Elisabeth to do as good a job as she herself did. Nor did she want her to make a hopeless mess out of everything, of course. But in between was a safe middle ground, and Lyn learned to gauge it. On those days when Madame Pugnant could find nothing genuine to criticize, she was snappish and out of sorts, so Lyn made sure there was always something for her to put straight. It made life pleasanter for everyone, and Lyn came to regard it as a kind of game. At least it offered a little diversion from the black fog that enveloped her most of the time now. Marguerite told her how much Maman looked forward to their daily sessions, and how cheerful she was afterward.

Lyn missed Donald acutely. In spite of his grumbling and despair, he was the one person who had understood exactly who she was and believed unconditionally in what had happened to her.

The new year began. It was 1745, and before the end of January Lyn would have been away for six months. Once, not very long ago although it seemed like lifetimes, she had toyed with the idea of taking a year off before college. Lots of kids did it—they found jobs, got some practical experience in what they called "the real world," earned some extra money, gave themselves time to think out their lives a little, decide what they wanted. But Lyn knew what she wanted: an undergraduate degree, then a master's in education or social work. The sooner she got the one, the sooner she'd get the other. What was the point in delaying? Dorrie, predictably, had left her the freedom to make up her own mind, but when Lyn announced her decision, she had been clearly relieved. She, too, saw no point in delaying if Lyn was sure.

And now—willy-nilly—here she was, taking a year off anyway. She had dropped further out than anyone could possibly imagine. When they asked her what she had done with her time, she could tell them she had spent it working in a bakery. It was an acceptable truth, tamer than collecting trash or driving a taxi or setting up her own business. Only Dorrie would know how much lay beneath the surface of that answer; she would know because presumably she was having to cope with Elisabeth Bernard while Lyn was missing. Try as she might, Lyn could not imagine what that must be like for either of them. She and Dorrie were going to have a lot to talk about.

On a particularly bleak Wednesday afternoon, Lyn trudged up the rue de l'Estang muffled to the eyes in her cloak. She was going to the Widow Jodouin with a meat pie Christophe had just taken out of the oven for her. It seemed to be snowing, but it was impossible to tell for sure because the wind was so strong it drove and tormented the snow that had already fallen, sending it in great blinding sheets up and down the streets and throwing it off rooftops with evil fury. It plastered the sides of houses with a freezing whitewash and flung up high, sharp-edged drifts in front of doors and across intersections. Lyn could feel the snow sifting into the folds of her cloak and filling her moccasins. She longed for her snow boots and down parka, her Ragg balaclava and mittens; how incredibly free and convenient twentieth-century women's clothes were: easy to wear, easy to keep clean. To take her mind off her discomfort, she began to outfit Elisabeth's family.

Marguerite would never wear slacks—Laura Ashley more like: feminine and slightly frilly with little flowers and ruffles. Louise, on the other hand, would love jeans—and turtlenecks. Suzanne would think synthetics a miracle—elastic waistbands, or those shapeless, bright-colored dresses large women seemed partial to. Lyn smiled as she imagined Joseph in a polyester suit—three pieces, with shiny threads running through it. Something tailored and quite severe for Madame Pugnant, and Jeanne would wear only the trendiest stuff, with designer labels, meant to last one season. She would spend a fortune on stylish, impractical maternity clothes, and discard everything as soon as she could.

Turning left into the rue d'Orleans, Lyn glimpsed another figure, struggling toward her through the shifting snow. The wind was behind him, coming in off the water, driving the hard little ice pellets into Lyn's face so she could barely see. It wasn't until they had passed each other that it struck her there was something familiar about him, but when she paused to look back, he had already almost blown into obscurity. She could hardly make out his shape. She glanced quickly at the ground; his footprints were filling over. He was being erased, as if he were a mistake in her afternoon. Her breath came short and her pulse beat in her ears. Impossible, she told herself, don't even think about it. The figure could not have been Michel. She steadied herself with several deep lungfuls of biting air, and resumed her journey. Playing fanciful games was dangerous, although she hadn't been thinking of Michel at all.

Madame Jodouin, widow of an officer, had been left in modest comfort by her husband. She lived in a snug little house on the rue d'Orleans and brought in a bit of extra money by boarding a shabby, cheerful young man who taught dancing, deportment, reading and writing to the young sons of other officers in Louisbourg. There was a timid girl who did the most menial chores—an orphan—and Monsieur Esnard chopped wood and shoveled snow for his landlady. Having no bake oven herself, she often brought things to the bakery.

Lyn found her alone in the kitchen. Monsieur Esnard was out tutoring one of his charges, and Madame Jodouin was eager to have Lyn stay for a cup of chocolate. Lyn was grateful for the chance to warm herself by the fire and wrap her cold fingers around a steaming cup. Madame Jodouin simply wanted company on such a wretched day. In the course of conversation, Lyn asked casually if she had heard of anyone newly arrived in town.

"Merciful heavens, no! It will be spring before we see any new faces in the streets. It is a very long time to wait, is it not?"

"Very long," agreed Lyn, thinking that was the end of it.

Jean Bernard had been to the house several times since Madame Pugnant's illness, but always Lyn managed to avoid him, contriving to be busy elsewhere as soon as she heard his gruff voice. It didn't matter—he didn't come to see her anyway. Whatever business he had was with Madame Pugnant. At first Marguerite was afraid he would upset the old woman, but it seemed quite the contrary. He and his mother-in-law had declared a truce, and if anything, his visits seemed to invigorate her. He even, Marguerite reported downstairs in amazement, made her laugh occasionally.

The day after visiting Madame Jodouin, late in the afternoon, when Lyn was tidying the shop with Louise, Jean Bernard came stamping into the hall and, instead of going upstairs directly, came into the bakeshop, tracking mud and melted snow, shaking his hat off onto the floor: a vigorous, disruptive presence. Louise went very still in her corner, and Lyn had no chance to escape.

"Aha!" He pinned her behind the counter. "I want a word with you, Elisabeth."

"I am very busy—"

"Has he seen you?"

"He? Who?" Startled, she thought at once of Donald.

"He has not tried to speak to you then? Eh? You will tell me the truth, girl. Do not think that you can lie to me and get away with it."

"Who?" she said again, her heart beginning to slam against her ribs.

His eyebrows drew together into a black tangle. "I do not believe that you do not know Martel has come back. Two days ago, on foot. You have not seen him?"

Dazed, she shook her head. Then it could have been Michel she had passed in the snow. It was. But why? What were they doing here? Why had she not known?

"I heard that he has lost his boat again. For good this time. It is a pity that he did not lose himself with it!" growled Jean Bernard.

"Has he—have *you* seen him?"

"I have. And I have told him plainly that if he knows what is good for him, he will stay out of my way hereafter. And he will have nothing to do with you. I will not allow it, do you understand?"

"Yes," said Lyn bitterly. "You have made that quite clear."

He grunted. "You remember it. Give no more thought to that Martel—he is not worth it. If it takes so little to send him packing he is a sorry excuse for—"

"So little!"

"He is a coward, Elisabeth. I was a fool to waste my time on him," he said angrily. "We are well rid of him." He stumped out and up the stairs.

"Did you really not know?" asked Louise, once his footsteps died away.

"How should I?"

"It is just—I thought that you might have seen Michel."

"In the street, yesterday—but I was not sure. He did not speak."

She turned to Louise, suspicion creeping into her voice. "Michel has not been here, has he?"

"Do you believe that he would dare to show his face? After running away?"

Which, Lyn reflected later, was hardly an answer to the question. But it was all Louise would say, and Lyn was too busy struggling to assimilate what she had just learned to press her further. The hardest part was that Mathieu had been in Louisbourg for two days and she had not known. He had not found some way to tell her. He knew where she was. No matter how hard she tried to rationalize his failure to see her, or to send word, she couldn't avoid the conclusion that she simply did not mean enough to him to risk another brush with Elisabeth's father. He must have come back only because he had no choice—his boat was gone.

She spent a long, restless night chasing herself in circles. In a town of only six hundred civilians, it would be impossible for Mathieu to avoid her altogether between now and spring. Sooner or later they would meet somewhere. At least she had some warning; she would not come upon him unexpectedly around a corner, and suffer the ultimate humiliation of falling apart on the spot, where he could see. By morning she had decided that she should be grateful to Jean Bernard in this instance for playing the heavy-handed father.

Blaize was unusually impatient to go out after breakfast. He contained himself through prayers, but didn't wait for Lyn to finish her bread and cheese before he was off to the cowshed. The air outside was sharp and still; it stung her nostrils. Overhead, clouds lay like slate across the sky in gray striations, too high and flat for snow. The courtyard paths were trampled with footprints: to the woodpile, to the back gate, to the privy, to the cowshed and hen-house. The privy door stood half open, so it didn't surprise Lyn to find Blaize already with the cow. She was knocked breathless, however, to discover Michel with him. Blaize's face shone with delight when he saw her. His eyes dancing, he put his finger against his lips, and would not be satisfied until she gave back the sign.

"So," said Michel. "You have been looking after my cow."

She nodded, feeling stupid.

"And"—he looked at Blaize—"looking after my friend, too." Blaize squirmed with pleasure.

"So it *was* you I saw Wednesday." Lyn's head began to work.

"What happened? Where have you been? How did you lose the boat? How did you get back?"

"Do not ask so many questions. I cannot stay long. I tried to see you yesterday, but you were with Madame. I saw only Louise." He frowned. "I have never understood—why is she so angry with you?"

Lyn sighed. "I do not think I can explain."

Michel eyed her calculatingly, but all he said was, "I must soon go back to work or I will lose my job."

"Where? Where do you work?" asked Lyn, astonished.

Michel grinned. "Next door. For the Widow Grandchamp. I scrub pots and chop wood and she gives me food and spruce beer and lets me sleep by the fire. It suits me. Suzanne is *very* cross."

There was a private battle going on inside Lyn. Michel watched her, the grin still bright in his eyes. The cow shifted her weight and blew through her great, moist nose, in case Lyn had forgotten what she was there for. "I must milk her." Lyn seized the diversion gladly.

"Well, now that you know I am safe you do not need to worry any longer. I only came to reassure you," said Michel from the doorway.

Lyn bit her lip, wanting and not wanting. The wanting won. "Michel—" She stood up, knocking the stool over.

"Yes?" He poked his head inside. He knew perfectly well what she was trying not to ask.

"Merde!" She gave in. "What about Mathieu?"

"Mathieu? Did I not say? I must have forgotten."

She glared at him across the cow's rump.

He shrugged. "Mathieu is all right." Blaize grabbed him by the hand and tugged, and Michel came back around the door. "He has found lodging with Georges Aubert, the carpenter on the rue d'Orleans." He paused, then said grudgingly, "He told me to come and see you. He did not think it wise to come yet himself."

A dam burst, flooding Lyn with a warm, sweet tide. She leaned against the cow and closed her eyes. "Tell him I am glad he is safe," she said. "Tell him—"

"I will tell him I have done what he asked of me," said Michel austerely. "Anything else *you* must find a way to tell him yourself." And he vanished, leaving her gripping the cow's tail, grinning like an idiot. The cow, who did not understand the irrational behavior of human beings, rolled her eyes and lowed in mild protest.

For the time being, it was enough to know that Mathieu was well, had found a place to live in the town, and above all, was thinking about her. Lyn resolved not to go rushing off half-cocked and risk another explosion of Jean Bernard's wrath. She must be patient, careful. But no longer did she dread the prospect of meeting Mathieu accidentally on the street; she longed for it to happen.

She saw him first at Mass on Sunday. She had never known Mathieu to attend Mass before, so she didn't believe her radar when the nape of her neck began to prickle. After so much time, she mistrusted it when it told her he was there, somewhere in the congregation behind her. But as they left the chapel, she caught sight of his familiar shape and her heart rammed itself into her throat. At that instant he turned his head and their eyes met and she thought for a moment she would choke. His mouth twitched upward, then he looked away. That was all.

Marguerite pulled her back into the family as they greeted friends and acquaintances—with the town so shrunken there were no strangers—and answered enquiries about the state of Madame Pugnant's health. Louise gave Lyn a black look; she too had noticed Mathieu. Lyn had to content herself with that one glimpse, but on it she sailed through the rest of the day, oblivious to Jeanne's fretful complaints and Suzanne's grumbling, not bothering to listen to Joseph's pronouncements on the garrison and its politics, which usually made her bite her tongue with impatience. She was happier than she had been for weeks, and all because a man she knew had almost smiled at her.

It turned out not to be very difficult to *see* Mathieu. The hard part was finding snatches of time when they could talk to each other. Georges Aubert lived with his wife and brother and seven children almost at the end of the rue d'Orleans, near the Maurepas Gate. Behind the house was a large yard enclosed by a high palisade fence in which he kept heaps of lumber and rough logs. In addition to building houses, he sold firewood by the cord. He also owned one of the few teams of oxen in Louisbourg, and when he was not

288

working them himself, he hired them out. Mathieu did a little of everything for him: odd bits of carpentry around the town, mending windows and shutters for people who couldn't or didn't need to do it themselves; sawing, splitting and carting firewood; going out with the team to do a job for someone else. Aubert was very careful of his beasts; they represented an enormous investment and a good source of income, so he did not send them alone.

Lyn and Mathieu took up their game again, spotting one another in the streets, grabbing any chance for a few words, never finding enough time. Once in a while, behind a cartload of wood or on a blind corner in the snow, he would kiss her, hard and quick, and she would hug him fiercely, desperate for contact. But the house in which he lived was small and very full, and there was always the specter of Jean Bernard charging up behind them, uttering threats. Mathieu never came to the bakery.

"What would he do this time, do you think?" asked Lyn as they walked together through the snow-cloaked streets.

"Come after me with his roofing hook. He has told me so."

"He has? When?"

"The first day. Michel advised me to listen. He reminded me of the damage Jean Bernard did with his bare hands the last time he and I discussed you."

She felt a confusion of anxiety and happiness. "I do not see, if you were his friend as he said, why he should mind."

"It is because I was his friend. He thinks that I used him." Mathieu sounded sad. "I had his trust, and now—"

"But I am not even his daughter!" said Lyn crossly.

"If I thought you were," replied Mathieu, "then none of this would have happened."

She studied him for a moment. "So you do believe me."

"I have tried very hard not to," he confessed. "It would be so much easier, and as I have said, I—"

"—do not want trouble."

He smiled, his face lighting like a bonfire. "So. You must go, and I must deliver my load."

"I wish—"

"Ah! That is what caused the trouble last time, is it not. Do not wish, as a special favor to me."

The next time she met him, she said, "If only you had a room somewhere else. Instead of in a house with so many people. Why did you choose to go there?''

"Aubert owes me a favor, and he has work. Besides, it does not matter. Wherever we go there are eyes. You should know that by this time. It was one of the men in the tavern who told Jean we were there. Did you not realize?''

She shook her head. "It is not like where I come from. There is so much more freedom there. I never thought about it when I had it.''

"Is that good?'' He sounded doubtful.

"Yes, of course it is. Well, usually.''

"You must be patient. You must wait.''

"For what?''

"Warm weather,'' he said, grinning at her exasperation.

She did not tell him about Donald, and Mathieu did not mention him. Initially she had thought to ask Mathieu if he could find out anything more about Gerard Grossin—if anyone had seen him in any of the fishing settlements along the coast, or up on the Mira River. But she held back, partly because she suspected it was useless, and partly because when it came to the point, she didn't want to discuss Donald with Mathieu, any more than she wanted to discuss Mathieu with Donald. If she asked Mathieu for help again, she was sure he would give it, but between now and the first time she had asked, their relationship had undergone a fundamental change, one that actually frightened her when she remembered who she was and where she belonged. Since Mathieu's return, she deliberately chose not to think about the future, preferring to go from day to day, being with him whenever she could.

She had never experienced such feelings before, never with Mike. Poor Mike—he did not stand comparison with Mathieu. Perhaps, she thought—when she thought of Mike at all—he had found a nice conventional Catholic girlfriend, one of whom his mother could at least halfheartedly approve, with the orthodox number of legally married parents and lots of siblings. She didn't want to consider what she would lose now by going home. Separation from Mathieu wouldn't be in miles, it would be forever.

Face it when it happens, she told herself firmly; in the meantime be thankful for what you have, Carolyn Paget, even if it means hanging around on bone-rattling, bitter-cold street corners, while

290

your nose runs and your feet go numb, hoping for five minutes with Mathieu to last until the next time you see him.

At the frozen end of January, Lyn came back to the bakery through the lowering afternoon with the wind in her cloak, still feeling Mathieu's arms around her, keeping her warm. He had made her laugh by telling her about the locksmith's wife, who had become so enraged at her husband's gambling that she had hit him with a frozen codfish and knocked him senseless, there in the tavern where he'd been playing cards.

"You are making that up," she accused him.

"I am not. A codfish is a formidable weapon in the right hands."

"Then if this war between England and France is over fish, perhaps it should be fought with them."

"They could be fired from cannon," Mathieu suggested.

"Everyone must be granted the right to bear fish."

He shook his head at her. "The cold is freezing your brain. You must go and sit by the fire and think pious thoughts before supper." He gave her a swift kiss and sent her off, her head still filled with thoughts of frozen codfish, and the way his eyes softened when he smiled. She had no room for piety.

Christophe was waiting for her. As soon as she came in, before she could shake off her cloak and hang it on its peg, he met her.

"Christophe, have you heard about Madame Therreau and the codfish?" she asked.

"No. Mademoiselle, I have been watching for you."

It was dark in the hall, but something in his voice made her turn and peer at him. "What is it? Something is wrong—is it Grand-mother?"

"No."

"Not Marguerite? Or one of the babies?"

He shook his head. "Will you come with me into the bakery, Mademoiselle? I have bad news for you, I am afraid."

She could not imagine what he had to tell her, but her muscles tensed with apprehension and her scalp tightened. The bakery was empty, work over until the fires were laid for the next morning's bread. It was warm in the long room, and the air was laden with the moist rich aroma of yeast. "What is it, Christophe?" she asked, her voice steady.

291

"I am sorry—truly. I do not want—I thought that I should tell you first. A company of soldiers went out early this morning scavenging for game. About six miles to the southwest they found the body of another soldier. He had been dead for some time, but they believe—"

"Oh, God," whispered Lyn.

⇥⟫ 22 ⟪⇤

IT WAS VERY PECULIAR; IT WAS AS IF A LITTLE PIECE OF HER HAD broken off and was perched somewhere outside, observing: So this is what it feels like to be in shock. So this is how I deal with death. Why don't I cry? What should I do next? What will happen to me? It prodded and poked her to see if she would squirm, and where it hurt worst, and all the while inside her head she was shouting, It can't be true! It can't! Not Donald—he can't be dead!

From somewhere Marguerite came to her and pried her fingers loose from the dough trough. Whispering the same soothing nonsense words she whispered to her babies, she guided Lyn up the stairs to her room and sat her on the bed, kneeling in front of her.

"Elisabeth. Elisabeth—you must hear me. You must speak to me. Tell me—what can I do to help you?"

Dazedly, Lyn looked into Marguerite's face and the fragment of herself noticed the love and distress, but she was too numb to respond. Marguerite chafed her hands. "You are so cold, Elisabeth. Please let me help."

From far away, Lyn heard herself say in a flat voice, "There is nothing. No one can help." Following an earthquake, she remembered reading once, the aftershocks went on and on.

Marguerite said something to her, something that made no sense, then stood up and went away. Lyn sat still, afraid to move in case it jarred her mind loose and she began to think again. She felt very fragile; at any moment it would happen and she would fall off the edge. She would be forced to make sense of things she did not want to understand. It was cold in the room; she was cold right through.

"Here. Drink this, it will warm you." Marguerite curled Lyn's

292

stiff fingers around a cup and held them there, then raised them to her mouth. "Elisabeth, you must," she said firmly. "Come. It will warm you."

She took a sip, expecting one of Marguerite's foul-tasting brews, but this burnt a fiery track down her gullet and smoked out her sinuses. It was rum laced with honey and lemon: a hot toddy, she thought with detached surprise. Dorrie's favorite medicinal drink. Her hands gripped of their own accord and she took another comforting swallow.

"There." Marguerite sounded relieved. "Now. You must tell me what has happened. I know only a little from Christophe, but he could not say very much with other people around. He is very anxious, Elisabeth."

Lyn let out a long sigh. "What did he tell you?"

"That you were taken ill. And when I went back I told them that you have the ague and that you must rest." She sat down beside Lyn. "But it is not that."

"I am cold," said Lyn.

"Christophe told me about the poor soldier who has been found. He said that you knew this man. How is it that you do?"

"He came often to buy bread. He was very homesick and he would talk to me." There was a silence; Lyn could feel Marguerite waiting for more. At last Marguerite said, "But many people come to buy bread, Elisabeth. It is difficult when someone you know dies—I understand—but it happens. It is part of life, is it not. Perhaps if I knew—if you would tell me—"

Lyn finished the rum and felt a little strengthened, but she didn't know what to say. She didn't know how to begin to talk to Marguerite about Donald.

"Elisabeth, I am afraid for you. There was the trouble with Monsieur Martel—your papa was so angry. He does not know about this soldier, I think."

"No," said Lyn. "There is nothing for him to know."

"Are you quite certain? It is true that Maman is much stronger, but she depends on you. It would be very hard for her if she—if you—"

Suddenly Lyn understood what Marguerite was trying to ask. Any thoughts she might have had of attempting to explain Donald vanished. "No," she said wearily. "You need not worry, Marguerite. I did not—there will be no baby." And if there were, it would not be Donald's, but she didn't say that.

Marguerite gazed at her sadly. "But you did love him, this soldier?"

The question came at Lyn, unexpected. *Had* she loved Donald? She had certainly never felt about him as she felt about Mathieu—or Mike, for that matter. She felt responsible for him, sorry for him, bound to him in a vital way, but she didn't know what all that came to, and she didn't want to have to think about it. If only Marguerite could mend the day for her with those neat invisible stitches, the way she mended aprons and chemises and shirts, so that the ugly jagged rent Donald had made in it would no longer show.

"It is hard to love," said Marguerite softly, "but I think it is better than to feel nothing. Sometimes it is good, sometimes it hurts. It is the same for everyone, is it not?"

He had gotten only six miles from Louisbourg. He had with him a small supply of food, an army issue blanket and two gunny sacks. There had been no accident, there were no signs of injury or foul play. Gerard Gossin had died, the military court decided, of exposure. He would be buried hastily and without ceremony.

Only Lyn knew that he was not Gerard Grossin, he was Donald Stewart, a graduate student from Montreal. He should not have been there—it was a terrible mistake and his death made it irrevocable. That haunted her. She couldn't shake him loose. That he should die in this place was horrible; that he would be buried out on Rochefort Point without anyone knowing who he really was gave her nightmares. She woke sweating and trembling, feeling as if she were being squeezed in a giant vise. How would they ever know what had happened to him—his family, his friends, his fiancée? They would never find him, not even a trace of him. He had simply vanished, leaving a void in their lives, an enormous unanswered question.

"I must go to the funeral," she told Marguerite.

"Elisabeth, I do not think that is wise. What would Maman say?"

"She need not know unless you tell her. I must go."

"Then let me go with you."

But Lyn shook her head; she did not want company. She wanted no comfort or sympathy; however well-meant, it was based on

294

misconception. "You did not even know him. There would be no point."

"It is not good for you to be alone."

Instead of saying, It's what I want, Lyn said carefully, "Help Louise in the shop while I am gone. Please."

Unhappily Marguerite gave in. "Remember he is with God now, Elisabeth."

Lyn nodded, hoping it was true. If so, they were the only ones who knew who he really was, and where—she and God.

It was a raw, cheerless morning, unpleasant but unremarkable; one of a featureless string of gray winter days. The barracks chapel was cold and almost empty. Donald's body, wrapped in a plain dark shroud, lay in the middle surrounded by candles. Lyn recognized Père Athanase and the military chaplain, Père Isidore. The only other people were an officer—Captain Duhaget, whom she knew by sight but had never met—four glum-looking privates, an old woman enveloped in a worn black shawl, and, at the back, a tall dark-haired man. Lyn shivered. Why had Mathieu come? He had no reason to be there. She refused to look at him, wishing with all her strength he would disappear. This was hard enough without Mathieu to make it harder.

The handful of mourners stood during the Mass, silent, disconnected. When it was over, the four privates took up the bier, proceeding unevenly behind the friars and their assistant, who led the way carrying the cross and chanting in a monotonous hypnotic tone. The old woman in black vanished, leaving Captain Duhaget, Lyn and Mathieu to follow. Mathieu fell into step beside Lyn, but she did not acknowledge him. She was too far inside herself. They walked along the rue de France to the cemetery. The people they passed bowed their heads and crossed themselves, the men took off their hats.

A shallow grave had been hacked out of the frozen ground at the end of a row of plain wooden crosses. It was barely a foot deep. Here and there, where the snow had been scoured away by the wind, Lyn could make out the edges of coffins breaking the bare earth, pushed up by the frost. The cemetery was bleak and anonymous. But only meant for remains, she reminded herself fiercely, just a place to put what was left when life departed.

Père Isidore sprinkled holy water on the grave and on the long thin bundle that had been Donald. It was lowered into the narrow slit of a grave, and the soldiers covered it with clods of frozen dirt. Lyn closed her eyes and prayed with all her might for Donald Stewart, that he find his way back to where he belonged, that he find peace. She did not cry. She felt as cold and hard as the dirt under which his body now lay. Then she looked up and all around, memorizing the spot. She must hold it tight so that she could carry it back with her, so that she could tell them where Donald was when she returned. If—

She was being watched. On the far side of the grave, at some distance from the little group, stood another woman, holding herself stiffly, her face flat as a board. She met Lyn's eyes and looked away. When it was over and the procession moved off, following the cross back to the chapel, Lyn stayed, facing the woman. Mathieu waited, but she paid him no attention. At last the woman stirred.

"Why did you come?"

"I did not want him to die," said Agathe angrily. "I never wanted that."

"You did not help him," said Lyn.

"How could I? What could I have said? I would not go with him—I could not have stopped him." Her eyes narrowed. *"You* did not stop him."

"No." Lyn felt as if someone had tied a stone around her neck and dropped her into a well; down she sank into the cold black depths of despair. She didn't even see the woman leave.

"Elisabeth." Lyn looked up from the meager heap of troubled earth and shivered. "You cannot blame yourself. You could not have prevented his death."

"You do not know that!"

"What could you have done?"

She turned away. "I could have gone with him. He was looking for the way to get home."

"He did not find it," said Mathieu grimly. "If you had gone, you would only have died too. Where is the sense of that?"

She wanted to say, perhaps he would not have died, but she didn't believe it. "At least he would not have been alone. He should not have been alone."

"Elisabeth, look at me." When she did not, he took her by the shoulders, his fingers hard, and gave her a shake. "He did not have to do it. No one made him."

"You do not understand!"

"I am trying—"

She lifted her face to his. "Mathieu, I want to go *home*. Where I belong. I do not want to be Elisabeth anymore!"

"But you do not know how," he said. "No more did he. Perhaps it was what he wanted—to die rather than stay here. But I do not believe it is what *you* want. You would rather be alive, even here. He must have known that too."

She tore herself away from him and fled back to the middle of town. She was shaking all over, her teeth were chattering so that she bit her lip and tasted blood. Somehow she got back to the bakery, although she was aware of nothing on the way, and the blindness persisted in the days that followed. She functioned by rote, doing more or less what Elisabeth was expected to do. She barely spoke to anyone, she barely listened to anything around her. People began to treat her the way they had in the beginning: as slow-witted or tiresomely dull. Even Blaize deserted her, disappearing for hours on end.

Marguerite tried to reach her. From time to time, Lyn was dimly aware of her troubled face, a question, a hand on her arm, but she pulled away. She built walls around herself and moved far inside them, withdrawing into a kind of hibernation, slowing all her vital processes to the barest minimum necessary to keep her going. Most of all, she did not want to think.

"Elisabeth! Elisabeth, wait."

She was plodding up the rue Toulouse, bent against the wind, carrying a basket of rolls for the inn by the Place Royale. The innkeeper's wife had been taken ill and could do no baking. When she turned her head, she was surprised to find Mathieu beside her.

"Why do you ignore me?"

"I never see you."

"Because you do not look. I see *you*—every day. You will not speak to me." He was angry, his face full of hard, sharp lines. "Why?"

She shook her head helplessly. "There is nothing to say. You should not have gone to his funeral. You did not like him."

297

"I did not go for him. It was for you."

"Thank you," she said stiffly, and began to walk away. He would not let her. He walked with her. She was alarmed; he frightened her.

"Will you not let me help?" he asked, his voice gentler. "Is there nothing I can do?"

"No." She clenched her fingers on the basket handle so hard it hurt, and concentrated fiercely on that.

"Elisabeth, do not do this."

"I am doing nothing." She swallowed the panic in her throat.

He stopped. "Carolyn?"

She could not hold herself together. The street, the houses, swam before her eyes. She gulped and the tears poured hot and painful out of her and then she shook with sobs. The walls she had constructed for protection cracked, and her head felt as if it were bursting. Everything she had struggled so hard to suppress leaped out at her from all the dark corners inside. Mathieu put his arms around her and she sobbed against him as if she would never stop. "I did not know," he said softly. "I did not understand." Over and over. After a while, she began vaguely to wonder what he meant. She became aware that her nose was running and that she had made a large wet spot on the front of his jacket. She felt thick and dizzy and she pushed against his chest. He relaxed his hold and looked at her. "I am sorry." His eyes were somber. "I thought—I did not realize—that he meant so much to you."

The tears continued to drip down her cheeks. She gazed at him helplessly, unable to tell him that she wasn't crying for Donald. And that was one more reason for her to feel guilty about Donald, to feel she had betrayed him. Inexplicably, she was weeping for Gilbert— and Gilbert was only a cat. For months she hadn't thought of Gilbert, and suddenly, there in the wintry street, he had appeared to her so clearly she could see every hair on him, each gleaming white whisker. He had looked her straight in the face with his amber eyes and she had known in that instant, with absolute certainly, that she would never see him again.

That was what she had built her defenses against. That was what she had fought to shut out since Donald's death, and could shut out no longer. *She was not ever going to get back home.* "You do not know how," Mathieu had said to her in the cemetery, and she had run away—from it, from him. The tears were for everything she had lost—Dorrie and Mike and college, Waverley Street and the Red Sox, Gilbert, the fat man behind the counter in the post office, bathrooms and Sunday newspapers . . . the world that belonged to Lyn Paget. Always, in spite of everything, she had been sure she would have it all back again. There would be a sudden jolt and she'd be home. But Donald's death had changed that.

She blinked and there was Mathieu, arms hanging, his face angular with sadness. She wiped her eyes and nose on the hem of her cloak. "It is me," she said. "I am sorry."

She lay awake at night and wondered if the private wilderness she was lost in wasn't far worse than the wilderness outside, the one Donald had chosen. At least he had found a way out of his.

She made such a mess of the ledgers that Madame Pugnant, in a fit of genuine anger, forbade her to touch them again. "I do not know what has gotten into you, Elisabeth! What has happened to your brain? Can you not do the simplest thing right? *Look* at these figures—they make no sense at all. And here! Here is an account but no name. What am I to do with that, eh? Have you any excuse?"

Mutely, Lyn shook her head, and Madame Pugnant, who had by then progressed to sitting up for an hour or so at a time, peered at her in vexation. "It is not like you," she said irritably. "You have done some foolish things, but you are not stupid. Are you in trouble? For the love of heaven, girl, do not snivel! Life is seldom what we would have it be, but it is life. We must do the best we can, is it not. Or else give up. And where is the sense of that? Now go away. I am tired." Abruptly her eyes closed and she was asleep.

It often happened while she was sitting bolt upright. Her eyes would droop shut and she would be gone until her chin sagged. Then she would snort and wake herself up, glaring around, defying anyone present to have noticed. Marguerite watched over her as carefully as if she were one of the babies; and at times Madame Pugnant behaved rather like one, demanding attention, showing off her gradually increasing strength, fussing when she didn't like something or couldn't get what she wanted. She was very unsteady on her feet and had to be helped up and downstairs by Christophe or Joseph, complaining whenever she had enough breath.

299

"I do not know why she has to be so cross," said Jeanne crossly.

"It is because she has been frightened," Marguerite replied. "She is frightened that she should be so ill."

"Pah!" snorted Suzanne. "She will outlive us all, that one."

Concern for Madame Pugnant, and now relief at her gradual recovery, preoccupied the household; everyone seemed to have grown together. The tensions were still there, the underlying disputes and unhappinesses and dissatisfactions, but within the house they were a family. Lyn felt it keenly; she knew herself to be on the outside. Hard as she might try, she would never really be part of it, and the harder she tried the further she would move away from her self—the person she had been born. She didn't know what to do.

One morning in late February, Michel was once again in the cowshed, waiting for her when she came out to milk. Blaize greeted him joyfully and Michel leapt up to wrestle him into the straw, tickling him while he laughed his odd, explosive little laugh: "Uh! Uh! Uh!"

"You will upset the cow and the milk will turn. Why are you here?"

"I was sure you would be glad to see me." Michel brushed the straw out of Blaize's unruly hair.

Lyn sat down and began to pull the cow's teats. Blaize crouched beside her and opened his mouth, but she pretended not to notice, and after a few minutes he closed it and folded his legs under him, dejected.

"He wants to see you," said Michel abruptly.

"Who?"

"You know very well. I do not know why he bothers with you at all. But he wants to see you."

"Why does he not tell me himself?"

"How can he when you will not speak to him?"

Miserable, she shook her head. "It is no good. There is nothing to say."

Michel gave an irritable sigh. "You can listen for a change. *Sacredie!* What has he done?"

"Nothing. It is not Mathieu, Michel, it is me."

"I *told* him it was you." He made a sour face at her. "He will be in the woodyard behind Aubert's all afternoon. If you do not go and meet him, then he will come here to find you.''

''But that is stupid! He can*not* come here. If he is seen—''

Michel shrugged. ''So he is an idiot. That is what he says. If you do not go, he comes. And if Jean Bernard kills him for it this time, it is your fault.''

She felt the blood draining from her head and gave him a wild-eyed look.

''Well, it is true,'' he snapped.

She waited until her ears stopped buzzing. ''All right. Tell him I will come this afternoon.''

''I do not need to. He will know when you get there.''

''But—''

Suddenly he scowled at her. ''And you had better look after Blaize.''

''What do you mean?''

''I do not mind that he spends time with me in the tavern, but if his uncle catches him, there will be the devil to pay.''

''I did not know—''

''No, of course not. You do not know anything these days, I think.'' And with that he left.

She glanced at Blaize; he was absorbed in making himself a nest in the straw, patting and pulling it carefully into walls. But it's no good, she thought despairingly. Why don't they all leave me alone?

She had no business on the rue d'Orleans that afternoon. It was a long way from Monsieur Verrier's where she had delivered three loaves of white bread. But Michel had plainly meant it when he told her that Mathieu would come to the bakery if she did not go to see him, and she could not risk that. The responsibility for Donald lay smothering on her; she could not bear the thought of putting Mathieu at risk. Jean Bernard would not actually kill him, in spite of Michel's dire prediction, but he would make a terrible scene and Mathieu would only get hurt again. And for no reason.

It had to happen. She had known that sooner or later she would have to face up to Mathieu and finish things, but she had allowed herself to put it off, dreading the confrontation. When she reached the corner of Aubert's house and saw him working in the yard, she had to stop and catch her breath and steel herself. She was not a

301

coward; she had always believed that the best way to deal with a situation, no matter how unpleasant, or sad, or difficult, was to meet it squarely as soon as possible. Postponing it only made it worse.

Mathieu was forking dirty straw out of the oxen's stalls into a heap in the yard. It steamed gently in the cold air. He looked up as she entered the yard, giving her no chance to change her mind and sneak away. She lifted her chin.

"Good afternoon," he said neutrally, dropping another forkful.

"Good afternoon." She clutched her courage with both hands. "Michel told me that you wanted to see me."

He nodded. "It is good of you to come."

"I did not think much of the choice."

The corner of his mouth twitched and she bit her lip. She had to keep the conversation steady, to remember what she had to say to him and say it, not to let him distract her.

"I am glad you took me at my word. I must talk to you, and you will never let me near."

"Last time when I was the one who wanted to talk—do you not remember what happened?"

He regarded her levelly. "Indeed, very well. But it is too late to worry about that now."

"Mathieu, it is too late for everything. That is what I have come to tell you." She hesitated, but he said nothing. He gave the dung heap a vigorous poke with his fork and left her to stumble on. "It would have been easier if—you had not come back. If only you had not lost your boat—"

"I thought that you were glad to see me."

"I *was*. Of course I was. How can I make you understand? That was before—before I knew Donald—Gerard—had died. Now everything is different."

"I have tried to understand about him." There was an edge in his voice. "I know his death is hard for you, but it is a fact and you must accept it. You cannot waste your life mourning for him. That is stupid. But that is not what I have to speak to you about. Until the winter is over we are safe here. But when the sea is open—there is a war out there. I hear people saying that Louisbourg will be attacked in the spring. They are people I trust."

She nodded slowly. "It is true. You must believe them. If you do not want to be caught here you must leave as early as you can."

He stared at her with a troubled expression, as if he were trying to penetrate her skull, to see what was inside.

"I *know,* Mathieu. It happened two hundred years before I was born. The English sent ships from Boston. At the beginning of May they landed south of Louisbourg. The soldiers came overland, not from the sea, and they captured the town. In my time it is history. It cannot be changed."

He looked from her across the snowy yard. "And the people? What is to become of them?" he asked finally.

"Most of them were sent to France. That is all I can tell you. I never thought it would be necessary for me to know more."

"So. We must be gone as soon as the ice is out—by the middle of April at the latest," he said, accepting what she told him. He cocked an eyebrow at her. "I do not suppose you know what the weather will be like?" She shook her head. "It does not matter. I had planned to leave in the spring—not quite so early, but . . ." He shrugged. "That is why I want to talk to you."

"You told me months ago you would leave," said Lyn. "I did not expect to see you again, after Jean Bernard—I am sorry you have lost the boat."

"Forget the boat," he said impatiently. "That is not why I am here."

"No? But I thought—without it—"

"I do not know who told you that we lost her—it is not so. Michel and I, we took her up the coast—far up—to Petit Labrador, where she would be safe over the winter, and we left her there."

"If the boat is safe—then—you meant to come back?"

"Of course I meant to. Did you really believe that it was only an accident?"

"I do not know," she said. Then in a small voice, "Yes."

"I see."

But she knew he didn't. "I thought—I was sure that I would soon be gone, too," she said lamely, not knowing how to explain that his leaving had been tangled up in her own sense of impermanence. That she hadn't wanted him to go, but she had believed that one way or another their separation was inevitable.

"Back to your own place," he said and she nodded. "Do you still believe it will happen?"

She forced herself not to duck the question. "No." She waited for him to ask her why, holding on for dear life, but he didn't. Instead, he said, "Then you are free to leave with me in the spring. That is why I came back."

She felt her jaw drop. "I did not—Mathieu, how can I?"

"Why not? You say yourself that you do not belong here."

"But that is not what I meant. It is not the same thing at all. I do not belong *any*where in this time, Mathieu. I would not belong in Massachusetts. I do not think the way people here think. I cannot see the world through their eyes—*your* eyes. Everything is strange to me—I do not know how to live here."

"Can you not learn? I have told you I will help."

"I am not Elisabeth Bernard. I will never be," she said, her voice unsteady.

He shook his head impatiently. "I do not ask you to be. It is not Elisabeth Bernard I came back for. I do not know who she is."

"Do you know who I am? Even I am no longer sure."

"Then we will find out."

"Mathieu, I will be trouble for you as long as we are together."

At that he grinned. "It is true, and I am prepared for it. But wait—do not answer me now. Think first. Promise me that you will think hard."

"I promise, but—"

"Always with you it is but. Listen. I do not mean to be here in the spring. I want no part of this war. If I must leave without you, I will. But I do not want to."

She thought she was coming down with the flu: one moment shaking with cold, the next burning hot, then both at once. How could she consider leaving with Mathieu, when she had refused to go away with Donald? Donald had needed her—Mathieu didn't. Donald had relied on her for support and help, to prop him up and give him courage. Mathieu was self-sufficient.

She shivered. There had been times when she had utterly forgotten Donald, when she had become so involved in Elisabeth's life she hadn't given him a thought. He'd been gone for several days before she had even missed him—perhaps he had already been dead. Her skin was clammy with sweat. In the end she had failed him and it had been fatal. Right after he'd been to Agathe he had withdrawn from her; with the wisdom of hindsight, she realized he had made up his mind. But he hadn't told her—he had stopped asking. He knew she wouldn't risk it, she wasn't brave enough.

But brave enough for what? To be willing to die? For Donald it was either the way back or the way out. But Mathieu was right, she didn't want to die. Why should she feel so guilty about making a choice? Donald had made his: he had chosen to leave Louisbourg, no matter what might happen to him. He had decided it was better than staying.

So had Mathieu. He was going out into that same enormous, unknown wilderness. The difference was that Mathieu had no intention of dying. He knew what he would face and he was equipped to meet it, as poor Donald could never have been. If she agreed to go with Mathieu she was very likely to survive.

She would survive in Mathieu's world; that was the catch. She would be committing herself to a lifetime here: endless hard work, babies, making do with so little, threatened by disease and all manner of natural dangers, discomfort, inconvenience, isolation, a rigid social structure she would never be able to accept. She would be severing her last ties with Carolyn Paget's time. However tenuous those ties were, they were in Louisbourg. She was convinced of that, just as Agathe was.

So she could refuse Mathieu, and wait like Agathe, finding some way to stay behind next summer when the French left, clutching desperately at a tiny patch of ground, never knowing, always hoping, straddling two times—neither of one nor of the other—until— What? What if nothing ever happened? What if she spent her life here waiting, until there was nothing left of it but regret for everything she had not done?

There were no answers, only harder and harder questions. In the morning she felt, if anything, worse than she had all night. Suppose she did nothing at all? Stuck her head in the sand, and let whatever happened happen. For a moment the chaos subsided and she was flooded with relief. But it was only temporary. As she leaned her head into the hollow under the cow's flank, she knew it wasn't an answer. Even Donald had done better than that—he had made a choice and accepted the consequences of it. Almost eighteen years ago, Dorrie had made a choice, with no one to help and no easy answer. She had decided to have and keep her baby. And Lyn's father had chosen. Lyn always thought, buried far down inside

305

herself, that he had chosen wrong. But suppose he had stayed with Dorrie out of a sense of obligation? Suppose Lyn had grown up watching her parents argue and fight and make each other miserable? Would that have been worth having a father?

You spent all those years at school being brainwashed into believing in right answers; if you thought hard enough, if you knew the material, you'd sail through. Then you graduated and the rules changed. How did *any*one survive, she wondered bleakly.

This time she saw Mathieu before he saw her. She saw him immediately, through the bakeshop window. He was walking along the quay with the oxcart, and she saw him because, without thinking about it, she had been looking for him. The fog in her head vanished. What it came down to was that by choosing to go with Donald, she would have had to accept the reality of death; but choosing Mathieu, she was accepting the reality of life. Whatever life she made for herself in Mathieu's world. It would be hard—this future was not one she could ever have foreseen—but there would be joy and companionship and laughter in it as well as difficulty. She felt the stir of excitement. And Mathieu to love her. He loved *her*, not Elisabeth. She knew what she wanted to say to him, and she had to say it right then, at that moment. She couldn't wait.

Without a word to Louise, who looked at her as if she were demented, she set down the loaf she had been weighing for Madame Berton, ran out of the shop, out of the house, after the cart.

Mathieu did not even hear her come. He jumped when she caught his arm, and opened his mouth to speak, but before he could, she said, "Yes!"

The smile was instantaneous. He wrapped his arms around her tight and hugged her so hard she had no breath left. "You will not change your mind?"

She fought for air. "No! You will not change yours?"

He shook his head. "Are you ready to leave Grossin behind?"

Her eyes clouded for an instant. She would never completely leave Donald behind. It was not possible. But that wasn't what Mathieu was asking her. "I did not love him, Mathieu. I love you."

He searched her face. Whatever he found satisfied him; he kissed her and let her go. "Then it is settled."

"But, Mathieu—"

"Again, but?" He raised his eyebrows quizzically.

"It is Blaize. I cannot leave him behind, Mathieu. We are his only friends, Michel and I. If we go—"

"So? He shall come with us. I will fix it when we speak to Jean Bernard."

"Jean Bernard! Speak to him about what?"

"About getting married."

She couldn't help it, she burst into astonished laughter. "Married? You and me?"

His face turned dark and angular. "Do not repeat everything I say. Of course you and I. Who else would I mean?"

With an effort she swallowed her laughter and straightened her face. "It is just—I never—I did not think you meant—"

"But I asked you to go away with me."

She nodded earnestly. "Yes, and I have told you I will."

"But you will not marry me? Is that what you are saying?"

It had never occurred to her that he had been proposing. It was such a surprise to her, she did not know what she thought about it. "No—it is not that. I did not expect—I must think about it a little, Mathieu."

"Then what *have* you been thinking about?" he demanded crossly.

"Anyway, I keep telling you, he is not my father," she said, sidestepping the question. "We do not need to tell him anything."

"And I keep telling you, he believes that he is your father. Just as they"—he nodded toward the bakery—"believe they are your family. Me—I do not know. But Jean did me a favor when I was badly in need of one. Whatever you may think of him, in spite of his temper, he is a good man."

"Suppose he says no? Suppose he goes after you again?"

"Do not think I have not considered it," he said with a reluctant smile. "*You* need not worry. He will only shout at you. It is me he will attack."

"I thought that we could just go," said Lyn wistfully.

"It would not be right." Mathieu was firm. "Until you are twenty-five you must have Jean Bernard's consent."

"Twenty-five?" Lyn was appalled. "Do you know that my mother was not married to my father at all?"

"Not married? But Jean—how could that—" He caught himself.

307

"Sometimes I believe Michel is right. I am an idiot. It does not matter now anyway. Look."

She turned and saw Joseph on the steps of the bakery with Christophe behind him, and Louise peering out of the door.

"Trouble," she said.

"Trouble," said Mathieu. "And it is only the beginning."